MISSING PEACE

A NOVEL

N. K. HOLT

HMG PRESS

DEDICATION

To Luanne Jacobsmeier Pruett
Mother, Catholic, Iowan, Angel

There's a lot of you in this story, Mom.
A lot of Grandpa J, too.
I love you.

♥

AUTHOR'S NOTE

Missing Peace is set mostly in the fictional town of River Haven, Iowa. Many of the settings in Chicago, Illinois, are also fictional, as are some in the Middle East. I hope you enjoy the fictionalized land-scapes inhabited by my characters. I had great fun creating a world that suited my storytelling.

CHAPTER ONE

September 1993
River Haven, Iowa

Only terrible things happened at three in the morning. Monsters. Nightmares. Premonitions.

The alarm clock on the bedside table flickered past 3:09 AM as eight-year-old John McKay debated waking his sister. Six-year-old Janey had been sick all week. The doctor said croup was contagious, so Janey had been quarantined upstairs since Mom was much sicker after her last chemotherapy.

With the brat in solitary confinement, John had a captive, gullible audience for his growing repertoire of magic tricks.

"Do it again!" Janey had cough-requested after he pulled a quarter from her ear.

He also schlepped his sister's drawings and stories down the stairs before returning with fabricated praise. *What a wild imagination you have. You'll make an outstanding writer someday.* Things Mom might have said if she'd been awake, so it wasn't lying.

Dad said Janey was too young to understand the truth, but John knew better. Yesterday, his sister asked him what terminal meant. He'd lied about that, said he didn't know, but she'd made him pinky swear to tell her if anything changed with their mother.

Right now, that promise wedged beneath his rib cage like a rock. He'd also promised Mom he'd shield Janey from the harsher side of their mother's sickness.

He moved into his sister's room and shoved her shoulder. "Janey. Wake up."

She raised her puny head, grimaced and fell back on her pillow. "What?"

"Mom's gone to the hospital."

Janey bolted upright. "Where's Daddy?"

"He's gone, too. Followed the ambulance."

She whimpered, her voice hoarse. "Where's Perry?"

"Matt and Perry are meeting Dad at the hospital. Lisa's here." Their twin brothers were sixteen years older than John but lived nearby. Lisa and Perry had married a few months ago.

"They left me?" Janey's sobs triggered a coughing fit.

"Quit crying. I'm here, aren't I?" John made it sound as if he'd chosen to stay, but he'd been given no choice.

He'd awakened over an hour ago to the sound of crunching rocks as a vehicle pulled up the farm's gravel driveway. At first, he'd felt relieved to wake up since he'd been having one of those dreams. *Monsters. Nightmares. Premonitions.*

Then he looked out his bedroom window and spotted an ambulance. He made it downstairs just as two EMTs pushed a gurney into his parents' bedroom. John followed, but Dad stepped into the doorframe, blocking the entrance.

"You'll be in the way, Son."

"Why are they here? What's wrong?"

"Your mother needs to go to the hospital."

"I'm going, too. I'm her knight." Mom called John her mighty protector.

"No. You're going back upstairs to watch your sister. Lisa will be here any second." Dad kept glancing over his shoulder, growing more impatient. "Do as I say, John. Now."

The door shut in his face, forcing him to retreat and wait for the rest of the horrible scene to unfold below his bedroom window.

A few minutes later, the EMTs wheeled the gurney carrying his unmoving mother to the back of the ambulance. The oxygen mask covered most of her face. John waved, even though he doubted she could see him in the dark.

Dad shouted to Lisa before disappearing around the side of the house. The ambulance turned on the swirling red lights before taking off, its headlights sweeping the dark wall of tall cornstalks in the fields surrounding the farmhouse. As soon as the ambulance pulled onto the road, the siren began a slow wail. Five-seconds later, his father's pickup raced past.

Just like in John's dream.

"How long have they been gone?" Janey asked.

"An hour. Maybe less." He didn't want her to be mad that he hadn't awakened her sooner.

"Did you see Mom 'fore she left?"

"Yup. She waved. Said for you to mind me."

"She'll be back by morning, won't she?"

John shrugged. The stupid dream had ended right after the ambulance took off, but it left a dreadful shadow. *Don't think about it.*

He moved to sit cross-legged on the far end of her bed before patting the middle of the mattress. Fuller, their collie puppy, leaped up in the space between them, wiggling in excitement.

"You snuck her in the house." Janey kicked free of her blankets and scooted closer to the pup. Fuller licked her cheeks.

"Yeah, but I have to sneak her out before Dad gets back." Dogs had been deemed another carrier of germs.

From below, the clatter of the backdoor closing echoed, followed by muffled voices. Janey perked up. "Mom's back. But what about Fuller?"

John pressed a finger to his lips and stood. "You keep Fuller here. I'll see what's going on."

Creeping down the stairs, he slid quietly toward the kitchen but paused in the murky shadows in the hall. Dad sat at the table, his head buried in his hands. Matt and Perry crowded close on Dad's right side, Uncle Nick on the left. A Catholic priest, Nick was Mom's younger brother. That John's brothers were crying meant something horrible. And priests never cried.

John burst into the room. "What's wrong?"

Dad straightened and exchanged glances with Uncle Nick before drawing a deep breath. "It's your mother. She... She died in the ambulance, Son. I'm sorry."

John shook his head. "Sorry? You should have let me go! I should have been with her. I could have saved her!"

Without warning, Janey darted into the room. He should have known she'd follow.

She shoved up next to John. "Saved who? Why are you yelling?" Her eyes widened as they darted from person to person before settling back on him. "Where's Momma? Is she in her room?"

Dad cleared his throat. "Come here, sweetheart."

Janey took a single step closer but didn't speak.

"Your mom passed away. She's gone to Heaven, Janey-girl," Dad said.

"No! She'd never leave without telling me goodbye. She swore!" Janey turned to John, her hands clasped in begging. "Do your magic. Make them take us to her. We'll bring Momma back. Please!"

Tears burned John's eyes as he dropped his gaze to the ground. There was no lie big enough to make this better, no sleight of hand to make death disappear.

At her anguished cry-cough, John raised his head as she bolted from the room, her bare feet beating a path toward the staircase. He turned to follow. He promised Mom he'd always watch over Janey.

"Give her a minute, Son," Dad said. "Then I'll go talk to her."

"But—"

The front door slammed so hard the glass in the windowpanes rattled. The adults exchanged confused looks.

John raced straight for the door. "Janey, wait! Don't leave me!"

CHAPTER TWO

Eleven years later – May 2005
River Haven, Iowa

It was the party no one wanted to miss, held at the best place in southeast Iowa for underage drinkers to cut loose and get wild — the pasture behind Mohler's farm pond. The towering orange bonfire promised loud music, icy beer, and hot women. Over a hundred people had shown up for US Army Specialist John McKay's going away bash, with more pulling in despite the late hour. And after midnight, things got interesting in the corn wilds.

Rita, the cute redhead dancing with John, dashed toward the field outhouse as soon as the song ended. They'd just met earlier that evening at the county fair and could barely keep their hands off each other.

"I'll grab us another cold one!" John called after her. That Rita glanced back over one shoulder and winked boded well. Tonight was his final night of leave and getting laid before deploying was his top priority.

He staggered toward the flatbed trailer loaded with coolers. The crowd encircling Beer Central gave him an enthusiastic welcome. Being the guest of honor meant everyone offered him a beer, a shot, or a slap on the back — most times all three.

Even though he'd graduated two years ago, he recognized plenty of faces from his high school days. Funny how many of them hadn't realized John joined the Army eighteen months ago. Then again, the fact he'd had the poor luck to get stationed at Fort DeWald, Illinois, for advanced training — a mere four hours away — meant he'd been back to River Haven enough to always know where the next party would be.

Everyone had questions ranging from serious to inane.

"Where are you going?" *Iraq.*

"How long you gonna be gone?" *One year.*

"Will you send me a picture of you on a camel?" *No.*

"Will you miss us?" *Double no.*

This was the last time he'd be partying on the edge of a cornfield, watching the same stupid people get drunk, puke, and stumble perilously close to the fire. All the stuff he'd joined the military to escape. The Army promised a future outside of farming and the McKay family businesses. Uncle Sam also offered exciting duty posts, like Hawaii and California, which suited John's desire to see more of the country. Sure, that meant pulling a tour in Iraq first, but he and his platoon were ready. Locked and loaded, eager to serve. No reservations.

Except for that blasted recurring dream—

"I need another drink!" John jettisoned his empty beer bottle into a trash barrel.

"I got you covered, man." Sammy Mohler shoved a red plastic cup into John's hand before half-filling it with tequila. "Dude, where's your buddy, Layton? We need to get in one last toast before everyone scatters."

"He's...somewhere." John glanced around. Layton was undoubtedly wrapped in a blanket at the far edge of the pond, prioritizing. A Texas native, Layton Burnet attracted a harem wherever he went, and these Midwestern girls had no immunity to his southern charm.

John first met Layton eighteen months ago in basic where Layton had introduced himself as a sixth-generation Texan, which meant "everything's bigger" was his favorite topic of conversation and his signature pick up line. The generation thing was lost on everyone except other true Texans, who each pretended they could trace their lineage back to Steven F. Austin or Sam Houston. Texans were weird that way, but darn if it didn't make them more likable. When John introduced himself as a seventh-generation Iowan, Layton asked where Idaho was. Even made potato jokes.

The two men became close friends. Together, they'd survived tough drill sergeants, advanced combat training and extreme partying. More than battle buddies and friends, they were brothers to the end. The Texan had come back to Iowa with John every time they could wrangle leave. Layton fit in so well you'd think he'd been born here.

Sammy held the tequila bottle aloft and shouted for attention. The music quieted. "Let's hear it for John and Layton. Fighting to defend the United States. Go over there and show those stupid terrorists who's boss. Then get your butts back here safe and sound. *Hooah!*"

The crowd repeated the Army cry, *"Hooah!"* and when Toby Keith's song, *American Soldier*, started playing everyone raised their drink in John's direction while sing-shouting along.

That several people appeared ready to cry made John look away. Geez, if these people got to him, how hard would it be to say goodbye to his family? He upended the cheap tequila, barely noticing the burn.

A white pickup wheeled in, spinning up dust before nearly sideswiping another parked truck as it rolled to a stop. John's eyes narrowed at the truck's front vanity plate. A US flag in flames overlaid with a skull and crossbones was the logo for the Justice Freedom

Association, an anarchist organization spawned by the hate-fueled shock radio network that shared its name.

Three men climbed out of the truck. The tallest was his arch enemy, Randy Keener. John and Keener had tangled regularly back in high school, a rivalry that went deeper than Catholic High School versus Public High. The acrimony between the Keeners and the McKays was my-dad-beat-up-your-dad ancient. Like the Hatfields and McCoys, but spelled differently, his brothers joked.

Keener and his pals wore JFA T-shirts. *Justice Freaking A-holes.* John crushed the cup in his fist as they approached.

Keener stopped when he spotted John. "Thought you'd shipped out already."

John straightened to his full six-three. "Thinking never was your strong suit."

Keener snarled. "At least I was smart enough not to enlist during war time."

"Since the Army doesn't take felons or losers, you were safe." Snickers rippled through the crowd gathered behind John. Sensing blood in the water, folks were already choosing sides.

Sammy Mohler pushed his way between them, arms out. "If you came to start trouble, Keener, leave."

"Me? What about him?" Keener pointed to John.

"Party's in his honor," Sammy said. "Show some respect."

"McKays are a bunch of cheating liars," Keener said. "They don't deserve respect."

That the slur wasn't new made it easier to ignore. Everyone here knew the McKays' impeccable reputation and the Keeners' lack thereof. "I see your big mouth still starts talking before your brain engages." John turned away.

"Well, at least me and my big mouth will still be here partying while you're over there playing GI Joe in a sandbox. You and that redneck Texan are nothing more than government patsies and terrorist targets. Pawns in a war we'll never win. Ten bucks says you both come home in boxes."

The remark hit too close. John wheeled around. "Take your anti-war rhetoric somewhere else, Keener. No one here wants to hear it."

"I'm not anti-war, soldier-boy. I'm anti-government. Big difference." Keener's shoulders leveled. "And don't even get me started on that self-righteous idgit in the White House. He's leading this country straight to Hell."

Dissension swelled openly amongst the partygoers. This part of the country wore their patriotism on their sleeves. They fully supported the President and his war efforts.

One of Keener's pals noticed the crowd's mood and elbowed Keener. "Maybe this ain't the time."

"You're right, you're right." Keener made a half bow toward John. "No hard feelings, McKay. And to prove it, while you're gone, I'll make a point of taking good care of your hot little sister." He made a show of grabbing his crotch.

John's fist connected with Keener's mouth before he completed the lewd thrust.

Keener recovered quickly and charged. The two men hit the ground in a tequila-tinged blur of fists. Though equally matched in height, build, and blood-alcohol levels, John ended up on top, repeatedly punching Keener's face with both fists. The fight ended abruptly when Layton and two others yanked John off.

"He's had enough." Layton stepped in front of John, blocking his view. "You hear me?"

Adrenaline pulsed through John's system. He was still jacked, still ready to fight, but he knew to heed Layton. *Brothers to the end.*

Blood streamed from Keener's nose and face as his friends pulled him to his feet and helped him stand. "This isn't over, McKay!"

John glared over Layton's shoulder as Keener's friends dragged him away. "I agree. Practice is over. Let's dance!"

"Easy." Layton raised a hand. "He's just posturing. Let it go."

Sammy Mohler started swearing as flashing blue lights slowed on the highway near the main gate entrance. "Who called the cops?"

"I did," Keener's buddy shouted before disappearing into the dark. "McKay is crazy. He deserves to be arrested."

"Get the wagon out of here!" Even as Sammy shouted, the flatbed trailer with the coolers was being towed off along with the drunkest of the underage drinkers.

"Better pull your act together, bro," Layton warned.

John nodded. Just the thought of calling their sergeant from jail sobered him. Neither he nor Layton were twenty-one yet, and an arrest could jeopardize their deployment and Army careers.

"Everybody act cool. Nothing to see here," Sammy joked as a sheriff's patrol car pulled in and stopped.

Two deputies climbed out. John released a tense breath. Deputy Blake Evans had graduated with John's and Sammy's older brothers. Their families went way back.

"We got this," John whispered to Layton.

Blake scanned the crowd, nodding once in John's direction before addressing Sammy. "We got a call regarding a fight. False alarm?"

Before Sammy could respond, Randy Keener stumbled out from between two trucks, waving a tire iron, while shaking off his friends' attempts to hold him back.

Someone yelled, "Look out!"

"Yeah, he better look out," Keener shouted.

Blake Evans shifted away from the crowd and faced Keener with one hand on his pistol, his other arm held straight out, palm up. "Drop it and freeze, Keener! Now!"

At the deputy's order, Keener paused, using the tire iron as a pointer. "Don't you dare take McKay's side. Look at my face. My nose is broken."

"I said drop it," Blake thundered as he unsnapped the restraint on his holster.

"Sure thing, officer." Keener lowered his arm and then raised it again. "Right after I crowbar McKay's heart out—Owww!"

The other deputy who had silently rushed in from behind,

slammed Keener to the ground and disarmed him. "You're under arrest," the deputy said before snapping handcuffs on Keener.

"This is police brutality!" Keener protested as he was pulled upright. "I didn't do anything."

The other deputy shook his head. "You failed to obey an officer of the law. You threatened bodily harm. You're drunk and disorderly. That's just for starters."

"I'll show you starters." Keener tried to kick the deputy but lost his balance and nearly fell.

"And assaulting an officer." The deputy began reciting the Miranda rights as he steered Keener away.

Keener dug in his heels, twisting to glare back at John. "I hope someone blows your head off over there and saves me the trouble—"

The other deputy shoved Keener into the back of the patrol car, cutting off his tirade.

Blake Evans secured his weapon before approaching John and Layton. "That apple didn't fall far. His old man's a nasty drunk, too." Growing serious, Blake offered each of them a handshake before addressing John. "I saw your brothers earlier. They said you take off tomorrow. Man, I'm proud of you. But you two watch your six over there."

"Yes, sir."

Blake nodded before moving away. "Need to talk to you, Sammy."

Layton let out a low whistle once the deputy moved out of earshot. "You weren't even nervous, were you?"

John shook his head but stopped as nausea tilted his stomach. He'd had a lot to drink and it didn't help that Keener landed a few solid punches in his gut.

A blond came up and latched onto Layton's arm. "There you are. We've got unfinished business, cowboy. Come on."

Layton looked at John. "You good?"

"Yes," John lied. "I'll catch you later."

As soon as the blond tugged Layton away, John headed toward

the rear of the old barn. If he was going to puke, he didn't want any witnesses.

But someone had beaten him to the spot.

Forcing himself to hold the urge at bay, John circled toward the parking lot. In the dark, the sea of trucks looked alike. If he'd been drinking to forget, it had worked. Where had he parked?

He made it to the tree line before the booze cashed in all its chips. Throwing up left him wobbly. What had he been thinking, chasing beer with tequila? *Ten foot tall and stupid.* When he found his truck, he crawled inside and slumped against the seat, fighting vertigo.

When he opened his eyes again, the double vision had passed along with most of the dizziness, but he felt awful. The dash clock read 2:17. He thought of going to find Rita, the redhead, but worried he'd embarrass himself. The only thing he wanted now was his own bed. He sent Layton a text. No telling what it said between the tequila and autocorrect, though.

Cranking up his truck, he made his way to the main road. This wasn't the first time he'd driven home drunk. Fortunately, the McKay family farm was less than three miles away. With the cops en route to the county jail, the biggest things he had to watch for were other drunks and deer.

The highway was deserted, so he floored it. The tachometer surged ahead of the speedometer, but a bright flash of light on the horizon had him backing off the gas. At first, he thought it was lightning. When the light went on and off twice more, John realized someone up ahead was driving in stealth mode, turning on their headlights just long enough to see the next stretch of highway.

He flashed his high beams a couple times to alert the other driver. He expected the other vehicle's lights to come back on and stay on, but they didn't. Had the car pulled off the road? Worse, had it wrecked? Concerned, he sped up.

The light came on again suddenly, a couple hundred feet away. Too late he realized he'd crossed the center line. A car swerved around his truck, avoiding a head-on collision. Swearing, John slammed on the brakes and overcorrected. His truck started to flip, was already airborne. A desperate sense of *do something* clenched his chest as he grabbed for the seat belt.

Up ahead, a flash of green light burst like a fireball before shooting toward the sky and winking out. His truck bounced on the asphalt and lurched to a stop without flipping.

What just happened? How in the world had he not wrecked?

John stuck his head out the window and craned his neck. The other car, the green light, had all disappeared. There were no headlights except his own illuminating the night. Was John so drunk he'd hallucinated?

Spooked, he looked around again. Nothing appeared familiar. A mild panic had him clutching the wheel. *Where am I? Think, blast it.*

Dropping his gaze, John scanned the horizon once more, this time looking for another light. A star to guide him. Back in the day, Perry and Matt permanently mounted Christmas lights in the shape of a star on the tallest McKay silo to help them find their way home. For years it was a family joke, but as John spotted it due east, he had to admit his older brothers were geniuses. With several bulbs burnt out, it now resembled a lopsided triangle but still did the trick.

A few minutes later, John arrived home. Before turning into the farm driveway, he cut off his headlights and pulled onto the side road that led to the bunkhouse. Another brilliant move by his brothers was talking Dad into building a two-bedroom bunkhouse addition onto the hay barn far enough from the main house to allow total privacy. While his brothers had long since married and moved to their own farms, John had claimed one of the bunkhouse rooms in high school and kept it after enlisting. Layton used the second bedroom frequently enough to claim it.

No sooner had John parked than a dim flashlight beam extinguished behind the bunkhouse. He caught shadowy movement as someone ducked around the edge of the building, hiding.

A rush of adrenaline granted him a moment of sober clarity. He'd bet it was Keener's friends, intent on ambushing him to even the score. It had probably been them playing tricks back there on the highway. He'd teach them to not mess with a McKay.

Slipping out of the car, John crouched low and headed in the opposite direction. Years of sneaking in and out paid off as he circled around the far side of the hay barn and approached the bunkhouse noiselessly from behind. Oblivious to John's approach, the other person moved out of the shadows ahead to peer around the corner at John's truck.

Rushing forward, John attempted a choke hold, but stumbled as he knocked the person flat. A fist jabbed him solidly in the eye. Ignoring the sharp pain radiating from his cheekbone, he drew back to retaliate.

"John! It's me!"

He stopped his fist a moment before punching his sister in the jaw.

"Janey! What are you doing out here?" John rolled away and pushed unsteadily to his feet.

She didn't reply right away, her breath catching in a sob. Crap! He'd probably broken her when he'd slammed her to the ground.

Furious to realize how close he'd come to decking her, he tugged her to her feet, and then dragged her into the bunkhouse and in his bedroom. The overhead light half-blinded him when he flipped it on.

"Are you okay?" he barked.

Janey tugged her arm free. "Yes, you jerk! Look what you did!" She whipped her hands toward him, flinging mud across his shirt and onto the floor.

John did a double take. Janey was wearing a short, bare-shouldered dress that was now covered in muck. "What are you dressed up for? Wait. Were you sneaking out? Or in?"

While his sister still lived in the big farmhouse with their widowed father, John had no one but himself to blame for her ninja-like skills that had allowed them to slip in and out as children.

"Neither," she snapped. "Where is Layton?"

"I left him at Sammy's party." John took in her defensive stance, her heavy eye makeup. "Whoa. Why are you asking about Layton?"

Her chin lifted. "None of your business."

"Layton's my best friend and you're my sister. That makes it my business." He leaned closer and caught a whiff of perfume. "What are you hiding behind your back?"

"Nothing." She stepped sideways. "You're drunk. I'm going back to the house to change."

As Janey turned away, John spotted the red envelope in her hand and snatched it away. Layton's name was emblazoned in curlicues and hearts across the front. It reeked of her cologne. A blind man could have connected those dots.

"Give me that!" she demanded.

He held the envelope above his head, out of her reach. "So help me, if this is what I think it is."

She blushed, confirming his suspicions.

John didn't need this. Not tonight. "You are not giving Layton a love letter."

"Who says that's what it is?"

"If it's not, then I'm opening it."

"Don't you dare!"

He dropped his hand but immediately raised it when she dove for the envelope. Blast it. His baby sister had a crush on his best friend. Why hadn't he seen this coming? Given the amount of time Janey and Layton spent together when they'd been home on leave, it shouldn't surprise him, but John was so accustomed to Janey following him everywhere that he never thought twice that she tagged along with Layton and him. A mistake he would rectify right now.

"Whatever you think you feel for Layton, it's not mutual, Janey. He thinks of you as my pain-in-the-neck baby sister."

"He thinks I'm special. And cute."

"Baby calves with milk on their faces are cute. They're also too stupid to fend for themselves."

"You know nothing about Layton."

"I know everything. I room with the guy." He looked pointedly at the top of her head. Janey had the McKay trademark hair — midnight black. "Layton likes his women fast, hot, and blond. And he has no trouble finding them. Trust me, he's not interested in dark-haired little girls."

Her eyes narrowed to arrow slits. "Quit with the little girl crap. News flash: I graduate in three weeks and I'll be eighteen in two months. I'm going off to college in the fall. But, oh wait — you'll be gone for that."

The reminder stung. "You still need to forget about Layton."

"Because you said so? It's not your choice. And I'm sick of you trash talking every guy I have an interest in."

"Fine. You want to see Layton tonight? Let's drive out to Mohler's pond. He's there with Abby Wells. A blond. And don't forget his girlfriend in Texas. Remember Sharlene, the rodeo queen? Did I mention she's blond?"

"They broke up."

"For what? The hundredth time? They were engaged." His words might be slurred, but he knew what was right for his sister. "Grow up, Janey. Save the silly romance for your novels. You're not Layton's type and you never will be."

For a moment she looked as if she'd been struck. That quickly, she morphed back into full blown pissed off. "You know nothing. Give me that letter."

"I'm burning this letter. And don't even try writing another one, or I'll make sure to permanently embarrass you with Layton."

Her lack of response startled John. He and Janey had epic arguments, each determined to out-insult, out-shout the other in a race to score the last word. This time, though, revulsion blazed in her eyes, the silence between them deadly. Belatedly, he realized he'd crossed a line, the one about never interfering in someone's love life. A line meant to deter *her* interference, not his. Worse, he'd just insulted her writing and intelligence, too.

"Give my letter back." She looked ready to cry.

The heartbreak in her eyes telegraphed the seriousness of the matter. This was far worse than a crush. This hearkened back to the stories their mother told. "He's not your one. You've got to trust me on this, Janey." He reached out.

She smacked his hand and edged backwards. "Trust? I'll never trust you again. I hate you, John."

"You'll thank me someday, and—"

The door slammed before he finished. He started after her, but the roiling in his stomach reminded him how much he'd had to drink. He glanced around for the trash can and pulled it to the bed as dizziness overtook him. He sank onto the mattress, his elbows on his knees and his head in his hands.

It was just as well she'd left. If he said more, he'd regret it. Maybe it was time she learned the world didn't revolve around her. That he wasn't always going to be around to fix everything.

Leaning forward, he grabbed the trash can and prayed he'd pass out soon. Arguing with Janey had sobered him up just enough to remember what he'd drank to forget. The awful premonition. The one he couldn't tell anyone.

That Layton was going to die.

CHAPTER THREE

May 2005
River Haven, Iowa

An hour later, Janey McKay returned to the bunkhouse for round two with John. She found him passed out. Seeing his bruised eye gave her a bit of satisfaction, though she was tempted to blacken his other eye after a search of his room failed to produce the letter he'd stolen.

She'd risked everything in that letter, letting desperation erode her caution and pride as she poured heart and soul into words meant for Layton Burnet's eyes only. She would never forgive John if he'd read it.

Her brother's cruel remarks — *not Layton's type, likes his women fast, hot, and blond* — replayed as she hunkered down outside the bunkhouse waiting for Layton to return. How dare her idiot brother suggest Layton wasn't her *one?* John did not understand what Layton meant to her and what she suspected — hoped — she meant to Layton. She'd known from the first moment she'd met him a year and a half ago that he was the one her mother had promised she'd meet someday. *"You'll feel something in your heart, and then you'll get an unmistakable sign."*

The feeling and the sign had both been unmistakable.

Despite her brother's interference, time remained the bigger enemy. Their looming deployment meant Janey had less than twenty-four hours to finish what Layton had started the evening before at the county fair.

She, John, and Layton had gone to the fair to watch her nephew participate in the 4-H livestock show. Determined to spend every moment she could with Layton, Janey had rejoiced when John wandered off with a flirty redhead he met at the fairgrounds. She and Layton rode all the adult rides twice. Inside the haunted house, he'd slipped away in the darkness only to jump out a few moments later. When she'd screamed in fright, he'd tugged her into his arms and apologized over and over while holding her tight.

She would have stayed in that attraction forever if the carny hadn't come in and run them off. Back out on the midway, Layton promised to make it up. He bought her a massive bag of cotton candy and when she pretended to refuse to share, he tickled her.

"God, I love to hear you laugh," he teased. She focused on the three words, *I. Love. You.* He tried and failed to win her a stuffed bear. After complaining that the games were rigged, he finally won a split-heart necklace, complete with two chains. TOGETHER FOREVER the stamped metal heart read when the halves were conjoined.

"I'm ashamed I didn't win something bigger," Layton said as he'd struggled to fasten the chain around her neck at her insistence.

"This is perfect."

"Hardly. But keep it and think of me while I'm overseas."

At the time she'd been so overwhelmed by the gesture she could only press the other half-heart necklace into his palm and whisper, "ditto."

John and the redhead had the pitiful timing to return just then, blowing Janey's moment with Layton by announcing it was party time.

She'd grabbed Layton's arm. "I'm going, too."

"That's a big no." John took a sip from the flask the redhead held out. "I am not babysitting on my last night of freedom." The redhead giggled and pressed her boobs against his arm.

Despite Janey's protests, she had been left at the farm where she'd spent over six hours composing that letter to Layton.

She touched the half heart around her neck as she waited outside the bunkhouse beneath the stars. With Layton likely returning any moment, there was no time to rewrite her letter. Her only option was to tell him face-to-face, tonight, that she loved him. With family coming over after Mass in the morning, this would be their last shot at privacy.

Except Layton never returned that night. *He's with Abby Wells.* Janey cursed John for telling her that. Just before dawn, she made a resolution to never speak to either of them.

Avoiding John and Layton the next morning was simple. John told their father he had food-poisoning and couldn't attend Sunday Mass. Translation: the jerk had a hangover. And Layton supposedly left early that morning to run some last-minute errands. Translation: he still hadn't made it home from last night's party. Janey fumed through the church service, half expecting to be struck by lightning for her bad thoughts.

When she and Dad returned, they found Layton sipping coffee in the kitchen. Her ire melted in the warmth of his smile. How would she survive not seeing him for an entire year? Worrying twenty-four-seven if he was safe when stories of the war in Iraq dominated the news?

Dad excused himself to change clothes, leaving Janey and Layton alone.

"Good morning, cupcake." Layton tipped his cup toward her. "Sleep well?"

Her temper spiked. "I slept fine. How's Abby doing?"

Layton looked confused. "Abby? Who's Abby?"

She narrowed her eyes. Had John lied about Layton being with Abby Wells last night? Was her brother that determined to thwart her? "Never mind."

Layton moved closer. "Do we have time for one last ride?"

The request startled and saddened her. *One last ride.* "Of course." She grabbed his hand and tugged him out the back door, eager to get away.

"Easy, tiger. We're not in a race."

Oh yes, we are. "McKays don't do slow." She'd recited her family's racing motto hundreds of times, but today it carried new meaning.

Out in the machine barn, she climbed in the passenger side of one of the bigger ATV buggies with bench seats. Letting Layton drive was significant. McKays always drove. He took off through the west pasture, headed toward her favorite place on the entire farm: the pond. Had he chosen the destination on purpose?

Every time John and Layton came home on leave, she and Layton spent countless hours traversing the fields and consequently he knew the McKay farm as well as she did. He questioned her about everything, occasionally sharing brief snippets from his childhood spent on his late grandfather's ranch in Texas. While he went out of his way to not contradict her brother, Layton seemed to appreciate the land and Iowa's quiet lifestyle.

They rode in easy silence, the day's light so clear it hurt her eyes. The unfussy magic of being with him brushed over her skin like a honeysuckle-drenched breeze. He stopped the ATV beneath the big maple beside the pond.

He leaned back and sighed, eyes wide as if trying to take in the whole panorama. Then he glanced at her. "I will miss this place. It's like home to me, you know?"

"I don't want you to leave." Her eyes filled with tears as she looked away.

Layton gently grasped her shoulders and tugged her closer across the seat. "Aww, don't cry, little darlin'. This deployment will fly by, and we'll be back here bugging you in no time."

"But I won't see you for an entire year."

"We can still keep in touch. Look, I'm not the best at correspondence, but I'd love it if you'd write me. And I promise to write back."

I'd love it... She clung to his words. She'd used similar words in her letter.

Twisting toward him, she reached up and framed his face between her hands, memorizing every handsome detail. His dark blond hair kept military short. The deep green of his eyes. Those full lips. She mourned that the moment was too serious for the dimples that bracketed the world's sexiest smile.

"I need to tell you something important." Gathering all her courage, Janey moved into his personal space. "I think I love you, Layton Burnet," she whispered just before kissing him.

While she'd daydreamed endlessly about The Kiss, the reality of it was mind boggling. Before meeting Layton, she'd lamented how her three overprotective, overbearing brothers kept her distanced from the intimacies her classmates shared. But once she met Layton and knew he was her one — she'd been glad to save her kisses. For this moment.

A sudden panic overtook her as her inexperience kicked in. She'd started the kiss, but what to do next?

Her anxiety melted when Layton's hands speared through her long hair, letting it fall forward across his cheek, a dark silky curtain that cocooned them. Holding her tight, he took over the kiss and deepened it. His tongue probed into her mouth.

This kiss... Her pulse elevated as she pressed closer against his chest.

Abruptly he pulled away and shoved her back across the seat. "I'm so sorry, Janey. I don't know what I was thinking."

Confused, she scooted close and tried to hook her arms around his neck again. "Didn't you hear what I said? I love—"

"Yes, I heard. And no, you don't." He cut her off as he gripped her forearms and extricated himself from her embrace.

Stung by his rejection, Janey blinked against the blinding urge to cry. Embarrassment flushed her cheeks as she struggled to get away.

Layton didn't release his grip, holding her at arm's length. "Wait. Please look at me. Please? We – I can't do this right now, Janey. We're going off to war. John is like a brother to me and you're so young."

"I'm almost eighteen. And you're what? Nineteen?"

"It's more." He stopped talking as the sound of a motorcycle racing in from behind grew loud.

Angered and relieved, Janey took advantage of the interruption and slid as far from Layton as she could get just before John pulled in next to them, spinning up dirt as he slid into a sideways halt.

"There you are." John wore dark sunglasses, making it hard to read his expression, but his lips stayed pissed-flat as he spoke. "Matt and Perry just arrived, and everyone wants to see Layton. Robin and Lisa are putting dinner on the table as we speak."

Janey hopped out of the ATV. "Let me have the bike so I can get back to help them."

John swung off the motorcycle so fast she was afraid he'd drop it. "Tell Dad that Layton and I will move the cattle while we're out here."

Grateful to escape, she avoided looking at either of them. Her heart felt bruised, her ego battered. Back at the barn, she paced, needing time to pull it together before facing the rest of her family. Years of motocross racing had taught her the art of sucking it up, but that seemed easy compared to this.

Despite his protests, she knew Layton had felt the spark between them. But how did they overcome a war? A ticking clock? How could she make him see her as a woman versus John's younger sister? Make him give her — them — a chance when he only had a few hours before leaving?

By the time John and Layton returned, Janey's anger had restored her equilibrium and boosted her ability to ignore them, which wasn't easy. Everything about this day centered on John and Layton. The farm's crowded kitchen teemed with activities orchestrated by her sisters-in-law. Robin and Lisa had prepared a spread that rivaled Thanksgiving. A clove-studded ham, a roasted turkey stuffed with apples, and platters of golden fried chicken with milk gravy — because that was Layton's favorite — sat like jewels in a king's crown, surrounded by mounds of potatoes, casseroles, and veggies.

Janey's nephews swarmed about, competing for John's and Layton's attention. Lisa and Robin had six boys between the two of them, aged ten through two. While the younger children didn't understand what deployment meant, they picked up on the tense significance of the day.

It took Matt's ear-splitting whistle to get everyone to take their seat around the kitchen table. Janey sat as far from Layton as she could and feigned interest in the food. Everyone bowed their heads as Dad offered a formal blessing.

When Matt razzed John about his black eye, John made the-other-guy-looks-worse jokes that even had Dad laughing. Janey seethed, longing to claim responsibility and to call him out for stealing her letter. As far as her family was concerned, John and Layton were heroes. Today they were made of Teflon, and nothing would stick to the rats.

Plates full, conversation gave way to the scrape of knives and forks and "*mmm-mmm*" compliments between mouthfuls. Janey pushed garden peas around on her plate, paying an inordinate amount of attention to her nephews' antics. What little she ate felt like lead pellets in her stomach.

Dessert was a selection of pies — apple, pumpkin, and cherry. After eating a slice of each, John stood and cleared his throat. "Time to go."

That one sentence stopped all movement and conversation in the room. Heads and hands stilled in a moment of silence that left Janey cold. Dad rose from his chair, a sign for everyone else to do the same.

Matt grabbed a picture of their mother off the buffet. Mom would be with them during this, even though she'd been dead twelve years.

Janey lagged behind as they single-filed out the front door and crowded along the porch rail. Once outside, she regretted her choice to be last. End of the line meant watching and waiting. Enduring the hurt of the long goodbye. John and Layton began at the far side of the porch, bidding farewell to Matt and Perry, then peeling toddlers off their legs before stepping away.

When Layton moved in front of her father, he straightened to attention before extending a hand. "Sir, thank you for your hospitality."

"Oh, for Pete's sake. You've been here, what? A dozen times?" Dad asked.

Fifteen. Janey hated that she knew that.

"Bottom line, you're as good as family. Except for that awful accent." Her father shook Layton's hand, then bear-hugged him.

As John shifted close to their father, his shoulders also leveled.

"Call me sir, and I'll thrash your butt." Dad sounded gruff, but he'd never raised a hand to anyone. Forced into single parenthood late in life, Ward McKay juggled a farm and a business but never missed an evening meal.

Janey turned away as John wrapped his arms around their father.

"Your mother would be so proud," Dad said. "I can feel her watching from Heaven."

Her eyelids stung as John cleared his throat and said, "I love you, Dad."

"Love you, too, Son."

Now John and Layton stood before Janey, but the ache in her chest prevented her from looking directly at either of them.

"Janey, I—" John and Layton spoke at once, then stopped and gave the other a go-ahead motion.

The sound of gravel churning had everyone turning as a car pulled in the drive.

Her Uncle Nick, the leader of their local parish for over ten years, bounded up the steps two at a time. "I apologize for missing dinner, Ward."

"No problem," Dad said. "We understand. Duty calls."

Janey wanted to run to her uncle and be enveloped in his hug. Since Mom's death, they'd grown especially close. Instead, she held back and watched as Layton and her uncle competed in a quick squeeze-off handshake in lieu of farewell. Uncle Nick claimed his priest's collar gave him superpowers, and he always won.

Uncle Nick turned to John next. "I'm sorry. I got called away with an emergency. You wanted to talk? Do we still have time?"

Janey could have sworn that John looked guilty, but he shook his head. "I just wanted to ask you to keep me and my squad in your prayers."

"Always. You guys will be back before you know it," Nick said.

Robin touched Nick's shoulder. "You're just in time for family pictures." She held up a camera.

"Here." Layton extended his hand. "Let me take them."

Everyone filed down the steps and lined up by the rock-edged flower beds. The climbing rose half-covered the concrete garden-Madonna that her brothers called their Silent Sister because she showed up in decades of family photos. The profusion of yellow roses seemed to mock Janey. Once upon a time she'd been so certain they were the sign that Layton was her *one*. How could she have been so wrong?

Janey squeezed in between Matt and Perry, as far from John as she could get. And Heaven help Layton if he dared to say, "smile."

"On three, everyone say, 'John's eye is ugly.'" Layton's remark made everyone but her laugh.

After a few shots, Dad grew exasperated. "Enough. These boys have to go."

"I want one more," John announced. "With Janey."

She slid him the sideways stink eye when he moved in and hooked her arm, confident she wouldn't make a scene in front of everyone.

"Don't be mad." John kept his voice low. "Not on my last day."

She didn't respond, not ready to make nice. Not after what he'd done.

A wet nose pressed into Janey's hand as Fuller, the family collie, scooted in and sat near their feet. John petted the collie. Another family photo anomaly was Fuller's presence only in pictures with John and Janey.

After two shots, she tried to jerk free, but John held her arm.

"Janey, I..."

"You're what? Sorry?" Razors lined her hushed voice.

"You know McKays don't apologize."

"They also don't steal. Oh, wait..."

"I wanted to protect you."

"I can protect myself. I don't need you anymore." Tears welled in her eyes.

"Geez! Don't cry!" John hissed in her ear. "You're a McKay. Act like one."

It was a throwback to their motocross racing days. Back when she'd have done anything he asked.

"Leave me alone." She slugged him in the solar plexus and was grateful to see him wince in pain. Her brothers had taught her well. *Don't fight like a girl.* "Just go."

He sighed. "Look, we've got a few minutes. Let me get a picture of you and Layton."

Janey rose to the balls of feet, ready to flee, but Layton had already moved in and casually draped an arm across her shoulders as John moved away. Her spine stiffened in indignation.

"I hate that we had a misunderstanding," Layton whispered.

That's all it was to him? A misunderstanding? She reached to unfasten the half-heart necklace around her neck. "I thought this meant something."

He stilled her hand. "It does mean something. Maybe just not what you want right now. Keep it until I'm back. Let's see if you feel the same in a year. Then we'll talk. Okay?"

She met his gaze and struggled not to melt into a puddle at his feet. Hating her brother was easy, but this man? Never.

Before she could say anything, John shouted. "Got to go!"

They were out of time. Rising onto tiptoes, she hugged Layton, pressed a kiss to his cheek. "Keep my stupid brother safe. And you, too." His hands tightened on her waist, but he let go too soon. Through tears, she watched him walk away.

Her brother high-fived all six of their nephews before heading to the car. When he opened the passenger door, the terribleness of being left behind overwhelmed Janey. She shot forward, Fuller close on her heels. "John. Wait."

John paused and then opened his arms as she ran up. "Please, Janey—"

"Shut up." She pressed her forehead against his shoulder. "I hate what you did, and I'll never forgive you. But I also hate that you're going overseas to fight. That scares me."

"I'm not worried and you shouldn't be, either. We're golden, remember?"

"Take care of you — and Layton. Until you're home again." With those last four words she invoked their childhood pledge to only say goodbye if you were never coming back.

He kissed the top of her head. "Love you more, Sis." Those four words were his way of acknowledging the three words she was still too mad to say.

Fuller barked. John reached down to scratch the spot behind the collie's ear. "I'll miss you too, girl." He gave the dog a hand signal to return before he, too, moved away.

Janey wept as she returned to the porch and watched them pull out. Layton hit the car horn three times, breaking her heart all over again.

"Come back to me," she whispered as the car disappeared. *Until you're home again.*

CHAPTER FOUR

Fourteen months later – July 2006
Baghdad, Iraq

July in Iraq must have been the prototype for Hell, John McKay decided. Unending days combined with unbearable heat. *Check.* Constant wind from the north that felt about as good as a blow dryer on high pointed directly at his face. *Double check.* Foot patrols carrying a thirty-pound rucksack and a weapon while wearing body armor and a head-oven helmet. *Nailed it.*

God, he couldn't wait to wrap up this deployment. Just four more weeks. As their one-year tour of duty extended into fifteen months, John's perspective had transformed. Like everyone in his squad, he was sick of war, sick of sand, sick of nightmares instead of sleep.

It was late afternoon, closing in on twelve hours since his team started the day's mission. Heat shimmers radiated from the hard-packed earth, the ground refusing to absorb the one-twenty-plus temperatures. Beneath his uniform, it felt more like two-twenty. He'd never get used to the heat, though he'd learned to endure it. Same way he endured being away from home.

Home.

Funny how the more Iraq resembled Hell, the more Iowa resembled Heaven. Layton was right: *"You don't know what you got till someone else has it."*

Could John crawl back home, the prodigal soldier, and beg his family's forgiveness for leaving? Offer one big *mea culpa* for all offenses? This deployment had changed him, mostly for the good, but was it enough? Would they believe he'd reformed?

After adjusting his pack, John lengthened his stride. While he no longer believed one man could save the world — he no longer believed lots of things — he had to admit the Army's strategy of winning the hearts and minds of the Iraqi people appeared to be paying off. Oh sure, they still had the occasional troublemaker throw a rock or take a potshot at them, but overall, for the last several weeks there had been no explosions or sniper activity in their sector. Even the radical groups had been quiet, staying out of the area for a change. Not that anyone expected that to last. Those rogue fundamentalist groups were also out to capture local hearts and minds, and not in good ways. John's squad took every advantage of the peacefulness, working hard to build a decent rapport in the neighborhoods and making nice with the general population.

Today's shift had been uneventful. His nine-man team spent the morning providing security at one of the larger, open-air marketplaces near the outskirts of Baghdad. Later, they scored big points with the locals by doling out lumber. It surprised John to see how cheerful people got when he handed them two-by-fours. For most of Baghdad's residents, lumber was a high-value commodity. No big box hardware stores here.

His leader, Sergeant Boswell, had even ferreted out a snippet of intelligence to pass along to the intel section when they returned to their Forward Operating Base, which was where they headed now. No one protested taking a shortcut through a wide alley they'd patrolled earlier in the day. This alley was another hard-won strategic mission which provided a safe passageway for residents to get to and from the market.

John checked the time, eager to get back to base to make a phone call. Today was Janey's nineteenth birthday, and he didn't want to miss it as he had her eighteenth — provided anyone was home, that is. Much had changed in Iowa since his deployment. Dad remarried a month ago. His brothers had given him two more nephews and opened another farm equipment store across the Mississippi River. Uncle Nick was transferring to another parish and Janey had gone off to the University of Iowa, seeming as determined to flee the farm as he'd once been.

Up ahead, John heard voices and saw a group of Iraqi boys playing soccer. As soon as they spotted the soldiers, the boys scattered. They always did. John tried to imagine life from these children's viewpoint, but his own idyllic childhood back in Iowa seemed as foreign as this country.

Someone behind him called out. "Looks like we'll get back in time for chow. *Hooah!*"

John grinned and echoed the cry. Who would have believed dinner in a mess tent was the highlight of a soldier's day?

Eighty meters into the alley, they stopped so Layton could get a rock out of his boot. Layton was a SAW gunner — squad automatic weapons — and a top marksman. Their squad had two heavy weapons gunners: Layton and Corporal Chris Worth, another native Texan who liked to talk about being from the Lone Star State as much as Layton did.

While they waited, John scanned the windows and rooftops of the shrapnel-pocked, three-story buildings that lined the alley, watching for any movement. Even though his squad had patrolled this section so many times he recognized most of the beggars who slept here, no one lowered their guard.

"Speed it up, Layton!" Sergeant Boswell shouted.

On reflex, John snapped to full attention at the Sergeant's bellow. *Pop! Whiz!*

"What the—" John scrambled for cover as two more rifle shots landed close. The first bullet felt as if it had passed within inches of his face. The knee-jerk reaction to the Sergeant's yell saved John's life.

Adrenaline surging, John swung his M-4 to the left and searched for a target. "Contact. Straight ahead," he called over his shoulder. That the shooter was further up the alley, protected by the corner of a building, didn't stop John from firing. The jerk nearly killed him.

The air grew heavier, the scent of spent powder mixed with the stench of garbage and dust. John wanted to gag but remained focused on his target.

"Fall back," Boswell ordered.

"Not an option, Sergeant." Layton slid in beside John and Sergeant Boswell. "We're pinned down. There are two more shooters at the other end of the alley."

Boswell started swearing. "Get on that SAW!"

John kept firing at the gunman ahead, giving Layton a chance to follow orders. Volleys of gunfire blasted behind him as others in his squad set sights on the other two shooters.

"Call in a SITREP to HQ," Boswell shouted as he, too, started firing.

John lowered his weapon long enough to radio in their location and situation. In close sectors such as this alley, a rapid reaction force would have to come by ground. Choppers could be easily hit by RPGs and small arms fire from the rooftops.

"Third Squad is closest. They're en route from the north," John reported. "ETA three minutes."

"Blast it." Boswell jerked his head toward the right. "Where did he come from?"

He was a gray-bearded beggar, lying face down in the middle of the alley where they took the heaviest fire. As John watched, the old man tried to push himself up onto all fours. Dirt sprayed as bullets perforated the ground around the terrified beggar. That the shooters hadn't obliterated him meant they were baiting the soldiers.

John yelled to the old man. "Stay down!"

The old man ignored him, most likely did not understand English. The old man's outstretched hand scrabbled for a crutch just beyond his reach.

"I'm going for the old man," Layton shouted.

John shook his head in disbelief. *No way.* This scene was straight out of his recurring nightmare where Layton took multiple shots after rescuing an old man.

"Stay on that SAW," John yelled. "I'm closer. Moving now!" Keeping low, he bolted forward.

Behind him, the gunfire peaked as the others in his squad laid down cover, concentrating their fire to keep the shooters suppressed. John raced to the old man and grabbed beneath his shoulders. The man weighed less than a child and appeared even older than John thought.

"Hold on, buddy. I got you." John dragged the old man to the closest boarded-up doorway for what little cover it provided. Then he shoved the man behind him, against the base of the building before grabbing his M-4. Once again, he focused on the shooters and on protecting the others in his squad. Fear and stress peaked as he squeezed off shots.

Every prayer he'd learned during his twelve years of parochial school echoed in his head. At these times, all of John's reflexes were seventh-generation Catholic, sprinkled with cussing that would make the devil proud.

The roar of heavy diesel engines filled the alley from the west as support finally arrived. Third Squad's Humvees charged in, adding depth to the soundtrack of war. Fifty-calibers blazed from the armored vehicles, forcing everyone to keep their heads down.

The first enemy shooter turned and ran away, firing shots to cover himself.

"Lily-livered chicken!" John shouted, returning fire at the retreating gunman.

The other two shooters hadn't budged. Obvious hard-liners, they fired at the Humvee. But there was no hiding from fifty-cal rounds behind walls of mud and mortar. The Humvee's agile cupola swung one-eighty degrees and quickly neutralized the gunmen in a haze of pink mist behind exploding walls.

"Cease fire!" Sergeant Boswell shouted. "Cease fire!"

The gunfire stopped, but the ringing in John's ears continued as he pushed to his feet to survey the scene and account for the rest of his squad. Had anyone been hit? His pulse thudded as he searched for Layton. It leveled in relief when he confirmed his friend was still with Sergeant Boswell. John kept quiet as the Sergeant yelled out last names one by one and waited for their response.

"McKay?"

"All good," John shouted. No one injured, in tight quarters, with three different shooters, was the first miracle. That he'd also kept Layton safe, again, was another. "Thank you, Lord," he added under his breath. No atheists in this foxhole.

Eager to rejoin his team and go thank the other soldiers from Third Squad for their aid, John turned to check on the beggar. The old man sat upright, his head cloth askew as he brushed dust from his threadbare robe. As John looked more closely at the old man, he noticed that only one foot poked out from beneath the man's robe.

The old man brushed away blood trickling from a cut on his nose, undoubtedly where John had accidentally head-butted him in the scramble to get to safety. But better that than dead.

John pointed to the old man's face, tried to use hand signals. "Sorry about that. Your nose. Needs a bandage." He wished he had remembered to replace his lost pointee-talkee, a picture/word graphic for basic English/Arabic communication. "I'll get my first aid kit."

The old man muttered unintelligible words as he pointed to the bullet holes just above where they'd huddled.

"Uh, yeah, close call," John said.

The man burst into a frantic chatter of Arabic, extending his arm and shaking it with each passionate word.

"I get it. You're pissed, but I don't understand you any more than you understand me." John stepped backward. "Be right back."

"Allahu Akbar!"

John paused. Now that phrase he recognized, had heard it repeated often at prayer times here. It translated to 'God is greater.' A few people might attribute negative connotations to the words, but John thought he understood its context in the moment. "Yes, your Allah and my God watched out for us today."

The old man's voice grew insistent as he extended his arm once again and thrust a strand of dirty beads forward, clearly wanting John to take them.

John shook his head, dismissing the old man's offering as he turned away. "Just doing my job."

Layton ran up just then. Red-faced, he shoved John's chest with both hands, knocking him off balance. "That was my save! Didn't you hear me yell?"

John recovered and shoved him right back. "We needed you on the SAW!"

Layton's next push came harder. "Yeah, but when you dove down, I couldn't see a thing. Didn't know if you were dead or alive."

John leaned in, nose to nose and ready to tango, but before he replied, Sergeant Boswell appeared. At once, John and Layton straightened to attention. *You're welcome, jerk,* John thought.

"Here's the old man's crutch and grocery sack. What's left of it anyway." The Sergeant nodded to the bullet hole riddled burlap bag he held out to the beggar. "That could have been you."

John knew the last was meant for him. He also knew his Sergeant or any of the others would have done the same thing. Protecting innocent Iraqi citizens was part of their mission. John had the additional burden of safeguarding a big, stupid Texan.

The old man poked John's ankle with his crutch before flinging the beads up in outstretched hands. Then he started wailing at the top of his lungs in an ear-piercing screech.

"Oh, for cripes sake, McKay, just take the trinket and shut him up," Sergeant Boswell snapped. "You can ditch it later. Now give me the radio, so I can update Command."

"Yes, Sergeant." As soon as John accepted the beads, the beggar clapped his hands and gave a toothless smile to the Sergeant.

"Whatever," Boswell said. "McKay, get Carpenter to look at the old man. Layton, tell Fallon to get pictures of the dead shooters for identification."

John offered the beads to Layton. "Here you go, bro. If he was your save, then you should have these."

Ignoring the beads, Layton shouldered roughly past, trying to knock John off balance. If John's thing was *last word*, Layton's was *last punch*.

John jogged over to Specialist Danny Carpenter and told the medic about the old man. "Sarge said to check him over."

Before moving away, Carpenter fist-bumped John's upper arm. "Good one, dude, saving that old man."

John nodded as another Humvee lumbered up the alley. Overhead, two Apache gunships zigzagged, the two-man attack helicopters as graceful as they were deadly. Now that backup had arrived, someone would search the deceased gunmen hoping to find ID. Odds were strong they'd find nothing more than extra magazines filled with ammunition, which meant taking pictures back to the marketplace to ask if anyone could identify the shooters, a useless endeavor that would stretch their day even longer.

Carpenter called out. "McKay! Where'd the old man go?"

John hurried back across the alley. "He was right there a minute ago."

"I turned away to grab a bandage and poof. Now he's gone." Carpenter shrugged. "I don't get it."

John noticed the old man's bag and crutch were gone, too. He looked around. Teddy Fallon and the Sergeant stood a few feet away. "Hey, Sergeant, where'd the old man go?"

"Beats me." Boswell handed John the radio. "Just as well. We're rolling out."

Fallon hung around after the Sergeant left. "Did you see that?"

"See what?" John asked.

"The old man. He disappeared in a flash of green light that shot straight into the air. Poof! Just like Carpenter said." Fallon crossed himself, his voice drifting off uncertainly.

"Whoa," Carpenter said. "I didn't mean that literally. The old guy probably crawled off when I turned my back."

Fallon's words spooked John. Once again, he recalled bits of the incident after Mohler's party. A flash of green light. John had never mentioned the incident to anyone, yet Fallon's description was too specific to be a coincidence. "The light. Did it go off and on first?"

"You saw it, too?" Fallon sounded relieved.

Danny Carpenter frowned at Fallon. "Easy buddy."

"No, hang on." John pressed Fallon for details. "Tell me about the green light."

"Don't do that. Don't egg him on," Carpenter hissed as he brushed past John. Carpenter put a hand on Fallon's shoulder. "Let's get you back to base and down off the adrenaline."

"Nah. I'm fine." Suddenly embarrassed, Fallon shrugged free and moved away.

"I'll keep eyes on him," Carpenter said as he faced John. "Battle stress combined with being an expectant father will do strange things to the mind." Carpenter's gaze narrowed. "How about you? You good?"

"Yep." John didn't want anyone questioning his stress or mental fortitude.

"Fallon was right about one thing. Who'd have guessed that old fart could move so fast?" Carpenter joked as he strode off. "Let's boogie."

John hung back, eyeing the alley's shadows one last time, but he found no sign of the beggar. "You're welcome, old man."

His eyes skimmed across the fresh line of bullet holes scant inches above where he'd huddled. That was two close calls he'd survived today. Now he just had to stay golden for three more weeks.

CHAPTER FIVE

July 2006
Baghdad, Iraq

By the time John's squad returned to base, it was dark. As expected, the trip back to the marketplace yielded no clues about the identity of the dead shooters. None of the Iraqis would risk being seen publicly cooperating with US soldiers, the threat of reprisal meted out by certain local sects too pervasive. Still, word would spread, and someone might come forward later.

At the chow hall, John wolfed down two plates of heat-lamp desiccated leftovers. Then he hit the shower and scrubbed off nineteen hours of sweat and sand before returning to the tent he shared with his squad. Quarters here were tight, privacy nonexistent. Each soldier had a bunk and a chair. Space for footlockers was minimal, so he and Layton shared one.

Overall, his squad was a good group. Everyone got along, pulled their weight, and covered each other's backside when things got rough. In Iowa, John had been a big duck on a small pond. High school quarterback. A top-ranked motocross daredevil.

Here, there were lots of big ducks. Preach Sheridan led his high school basketball team to a division title four years in a row. Donald Livingston had been the top Colorado wrestler. The list of champs stretched long.

Tonight, though, everyone was wired. Today's battle proved a jagged reminder that The Grim Reaper lurked around every corner.

John opened his locker and grabbed his laptop. The barracks glowed from the light of computer screens as each man sought distraction. Some wore headphones as they watched movies or played video games. Others talked via Skype to loved ones — family, wives, and girlfriends — their voices low. John heard the heaviness in Danny Carpenter's voice as Carpenter talked to his girlfriend back in Connecticut. Those two shared a genuine bond, an intimacy that every soldier in their platoon envied.

While John and Layton generally high-fived the single life, John sometimes wished he had a significant other like Carpenter. John suspected Layton did, too. Though the Texan swore he and Sharlene were done for good, John noticed the wistful expressions that often crossed Layton's face. There was no mistaking that look — it always involved regret and a woman.

John hadn't been seriously involved with anyone since his high school sweetheart broke up with him right after he enlisted. At the time, he'd wanted no responsibilities, no strings. But over the past year there had been plenty of time for introspection and regrets. Romantic ties could be lifelines or anchors.

On the upside, being single meant he wasn't missing kids' soccer games or worried over his wife's chemotherapy like his sergeant. He also wasn't going through separation anxiety like Fallon. Fallon went home for three days of emergency leave when his father died six months ago, and now his girlfriend was pregnant. Fallon spent the first ten minutes of his calls home grilling his girlfriend about who she was seeing. The last ten minutes passed in a flurry of tears as Fallon promised they'd marry as soon as he got home.

While John waited for his laptop to reboot and his email to load, he thought of his own list of promises. *When I get home, I'll—* He frowned. His current list of do-overs could choke Dad's prize bull.

Seeing a message from his sister lightened his mood. Despite their falling out, Janey still wrote him regularly. Funny how much he looked forward to her accounts of life back in Iowa. Her colorful laments of Podunk revisited were amusing but distant. He missed the teenage angst-filled emails she used to write when he first enlisted. Back when she'd asked his advice on everything.

Janey hadn't forgiven him for taking the letter she'd written to Layton, and as McKays were known to take grudges to the grave, she might never absolve him. John hadn't apologized for filching it either, so the topic was never brought up despite the overwhelming smell of elephant manure in the divide between them.

She refused to discuss it unless he apologized first. Another throwback to their childhood, when not speaking to the other person was the penultimate snub. Back then, he always won. She'd cave and give in. This time, however, Janey held on. He'd kept quiet, holding out.

Tonight, Janey's email was brief. Check Myspace for a link to my New York pictures.

Janey and her best friend, Gemma, kicked off their summer break with a week in New York City. For a girl who swore she'd never leave the farm, Janey's social life quadrupled since she'd left for college last fall. She wasn't the reckless party animal John had been, but it seemed she dated a different guy every month and was constantly on the go with Gemma.

When he logged onto his Myspace social media account, he found Janey's post front and center. The first photograph showed her in a short strapless dress, feet bare. Central Park Art Festival, the caption read. She laughed at something off-frame, a pair of high heels dangled from one hand, her other hand holding back her overlong black hair. The wind had kicked up the hem of her dress. Not indecent, but—

What happened to the scrawny tomboy he'd left behind? She'd

lost her braces, grown three inches taller and filled out. Too out. When had she gone from cute to beautiful? Yesterday she'd been a six-year-old tyrant who'd wanted to quit first grade. Now she was nineteen. A legit adult. Thanks to this never-ending deployment, he'd missed two of her birthdays and her high school graduation. She'd shrugged it off as no big deal, but when had his absence become acceptable? They used to be there for each other's everything.

"Whoa!" Layton came up and leaned over John's shoulder, while pointing at the screen. "Dude, if she weren't your sister..." He whistled.

If you only knew. Buzzards of guilt landed on John's shoulders. He scrolled backwards through the photographs. "I need to upload a few of her motocross race shots. The ones with mud on her face and braces shining like the grill of a new Ford truck. Anything to discourage all the wannabe Romeos drooling in the comment section."

Layton laughed. "I doubt the big brother scare tactics will work. Reality check: your sister is drop-dead gorgeous, and she's no longer a baby. My offer stands, though. I'll help you kill any freaks who try to marry her."

John and Layton made many drunken pacts, both serious and crazy, including the one where if the worst happened to John, Layton would return to Iowa, shoot Randy Keener, and watch over Janey. A loyal friend, Layton asked where to shoot him.

And if something happened to Layton — he better never die — John swore to go to Texas to look after Layton's grandmother. "She's meaner than a cornered one-eyed rattlesnake and hates my guts," Layton had explained. "Let her know you control my life insurance, though, and she'll behave."

When John traveled to Texas for Layton's mom's funeral, he'd met Grandma Rattler. Small wonder Layton now avoided Texas.

John checked the time. Despite the late hour, it was early morning back in Iowa. He hit the SKYPE icon. "It's Janey's nineteenth birthday," he said to Layton. "If she answers, help me sing."

It took a few minutes, but as soon as Janey's face appeared on the screen he and Layton started to sing. Layton even broke into an impromptu, booty-shaking Texas two-step which Janey applauded. By the time they reached the final chorus of "happy birthday to you!" several others in the tent joined in, the refrain mostly shouted.

Janey looked delighted, and for a moment John's weariness lifted.

"Thanks, Johnny. And tell Layton I said hi."

"Hear that, buddy?" John tilted the screen toward his friend. "Say hello, Layton."

"Hello Layton." Layton waved. "Happy birthday, darlin'."

"Did you see my New York pictures?" she asked.

As Layton moved away, John resettled the laptop. A scowl played across Janey's face but promptly disappeared. Despite the boyfriend-of-the-week act, John knew his little sister. She still longed for Layton.

John acted as if the question was meant for him. "Yeah. I did. And so did half the male population on Myspace."

"Right." Janey rolled her eyes.

"Got any exciting plans for the day?" John asked. "How are you celebrating?"

"Gemma and I are driving to Iowa City to look at apartments. For my birthday, Dad's paying my half of the first year's rent, so it's goodbye dorm life. When we get back, Dad and Eileen are taking us out to eat."

"How are things with you and Eileen?" Eileen was Dad's new wife, and Janey was adjusting to not being the sole female in their father's life.

"I'm trying for Dad's sake, but it's tough. Eileen is taking down all of Mom's stuff so she can remodel the kitchen."

"And you want nothing to change. I feel you, kiddo. So, what's up with you and Stretch McFetch? Or is he still a thing?" Janey's last boyfriend had been a varsity basketball player.

"We were never a thing."

"Good. He was a dork. A tall dork."

Janey's eyes narrowed. "If I want your opinion on a guy, I'll ask for it."

"If you'd asked my opinion on the last two chuckle heads—"

She leaned back, away from the screen. "Okay, I'm hanging up now."

"Don't." His sister was still pissed, but he was making progress. At least she hadn't simply disconnected.

"Why?" she snapped.

They used to tease. Argue. *Before.* "I want to tell you about this—"

Janey's image pixelated and blurred. Then the call cut off.

Everyone in the barracks groaned as the internet shut down. A regular occurrence there. It was just as well. He needed to catch some sleep. Each day's patrol seemed to start earlier.

Stowing his computer, John battled a wave of homesickness. He reached for his helmet that hung on the chair and tugged out the laminated photo he kept tucked in the liner. It was a shot of Janey and him, taken just before he deployed. He stared at the sunlit corn fields in the photo's background. Fuller was in the shot, the collie leaned against John's leg. After thirteen years, the collie's muzzle was graying.

Man, he missed that dog. He and his mom spent hours training Fuller to respond to silent commands, and after Mom died, the dog had been John's childhood confidant. The dog knew all the secrets he couldn't tell his dad, the dreams Janey wouldn't understand.

Unsettled, he tucked the photo back into his helmet. The tent was quiet now, most lights off. Layton was the exception, tapping on his keyboard, no doubt doing homework for his online class. Layton had big plans and dreams, like buying back his grandfather's ranch in rural Texas even if it was years before he moved back there. Layton's career trajectory with the Army was cast in stone.

"Get a degree. Apply to Officer Candidate School, like me," Layton advised. "Unless you want to be an enlisted grunt all your life."

Except, John wasn't college material. He'd loved sports, hated academics. Like Layton, John initially imagined himself retiring after twenty years of military service. But that was before he deployed, before he witnessed death and destruction. War changed everything and nothing. And it never ended.

If John didn't reenlist, what would he do? The only big plan he'd ever made was to hike all fifty states. Then what? Sure, Matt and Perry would make room for John in the family business, which would give him a chance to figure it out. And Layton frequently reminded John that he had a sweet deal waiting back in Iowa, referring to the neighboring farm Dad had bought at auction. Three hundred acres and a homestead adjacent to the McKay farm. *"It's yours, Son."*

The gift triggered the argument that pushed John to enlist. He didn't want to be a farmer. Or did he?

He yawned so hard his jaw popped. For now, his goal was simple: make sure he and Layton made it home. For a few minutes today, it felt like John had changed destiny, as if saving the old man assured Layton's well-being. Maybe now that blasted recurring dream would go away for good.

Rolling onto his side, John closed his eyes and gave in to weariness.

Within moments the nightmare took over, dropping him back in battle. It was always the same. Gunfire blasted all around. He ran but was never fast enough to save his friend. Shots rang out and Layton went down.

This time, though, the old beggar appeared out of nowhere and shook dirty beads in John's face.

John pleaded with the old man. "Help me find my friend. Please."

"Find what's missing," the old man ranted, switching from English to foreign tongues, then back to English. "The missing piece."

The beads were thrust forward again, and John had the impression he needed those beads to find and save Layton. But when John tried to reach for them, the old man disappeared in a fiery explosion that seared John's skin.

Wake up! Desperate to ground himself, John forced his eyes to open. Then he clenched the metal side rail of his bed. He looked around to see if he'd woken anyone by crying out.

Get a grip. It's only a dream. Willing his pulse to slow, he silently repeated the mantra as he rubbed his eyes and inhaled through his nose. All the usual tricks to reassure himself he was safe. Alive. Awake. He concentrated on the orchestra of snores around him. Outside the tent, generators hummed. A helicopter swooped low overhead. Sounds of life drowned the dreams of death.

It took a few moments for the crushing pressure in his chest to ease. Several others in his squad had similar nightmares, but everyone's hell was unique. Danny Carpenter was claustrophobic and dreamed of dying in tiny airless spaces. Chris Worth feared fire and dreamed of flames. John feared not saving Layton, of being too late to save his best friend.

Tonight, though, the nightmare had been different. What was up with the old beggar hijacking his dreams? The old man's sense of urgency made no sense. *Find what's missing. The missing piece.* John leaned up on his elbows, trying to ease the anxiety in his gut. The old man had rattled the beads while talking and now John couldn't shake the feeling that those beads had something to do with saving Layton.

But did John even have the beads anymore? He hadn't wanted them to begin with, and even the sergeant said to toss them.

Reaching for where his jacket hung on the chair, he patted each pocket. His fingers brushed an unfamiliar bulge in a side pocket. He reached in and pulled out the beads. The strand was longer, the beads larger, than he'd remembered. The beads also felt warm, as if they'd been resting against a heated surface or the warmth of a body. Only they'd been in the jacket, hanging on the chair.

Grabbing a penlight, John ducked under the sheet to examine the beads. What he saw confused him, yet there was no mistaking the shape. It was a rosary. But why would a beggar in Iraq – who'd openly praised Allah – have a Catholic rosary?

John scrutinized the piece beneath the narrow flashlight beam. He would have guessed the beggar gave him Muslim prayer beads, except those certainly wouldn't have included a crucifix and a medallion with the Virgin Mary.

One bead reflected light. Using his thumbnail, he flicked the dried dirt loose and found a black faceted crystal that glinted like moonlight trapped in a diamond. The bead was inlaid with intricate bits of silver. He brushed off several more. Some of the silver designs resembled Arabic letters but were likely just a decorative insignia.

Puzzled, John switched off his light and quietly gathered the rosary into his hands as he settled back in the dark. The warmth and heft of the beads struck him anew.

Simultaneously, he flashed back to a memory from his childhood. He was inside St. Francis Catholic Church in River Haven. The occasion was his fourth birthday, and he sat in his grandfather's lap, waiting for Sunday Mass to begin. The church's gothic interior, with its gilt-spired altars and statues, seemed cavernous and spooky to John as a child, yet in memory he felt awe. Moments earlier, the parish priest blessed the miniature rosary Grandpa had given him.

"I received my first rosary on my fourth birthday, too," Grandpa whispered.

Gnarled fingers closed over John's small fingers as Grandpa softly recited the Hail Mary in Latin. "*Ave Maris, gratia plena, Dominus tecum...*" John didn't understand the language, but he'd heard the words often, the syllables hypnotic, his grandfather's voice reverent.

Sensory recall overwhelmed John. The click of beads, the hissing flicker of votive candles. People crowding into pews as Mass started. The lingering scents of incense and Grandpa's pipe tobacco seemed as vivid as his grandfather's loving, protective embrace.

Emotion welled in John's chest as the scene faded. His grandfather died before John's fifth birthday. He had few distinct memories of his grandfather — most were images from photographs. But that particular moment existed in a space of time known only to John and his grandfather.

John clutched the strange rosary now, grateful for a peaceful interlude after the nightmare. As his fingers advanced from one rosary bead to another, he mentally grasped for more wisps of the past, another memory. Once again, his grandfather's voice came back through time. *"We start at the crucifix, little one, and make the sign of the cross."*

———

JOHN AWOKE to someone calling his name. At first it sounded like his grandfather. Then the voice became more guttural, speaking in sharp Arabic tones that morphed into English. The frantic words of the old beggar — "find the missing piece" — replayed over and over, not making any more sense the eighteenth time than the first.

Get out of my head, old man. John opened his eyes.

It was still dark, the tent an echo chamber for the snorts and wheezes as the others slept. John sat up and discovered the strange rosary entangled in his fingers. He had a vague memory of trying to pray with it. Had he even made it through the first decade of ten beads?

He checked the time, surprised to see it was oh-five-hundred hours. It had been past midnight when he'd gotten to bed and then he'd been up again after his nightmare, after he'd retrieved the rosary from his jacket. Yet right now he felt rested, as if he'd slept soundly for hours. When was the last time that happened?

A phone buzzed. Across the room Carpenter answered and grunted, "Yes, sir," before disconnecting.

"We can sleep in," Carpenter announced. "No patrol this morning."

Bed frames squeaked as bodies shifted to enjoy the rare reprieve. The Army changed patrol routines to minimize the chance of ambush, but yesterday's attack proved that didn't always help. Wide awake, John rolled to his feet. This was the first time he'd had a Sunday morning off in months. He could hit the gym, grab breakfast and go to a church service.

After getting dressed, he felt compelled to grab the old beggar's strange rosary. It brought his grandfather back for a few minutes and brought a good night's sleep. Perhaps it would help him understand the meaning of the strange dream.

A short time later, John made his way across the compound to the makeshift chapel-tent. The Army provided space for those who wanted to attend religious services, but the last chaplain had been a Lutheran minister. Their new chaplain, Father Donovan, was a Catholic priest and offered a traditional early Mass and two non-denominational services later in the morning. Sunday evening the priest heard confessions.

Back in Iowa, John attended Mass weekly. He never questioned it. Mass was something his family did every Sunday, yet he didn't recall feeling especially moved by it. And having a priest for an uncle meant he couldn't skip out like most of his high school buddies. Funny how Sunday Mass became one thing John missed most after deployment. In the face of war, he craved the rituals and everyday reassurances of life.

The early church service was already crowded. He made his way to an empty folding chair near the front of the tent. The premium seats, the ones closest to the exit, always filled first. Tinny music, all the old traditional hymns he'd never admit to knowing by heart, poured out of a decrepit CD player to lend the space a worshipful atmosphere. John spotted Teddy Fallon and waved him over.

Fallon sat. "Hey man, about yesterday—"

A warning announcement blared across the PA system outside. "Incoming!"

Chatter ceased immediately as everyone hit the floor, a frequent enough occurrence that the move was instinctive. The room collectively tensed as rapid-fire artillery echoed from the Vulcan mini guns on the southern perimeter of the base, sounding like an electric buzz saw on crack.

Just as quickly, the "all clear" was given. They stood, but the undercurrent of angst remained. It never fully went away. John straightened his uniform and turned toward Fallon, but they were interrupted again as Father Donovan cleared his throat and stepped up to the folding table-cum-altar as if nothing were amiss.

"Let us begin," the priest said.

Fallon gave a dismissive shrug before making the sign of the cross.

"The Lord be with you," Father Donovan continued.

"And also with you." The appropriate liturgical responses came forth of their own volition despite the unconventional setting. The familiar routine of Mass lifted John's spirits.

If Father Donovan's accent didn't give him away as a New Yorker, his closing line after the final blessing did. "And God bless the Yankees." Chuckles preceded the final, "Amen."

John lingered after the service. So did Fallon. When Father Donovan turned to them, John gave Fallon a you-first motion.

Fallon shook his head. "Go ahead, man."

Self-conscious, John kept his voice low. "Do you have a moment, Father?"

The priest nodded, his eyes dropping to John's name tag. "McKay. Your squad came under fire yesterday, didn't it?"

That was one attribute everyone, regardless of religious preference, loved about Father Donovan. He had a knack for personal details, keeping track of expected babies or sick parents and was a source of solace for believers and non-believers. His reputation for universal compassion was clear as he included the Iraqi people in his special-intention prayers. The priest also kept a check on all patrols, knew about all incidents.

"Yes, sir. We were lucky, no injuries." John paused, uncertain how to bring up the rosary. "I, uh, met this weird old man."

"I heard you saved his life."

"It was nothing."

"Saving a soul always has a deep meaning."

"Yes, sir. The old man gave me some beads, but I didn't realize until later that it was a rosary." John noticed that Fallon leaned in to eavesdrop. If Fallon was concerned John would mention yesterday's flash-of-light incident, he could relax.

"A rosary? You don't say." Father Donovan pointed upward. "God works in mysterious ways."

"But it's not your usual rosary. It's different. Here." John tugged the beads out. Even with the muted light, the beads sparkled.

Father Donovan's smile widened as he reached for it. "What a magnificent rosary."

Before the priest could touch it, Fallon shouldered closer, bumping John's arm. The beads slid from John's grasp, but Fallon caught them before they hit the ground.

"Sweet Mother of God." Fallon's eyes widened. He looked from John to the priest. "Sorry, Father."

John scowled and snatched the beads away from Fallon before turning back to the priest. "I'm wondering how the old beggar got this."

"How the man came to possess the rosary is unimportant. Maybe he found it. Maybe he stole it. Perhaps he is Christian or wants to convert. Perhaps the beads were meant as a gesture of peace." Father Donovan placed a hand on John's shoulder. "Truth is, the man could have faced punishment had he been caught by an Iraqi cleric with it. He might have given you the beads to forestall trouble."

John knew some Muslims considered Christian items like medals, rosaries, and religious art to be abominations. And the Middle East wasn't exactly known for its Christian enclaves. Still, nothing in the priest's explanation satisfied John's questions. Something about the beggar and the beads haunted him, but with Fallon so close, he didn't want to mention the old man's dream appearance.

"So, what should I do with the rosary, Father?" John asked.

"Besides pray it?" The priest winked. "Keep it as a spiritual souvenir, John McKay. The Lord made certain that rosary ended up with a good Catholic boy. I have faith the reason will be made clear."

Another soldier came up then, hesitated and stepped backwards behind Fallon, reminding John that others waited to see Father Donovan. John bid the priest goodbye. "I hope you're right, sir."

Back at the now empty barracks, John dug around in his footlocker until he found the smaller rosary his uncle gave him before he'd deployed. It was plain, black, and fit flat in a pocket. John fingered the simple beads. He'd quit carrying his uncle's rosary right after his first battle. It felt sacrilegious on the war field. It also made him feel hypocritical. Did he only believe in the Almighty when bullets flew?

John tucked his uncle's rosary back into his jacket and set the ornate rosary aside. The light on the old beggar's beads undulated, making the silver inlay pulse, like it was sending a frantic Morse code message. His mom once said every rosary had a unique purpose and story. He'd dismissed it as another Catholic Mom-ily, but now it raised his curiosity. What was this rosary's story and why was John so certain it even had a history, that the silver markings meant something? If he could find out who made the rosary, could he figure out how the old beggar came to possess it?

He had a sudden urge to send the beggar's rosary to Janey. If anyone could ferret out info on the beads, his sister could. A budding journalist with a growing list of bylines, Janey had bird dog instincts and the McKay tenacity. If she hit any snags, Uncle Nick could help. In fact, if John sent it now, he bet she'd have a complete dossier in a week.

He grabbed a notepad and started a letter. **Dear Pest—**

Recalling Janey's nickname made him smile. As a child, he'd thought that if only he had kept his mother in sight, she wouldn't have died. It had been a long time before he let Janey out of sight, which hadn't been an issue until John started dating. That's when she earned the name Pest.

Greetings from the land of sand. Before you get all excited about
what I'm sending, I'll warn you it's not a gift. I'm sending this
rosary to you for safekeeping until I get home. There's something
special about this piece, and you'll never believe how I got it...

When he finished the letter, he folded the pages and picked up
the rosary. Heat still radiated from it, searing his fingertips. He almost
dropped it as Fallon had earlier. Had Fallon felt it too? What was
with this rosary? Not only did it feel weird, but something about it
moved John, made him want to pray. He didn't like that. He was okay
being a casual Catholic, and he made a terrific sinner. The last thing
he wanted was a desire for devotion or a calling to peace.

Peace. There was that word again. Father Donovan mentioned it
and John wrote about peace in his letter to Janey. Now, however, he
wondered if he'd misunderstood the beggar's words in his dream.
Had the old man meant peace? Or piece?

The distinction seemed vital. Exactly what had the beggar said?
Most of the old man's words had been in Arabic, but one English
phrase had been repeated. *Find the missing piece.*

Or is it the missing *peace*? Peace was absent in parts of the
Middle East. Heck, it was missing in much of the world.

The rosary grew warm as if in affirmation, raising goosebumps on
John's arms. He shoved the beads away, overcome with a desperate
urge to talk with the old man again.

"Dude! Snap out of it!" Layton shouted as he shook John's
shoulder.

He noticed that Layton stepped backwards. Standard procedure
for dealing with someone caught in a PTSD flashback who might
come up swinging. Embarrassed, John gave him a thumbs up. "Sorry.
Lost in thought."

"You were mumbling in what sounded like Arabic, man. You
taking language lessons on the side?"

"Hardly." John grabbed the rosary and thrust it toward Layton.

"Remember that old beggar in the alley yesterday? This is what he gave me."

Layton barely touched the beads before drawing his hand away. "No disrespect, but a lot of that Catholic stuff creeps me out. You're not keeping it, are you?"

"Yes, but I'm sending it to Janey."

Layton shrugged. "I came to tell you the sergeant's called a meeting. We have ten minutes to find the others."

CHAPTER SIX

July 2006
Baghdad, Iraq

Layton Burnet made his way toward the mess hall, grateful for a few moments alone. Back at the barracks, he'd experienced a familiar stab of conscience when John mentioned Janey. *You should have told him.*

Right. *Hey bro, your sister kissed me before we left Iowa, and I can't quit thinking of her.*

Liar, liar. It was so much worse. Like, enroll in college, apply to Officer Candidate School, worse. John razzed him, called him Mr. Ambition. Would John still think that if he knew it was all for Janey, to be the type of man the McKays would approve?

He winced, recalling all the cracks John made about Layton being a ladies' man, an image his ego never cared to correct. Until now. Until fourteen months ago.

Layton hadn't stopped dreaming of Janey since their kiss. He tortured himself by checking her posts and photos on social media. Her friend, Gemma, shared poolside shots from their New York trip.

That Janey looked hotter than a Texas summer left Layton panting one moment and jealous of anyone viewing the photos next.

Regret dogged him. What if he hadn't stopped kissing her that day? What if he'd just gone along, let it play out instead of shutting her down so quickly? He hadn't even let her finish talking. *"I think I love you,"* was a serious declaration, and he'd reacted terribly.

She'd caught him off guard with her kiss. Then instinct kicked in and took over. He'd barely been able to pull back. Pushing her away had been one of the hardest things he'd ever done. Janey was smart, bold, and gorgeous, but she was also his best friend's little sister. Which meant she was off-limits for a lot of reasons.

If John had come along a few minutes sooner, he would have lost his mind to see Layton kissing Janey. And Layton didn't want that as they were going off to war. *Brothers to the end.*

Though Layton thought he and Janey agreed to talk when he returned, she seemed to have forgotten the incident. She'd gone off to college, dated, partied. She sent him notes, showed she cared — but as what? A family friend? Did she even remember their kiss?

Sure, he'd followed Janey's lead, flirting with Sharlene via social media while deployed, but Sharlene wasn't the woman who haunted his sleep. Only Janey McKay did that. He recalled their early morning rides at the farm, how she'd climb on the back of his ATV and lean close as they rode. It had been their private ritual. They'd watch the sun rise over the pond and talk about family and farming. She'd shared her heartache over her mother's death; he'd revealed some of his own inner thoughts. She was easy to be with, had the same values and interests.

Which meant *nada*. If it was just a passing thing for her, then the question of asking John about dating her was moot.

Dejected, Layton focused on his search for the others on his team.

A few minutes later, their squad gathered near the chow hall. Sergeant Boswell looked grim as he came up. "Listen up. They got an

ID on one of the dead shooters. Turns out he was the eldest son of Farid Zaman."

Layton recognized the name. Farid Zaman was a local warlord known for his dislike of the US and NATO occupation. The self-proclaimed leader of the radical group dubbed Black Death, Zaman and his followers were a plague to soldiers and Iraqi citizens. Zaman openly embraced terrorism and recently aligned with a hard-line fundamentalist cleric whose beliefs would send Iraq back to the dark ages.

"It gets worse," Boswell went on. "Now Zaman's declared a *fatwa* against our squad and put a bounty on our heads."

"What's next? Wanted posters?" Chris Worth's joke garnered a few nervous laughs.

"Bingo. Someone snapped pictures of us asking questions at the marketplace yesterday. Intel intercepted a few that were being circulated this morning." Boswell held up several grainy, photocopied images. A shot of Layton and John was on top.

CHAPTER SEVEN

July 2006
Baghdad, Iraq

The weeks that followed spiraled downward for John as anti-US-military violence ballooned around the outskirts of Baghdad after Farid Zaman swore a hundred-fold vengeance for the fatal shooting of his son. Zaman's group, Black Death, also claimed responsibility for the murders of innocent Iraqi locals purported to be conspiring with the Americans.

The Army increased patrols in frequency and size, which wasn't easy as a severe intestinal virus swept through the base affecting nearly half the personnel. John and the other soldiers who didn't succumb to the Baghdad Crud were forced to maintain longer duty hours.

While grateful to avoid the debilitating sickness, John was exhausted from the extended missions. The few cat naps he could grab between each operation were riddled with dreams of the old beggar holding out the rosary and demanding that John find a missing piece. Or peace.

One dream haunted John, however. The old beggar claimed to know his mother's last words. "She said to tell you—"

John awoke before the old man finished speaking. That shook John. For years he and Janey fretted that Mom had died alone. They imagined her calling out to them and conjectured her last words.

His dreams fueled a growing obsession with finding the old man again. But how? The beggar had disappeared before anyone got his name or asked for ID, and his squad hadn't been back to that sector since the shooting. John asked other patrols to watch for the old beggar but got no leads and his late-night Google searches on the rosary yielded nothing except increased frustration.

Today, however, John got an unexpected break. Finally back on daytime rotation, he walked up to one of the transport trucks the others were boarding and learned that his squad was returning to the marketplace, close to the alley where he'd met the old beggar. Eagerness boosted his attitude. Maybe he'd get answers.

"Good morning, sunshine." Layton came up behind John and clasped his shoulder. "Miss me?" Layton had been confined to the infirmary the last forty-eight hours puking his guts out.

John dropped his pack next to the truck and turned around. "You look like crap. Go back."

"No way you're going back to that neighborhood and pulling your John Wayne act without me to cover you," Layton said.

Before John could respond, Corporal Lovett walked up. Lovett was also pulling double duty for Sergeant Boswell and another sergeant who were both in quarantine. Behind Lovett was Ollie Fitz, an interpreter fluent in the local dialect.

Lovett kept his briefing short and John made a point to sit beside Ollie in the truck as their small convoy left base.

"I need your help." John explained to Ollie how he met the old man and received the beads but didn't mention the dreams. "I can't shake the sense that there's more to the story. As weird as it sounds, I think the old man was trying to tell me something important about the rosary that affects our mission. If I can get a lead on his where-abouts, I'd like to talk to him again."

"Weird?" Ollie shrugged. "You finding a Christian rosary in a Muslim community is downright absurd. That the old man is missing a foot makes him easier to watch for and describe. Just don't expect much."

The convoy made several stops for possible improvised explosive devices – IEDs – before arriving at the busy open-air market that stretched along several city blocks. Most shoppers cleared out when the soldiers arrived. The few that remained avoided eye contact and crossed streets to avoid them.

An odd silence preceded the soldiers as they made their way along the street. There was no laughter, no hum of busy customers, no sounds of commerce or women giggling — not even a dog barking. The underlying sense of hostility and distrust was pronounced. John had never felt more like an interloper.

The vendors made a show of ignoring the soldiers by turning their backs to them. Each time Ollie cornered someone to ask about the old man, he received a terse head shake and a sharp *go away* wave of the hand. At one shop, a vendor spat before vehemently shouting the name of Zaman's dead son. Everyone in the squad tensed.

"Relax," Ollie said. "It was one of those fleas-of-thousand-camels general curses. No biggie."

By the time they returned to their transport vehicle two hours later, it was 10:00. The sun perched high in a cloudless sky with the temperatures already one-fifteen and climbing.

Layton came up and handed John a bottle of water. "Any luck with Ollie?"

"Nope." John tried to joke. "Who would have thought one old crippled guy could be so hard to find? Except you." Layton had been openly skeptical of John's desire to find the old man. And maybe his friend was right. Maybe John was trying too hard to see something sacred in the sand, trying too hard to make sense of nonsensical dreams. "Look, I've been obsessed, and I know it. Guess it's my McKay stubbornness."

Layton shoved his helmet back and wiped his forehead. "Texans are just as hardheaded as McKays. For what it's worth, I believe that if you're meant to find the old buzzard, he'll show up. When you least expect it. While I don't get the whole rosary thing, even I have to admit those beads were freaking bizarre. And I'm going to Hell for saying that, aren't I?"

"Straight to the devil. Both of us," John agreed.

Their armored vehicle lurched forward, gears grinding as they headed south. Twenty minutes later, they stopped near an abandoned elementary school that had been damaged by mortars two years ago.

As part of the effort to shore up local support, the Army had expedited plans to rehab the school building. This site was considered a double win because it provided two critical foundations of community: education and employment. Local Iraqi contractors would be used for much of the job. They were scheduled to meet the local crane operator and rigger today.

Out on the street, Corporal Lovett unrolled a blueprint across the vehicle's hood. "The equipment will be set up here. A supply trailer there." Lovett stabbed two circled spots on the drawing. "We need to confirm that both entrances are clear and accessible. Shouldn't take long."

They split into three groups, Layton leading one, Chris Worth leading another. Since he had the radio, John fell in behind Corporal Lovett, Ollie, and another soldier. As they swept out toward the East, Ollie nudged John and pointed. Just ahead, an Iraqi man pulled a wooden cart balanced on mismatched rubber tires.

"Bet he's headed to the marketplace," Ollie said. "We can ask about your old man. This guy might be more talkative away from the crowds."

"Couldn't hurt," John said.

"Keep it quick," Corporal Lovett said. "We'll go find that crane operator."

The Iraqi man slowed when Ollie called out. As they drew closer, John noted the wooden cart was loaded with dates.

The man took a defensive stance, his mistrustful gaze going from Ollie to John. When their eyes met, John felt a tingling of awareness. *I know him.* But from where? He never forgot a face, yet he couldn't place this man. The man gave no indication of recognizing them.

John guessed the man to be in his late thirties. A small boy, age four or five, peeked from behind the man's legs.

Ollie addressed the man in Arabic. "His name is Jamal." Ollie interpreted the man's responses. "He lives a kilometer from here."

Ollie continued talking, but this time he used his hands, approximating the beggar's height and mimicking the use of crutches.

Jamal seemed to listen half-heartedly before responding with a single syllable reply and a shake of his head. That's when John noticed that Jamal's left cheek was scarred. Purposely. This man had been marked as a potential traitor, most likely while Saddam Hussein's party struggled for control in the early days of the war.

John spoke to Jamal directly. "Do you speak English, sir?"

Jamal glared at John before turning back to Ollie and answering in sharp-toned Arabic.

"He was a professor," Ollie translated. "At the university. He said his ability to speak English earned him the mark on his face. He will not speak it again and risk reprisal against his family."

The boy, who'd remained silent, let out a cry and then shuffled closer to Jamal. The child wore a metal brace on his left leg, which reminded John of his nephew, Lucas, who'd worn a brace for a club foot. Lucas had undergone surgery two months ago.

John extended his hand, intent only on soothing the child. Jamal pulled the boy out of reach before swinging him onto the cart.

This time when Jamal spoke to Ollie, his voice shook with fury. "He doesn't think we should frighten young children or pick on helpless old men," Ollie translated.

John straightened and looked at Jamal. "I apologize. I did not mean to scare your son. And the old man isn't in any trouble. He gave me a gift, a very important one that I need to know more about." As he spoke, John tugged out the small rosary from his uncle. "The old man gave me beads similar to these, except the stones are bigger. The old man rambled on about a missing piece and something else, but I couldn't understand his message."

For a second, Jamal's eyes widened, but he shook his head.

John leaned closer. "You know who I'm talking about, don't you?"

Scowling, Jamal turned back to Ollie.

"He has never seen such beads and doesn't know your old man." Ollie spoke quickly to keep up. "He's pissed and wants to leave."

"Yeah. I got that. Tell him I said thanks." Not for the first time, John felt foolish for wasting time chasing dream conversations and wished he'd never met the old beggar.

He stepped away. He and Ollie needed to rejoin their squad.

"Wait!" Ollie caught up. "For what it's worth, I think Jamal told the truth about not knowing the old man."

"Look, thanks for asking. I won't—"

An explosion behind them cut off John's words. The force pitched him onto one knee. He quickly recovered and swung his M-4 forward as he turned and saw that Jamal's cart was on fire. Had the man's cart hit an improvised explosive device?

"They need help," Ollie shouted.

"Come on." John ran toward the burning cart.

The smoke made it hard to see, but he heard the child's cries. They found Jamal and his son pinned beneath fiery debris. Jamal's face was covered in blood, and he didn't move. The child continued to scream.

"Grab the axle," John yelled.

Together they flipped the wreckage to one side. John extinguished the child's flaming robe, and then lifted him to safety. The child writhed in agony, crying and screaming. Raw patches of severely burned skin covered the child's torso, arms, and legs. The brutal inequality of the situation angered John.

Instinctively, he tried to pray, but for the first time in his life, the words that had been drummed in since birth eluded him. How did one pray without prose? Without language?

A vision of the mysterious rosary came to mind and he desperately latched onto its symbolism. *God help this innocent child.*

"His father's alive." Ollie rushed toward John, supporting Jamal. As soon as Jamal spotted his son in John's arms, he surged forward unsteadily.

Two more explosions sounded further away, by the school building. John exchanged a glance with Ollie. That wasn't an IED. Those were rockets. They were under attack.

John swung the injured child into Jamal's outstretched arms. "Go! He needs a hospital."

Jamal took off with his son as John and Ollie raced back to the squad.

"This way," Ollie yelled.

As they ran, John tugged his radio out and called in their situation. "We're under heavy rocket fire. Need immediate support."

One of their transport trucks exploded when they drew close. More rocket-powered grenades came in from multiple directions, demolishing the other truck. Debris flew as John and Ollie scrambled for cover.

John continued to shout updates into the radio. "We're surrounded. Unknown number of assailants."

He searched for the others in his squad as they ran. Danny Carpenter fired from behind a low wall. What about Layton and the others?

Up ahead, Chris Worth called out. "Over here!" Preach and Lovett were with him, about ten yards away.

Ollie zigzagged along the edge of the courtyard, John right behind him. Gunshots surrounded them, making it impossible to determine friendly fire from enemy rounds.

Corporal Lovett screamed. "I've been shot. Preach is down, too."

Ollie fired as he sprinted. "We're almost there. Hang on."

An enormous explosion shook the ground. The school building imploded right in front of them, forcing John and Ollie into the open.

Ollie listed to one side. "I'm hit."

"Got you." John grabbed Ollie beneath one arm and lunged onward, ignoring Ollie's groans.

Grit had John's eyes burning, making it hard to see the others in his squad. Where was Layton? Where was support? Smoke and dust from the explosions billowed, forming a wall that looked impenetrable and robbed John's sense of direction. Which way to safety?

"Won't make it." Ollie slumped.

"You will." John jerked Ollie into a fireman's carry over one shoulder and lurched forward.

A rocket came whistling in. John surged ahead, summoning forth every ounce of his strength. *Going to be close.* A second before the rocket landed, he shoved Ollie away and tried to jump. The ordnance exploded, lifting John in a blast of scalding heat.

Time stuttered. Light strobed off and on, synced to a cascade of smaller explosions. Fire ripped through his lower torso. John tried to breathe, but the air was too hot. Sound amplified, then ceased as he slammed to the ground.

When John came to, he screamed Ollie's name, but he couldn't hear his own voice. Then with a popping noise, the percussion deafness cleared. At first, he only heard muffled sounds, incoherent shouts, and thunder that wasn't thunder.

How long had he been passed out? Where was Ollie? The others? Dazed, John blinked to focus his vision and tried to assess. His weapon, his radio, were both gone. He attempted to move but found his left arm unresponsive. Worse, he felt nothing below his waist.

Gathering his energy, John rose slightly and looked down at his body. His shirt and jacket were torn away, exposing a gaping bloody wound in his stomach. Blood seemed to spurt with each heartbeat, slow but steady.

"Oh no. No..." John had seen wounds like this before, heard medics whisper *won't make it.* Not on a battlefield with no help in sight.

As he collapsed back, his hand hit something. His weapon. He pulled it close. To his left, a burst of fierce gunfire sounded. Then he heard his name shouted and recognized Layton's voice.

With effort, John twisted his head and spotted Layton behind a section of wall, bent over someone. *Fallon.* Layton kneeled, keeping one hand pressed against Fallon's body, while firing his weapon with the other. Courage the size of Texas.

Behind Layton, Danny Carpenter dug through rubble with a franticness that spoke of disaster. Was John seeing correctly? Out of twelve men, only two remained standing? *God help us.*

John's gaze locked on the eerily familiar buildings silhouetted behind Layton. This scene was straight out of John's premonition and he knew what came next. Just like in his nightmares, a black-clad figure crept in and aimed a weapon toward Layton.

"Not. Today. A-hole." Rallying his strength, John raised his M-4 and fired a single burst. The assailant fell. Unable to hold the weapon up any longer, John let it drop to his chest.

Layton yelled. "I'll be there in a minute, buddy."

John thought of Fallon's pregnant girlfriend and knew a sudden clarity. *Prioritize. Protect. Don't waste time saving a dead man.* "I'm fine. Don't let Fallon die."

"Where is support?" Layton continued. "Can't hold them off much longer."

"Yes, you can. They're coming." John hoped he'd given the correct coordinates.

Cold crept up his chest. With his good hand, he loosened his helmet and fumbled for the photo tucked inside. He held it inches from his face. Janey. He swallowed a cry, knowing he'd never get to tell her goodbye. That he'd never get to apologize. He realized his own pigheadedness had cost him the opportunity to hear her say, *I forgive you.*

Layton shouted again. "John! Look out at one o'clock!"

Squinting, John tried to raise his weapon, determined to do whatever he could to protect his squad.

The scarred man, Jamal, moved into John's line of sight. Jamal had his hands held upwards, showing he was unarmed.

"He's friendly. Don't shoot," John yelled to Layton before his voice gave out to a coughing fit.

Belatedly, John recognized his mistake. That Jamal was alone meant his child had died. Had the man returned seeking retribution?

Jamal rushed forward now, speaking in frantic English. "I've come to help. The old man you sought—praise Allah—found us. Thank you for sending him."

John shook his head. "I sent no one."

Jamal kneeled beside him. "You did. And he saved my son. He said I must come help you. But..." Jamal's voice faded as his gaze swept over John's injuries.

John saw his own death mirrored in Jamal's horrified expression. Time was short. "You. Must go." John held out the photograph of Janey. "Take this. Don't want...bad guys to..."

"The old man will save you, too." Jamal was adamant. "I saw him do it."

"It's too late. Get your son and go." John thrust the photograph forward one last time. "Take this. Please."

Grateful to feel the photograph slide from his fingers, John closed his eyes and hoped that Jamal and his son made it home.

Home.

A tear slid down John's cheek as he thought of his family and wished he wasn't...alone. Had it been like this for Mother – drawing her last breath alone?

The sounds of war escalated, gunfire and bombs a hellish requiem. He prayed for death to come swiftly. Prayed he would not cry out and distract Layton and Carpenter. Prayed the coldness passed quickly.

Someone squeezed his fingers.

John tried to focus his hazy eyesight. Jamal was still there, bowed close, keeping John's hand in his as he chanted. The cadence of Jamal's Arabic was soothing, prayer a universal language of spirit.

Warmth enveloped John as his labored breathing ceased. He felt weightless as his soul slipped free of his body.

John looked back down at the battlefield as if from above. He saw Jamal still bent low in prayer; he saw Layton kneeling beside Fallon, still holding a compression bandage with one hand. There was a volley of gunfire. John watched as if from a distance as Layton took an upper body hit and fell forward. Layton stayed down, then struggled to rise, to correct, before slumping forward again.

I failed to keep him safe. Immediately, John's sad thoughts were replaced with an overwhelming sense of love. Creatures of brightness surrounded him, and he knew they were there to accompanying him to—

"No." John struggled to get away. "Please. Not. Yet."

Gasping for air, John grabbed Jamal's hand. "Tell Janey..."

CHAPTER EIGHT

July 2006
Thirty miles north of Baghdad, Iraq

The jackal felt trapped. Cleric Ibrahim Yassin watched Farid Zaman pace the length of the small room. They had been on the move from village to village, hiding from American soldiers while waiting to hear the outcome of the ambush.

Today's battle was pivotal. Despite losses on their side, the daring attack would increase Zaman's stature. The West would view him as an even greater threat, a powerful, dangerous leader who could rally forces against them. It was the exact image Yassin needed to get Zaman re-focused on their objective.

Unfortunately, Zaman's thirst for revenge made it difficult to keep him fixated on the true way. They had just met with several local tribal leaders, and Zaman's displeasure with the other leaders' failure to commit hung in the air like a hangman's noose.

"How dare Rehab question my moves?" Zaman smashed his fist to the table. "How dare his brother question my authority or suggest I withdraw the *fatwa* now?"

"Rehab and the others are still measuring their power and influence against yours." Yassin's voice projected calm authority. As Zaman's spiritual advisor and trusted confidant, Yassin's sway held more merit than even Zaman's military counselors. "Rehab is accustomed to being a leader. As your influence grows, the other warlords will have no choice but to back you."

"Or be the next to perish." Zaman's temper was shorter than usual. "I should have Rehab executed like the dog that he is."

"Rehab is more valuable alive. The smaller tribes listen to him." Yassin switched tactics, appealing to Zaman's ego. "Rehab knows your power. He sees how readily you draw in new followers. The Westerners' hatred of you for your successful attacks against their military will fan excitement in the true believers. As word of this bloody victory spreads, offers of backing from supporters in Iran and Syria will pour in. With more money and weapons, Rehab and the others will give in. I advise patience."

"Patience is for old men like Rehab," Zaman shot back. "The moment the infidels lower their guard, I intend to wipe them from our land."

"The plan is to wipe them from the face of the earth, not just our land," Yassin reminded. "That is what the other warlords want to hear. Your vengeance doesn't feed their families or increase their wealth. They want the hope of more territory, of more power for their followers. They want to witness the rise of Islam's might."

Zaman stormed across the room and took a seat. "Very well. Expedite the offers of support you spoke of. I want all the money and arms you can muster. Then tell the warlords whatever they need to hear. But I want one thing to be clear. The *fatwa* remains. I demand vengeance for my murdered son. I will not rest until those infidels' blood fills the streets here and in their homes."

CHAPTER NINE

July 2006
River Haven, Iowa

Janey McKay hustled to tie down the alfalfa bales perched atop the forty-pound bags of horse feed crammed into the bed of Mrs. Halliday's truck.

Mrs. Halliday fanned herself with a sales flyer. "Look at you! Why don't they have those boys in the parts department out here doing this?"

"They couldn't handle this heat." Janey tried to joke as she secured the load with orange baling twine, but the implication was clear. *Look at you... all hot and sweaty. Look at you... a girl.* And wait for it...

"But you're a McKay!"

Which, here, meant absolutely nothing. Janey had worked at the McKay equipment and farm store since junior high. She earned minimum wage, with no benefits. Being a McKay meant she was expected to work harder than anyone, even during college breaks.

And forget gender. Being female gave her a little benefit with her father, but with her brothers? They were slave drivers.

"Matt and Perry remind me daily that they started out sweeping floors and scrubbing toilets," Janey said. "I'm not about to complain." An outdoor person, she preferred the loading docks to being penned up in the parts warehouse. Plus, it was temporary. She'd be back at college by the end of August.

Mrs. Halliday shook her head. "I always thought you'd enter beauty contests, like your mother. She could have won Miss America if she hadn't got married."

Janey slammed the tailgate harder than necessary. Mrs. Halliday went to high school with Anna McKay and always brought it up. Some days it was hard not to resent people who had known her mother longer than Janey had.

One of the forklift drivers wheeled close enough to shout. "They're paging you, Janey. Call on line two."

Grateful for the interruption, she held out a clipboard for the woman to sign. "Drive safe going home."

Ducking inside, Janey let the air conditioning rejuvenate her as she headed for the executive suites. Her brothers were due back from a trade show today, but flight delays meant she could still assert familial advantage and use Perry's office. She sat in her brother's over-sized leather chair and put her booted feet up on his credenza before answering.

"This is Janey McKay. How can I help you?"

"It's Wayne. Do you have a moment?"

"Yes, sir." Wayne Franklin was her editor at The River Press, the local newspaper. Under Wayne's tutelage, the occasional freelance article Janey wrote morphed into a biweekly, patriotic-themed column. The bylines helped build her portfolio as she worked on a journalism degree.

"I've got good news," Wayne said. "The publisher would like to see more articles from you and is offering a temporary, paid internship as a cub reporter. It'll run four weeks, or until you head back to school. Are you interested?"

"Yes!" A paid position at the paper meant fewer hours here and more hours writing.

"Let's meet Tuesday afternoon to discuss details," Wayne said.

Janey hung up and pushed back to spin circles in Perry's chair. "Yes!"

"Yes, what?" Her brother flashed in and out of view as the chair twirled.

She dropped her feet, jerking to a stop. "You're back."

Perry chuckled as he crossed the room. "Just in time it seems. Better get back to work, slacker. Before the boss catches you."

"Ha, ha." She stood. "While you're here, we need to discuss my schedule."

"Looks like we need to find more for you to do."

"Nope. The River Press just offered me a paid internship for the rest of the summer."

"Congratulations, kiddo!" Perry slipped into big brother mode and gave her a hug. With John in the Army, Perry became the biggest supporter of her writing dreams. "When do you start?"

"Soon. I'll know more next Tuesday."

Perry shifted back into boss mode. "In the meantime, you're still our delivery girl. Ethan in parts is looking for you."

Janey rolled her eyes. "Delivery *person*. First tell me about your Kansas City trip."

"It was productive. We met with—"

The intercom buzzed. "Your father's on line one, Mr. McKay," the receptionist announced.

"You know Dad wants a full report on the trade show. He hated missing it." Janey headed toward the door. "Don't tell him my news, though."

"Scram! Go see Ethan!"

The counter at the parts department was deserted. A bag sat in the delivery basket. GASKETS FOR MR. SMITH, the tag read. She hit the bell on the counter and shouted, "Got it!" before beelining toward the side exit. If she hung around, someone would ask her to pick up food or coffee while she was out, and this close to quitting time she had no intention of returning.

Outside, the summer sun dominated the afternoon sky, parboiling the earth for day five of a triple digit heatwave. Even the asphalt in the crowded parking lot felt spongy. She climbed into the McKay Equipment truck — not a perk because they always stuck her with the oldest pickup — and twisted the AC knob to MAX.

The temptation to curse the heat died as soon as she eyed the two photographs she kept clipped to the visor, one of John, the other of Layton Burnet. No matter how high the temperatures here, it was hotter in Iraq. "Everything's worse in Baghdad," John frequently complained.

Yeah, well, wait until you're home. While he was overseas, she tried to not pick a fight. But they still had a score to settle, and Janey wasn't about to let him off the hook without an apology. He had no right to steal her letter. And if he'd read it, she'd kill him. That it was just as well Layton never saw her letter didn't absolve John.

While her feelings for Layton hadn't changed, after fourteen months with no encouragement from him, she was disillusioned. She stalked Layton's posts on social media since he'd deployed, paying special attention to his relationship status. Over the last year it bounced from his platinum-blond ex-fiancée, Sharlene, to it's complicated, to his latest status: single. Who knew what it would be when John and Layton's deployment ended?

Her hand went for the half-heart necklace beneath her shirt as her gaze lingered on Layton's image. She'd quit wearing the necklace a dozen times since he'd been gone, but darn if it didn't end up around her neck repeatedly. He was her *one*. The sign had been unmistakable.

Or so she'd thought. To her credit, she tried to move on, diving into the University of Iowa's hyperactive social scene. She'd dated, but as her best friend Gemma noted, no one could compete with Layton. That truth hurt.

Flipping the visor up, she sped off. A few minutes later, she pulled into the Smith dairy farm. Mrs. Smith met her at the back door. Janey held up the bag. "I've got a tractor part for your husband."

"Gerald's in the field. I'll run it out to him." Mrs. Smith signed the ticket. "We received the invitation to John's homecoming party. And I see the signs are back up around town. Your family must be excited."

Janey nodded. Welcome Home signs and yellow ribbons had first appeared in River Haven's store windows and people's yards three months ago, but after John's deployment got extended, they disappeared. Their revival meant this fifteen-month stretch of worry would soon be history. The American Legion parade was back on, and the McKay family planned a huge homecoming event with live music and a barbecue to honor John and Layton.

Provided Layton came back to Iowa. John was noncommittal about Layton's plans, and Janey refused to ask more than once. The telltale would be if Layton returned to Texas instead of Iowa. She hadn't forgotten his promise that they'd talk when he returned, and if he'd just said that to be nice, she'd shoot him. McKays didn't do nice. They got even.

Feeling depressed after leaving the Smith's, Janey headed north on Highway 61. It was the long way home, but when driven by a McKay was quickest. John once told her that the faster he drove, the clearer his thoughts became. She agreed. It was one thing she missed about motocross racing. That and—

A white truck zoomed up behind her, blasting its horn. She glanced at her speedometer, wondering if she'd slowed while lost in thought. Except she was running sixty-seven in a fifty-five zone.

The truck remained right on her tailgate, honking and flashing its headlights. She glanced into her rearview mirror. Was the other driver drunk or just a jerk? Had she been in her own car, she would have flipped off the driver and sped away. Driving a pickup with

MCKAY FARM EQUIPMENT plastered all over it and a HOW'S
MY DRIVING? sticker on the bumper, meant she had to suck it up.
Perry threatened to slap a governor on the truck if she got one more
speeding ticket.

She slowed and moved onto the shoulder, giving the other truck
ample room to pass. Which the idiot could have already done. Except
for the two of them, there were no vehicles visible for miles.

The white truck swung partly into the left lane and sped up, but
instead of moving on, the driver straddled the center line and drove
parallel to her. What was this road hog's problem?

The dark-tinted window on the other truck's passenger side
lowered. Janey's gut tightened when she saw who was behind the
wheel. Randy Keener. *Great.* The McKays and Keeners had a long-
standing feud stemming back to when Matt and Perry raced against
Randy's older brothers. After multiple violations for cheating with
illegally modified engines, Janey's father got the Keeners banned
from the motocross racing circuit. The Keeners blamed the McKays
for everything from withdrawn sponsorships to the subsequent loss
of their motorcycle franchise. Randy and John revived the feud by
tangling over the years, but Randy's last run-in with John got
Randy's parole revoked. Three strikes meant he'd stayed in jail.
Since getting out a month ago, Randy heckled Janey whenever he
saw her.

She looked at the stretch of highway ahead, ignoring Randy as
she let off the gas and dropped back. Instead of passing, he slowed his
truck, once again matching her speed. Then he drifted close, forcing
her further onto the shoulder as he blasted his horn nonstop. She
glared at his truck. He made a roll-down motion between honks.

Janey lowered her window half-way. "What do you want,
Randy?"

"Depends on what you're offering, sweet thing." He tugged off
his sunglasses to leer and wink. "I've got what you need right here."
He pointed down toward his lap.

"Pervert!" Disgusted, she started to raise her window, but he veered close, laying on the horn. Reaching across the seat, she fumbled in her bag. Where was her cell phone?

Her right front tire dropped off the roadbed. She kept an even grip on the steering wheel, her tire balanced on the edge of the ditch. They were doing over eighty now. She glanced ahead, hoping another car would come along.

"Go away and leave me alone," she shouted.

"When's that sorry brother of yours getting back?"

"I have three brothers, and none of them are sorry." She knew which one he was talking about.

"Me and my boys have been waiting over a year to stomp John's butt."

By his *boys*, Randy meant the rough neck bigots that hung out at the JFA office downtown. Randy was the leader of the Justice Freedom Association local chapter. That many members had been inducted into the JFA during Randy's stint in jail spoke volumes about the association's recruiting policies.

"John's going down for the count," he yelled.

Her temper spiked. *Never threaten a McKay.* "Good luck with that."

Taking her foot off the gas, she fell back a few feet and waited for Randy to follow suit. When he did, she punched the gas and pulled ahead.

Her lead didn't last. He came up beside her again and cut close, hitting her side mirror with his. Glass shattered as her truck's mirror housing crumpled.

"Look what you did!" he accused.

"Bite me, Randy."

No longer caring what vehicle she drove, she floored it. RPMs jumped as her truck shot forward, speeding up past one hundred. She might have the oldest truck in the fleet, but nothing a McKay owned lacked power. The older Ford's 385 horsepower V8 ate up pavement as the speedometer eased past one-ten. Randy's Chevy was only a six cylinder with half the horsepower and his truck receded in her rearview mirror. Though he didn't appear to be giving up, he didn't stand a chance.

A blinking light on the dash caught her attention. LOW FUEL.

No! Not now.

Janey eyed the fields on either side of the road. If she continued north, Randy would catch her before she reached a gas station. Her only option was to double back and hope she made it home.

Backing off the accelerator, she slowed before hitting the brakes. With a flick of her wrist, the truck did a controlled one-eighty spin, which popped her right back in the direction she'd come.

Randy had dropped into the correct lane, but when he saw her maneuver, he veered back over the centerline, racing toward her head-on.

There was no time to panic. That she felt calm was all thanks to her brother.

Though she had never played chicken, John had, and his advice rang in her ears. *Hold your lane and keep the fire in your eyes. Make the other guy back down.* She prayed her brother was right.

At the last second, Randy lost his nerve. He swerved back into his own lane moments before she shot past. She watched in her rearview as he over-corrected and slid off the road, wedging his truck into the ditch.

"Hope you stay stuck!" Janey called out the window.

She took the next turn, eager to get home. Perspiration drenched her shirt as the tension in her system crashed. Her hands trembled as she continued to check the road behind her. She debated calling the cops, but with no eyewitnesses, it was her word against his, and he'd likely claim she'd started it. No one would believe Randy, however her brothers wouldn't pass up the opportunity to lecture her. Perry would rant, but his fuse was longer than Matt's was. Matt would launch the moment he heard the name Keener.

The side mirror rattled where Randy had sideswiped her. If she could repair the truck mirror quickly, she wouldn't have to tell anyone.

As she cleared the ridge, the tallest of the McKay farm silos came into view but that sense of comfort deflated as she recalled her latest missteps with Eileen. She debated heading back to the store, except she needed gas. And she couldn't keep avoiding her father's new wife.

Everyone warned Janey to expect an adjustment period after Dad remarried, but Eileen's desire to "take care of Ward" meant monopolizing all his time. Feeling ostracized, Janey moved out of the farmhouse and into the spare bedroom in the bunkhouse, next to John's room. Things hit a crisis point, though, when she returned from New York and found all her mother's kitchen knickknacks, all the fragile memories of Janey's childhood, packed up for donation to the church thrift shop.

Janey hauled the precious boxes out to the bunkhouse to keep them out of the way until she could take them to Perry's for long-term storage. Perry, bless him, had understood her heartache, but cautioned against upsetting their father.

Dad's worsening heart problems were an enormous concern, but now with Eileen in the picture, he seemed secretive about doctors' appointments. Janey worried her father hid something about his health. Matt and Perry disagreed, insisting she overreacted. John seemed unconcerned, holding to his claim that since they'd lost their mother as young children, they were immune from further tragedy. He'd been right more than once. Janey survived life-threatening pneumonia; John had walked away unscathed from two horrendous motocross wrecks. Perry and Matt lived through a plane crash last year.

"Never doubt me," John chided when she shared her hyper-vigilant concern about their only surviving parent. "I'm telling you; we're golden."

She lowered the visor and glanced at her brother's photograph. "You better be right about Dad, John."

At the big MCKAY FAMILY FARM sign, Janey stopped. A

large, dust-covered postal truck sat next to the mailbox, blocking the drive.

She lowered her window. "Afternoon, Mr. Dillon."

Harry Dillon had delivered their mail for as long as she could remember. He pointed to her truck's dangling-by-wires side mirror. "Tough day?"

"Hit a deer."

Harry chuckled and handed her a thick roll of mail and magazines held together by a half-dozen rubber bands. "Got something for you today, Janey." He gave her a small box. "Looks like another package from your brother. He ought to be home soon, right?"

Janey tipped the box and heard the soft clink of metal that telegraphed the contents. More boring battle coins for the trophy shelves in John's room. She dumped all the mail on the passenger seat. "Just two more weeks."

"Tell your father I'll see him tomorrow at your uncle's farewell party," Harry said before pulling away.

Janey grimaced at the reminder. Uncle Nick was being transferred to another parish, in Chicago. In fact, he'd be gone before John returned. The thought of her uncle leaving threatened to bring tears to her eyes. *I wish things would stop changing.*

More than friend/uncle/confidant/spiritual advisor, he was also a tie to her late mother. Uncle Nick was the voice of calm, of reassurance. She wouldn't have made it without him.

Her brothers' and their wives' cars lined the long gravel driveway leading up to the two-story farmhouse. Janey grinned. While Dad had not felt well enough to travel to Kansas City for the trade show, he would demand an immediate update of all the events and a full recap of whom Matt and Perry talked with, and what was discussed. Her brothers just thought they ran the show.

As soon as Janey parked, Fuller bounded up. The dog barked and then whined.

"What's wrong, girl?" Concerned, she dropped to one knee and scratched the collie's ruff. Her mother had raised champion show collies and Fuller came from the last litter. A family favorite, Fuller had been the only dog ever allowed in the house. Until Eileen moved in. Another reason Janey moved out to the bunkhouse. "That better not be a guilty bark. I hope you left Eileen's chickens alone today."

Eileen had decided the farm needed chickens. Fuller hated chickens. That Fuller had been on the farm a lot longer didn't matter. The chickens weren't the only ones with ruffled feathers. "Life doesn't revolve around us anymore, Fuller. I miss that."

Straightening, she noticed the riding mower abandoned mid-cut on the front lawn. Her gaze swept across the rock garden and paused at the concrete Madonna statue. The climbing rosebush that grew over the trellis appeared wilted, the flowers all drooped.

A sense of cold swept over her at the sight of the dying blooms. The rosebush had died the night her mother passed away. As Janey moved forward, she spotted an unfamiliar car, a navy-blue Ford Explorer with an Illinois license plate.

The front porch door opened, and Matt stepped out. "There you are." His perturbed tone made her wonder if Randy Keener had called. Matt held up her cell phone. "You left this on the loading dock."

"Sorry. I left in a hurry and..." Drawing closer she realized her brother had been crying. She dashed up the porch steps fearing the worst. "Oh, God! Is Daddy okay?"

"Dad's fine." Matt reached out to touch her shoulder. "It's John, honey."

Her hand went to her heart. *John.* "What's wrong?"

CHAPTER TEN

July 2006
River Haven, Iowa

"John was killed in battle." Matt's voice cracked as he spoke.

Killed. Anguish bolted through Janey's lungs. Distress took out her knees. "No!"

Matt stepped in and caught her, his silence a blood-freezing affirmation.

Uncontrollable trembling seized her muscles. *John. Killed.* She wanted to run away, but Matt wouldn't let go, steadying her, forcing her to acknowledge his words.

"I'm sorry, Janey. Come in the house. Dad's waiting."

She resisted, wanting no part of what lay ahead. He kept her tucked to his side, giving her no choice. As soon as they entered the living room, her father stood. He opened his arms wide, his expression one she hadn't seen since her mother died. Janey rushed to him.

Dad stroked the long braid of hair down her back as he also wept. "I know, baby."

"How?" She couldn't form sentences, grief a choking noose. "When?"

Her father cleared his throat. "This is Captain Hartman and Lieutenant Simmons. They are Casualty Notification Officers." Only now did Janey realize there were two strangers in their midst. The uniformed officers stood at attention next to Eileen. The Illinois car tags.

At her father's introduction, Captain Hartman shifted forward. The melancholy lines around his mouth bespoke grim experience. The Lieutenant was younger and not as adept at hiding his discomfort.

Captain Hartman spoke first. "On behalf of the Secretary of the Army, please accept the United States Army's deepest sympathy on your brother's death."

She shook her head. "I don't want sympathy. I want to know what happened to my brother."

Perry came up and hooked her arm before tugging her toward the sofa. "We all want to know. Give him a chance to explain."

"Specialist McKay's squad came under attack during a patrol in Iraq yesterday," Captain Hartman began.

Specialist? Janey cut him off. "His name is John."

The Captain looked her in the eyes and nodded. "Your brother, John, died from injuries received in combat when his squad was attacked by enemy forces."

Died from injuries. Attacked. Enemy forces. Her abdomen clenched as the words brought violent images to mind. The embedded journalists she followed covered the war from the front lines, but those carefully edited scenes concentrated on the shock and awe factor. The human losses were reported as statistics, numbers that lacked faces, names, visceral connections.

"Few details are available as the investigation is not complete," the Captain continued.

Janey saw an expression pass between Dad and the Captain and wondered if specifics were being omitted, details censored. Frantic questions surfaced in her mind. "That's all you can tell us? I want to know how my brother died. What was his squad doing when they came under attack?"

Dad held up a hand. "They don't have those answers, Janey. But I promise we will get them."

The Captain turned back toward Janey. "I wish I could tell you more. Unfortunately, we know little beyond what's being released to the news. Five soldiers died, and several others were injured. There were also civilian casualties."

Five dead soldiers. *Oh, please no!* "What about Layton Burnet? He's in John's squad." She couldn't lose both John and Layton.

The Lieutenant spoke up now. "We don't have any information on the others, ma'am. The Army is still notifying next of kin. I'm sorry. I understand from your father that Specialist Burnet is a family friend."

Friend? She nodded, afraid that if she spoke she'd blurt out a declaration of love. She pressed her hands to her temples, desperate to ease the pounding *no, no, no* echoing in her head. *Be alive, Layton.* She couldn't contemplate further loss.

"Captain Hartman promised to relay a message that we want full information on John, Layton, and all the others." Dad's voice cracked. "We may not know details, but I know my son. He would have died a hero."

"He lived a hero," Janey whispered. *My hero.*

Captain Hartman addressed her father. "I have some paperwork to review with you, sir."

Once again, that look exchanged between the men. If they were concerned about this upsetting her, it was too late. She sat straight up and leaned forward. *Act like a McKay.* "I'm not leaving."

"That's my girl," Dad said. "Go ahead."

Most of the questions verified John's personal data and were worded in past tense. Where was John born? Did he have a religious preference? Dad offered present tense responses. *John is a Roman Catholic.*

When the Captain reviewed the names of next of kin Janey bowed her head at the reminder that there were two new nephews who would never meet their uncle.

"A Casualty Assistance Officer will be in contact to let you know when your son's remains will be flown back and to help coordinate transfer to a local mortuary," the Captain said.

The lump in Janey's throat swelled. They couldn't be discussing John. He was too big, too real for an impersonal word like remains.

"We'll use Lloyd's Funeral Home," Dad said. "On First Avenue. Downtown."

Lloyd's had handled her mother's funeral. Janey shut her eyes against that memory as they continued to discuss the mundane. *Return all personal belongings here. Do not wash his clothing.* After her mother died, Janey had been sequestered from the details of death. The adults whispered in her presence or discussed it out of earshot. *She's too young,* morphed to *don't want to upset her.* Her family's good intentions left her inexperienced at handling emotional trauma.

When Janey opened her eyes again, the two officers were on their feet, preparing to leave, their part in this tragedy complete. The Captain reiterated his contact information before offering a last round of condolences.

"I'll see them out." Perry nodded to Matt.

Janey recognized her brothers' shorthand. Perry wanted to ask more questions, away from everyone. For the moment, that was okay. She'd corner Perry later.

When the screen door banged shut, her anger surfaced and turned into rage. "This wouldn't have happened if the Army had sent John home after one year. They shouldn't have extended his deployment!"

"We've all thought the same thing, honey." Matt's wife, Robin, moved in and pressed a tissue into Janey's hand.

"And none of it brings John back," Dad said. "As much as I hate to say it, your brother knew the risks of joining. Deep down, we all knew."

Janey wanted to deny it. Whenever news broke of military casualties in Iraq, her family held their breath and mourned. *There but for the grace of God...* That grace had run out. God had failed. So had the Army. And so had John and Layton, who'd each promised to look out for the other.

"Have you called Uncle Nick?" Janey asked.

"The church secretary is trying to reach him." Dad turned to Matt. "Can you contact Lloyd Nelson, see if we can meet in a couple hours? I have to put up the lawn mower. Then I need to make a few phone calls and—"

Her father stopped talking and swayed, his face vivid red.

Janey rushed forward, but Matt and Eileen were already at his sides.

Dad waved them off with a choking sound. "Just let me sit back down. It's my blood pressure." He glanced at her. "I'm fine, Janey-girl."

"You need to take it easy, Dad," Matt said.

"Don't coddle me, dang it," Dad snapped. "Doctor's been messing with my prescriptions again. That's all."

Janey glanced at Matt. Their father rarely raised his voice. Matt gave her a terse *not now* look.

Eileen patted Dad's arm. "The doctor warned there might be minor side effects, right Ward? Still, maybe five minutes in the recliner wouldn't hurt. It would sure make me feel better. In a bit, you can get the mower while I feed the chickens."

Dad relaxed as Eileen leaned in to press a kiss to his cheek. "I'm fine, sweetheart. But if it will give you ease — five minutes."

"Perry and I will get the mower and the chores, Dad," Matt said. "You take care of the phone calls."

Janey felt invisible, shut out, her once-familiar world upturned. "I'll get the chickens."

She followed Matt out the door. The officers' car was gone, but the pall remained. She wanted to hate them, to cast blame. Anything to lessen her pain. She didn't want to believe John was gone, and yet a coldness had leached into her chest that refused to ease. Refused to be denied.

She glanced at the rosebush over the Madonna. The leaves were curled and dropping. Just like after Mother died. The rosebush was also linked to Layton. Janey prayed it wasn't an omen of his death, too. *Please, no.*

Tears streamed down her cheeks. She grabbed Matt's hand as they walked across the drive. He squeezed her fingers twice. Their little code. *I'm here.*

"You okay, kiddo?"

"I'm worried about Dad. Did you see how red his face was?"

Matt wrapped an arm around her shoulders. "Dad will be okay, Sis. He just needs to get off his feet, which he's more likely to do if we're not in there hovering. Eileen will keep an eye on him."

"That's my job." Janey wiped her face with her arm. "Or used to be."

"It will always be your job. But none of us are here twenty-four-seven anymore. You're in college most of the year. Perry and I are traveling more. Eileen is a godsend. Why don't you go back inside and help Robin and Lisa?"

"I don't want to listen to them call and relay the news over and over." *I don't want it to be true.* "I need to feed Fuller, too."

At the curve in the driveway, Matt paused. "I will finish mowing. Perry will check the cattle. You know we're both here for you, right?"

Janey squeezed his hand before watching him walk away. An acute sense of foreboding welled up as he left, paralyzing her voice and preventing her from calling him back. Lost and alone, she looked at the sky; she had to shade her eyes against the pure bright blue. Fury boiled up anew. *Why did this happen? What about my prayers? What about Layton?* The lack of information about him increased her dread. How could she find out if the man she adored was dead or alive?

The Army might not release information, but there were others who knew, others who'd been deployed and fighting side-by-side with John and Layton. She tried to remember the names of John's squad mates. Carpenter. Fallon. Preach. John referred to all of them as brothers. Her stomach ached at the thought that some of them had died, too. Four more families were receiving visits from Casualty Notification Officers today while still others were being notified of injuries. Was there an Army officer out in Texas trying to reach Layton's next of kin? Janey wondered whom the Army would notify. To hear Layton talk, he had little family. An only child, both of his parents were deceased, and he wasn't close to his grandmother, who was in a care center. He'd mentioned a cousin once, but she didn't recall a name.

Inside the three-car garage behind the house, she pulled on rubber boots. Dad had added an elaborate chicken coop on one side to make it easier for Eileen to gather eggs in foul weather. After raking the run, Janey changed the water and scattered feed. The hens seemed subdued, clucking softly while keeping their distance, as if they sensed the sadness in the air.

When she finished, she headed to the bunkhouse, her mind turning over ways to find out what had happened to John, Layton, and the others. First, she'd check John's friend list on his Myspace page. He was connected online to most of his squad mates. Once she had names and hometowns, she'd search for contact information and make phone calls.

She would also get on Layton's Myspace page and reach out to anyone who could connect her with Layton's family, even his ex-girl-friends. Janey would beg if needed, pride be damned.

At the bunkhouse, though, Janey ignored her bedroom. Guilt over every cross word she and John had ever exchanged surfaced and its weight threatened to crush her. *You're dumber than a fence post. You're mean and suck eggs. I hate you. I'll never trust you again. I don't need you anymore...*

Slipping inside John's bedroom, she shut the door and cried. *I'm sorry. Please come back.*

Everything in John's room was just as he'd left it. The corkboard by his desk still had photos from his senior year of high school. Homecoming. Prom. Football banquet. She recalled John grousing about having to wear a suit, but he looked dashing. Handsome, like all McKay men.

She stared at the US map mounted beside the corkboard. Every state had at least one push pin in it, representing a significant trail he intended to hike. "I want to see all fifty states at least once before I settle down," he'd said. "Maybe twice. See what's beyond Iowa."

A grandiose dream that would never come true.

She ran her fingers across the montage of framed photos that captured highlights of his motocross races. Another wall held shelves loaded with first place trophies. His history of wins didn't include second or third place. John said those didn't count.

She recoiled when she spotted the row of commemorative battle coins he'd shipped from Iraq. His explanation about them had been vague. From what she gathered, they were small awards, some for his squad's accomplishments, some from senior officers who recognized his individual contributions to a mission. Janey had placed the metal medallions front and center on the middle shelf, so he'd notice them when he came home.

Except...

Tears blurred her vision as she recalled the box Mr. Dillon had handed her an hour ago. More stupid battle coins that John had mailed home, never expecting—

"God, why?" Her anguished voice echoed in the emptiness.

John. Layton.

While Janey's family shared her grief over John, they weren't aware of her romantic feelings for Layton. Didn't know he was her *one.* Her best friend knew, though.

Tugging out her cell phone, she called Gemma. It went straight to voicemail, so Janey left a brief message. "Gem, please call me."

Scratching sounded at the door. When she opened it, Fuller bounded in and leaped onto John's bed, whining as she circled frantically. The dog knew. The collie had a sixth sense when it came to Janey and John. When they were kids, Fuller followed them everywhere and served as an early warning system if danger lurked nearby and ratted them out to adults if they ignored her barks.

Janey wrapped both arms around the collie's neck, trying to soothe her. "Easy, girl. It's awful." Shifting to sit beside Fuller, she punched in her uncle's phone number.

His cell phone rang four times before his recording kicked in. "You've reached Father Nicholas of St. Francis' Parish—"

At the beep, Janey's voice broke. "Uncle Nick, please call. Something happened to John. We – I – need to talk to you."

CHAPTER ELEVEN

July 2006
River Haven, Iowa

Father Nick Shelton attended his final church board meeting in the tiny farm community of St. Paul, twenty miles north of River Haven. Like the other six churches in his parish, St. Paul's requested one last gathering with their soon-to-be-former pastor.

A native son, Nick cut his priestly teeth here in southeast Iowa. This parish, these people, were all he'd ever known as a priest. But the unheard-of thirteen-year tenure at one location came at a price. The devil's due was his next assignment. Chicago.

The mere thought constricted his lungs. *Don't panic. Breathe.* This wasn't the place for an anxiety attack. He gulped in air, counting silently as he followed the board members to the social hall where a crowd gathered for a farewell potluck meal. The head of the board, Deacon Hellweg, acted as an impromptu Master of Ceremony, addressing the crowd and granting Nick a few moments to pull it together.

Everyone grew silent when Nick led the group in prayer. The

noise amplified as he then led the stampede toward the buffet line. His stomach growled in anticipation, reminding him he'd skipped breakfast after getting an early morning call that he was needed at the nursing home.

The two long rows of linen-covered tables held every imaginable dish. Fork-tender roast beef. Garden fresh vegetables and apple-cinnamon dumplings the size of his fist. He spotted all his favorite casseroles and mourned the size of his plate. Iowans cooked with love and every recipe blessed the stomach and heart.

More than one person asked if he could pull strings to get tickets to the upcoming papal Mass in Chicago. Though still months away, everyone was excited over the Pontiff's Midwest stop.

"I'm not even sure I'll get one," Nick had to admit. His transfer had only been announced two weeks ago and passes for the Pope's highly anticipated visit had long since been snapped up.

Nick had only taken two bites when the church secretary approached and handed him a note marked Urgent. The tears in her eyes telegraphed tragedy. Instinctive compassion flooded his thoughts. What now?

He glanced at the note. That it was from his brother-in-law, Ward McKay, tightened his chest.

John has been killed in battle. Please call.

Sharp nausea had Nick pushing his plate away. He reread the note, taking in its painful message before bowing his head. As a Catholic priest, he stayed on a first name basis with death and had become inured to tragedy. This news bypassed that facade, exposing his secular frailty.

He tugged out his muted cell phone and discovered voice messages from Ward, Perry, and Janey. He needed privacy before listening to them.

Pushing to his feet, Nick waited for the hall to quiet. "I've just received news that my nephew John McKay was killed in Iraq."

Everyone gasped. Many of St. Paul's parishioners patronized the McKay farm equipment business. Some were distant relatives. But all recognized John's name. The parish churches kept a special intentions prayer list for active military members, a list that was recited every Sunday at Mass. The list included someone's niece from California, a cousin in Kansas, but their local soldiers were venerated as heroes.

Deacon Hellweg stood. "Our deepest condolences, Father. We'll head back to the church to recite the rosary for your nephew. You are welcome to join us."

"No time," Nick said. "I must leave."

Those words, *no time*, dogged his steps as he made his way through the parking lot. As one of two parish priests serving three schools and six churches within thirty square miles of River Haven, Nick traveled frequently, rotating weekday masses and Sunday services along with administering sacraments and other duties. Today's priests were administrators as well as shepherds. *No time* was part of his daily conversation.

Alone in his car, he broke down, weeping as he listened to each voicemail message. He and John had been close, their bond a sacred and rare blend of blood and friendship. Hearing Janey's distress amplified Nick's grief. He and Janey had an equally exceptional relationship, a closeness that made his departure even more difficult to contemplate.

Nick called his brother-in-law first. "I'm in shock, Ward. What happened?"

"Two notification officers came here about two hours ago." In broken words, Ward described the moment. "I opened the door and saw them standing there...and I knew. God help me, I knew. We're getting stonewalled on specific details, but it must have been bad. Five soldiers were killed and more injured."

Eyes closed, Nick slumped forward, imagining the worst. "Any word on Layton?" The Texan had become part of the McKay family, visiting Iowa as frequently as John did. Nick had been secretly determined to convert him.

"None. They won't release any information pending notification of all the families."

"How are you holding up?" Nick asked.

"It's gutted all of us. But you know how close Janey and John were. I didn't think anything would ever be worse than losing her mother. I was wrong."

Nick's heart squeezed at the mention of Anna. His last promise to his sister was to watch over John and Janey. With John's death, Nick failed. "Tell Janey I got her message. I'm leaving St. Paul's now, headed your way."

"We're going to Lloyd Nelson's." Ward's voice cracked. "It may sound crazy since we don't even know when John is coming home, but I don't know what else to do."

"How about I meet you there?"

Disconnecting, Nick tried to tamp down his sorrow, but tears welled in his eyes as he reached for one of the rosaries he kept looped around the rearview mirror. Since it seemed he did most of his praying while driving, he kept the beads there. Now their very handiness seemed another sad commentary on his spiritual life. Did he only reach for the beads in desolate times? Or had life devolved to a series of desolate events?

He made the sign of the cross before pressing the gas and taking off.

———

AS SOON AS Nick stepped inside Lloyd's Funeral Home, he knew a terrible moment of *déjà vu*. Thirteen years ago, he'd arrived at Lloyd's following the news that his only sister, Anna, succumbed to cancer.

That Anna's death had been expected hadn't made her loss any easier. Janey had been six years old and she ran to Nick that night, begging him to bring her mother back. To perform a miracle. "Like the story of Lazarus," she'd cried. Dear God, Nick wanted to. Then. And now, as Janey rushed to him again. That she didn't ask for a miracle relieved and saddened him.

He hugged his niece as anguish bled from her. "I'm so sorry, honey. And—"

"Don't. Don't tell me he's with God and Momma—" Janey pounded feebly at his chest before collapsing against him. "It's not fair! It's not right! I want them back."

Nick kept silent as he hugged her more tightly and wept with her. John's death was a surprising, vicious punch. There were no words to make this better.

After a moment, Janey straightened and wiped her cheeks. "We'll talk more later. The others are waiting to see you."

He marveled, watching as she reeled in her emotions. Anna had been that way, too, keeping her hurts private as she carried on, always putting others first. Did Janey know how much she was like her mother? Had Nick told Janey that, told her enough about Anna? Lord, he needed more time.

In the funeral home's office, Matt and Perry flanked Ward. One by one, the men embraced, seeking to comfort even as they sought comfort. Nick recalled how Ward once begged him to discourage John. "Tell him not to join the Army. He'll listen to you, Nick."

Thorns of guilt pierced Nick's heart. *If I hadn't encouraged John, would he still be alive?*

Right after high school graduation, John sought Nick's advice about whether to enlist. "I worry about leaving Janey," John had fretted. "Dad is already upset that I don't want to be a farmer." Ward bought the adjacent farm, expecting John to take over. Instead it seemed to kindle John's determination to leave.

"You can't put your dreams on hold for others," Nick had counseled. "Seek an answer in prayer and trust that Janey and your father will be fine." John called two days later to report that he'd gotten an unmistakable sign from God to enlist. Nick wished he'd asked what that sign was.

Ward's wife, Eileen, moved closer. "I regret I never got the chance to meet John in person. He'd been so adamant that we not postpone the wedding when his deployment was extended."

Nick patted Eileen's hand. "John wanted his father happy." Ward and Eileen had each been widowed for over ten years. Both were well into their sixties. This second chance at romance suited them. Especially now.

Finally, Nick greeted the funeral director, Lloyd Nelson. Still spry at age ninety, Lloyd knew death even more intimately than Nick.

Ward wiped his eyes with a handkerchief. "The Army hasn't confirmed when John's body will return. Lloyd warned us it could take a few weeks, but he will check with his contacts in the military. I know you're leaving, but John would want you to offer his funeral Mass, Nick."

"I'll be here for that. Count on it."

"We'll have a graveside military service. I will not let grief overshadow the fact that my son died serving this country."

"Full military honors," Lloyd said. "I'm handling everything."

"The Army is supposed to let us know whether a priest was available to administer Last Rites." Ward's voice rose with concern. "If they can't confirm it, will you do it, Nick? I'd feel better."

"Of course." The Catholic tradition of Last Rites was only done once, while the person was alive, but Nick wouldn't deny his devout brother-in-law the comfort of this Blessed Sacrament.

"Thank you." Ward shook hands with Lloyd, then turned back to Nick. "We'll talk more at the house."

When they arrived at the farm, cars already lined the driveway. The McKay family was well known in southeast Iowa, and as word spread, the influx of visitors grew. Nick appreciated the way members of St. Francis' Church mobilized to help. Prayer services were scheduled. The Ladies Altar Circle arrived to coordinate the inflow of food being delivered to the farm. Friends answered the phone and took messages.

Janey hovered in a corner of the kitchen, inconsolable and withdrawn. Nick was grateful that her best friend, Gemma, remained at her side, mirroring every emotion, yet acting as a buffer when moments grew awkward. And death was always awkward. Gemma also deflected many of the "poor Janey" remarks.

After the evening meal, Gemma had to leave for work. When Janey slipped outside alone, Nick followed. He caught up with her and Fuller as they walked toward the east pasture.

"Feel like company?" he asked.

She managed a sad smile. "No. But we'll make an exception for you."

They walked side by side along the wide path through the cornfields, straddling the chasm of grief in tandem. Sometimes grace was simply the gift of space.

When Janey finally spoke, her words surprised him. "Do you remember the night my mother died?"

How could he forget? "I remember you disappeared and scared everyone. Especially John."

"They said Mom was gone, and I took it literally. I thought if I was fast enough, I could catch up with her and bring her back. I ran through the fields until my legs gave out, and then I burrowed beneath the exposed roots of a tree at the creek bank. I heard everyone searching for me, calling out my name. But I didn't move. I knew they would make me come home, and I wanted to keep searching, to find Mom." Her steps faltered. "I thought that night would last forever. How could the sun come up when my world had been shattered? Yet it did. It still does."

Nick draped an arm along her shoulder. "Sometimes life sucks, honey."

"Yeah. I figured that one out. Just spare me the divine purpose sermon."

"Ouch. Does that mean you're not in the mood for my all-things-pass shtick either?"

"I don't want it to pass! Ever," she blurted. "I don't want anything to change, and I don't want anyone to forget John, like I sometimes forget Momma."

Nick let the mantle of silence resettle as they walked. He and Janey had talked of that before, how as time moves forward the dead remain frozen in the past. She'd been upset to realize that the older she got, the less she thought of her mother.

The path they followed ended at the pond. A welcome breeze kicked up, signaling dusk's approach, but for now there was plenty of light. As they'd done a hundred times before, he and Janey bent down simultaneously, collecting stones to skip across the water's surface. Fuller circled the old maple tree nearby and collapsed for a nap.

Nick watched Janey sling a test stone, and then he counted the beats. Seven. He needed to do eight. Or at least that's what he would have thought if John were there. John viewed everything as a game, a challenge. The stone dropped from Nick's hand. As he bent to pick it up, she spoke again.

"Is there any way you can stay? It's too much. Losing John and you."

Remorse over leaving surfaced anew, but he didn't voice his doubts. His promise to family sometimes ran counter to his promise to the church. And with his ordination vow, he became a priest first and uncle second.

"If I could stay, I would. But Chicago's not so far away, and I'll be back for visits. With the Lord's help, we'll all do fine."

Janey tossed a rock. Too hard, it sank. "The Lord's help is easier for you. You're a priest."

He snorted as his rock sank, too. "Everyone thinks God gives priests immunity tokens."

"He doesn't?"

"He gives grace. In equal measures — to everyone. Priests included."

"What do priests need grace for?"

"Everything. At some point we all fight the same battles, Janey."

"But you're better at it. You know all the right things to say."

If only she knew how empty feeling all the right words were. How many times had Nick tried to explain, to mothers, fathers, lone children left behind, that God had a greater plan for someone who passed away unexpectedly? Nick knew how hard it was to believe and understand. He struggled with the decisions of the divine, too. Convincing someone to have and keep their faith in the absence of tangible proof could crack the armor of even the most hardened believers. Were his own cracks visible?

He changed the subject. "If I know all the right things to say, then why am I so nervous about meeting new kids in Chicago? You're my inside source to all things cool, you know. What will I do without you to interpret?"

"Try not to act like a dork." Her retort made him smile. "And remember to ask for their playlists," Janey went on. "Connect with their music first."

She flung a rock. He counted. Eight, nine.

"Music, good. Dork, bad. Got it." He flicked his wrist, sent a stone skipping across the pond's surface. He groaned as he finished counting. "Seven."

"Loser."

Her remark, delivered without snark, left him wanting to laugh and cry at the same time. It's what John would have said if he'd been there. "It's getting dark. Let's go back."

By the time Nick returned to the rectory in River Haven, it was after ten PM. The church secretary had left his calendar open on his desk. The blank page startled him, the day normally crammed with entries and sticky notes. His only appointments tomorrow were a breakfast meeting with Father Martin, his assistant pastor — now the new acting pastor — and another farewell party in the evening. His secretary, bless her, noted that she'd cancelled both.

Nick opened a drawer, looking for the last photo taken of Anna and him before she died. The drawer was empty. He cleared the desk two days ago before, having his belongings shipped to his next post, Chicago's Prince of Peace parish. The thought further depressed him.

In seminary, Prince of Peace had been uncharitably referred to as an elephants' graveyard; the place old priests went to die. Located in one of Chicago's oldest neighborhoods, it surprised Nick to learn the small church was still open when so many others had been shuttered. Apparently, Prince of Peace's saving grace was the youth center it sponsored to help disadvantaged teens.

When word of his new post first arrived, Nick objected. What did he know about inner city life? *Nothing.* But the diocese quashed his arguments. The youth center licensing required someone with a psychology degree, and the bishop insisted they needed someone younger to promote change.

Tonight, Nick didn't feel younger. Grief overwhelmed him as he shuffled the stack of condolence messages the secretary left. The very last one was a note to call his superior at the Diocese office in Davenport. Despite the late hour, he picked up the phone. A night owl, Father David would still be up.

"Your secretary gave me the news," David said. "I'm sorry to hear about your nephew. How is your family?"

"As well as expected." Nick had repeated those words too many times today.

"Can I do anything?"

Nick sat forward. "Yes. This isn't a good time for me to leave. Is there any way they can reassign—"

Father David cut him off. "That you've stayed in one parish as long as you have is a miracle. I can arrange a slight amount of leave, but beyond that, no. I'm sorry your family is going through this, Nick. Sometimes our duty to God and the Church feels like a sacrifice to them. I urge you to pray they'll understand."

After hanging up, Nick leaned back in his chair, contemplating Father David's hasty rejection of his request to send someone else to

Chicago. If Nick opened up about the anxiety attacks he'd started having, would David reconsider? Perhaps. Except there was no guarantee Nick would remain in Iowa and there was an actual possibility of being reassigned even further away. At least Chicago was only a four-hour drive from River Haven. Did he risk an even greater sacrifice by speaking up?

His gaze landed on the ornate crucifix hanging above the office door. Immediately, he regretted his line of thinking. Nick's so-called sacrifice was nothing compared to Jesus'.

"Forgive me, Lord." Reaching into his pocket, Nick tugged out his rosary and cupped it in his palm as David's reminder to pray came back to mind.

Earlier today, when Nick prayed in the car, he'd been interrupted with phone calls. It was such a regular occurrence he never questioned it. Now, though, it weighed heavy on his mind. When was the last time he'd completed a full recitation of the rosary?

That he couldn't recall had Nick grasping the beads nervously. Closing his eyes, he forced his breath to slow and recalled a practice from seminary of becoming centered within prayer. *Be calm.*

It worked for three seconds, then grief and sorrow resurfaced, shattering his concentration.

Pray through it. Start again. Slowly, he made the sign of the cross and kissed the rosary's small crucifix.

The phone rang.

He sighed. He could let it go to voicemail but first opened one eye to glance at the caller ID.

The hospital. He answered.

"There's been a car wreck. Two students from your parish, both comatose," the hospital clerk began. "The families asked for a priest."

The last line hinted at an unfavorable prognosis. Tonight, would Nick have to explain to more grieving parents why their children were taken from them?

"I'm on my way." He pushed to his feet and once again tucked the beads of another incomplete rosary into his pocket.

CHAPTER TWELVE

August 2006
River Haven, Iowa

Janey resented the way the world continued despite her loss. The attack that killed John made one day's broadcast cycle before television news moved on to other tragedies. She quit watching, disconnecting from current events. Time lost meaning while her family remained sidelined, impatient for updates. She hadn't left the farm since they'd gotten the news, unable to talk without crying. She couldn't bear to have people look at her — or worse — hear them voice questions about how John died or ask about Layton. Knowing nothing about Layton kept her half-crazed, between worry and hope.

While the McKays had been warned to expect a delay in the return of John's body, it made the wait no easier to endure and perpetuated, for Janey at least, the false hope that a dreadful error occurred, that maybe John was unconscious in a hospital, under the wrong name, his body misidentified.

He wasn't.

It took seventy-two hours for the Army to publicly release the names of the soldiers killed in action. Seeing John's name on that list felt as painful as when she'd first heard. In contrast, the absence of Layton's name on the casualty list left her giddy. It was the first official confirmation that he hadn't died, too.

The relief at learning Layton was alive was soon usurped by fear about whether he'd been hurt. The lack of answers grew maddening. While the names and details regarding the injured soldiers continued to be withheld for privacy reasons, Janey ransacked Myspace for information. Her attempts at tracking down Layton's cousin failed, and online messages sent to Sharlene and another of Layton's ex-girlfriends went unanswered.

From memory and letters, Janey compiled a complete list of John's squad members, but none of their profile pages on Myspace had been updated since the attack. Gemma's uncle, a Marine who had previously deployed to Iraq, explained that a blackout had likely been imposed on Internet and phone lines following the attack, a standard security procedure.

Janey combed the Internet for details on the other deceased soldiers and finally contacted the sister of Donald Livingston, a soldier from Colorado who'd died that day with John. Like the McKay family, the Livingstons had no details about that final battle. Janey's dad spoke at length with Donald's father. The two men shared personal stories about their lost sons and commiserated on the frustrating lack of information from the Army.

Mr. Livingston also wanted to know about the others who'd been killed and injured. "Donald spoke of his squad as family. He would have fought to his last breath to protect them."

Janey reread all of John's letters and emails, desperate to find a sign, a hidden message that would give her forlorn spirit peace. Her brother ended every letter the same way — he loved her, he missed her, and he had so much to tell her when he came home. Words of life, not expectations of death. And nowhere had he kept his promise to not leave without saying goodbye.

How many times had she and John sworn that? Vowed to say all the things they hadn't been able to tell their mother before she passed away. Their agreement was their failsafe; that one last goodbye guaranteed them both a final do-over, a chance to beg forgiveness, declare love, and show gratitude. John joked it was his license to freely sin. Right now, though, Janey felt she'd been duped, that she'd taken the promise seriously while he had not.

It did no good to remind herself that he'd been overseas, fighting in a war. Or that they'd been kids when they made the pact. A promise was a promise, and McKays always kept their promises.

Not knowing exactly how John died bothered the entire family. What did "in battle" mean? Bullets? Bombs? Fire? Had he died instantly, or had he suffered? Janey pondered his last moments. What had he been doing before he died? What had he thought? Said? The need to know became an obsession, as it had after their mother died. She told herself that Layton would know, which made her search for news on Layton even more desperate.

"Be patient," Uncle Nick counseled.

But in grief, everything lost proportion. Droves of friends and neighbors continued to stop by the McKay farm daily, which seemed to help her father's spirits. He processed his grief verbally. Janey withdrew to solitude, especially after Uncle Nick left for his new post in Chicago. She roamed the fields with Fuller, a painful sojourn of feeling lost in the very places she knew by heart.

Every path had a memory.

Every stone, a story.

There had never been a time in her life when she hadn't known John. They shared more than blood; they shared the soil. Everything she knew about the farm she'd learned from him. He'd once bragged there wasn't a tree on the farm he hadn't climbed and carved his initial into, so Janey spent the summers of her ninth and tenth years climbing tree after tree, to search for his J – and adding her own. She climbed those trees now, searching for their past. Searching for the impossible. But the solace she sought – *John!* — was gone.

She had a thousand terrific memories of her brother, yet the awful memories seemed to get more playtime in her head. Especially their fight the night before he left. That she'd withheld absolution over the letter he stole; worse, that she'd continued to curse him almost daily for it, would be a lifelong regret.

The farm held all her memories of Layton, too. Every cherished moment, every laugh, every secret. Every hope. She'd fallen for him one breath at a time, right here in Iowa. Now all those months she'd spent agonizing over her unrequited love for Layton seemed a joyride compared to not hearing anything from him.

After a week of silence, Sharlene Sweeney responded with an email message:

> Oh my God, I hadn't even heard anything was wrong until I got your message and looked it up online. I am so sorry about your brother. I haven't heard from my darling Layton yet, but I'm sure I will. As far as next of kin, his grandmother is in an old folk's home, but I'll see if I can contact his cousin. Please let me know if you hear anything about Layton. I've been counting days until he's home.

Janey ignored that last line. Layton was hers. She continued searching for the other soldiers' families and significant others. She finally got a clue on Layton after connecting with the fiancée of Teddy Fallon. Teddy was hospitalized in Germany after losing a leg. His fiancée, Roxanne, just returned from an overseas trip with Teddy's mother and confirmed that Layton was also hospitalized in Landstuhl Regional Medical Center in Germany.

"No, I didn't actually see Layton," Roxanne clarified when Janey called her. "But the chaplain mentioned Layton's name to Teddy while I was there. Teddy said that Layton saved his life." Though Roxanne had no details on Layton's injuries or condition, she promised to ask Teddy the next time they spoke.

Knowing that Layton had been injured kept a heavy stone of distress lodged in Janey's gut. How badly had he been hurt? Was he conscious? In a coma? *Please call me* became her silent mantra, a substitution for the prayers she couldn't voice. Prayers failed to keep John safe. What good to offer them for Layton?

Matt and Perry stayed close, one of them at the farm with Dad, while the other one worked. The confirmation of Layton as injured shook Janey's entire family, who all cared deeply for the Texan. The ongoing lack of information from the Army left her father and brothers conjecturing about what occurred during that final battle, too.

"They were likely side-by-side when fighting erupted..."

"Probably both injured at the same time..."

"Layton will contact us as soon as he can..."

Janey's attempts to learn more about Layton hit a brick wall when Teddy's fiancée Roxanne's phone was inexplicably disconnected. When Layton's Myspace page disappeared, Janey freaked out, worried the worst had happened until she discovered that all the other soldiers' pages — including John's – disappeared, too. The Army Casualty Assistance Officer, the family's only point of contact, assured her it was likely a temporary security measure.

Janey's burgeoning grief riddled what little sleep she had with nightmares. She began dreaming of being at the battlefront, of hearing John call out amidst explosions, screaming at her to find the piece that was missing. Did he mean a piece of his body? The thought of her brother being physically blown apart was atrocious.

Ten days after John's death, they received word that his body was being returned. The McKays and Lloyd Nelson went to the Cedar Rapids airport to meet the plane carrying John's coffin. The military escort, a uniformed Army officer who accompanied the casket from Dover, held a salute as the crated casket moved slowly down the conveyor from the plane.

Janey's heart splintered as Perry placed a silver crucifix that belonged to their mother atop the crate before it was loaded into the waiting hearse. All activity on the tarmac stopped as airline employees and disembarking passengers bowed their heads and stood still.

Back at the funeral parlor in River Haven, the military escort met privately with Lloyd before meeting with the family in Lloyd's office.

The Army officer addressed Janey's father before opening a large brown envelope. "Sir, these are the personal effects carried by your son that final day."

Janey recognized each item. The black rosary from Uncle Nick. The engraved pen and pencil set from Matt and Perry. The silver St. Christopher medal inscribed "Hurry home," that Janey had given him. The wristwatch from Dad.

Last were John's dog tags, two engraved metal rectangles sheathed in black plastic that dangled from a thick ball chain. Dad's fist closed over them. "My son!" Sobs filled the gap of silence.

After the officer departed, Lloyd Nelson came in to reconfirm the funeral arrangements. Ten days ago, it stunned Janey to learn that John discussed final matters, like a closed casket and a high Mass, with her father and brothers before deploying. And even as she resented being excluded from yet another conversation, she realized she wouldn't have let John speak of not returning, would have never let him say, "*If the worst case happens.*"

She would have thrown his own words back in his face. *"We're golden."* Except...

They weren't golden. They were as tarnished as everyone else was in the world. That realization left Janey feeling more vulnerable. She still had a lot to lose.

Lloyd also reviewed a copy of the obituary, which confirmed that the wake would be the day after tomorrow, with burial in the family plot the following day.

"Everything with John – is okay?" Dad asked Lloyd. In keeping with John's wishes, the family agreed that only Lloyd would view the body.

Lloyd pressed a hand to her father's shoulder. "The military did a fine job, Ward. I couldn't have done better." Lloyd nodded toward

Perry, Matt, and Janey. "You can rest easy knowing your brother is all in one piece. He looks like he's sleeping."

"Thank you." She felt relieved, yet still she wept. She had told no one about her nightmares of John begging her to find something missing.

Janey, her father, and Eileen had barely returned to the farm when a courier arrived to deliver John's belongings from Iraq. The two, drab-olive duffel bags with MCKAY stenciled in black were the same ones her brother left with.

She stood beside her father as he signed for them. That they had been told to expect the bags made them no easier to see. Janey helped her father carry the bags to the bunkhouse, grateful that Eileen opted to stay behind.

Inside John's bedroom, Dad set the bag down, and then wiped tears from his cheeks. "I don't have the heart to unpack these right now."

She leaned in and hugged him. His choice of words — "don't have the heart" — fanned her concern. In the space of two weeks, her father had paled, seeming to move slower and more cautiously.

"We can leave it for another day, Daddy. These won't be in anyone's way out here."

Her father moved to the trophy shelves and brushed his fingers across the nameplate of one. "You know, I watched your brother win every single trophy in this room. Except for those." He pointed to the row of commemorative coins John sent home during his deployment. "If they're even trophies. Honestly, I don't even know what they're for. Do you?"

Janey shook her head as she glanced at the medallions imprinted with Army and military insignia. "I never understood their significance. John just asked me to put them out here until..." *Until he came home.*

"What do you think about giving these coins to Lloyd to bury with John? They were obviously personal military mementos, meaningful only to him. Now they are tokens of the war that took his life. Frankly, I don't want to see them every time I come out here."

Lloyd Nelson invited the family to bring items for him to place inside John's coffin. She took her tattered childhood teddy bear and Fuller's collar. "I agree, Daddy. And I bet Perry and Matt will too."

"I'll take these in the house then, and check with the boys tonight."

As her father gathered the loose medallions, Janey looked for the unopened box she'd placed on the shelf. It was gone.

Puzzled, she turned and spotted the box on the desk, highlighted by a beam of sunlight. That the box arrived the same day as the news of John's death left it tainted. It was one more painful reminder of John's famous last words, *"I'll tell you when I get home."*

She snatched up the box and held it out to her father. "Take this, too."

"Don't you want to open it first?"

She shook the box, heard the telltale metallic clink. "It's more of those stupid coins. It's all he ever sent, and he always said to just dump the boxes in his room, that he'd sort through them later. I thought I was doing him a favor by putting them on display."

Dad took the box from her just as they heard a car pull up outside in the driveway. "That's probably your brothers. I need to head in," he said.

"I'll be right behind you." Alone, Janey let her gaze wander around the room. With those coins and the box gone, the room looked exactly like John had left it.

Like he would still be coming home.

———

LATER THAT NIGHT, Sergeant Boswell, the leader of John's squad, called Janey's father to express condolences. The sergeant had just returned to Fort DeWald, Illinois, his deployment ended. That John also returned that day hit Janey in the solar plexus.

Matt and Perry were still at the farm and Dad put the call on speakerphone so they could all hear.

"Your son was one of the finest, bravest, soldiers I've had the privilege to serve with," Sergeant Boswell said. "Everyone in the platoon looked up to John."

"Can you tell us anything about that final fight?" Dad asked. "We keep getting told that the investigation is incomplete. I've lost a son, so I don't care about any investigation. We're also worried about John's buddy, Layton Burnet, who we've been told was injured. He and John were very close, and we consider Layton family."

"I know how close he and John were. Overseas, Layton spoke of Iowa more than Texas, if you can believe that," Boswell said. "I was not present at that last battle, but you deserve to know more, and I'll share what little I can. The Baghdad Crud – sorry, a severe stomach virus — wiped out half the post that last week, me included. John hadn't been affected by it, but Layton had just been released from quarantine and probably lied about being well enough to accompany them that day. Those two looked after each other. In fact, we'd been in a skirmish a week prior and John rescued an old beggar, beat Layton to the save."

"I bet Layton was furious," Matt said.

Janey swiped at her eyes, remembering how fiercely competitive John and Layton could be. Like actual brothers.

Boswell's voice lightened. "You know it. I'd have sworn John did it more to save Layton. As I said, I wasn't there for that final battle and while I can't speak to details, I understand John saved a couple civilians and another soldier before he was hit."

"Did..." Dad's voice broke. "I have to know. Did my son suffer?"

"I believe he went quickly, sir. I was told his injuries were catastrophic." Boswell cleared his throat. "I regret that I don't have more to tell you. When you've lost a loved one, it's tough to be told to be patient. But if you'll give the Army investigators a chance to complete their report, you will eventually get answers."

"Can you tell us anything about Layton's condition?" Janey

asked. "We've not heard anything other than he's still hospitalized. I'm — we're all worried."

Boswell paused before speaking. "I understand he was shot twice in the upper chest and shoulder area and that the wound was severe but not fatal. I'm sorry I can't say more. The Army's got a gag order in place and I've already revealed more than I should have."

"I understand," Dad said. "However, what you have shared makes it easier to breathe and I thank you for that."

Before disconnecting, the Sergeant offered his sympathy once more.

Afterwards, Janey researched everything she could find online about shoulder injuries. While the sergeant had disclosed little, it was *something*. The diagnosis by Dr. Google was harsh and overwhelming. Damage by bullets and rocket shrapnel could be minor or life-threatening. The prognosis depended on the extent of damage. She fell asleep clinging to the hope that Teddy Fallon's fiancée would get in touch again soon.

———

TWO DAYS LATER, they held John's wake. A huge crowd turned out. Janey stood with her family, shaking hands, accepting hugs and shedding more tears with each memory of John that was shared. She couldn't stop thinking of her mother's wake. Back then, Janey had been small and sickly. She'd cried so intensely that Perry carried her outside and walked around the funeral home's parking lot for two hours, holding her in his arms. He hadn't made promises. He didn't try to cheer her up. He just made crooning noises and let her cry. He stayed by her side tonight, too, squeezing her shoulder in silent support. Matt remained close to their father but nodded whenever she looked his way. What would she do without them?

When the wake ended and the last person left, two sheriff's deputies approached the family. Janey recognized Deputy Blake

Evans. A family friend, Blake graduated the same year as Matt and Perry.

"I apologize for disturbing you on this of all days, Ward," Blake said. "However, we wanted to let you know Randy Keener came by earlier. He claimed he was here to offer sympathy, but I know he and John were not friends. We escorted Randy off the property after he announced that the JFA filed for a permit to protest at the funeral tomorrow."

"He's not serious, is he?" Dad's face grew red. "Can you stop them?"

"Unfortunately, no," Blake said. "It looks like they've taken the proper legal steps and as long as they abide by the laws governing public gatherings, we can't do much except make sure they don't harass you or disrupt the service."

Matt leaned in. "Well, if I see any of those JFA jerks tomorrow, I'll run them over, then back up and do it again."

"That's exactly why you need to let us handle it, Matt," Blake said. "Keep your McKay temper under control. I don't want to arrest you for hurting someone, especially on the day of your brother's funeral."

Perry shifted closer to Matt. "We understand. Which doesn't mean we like it."

"I'll be surprised if anything comes of it," Blake said. "The JFA is notorious for making heinous claims just for publicity. Truth is, a tiny town like River Haven won't garner them any headlines. Still, I had to let you know, Ward."

"Thanks for that," Dad said.

Blake touched the brim of his hat. "I also want you to know that all off-duty deputies volunteered for honor patrol. We'll have plenty of uniforms in town tomorrow. If there's any trouble, I promise it will disappear quickly."

CHAPTER THIRTEEN

August 2006
River Haven, Iowa

The morning of John's funeral, the local news aired an interview with Randy Keener about the Justice Freedom Association's planned protest. Janey watched in revulsion as clips from JFA gatherings in other cities played on the screen.

"We're protesting the waste of our US tax dollars on a war that's been ramrodded down our throats," Randy told the reporter.

"Today is about John, not those idiots!" Janey's father ranted.

She had never seen him so angry and silently cheered when Matt and Perry showed up early. Perry, especially, had a calming effect, which everyone needed today.

At ten o'clock, two black Cadillacs arrived at the farm just as Lloyd Nelson promised. That a sheriff's patrol car escorted them was another stark reminder of the JFA's protest. Janey climbed into one vehicle with Matt's family. Dad and Eileen rode with Perry's crew.

The Cadillacs proceeded slowly into town, on a journey Janey didn't want to take. The forecasted rain held off, yet the skies remained appropriately gray. She noticed that all the Welcome Home signs had disappeared. Red, white, and blue ribbons had replaced the yellow ones. The difference caused the knot in her throat to swell.

At St. Francis, the hearse stood like a silent sentry in front of the church, an unmistakable symbol of the service that would take place there today. A military Honor Guard stood by, holding flags, adding pomp to a melancholy tableau. Cars lined the streets, the parking lot full. Lloyd Nelson told them that funerals for military heroes drew sizable crowds and judging by the traffic, the entire county had turned out. Janey mentally bolstered herself for signs of the protestors.

Matt's cell phone buzzed as they climbed from the car. When the quick call ended, he leaned close to whisper. "Good news. Blake said the JFA can't protest within five hundred feet of an elementary school." St. Francis Catholic School sat directly across from the church. "The sheriff's department set up barricades at five hundred feet and parked patrol cars in front of them to keep the protestors out of view."

Grateful, Janey pushed it from her mind as she followed Matt's family into the crowded church. There were two rows of pews reserved for them in front. Though she kept her eyes straight ahead, she couldn't avoid catching glimpses of pity. Like when she'd lost her mother. *Poor thing. So sad.*

When John's flag-draped casket was carried in, Janey sobbed. Six of his high school classmates served as pallbearers, with the other members of his Army squad named as honorary pallbearers *in absentia*.

Uncle Nick, who'd returned to River Haven late last night, and Father Martin, concelebrated the Mass. Janey continued to recall bits and pieces of her mother's funeral. Her uncle had concelebrated that Mass, too, but back then he'd openly wept. Now he just looked forlorn, his eyes red, his shoulders drooped. His voice cracked as he delivered a eulogy praising John as a son, brother, nephew, friend, and ultimately a hero.

Nick also called out the names of the other soldiers who'd been killed – Livingston, Sturk, Sheridan, and Worth. Janey's heart wrenched for those other military families who were also bidding unwanted goodbyes.

Even with the extra scripture readings and music, the formal high Mass went by too quickly. When it was time to leave the church, Matt and Perry flanked Janey as they proceeded down the aisle behind the pallbearers, arms linked. She couldn't take her eyes off John's casket.

Don't leave. Don't leave me.

As they stepped outside, the church's bells began to chime, a series of deep single bongs, the mournful sound so different from the bright ringing that heralded Sunday Mass.

Just beyond the bottom step, her father stopped and held up a hand as a second set of solemn chimes sounded from across town.

"That's St. Anne's," Dad said.

Even though the second parish church was two miles away, its bell tolled across the sky, out of sync in a perfect call and answer.

Then a third set of chimes rang in, and then another. Uncle Nick moved in close and pointed in different directions as he explained. "That's All Saints Methodist. And there's River Haven Baptist. St. Martin's Lutheran. And..."

Janey closed her eyes, overwhelmed by the unified resonance of church bells all over town, regardless of denomination, ringing in honor of her brother.

"Right now, the bells at the Houghton, St. Paul, and West Point churches are ringing, too," Uncle Nick whispered. "All for John."

The church had emptied, the crowd spilling into the street as everyone marveled at sounds never before heard. Janey leaned against Perry, her heart torn to bits by the haunting beauty of the cascading chimes.

Dad wiped his eyes. "It's a perfect send off. Let's go."

As the bells continued to echo, they climbed back into the Cadillacs and pulled away. Matt lowered the window so they could hear the chimes. Oncoming traffic stopped. Janey caught glimpses of drivers, their faces shadowed in sympathy, some saluting, others with hands folded in prayer, and knew she'd never pass another funeral procession without remembering this stabbing grief.

When they turned on to Main Street, Matt tapped her knee and pointed. "Look, honey."

Motorcycles lined the streets, dozens of them. Small US flags were mounted on handlebars and fenders. Men and women — some with hands linked, some with hands on their hearts — stood as the cortege passed.

"Blake mentioned that several groups mobilized to show support," Matt went on.

Some bikers held large flags aloft. Janey glimpsed a man holding a poster which was swiftly blocked from view by a flag. Away from the school grounds, a few JFA protesters were present, but the bikers moved en masse, keeping them hidden. Janey wondered how many other military families faced JFA protesters on days already overflowing with sorrow.

When the procession reached the arched entrance of Saint Francis Cemetery, just beyond the city limits, Janey's vision narrowed. All she saw was the tent awning set up on the distant rise. By the time they reached the parking area, the church bells had all silenced except St. Francis', the church where it had all begun. *Alpha and omega.* John had been baptized there and now...this. St. Francis' chimes tolled solo for a full minute after the family assembled at the gravesite. When it stopped, only her sobs were heard.

Even with guest speakers and the twenty-one-gun salute, the graveside service seemed brief. All fell silent as a lone bugler played Taps from forty yards away. A few moments after the last note, the solemn Honor Guard removed the flag from John's casket and folded it into a crisp triangle. A uniformed Army officer dropped in front of Janey's father and reverently presented the folded flag.

"On behalf of the President of the United States, the United States Army, and a grateful nation, please accept this flag as a symbol of our appreciation for your loved one's honorable and faithful service."

Dad's stoic expression of pride caved as his shaking hands closed over the flag's white stars. Janey's throat was raw as she, Perry, and Matt bowed over their father as he clutched John's flag.

"This concludes the public service," Uncle Nick announced. "The family will return to the church social hall shortly."

Taking their cue, the crowd dispersed. At Dad's request, only family was present for this last part as John's casket was lowered into the ground, right beside their mother's grave. Janey wanted to flee. To make it stop. But she was powerless against death.

When the pulleys grew quiet, the funeral personnel moved away. "Take as long as you like," Lloyd Nelson said before he, too, left.

In unison, the family stood and moved to the open grave. The only sound Janey heard was weeping. If they stayed there forever, would it all go away? She knew the permanence of leaving, of being left behind.

Uncle Nick reached for a handful of dirt and let it trickle from his fist as he offered one last blessing and quote in Latin – the same one he'd chanted at her mother's funeral. *"Non est ad astra mollis e terris via."* There is no easy way from the earth to the stars.

Then Nick helped Perry and Matt herd their boys back toward the Cadillacs.

Janey remained at the grave, holding her father's right arm, Eileen on his left side.

Dad looked toward the sky before making the sign of the cross. "It's time to go."

"I'll meet you back at the car," Janey said. "I need a moment."

Dad paused and then pressed a kiss to her cheek. "You heard Lloyd. Take as long as you need, Janey-girl."

As she stood alone, gazing into the black hole, memories of John crowded her mind.

Swimming lessons in the pond. *Paddle harder!*

Her first black eye. *You got to fight back. Make a fist like this.*

Her first race. *Just get out in front and stay there.*

Her vision blurred with wave after wave of anguished tears. She wouldn't be who she was without John. Didn't want to face a future without her brother. She glanced through tears at her mother's grave. John had been Janey's champion after Mom passed away and had promised to protect her from future tragedy. But in the end, Mom, John, God, had all abandoned her. She looked across the endless rows of headstones in the cemetery. Further proof that no one was ever safe.

Wiping her eyes, she cleared her throat. "Thank you for everything, John. I love you."

"He loved you more." Perry came up behind her and put a hand on her shoulder, his deep voice cracking.

"And he wouldn't want you to continue to grieve here like this." Matt moved in and took her hand, squeezed it twice. "He'd tell all of us to carry on."

Despite Matt's words, they stood for long moments, hands linked as they wept together. Then Perry took charge. "Let's go. We'll come back tomorrow when no one is waiting."

Even as she let him guide her away, Janey knew she'd never return.

———

BY THE TIME Janey's family headed back, the streets were clear again, allowing the McKays to make their way to the church luncheon quietly. One deputy who accompanied the family told Perry that the JFA had started some trouble with one group of bikers who blocked the protestors' signs. But when the JFA goons found out that three of the bikers were off-duty state troopers, they disbanded.

Inside the crowded social hall, people surrounded the McKay family. Janey watched her father offer comfort as well as receive it when some people recounted their own personal losses in lieu of condolences.

Gemma came up and wedged herself between Janey and one of John's old girlfriends. "Excuse me, but Janey's needed over here."

Over here was the far side of the hall where several of their former high school classmates congregated.

"Thanks for the rescue," Janey said.

"I know it was rude to cut her off, but who cares that John broke up with her in sixth grade?" Gemma replied.

As soon as Janey sat at the table, Gemma pushed a plate of food at her. "My mom made that noodle casserole you like. I told her to hide it in the kitchen."

"Good, because it's my favorite, too," Ben Hufstedler wheeled close and gave Janey a shoulder thump. Then he whispered. "Are you tired of hearing how sorry everyone is?"

Janey hugged his neck. "When does it stop?"

"Not soon enough."

Janey, Gemma, and Ben had been friends since kindergarten. Five years ago, Ben lost both legs in a farm accident, but a wheelchair hadn't slowed his fierceness.

"A change of subjects helps." Ben called out to another classmate and turned the topic to the fall college semester.

Gemma leaned in. "I'm going to get a soda. Want one?"

"I'll come with you." Janey didn't want to think about the fact that school would start soon. Normal life felt like a demon waiting in the wings, ready to leap out and smother the memory of those who'd passed.

They had barely taken a few steps when her cell phone vibrated. She glanced at the display, not recognizing the number. Her first instinct was to ignore it and let it go to voicemail. A sudden, powerful urge had her answering it instead.

"Hello?"

"Janey? It's me."

"Layton!" Relief bulldozed her senses. Light-headed, she clutched her side.

Gemma hooked her arm and herded her away from the noisy hall.

"Hello? Are you there?" Layton asked.

"Yes! I'm here! It's so good to hear your voice."

"It's better hearing yours."

Desperate to find a quiet spot, Janey pushed through the kitchen doors and ducked into the pantry. Gemma shut the door, closing Janey in.

Alone, she sank to the floor. "John's funeral was today."

"I'm so sorry about John." Layton's voice had a solemn tone, making him sound even more distant. "And I apologize that I'm not there. How are you holding up?"

"I'm... It's horrible. I can't believe he's gone. I still expect—" Her voice gave out.

Layton finished her sentence. "You still expect that he'll come strolling in the door wondering what we're all crying about. Me, too. God, I can't imagine what you're going through."

"What about you? We heard you were hospitalized in Germany. Are you okay?"

"I've had some shoulder reconstruction. Going under again tomorrow for what they claim is the last one."

"Tomorrow?" She let out a sharp sound. "How many surgeries have you had?"

"Too many. Look, I can't stay on long. I talked to your father and brothers a few minutes ago, but I needed to speak with you."

Janey closed her eyes. *I needed to speak with you.* Those six words resuscitated her soul and felt almost as powerful as a declaration of love. "I've been so worried. The Army won't release any information on anyone. We don't even know what happened to John. Or you, or anything."

"I know that part is difficult. And before you ask, I'm not allowed to talk about it while everything's under investigation." His words sounded hollow, obligatory.

"But why is it taking them so long?"

Silence amplified the distance. "I don't know. Look, as soon as I'm released, I'm headed back to the States. I'll get to Iowa as soon as I can."

Come back to me. "Promise?"

"I promise. What did John always say? I swear on—"

Static hissed across the line, cutting off his words. She panicked. "Hello?"

"You still there?"

"I'm here. Please don't hang up."

"I have to go. I know you have questions, but they must wait until we can talk in person."

Janey recalled times when John said he couldn't speak on a nonsecure phone line and hoped Layton wasn't simply blowing her off. "I can't wait to see you."

"And me, you. Take care and—"

The call cut off. She stared at the screen. CALL ENDED.

Knowing that Layton was not unconscious or comatose crumpled the last of her resolve. She cradled her head in her hands and bawled.

The pantry door opened. Gemma ended her sentry duty and kneeled beside Janey. "Is Layton all right?"

"I think so. He's still in the hospital in Germany, and he's having surgery again. He was vague. His voice sounded so monotone, Gemma."

"He's been through a lot."

"And still going through it." Janey's voice faltered. "He said he'll be here soon."

"Here, as in Iowa? When?"

"He didn't give any dates." Janey swiped at her eyes, unable to stop the tears. "And then we got cut off."

Gemma hugged her. "He called once. Have faith that he'll call again."

Faith? Right now all Janey felt was gaping emptiness. She missed the two people she loved most dearly: John and Layton. She climbed to her feet. All she wanted was to be home. She craved the familiar — her room, the barns, and her dog.

"I need to get out of here, but I don't want to bail on Dad." Janey started to say she didn't want to leave her father alone, but Eileen was there. And lately he seemed to prefer his new wife's company.

"Your brothers have it under control," Gemma said. "What about a short ride? I've got my car. It's a private place to scream."

And Gemma, bless her, knew when Janey needed to scream. Leaving the kitchen, they moved along the back wall toward a side exit.

Janey paused to talk to Perry. "Will you tell Dad I'll return shortly?" A throng of people were pressed around their father.

"When I can get to him. Looks like we'll be here a while," Perry said.

In Gemma's car, Janey slumped forward and rubbed her temples. Speaking to Layton had burst the dam of pent up emotion.

"Will music make it better or worse?" Gemma's hand hovered near the stereo controls.

It will never be better. "Worse."

"Let's head to the farm so you can grab some clothes and stay with me tonight," Gemma said. "We'll order pizza and watch movies. Or not."

"Sounds good. I want to check with my dad first." Chances were good he'd prefer Eileen's company over Janey's.

"Sure. Then—" Gemma hit the brakes. "What in the world?"

Janey sat up as the car slowed. Stretched wide across the highway's center median was an enormous banner.

ANOTHER DEAD SOLDIER EQUALS WASTED TAXPAYER DOLLARS.

The JFA's logo, a US flag in flames superimposed over a skull and crossbones, was prominently displayed.

"Stop! Pull over!" Janey saw a multitude of smaller signs

mounted on four-foot tall wooden stakes, planted closer to the road, right at a driver's eye level. These signs were more personal. More offensive.

WHEN JOHNNY COMES HOME AGAIN...WILL HE HAVE LEGS?

WHEN JOHNNY COMES HOME AGAIN...WILL HE BE IN A COFFIN?

Posted alongside these were a bevy of the town's familiar Welcome Home signs. All had been defaced with a large, red circle/slash.

Nausea roiled her stomach. "Those dirty, rotten..."

"Let me call Matt or Perry," Gemma said. "They'll know what to do."

Janey reached for the door handle. "I know what to do. Tear them down before my father sees them."

Gemma threw the car into PARK. "Wait for me."

Running along the shoulder of the highway, Janey uprooted signs as she went. Gemma moved parallel, snatching up signs like a mad woman. No traffic came by as they worked. With luck, she and Gemma had been the first to see them. Each sign fanned Janey's fury. What a cowardly act to leave them this close to the farm.

When all the small signs were down, she moved to help Gemma yank down the large banner.

Gemma pointed to the pile of signs she'd gathered. "What do we do with these?"

Janey grabbed the ones she'd pulled up. "Put them in the car and take me home. I'll pay those idiots a visit and return them."

"Not without me." Gemma flung her armload of signs into the trunk. "The JFA has an office downtown, right? Let's go."

Gemma did a U-turn, tires squealing as she raced back toward River Haven. Mid-afternoon traffic was light, the downtown sidewalks deserted. The JFA had a storefront in the vacant stretch of buildings next to Lander's Pool Hall. With so few businesses downtown, the landlords seemed less picky about tenants along this stretch.

The storefront's glass windows were blocked, covered from inside with paper handbills announcing JFA protests across the country. A hand-lettered poster on the door read HOME OF JFA DIVISION 176.

Janey went up to the door and yanked. Locked, it didn't budge. Making a fist, she pounded on the glass. No one answered.

"Now what?" Gemma asked.

Janey pointed to the trashcan in front of the building. "Let's pile their signs there. Where they belong."

When Gemma opened the trunk, Janey leaned in to grab a pile of the hateful signs.

"I knew you couldn't stay away."

Janey started at the voice. Spinning around, she found Randy Keener standing two feet away. His navy T-shirt and ball cap sported the JFA logo. That he had the nerve to smile galled her.

"You must want me bad. Admit it," Randy went on.

She ignored his sexual innuendo. "You left trash on the highway."

"What are you talking about?" Randy held his hands palms up, feigning innocence.

"Cut the act." Janey shoved the signs at him. "How dare you insult my brother's memory?"

Randy rammed the signs back. "What are you so hot about, sweet thing? Every word here is truth. Tax money that I paid was wasted on training and arms that got shipped overseas."

"Wasted? John gave his life fighting to defend our freedom. Even for gutless jerks like you."

Keener laughed. "Gave his life? Your brother was nothing more than target practice for jihadists."

"He was a hero."

"And look what that got him. A twenty-one-gun salute. Another waste of bullets."

Janey screamed in frustration and tightened her hands around the signs she still held.

Gemma moved close, her voice low. "He's out to make you mad. Don't give him that satisfaction."

Randy sidled in closer, ignoring Gemma. "Speaking of bullets, did you know that almost twenty-six hundred US soldiers have died in Iraq? Do you know what number your brother was? I didn't think so. The dead become statistics that nobody cares about. But not me. And not the JFA. We'll be celebrating at funerals every time another soldier dies."

Janey's temper spiked. "You and your organization are disgusting."

"No, I'll tell you what disgusting looks like. Jihadist groups celebrating US soldiers' deaths. Like that video from Farid Zaman's Black Death group expressing regret that John had not been captured alive." He grew more animated. "I wonder how long Johnny boy would have held up in their hands. As much as I hated your brother, even I wouldn't have wished that on him. Can you imagine being skinned alive and then set on fire? They invented torture over there."

Janey's stomach spasmed like she'd been punched. She wasn't sure what video he was talking about, but she could guess at its gruesomeness. "I'm not listening to any more of your lies."

She moved sideways to get away, but Randy shoved her back against Gemma's car and used his body to pin her.

"You started this fight, sweet thing, marching up here all self-righteous, like you own the world." Randy grasped a long section of her hair. "Might be fun teaching you some manners."

Janey let all the signs except one drop from her grip. "Get your hands off me."

Randy tugged her hair, trying to force her closer. "I want to hear you beg."

Never. Tightening her grip on the single wooden stake, she swung the sign up from the side and hit his head as hard as she could.

Then she swung her left fist up and slammed it into his jaw — just as John had taught her.

Randy wheeled backwards, releasing his hold. Pain pulsed through Janey's hand, but she ignored it and darted away.

Randy quickly regained his balance and tried to reach for her again.

Gemma leaped on his back. "Run, Janey!"

Randy shook Gemma off and swung an arm toward Janey. "You little witch! I ought to—"

"Back off, Keener!" Perry ran up and grabbed Randy, pushing him off to the side before stepping in front of Janey.

Two deputies rushed up behind her brother, one going to Gemma, the other holding Randy at bay.

"Did he hurt you?" Perry asked.

Janey shook her head. "What about Gemma?"

"She's fine," Perry confirmed. "I came as soon as I got her call."

Randy touched his head, wiped away blood. He turned to the deputy. "Did you see what she did to me? Arrest her!"

"Did I see two little girls kicking your tail? Sure did," the deputy responded. "You really want that to get out?"

"No!" Randy spat on the ground.

"Little girls?" Janey stepped forward.

Perry's hand clamped down on her shoulder. "Let them handle it."

One of the deputies stepped away to talk on his two-way radio.

"Handle it. Right." Randy looked from the deputy to Perry. "You McKays think you own the county. News flash: you don't!" He pointed to the signs on the ground. "Those were reported stolen this morning. And look who has them now. I'd call that possession of stolen property. Won't your sister look cute behind bars?"

The other deputy moved back in. "You're the only one looking through bars today, Keener. There's a warrant for your arrest for failure to report in to your probation officer again."

Randy started swearing as they handcuffed him. "You ain't seen the last of me, Janey McKay."

Perry shot forward and hissed something in Randy's ear that made him lose color and scramble backwards. While Perry was known as the level-headed one, Matt joked that his twin had a wolverine side that even scared him.

"And you better believe it," Perry said, his voice low and menacing.

Whatever Perry threatened, Janey hoped it would be enough to make Randy stay away from her family for good.

CHAPTER FOURTEEN

August 2006
Landstuhl Regional Medical Center, Germany

Layton Burnet stared at the ceiling of his darkened hospital room. Nights sucked, as time slowed, and minutes took hours to tick past. He kept the television off because his roommate was asleep, but he wouldn't have had it on if he'd been alone. If the nurse found him awake, she'd break out the sleeping pills, and the ones forced on him the first week caused some of the worst night terrors of his life.

He didn't need help in the nightmare department. Every time he shut his eyes, he fell back into a replay of that last battle. He heard injured friends scream for help, heard them cry out in pain he was helpless to assuage. The dying called for loved ones: mothers, wives, girlfriends they'd never see again. He heard shouts in anguished Arabic as the enemy, too, lay wounded, dying, Allah invoked as frequently as God. Everywhere voices yelled to Layton to do this, do that.

In the end, nothing he did mattered. Bullets shattered his bones, too. Made him wish he'd died on the battlefield. He'd had no thought of Heaven or Hell, just a simple wish that the surrounding horror would end.

The AC kicked on, rattling the overhead vent and stirring up dust. He fought the urge to sneeze, knowing it would make his shoulder throb more. While part of him welcomed the pain — his dead friends felt nothing — he wasn't trying to martyr himself. He just wanted free of the drug-induced stupor he'd been in since arriving in Landstuhl over three weeks and four — no, five — surgeries ago.

A week ago, he thought he was finally done with surgery, but bone fragments cost him another trip back to the operating room. Supposedly, the doctors were finished reconstructing his shoulder, though *best we can do* didn't sound one hundred percent convincing. Next up was rehab, which Layton would begin back in the States.

Getting back in shape was a top priority. His future with the Army, his career goals as an officer, depended on his ability to prove his fitness. His livelihood was the Army. Unlike others in his squad, he had no real family, no safety net. He had to rely on himself for support, which he'd been doing from age thirteen.

The difference was he'd thrived in the Army. For the first time in his life, he'd excelled in his studies and enjoyed being part of a team. His squad was the closest thing to family he'd known since his grandfather died when Layton was ten. Sure, the McKays all proclaimed Layton family, but he knew how fragile words were, especially now with John gone.

Grief sucker punched Layton. He still couldn't believe John hadn't made it. His friend was too big, too wild, too young to die, and Layton cursed whatever divine vagary that had decided to take John instead of Layton. He would have swapped fates with his best friend without thought.

Calling John's family had been tough. Yet Ward McKay seemed genuinely relieved to hear from him.

"I've been waiting for your call," Ward said. "We've been worried. How are you and when are you coming home?"

Home. People who had them used the word with easy entitlement.

John's older brother, Perry, bombarded Layton with questions, especially about John's final moments. "Was he in pain? Was he conscious? Talking? The Army won't tell us anything."

Layton dreaded answering. The last thing the eldest McKay brothers had said to him was, "Take care of John."

It hadn't been a casual request and Layton knew the disappointment and emotional distrust his reply would evoke. Guilt pounded another nail in his chest. *"I wasn't—"*

The call dropped before he could tell Perry that he'd been over fifty feet away from John. While waiting for the phone lines to reset, Layton decided not to call Perry back. Their conversation about John needed to happen face to face.

Layton almost skipped calling Janey that day, too, not sure he could handle her censure. Except Layton needed to hear her voice. He'd been told he'd screamed her name while out of it, which wasn't surprising. She had been the only thought that brought him any peace during all of this. A month ago, his biggest concern was how to ask John for permission to date his sister. That and wondering if Janey still had any interest in him.

Now? It didn't matter.

Layton closed his eyes. What happened between him and Janey seemed a lifetime ago, in a world that had since turned upside down. A world that had once revolved around her brother. If it had been difficult hearing Perry's questions, how bad would it be when she pressed for answers? She'd asked Layton to look out for John, too.

Alone in the dark, Layton once again second-guessed his actions on the battlefield. Would John have survived if Layton had got to him sooner? According to the doctors, Fallon would have bled out from the severed artery if Layton hadn't maintained pressure. They also said nothing could have saved John. Too much organ damage and blood loss. The sickening part was that Layton did not even know John had been so badly injured. John had been talking, told him to stay with Fallon. *"I'm fine."* Hell, John had even taken out an enemy shooter that was aiming for Layton.

Then Layton had been hit. Everything beyond that was blurred. He'd been unconscious when taken off the battlefield and hadn't been told for days about the casualties his squad suffered.

In the last twenty-four hours, as the medications wore off, Layton had tried to piece together the events of that final battle, tried to replay the scene over and over. What was he missing?

Earlier today, Army Criminal Investigation Division officers questioned Layton. From what Layton gathered, the CID believed the attack had been planned from the moment Farid Zaman learned his only son and heir died. Zaman had been patient, waiting for the perfect opportunity to launch an ambush. The day of the final battle, someone at the marketplace who knew of the *fatwa* and the bounty must have recognized their squad from the photographs that had been circulated and sent word to Farid Zaman's group.

Layton filled in the blanks. From the marketplace, his squad had likely been followed to the school site and had been there long enough for Zaman to move in snipers and launch a rocket attack.

CID also asked about an Iraqi man named Jamal who John and Ollie Fitz previously questioned. Apparently, that was the same man John identified as friendly. Layton hadn't seen much. One moment the man was with John, the next Layton blacked out.

When Layton asked the CID officers if anyone reported seeing the old beggar John rescued previously, they expressed surprise. "What old man?"

Layton's explanation ended up in two parts. First, he explained how John initially rescued the old beggar. Then Layton told them how Teddy Fallon screamed about the old man being at that last battle, pointing and calling out. Layton hadn't seen the old man, but with everything going on, a hundred old men could have been behind him.

Judging by the barrage of questions that followed, the CID found it suspicious that the old beggar had allegedly been present at both the skirmish that killed Zaman's son and the battle that killed John. One officer zeroed in with specific questions about the rosary the beggar gave John. Could the rosary have concealed a tracking device? Did John have the rosary with him in the last battle? Layton told them that John sent the beads back home to his sister before he'd died.

When Layton pressured the CID officers for more details on their investigation, they clammed up. Information was a one-way proposition with CID. The only thing they'd confirm was that Farid Zaman's group, Black Death, publicly claimed responsibility for the attack.

As soon as they left, Layton searched online for Zaman's video. It was brief and chilling. Using an interpreter, Zaman cursed the dead soldiers before implying that he had ties in the US and reiterating that the *fatwa* remained valid. Layton grimaced to think about the people who could be endangered.

The nurse came in just then to check Layton's vitals. "Can I get you more pain medication?" she asked.

He shook his head. He was having enough trouble remembering details and the more he recalled about the CID's visit and Zaman's *fatwa*, the more it triggered a sense of threat. Zaman claimed he wouldn't rest until everyone in Layton's squad and a hundred-fold were dead.

A hundred-fold more.

"On second thought, tell the doctors all I need is some aspirin and I'm good to go," Layton said.

He needed to get back to the States to protect his friends — his family? — and the woman who haunted his sleep.

CHAPTER FIFTEEN

August 2006
River Haven, Iowa

Janey battled an emotional tsunami in the days following the funeral.

When the JFA made national news for more protests, Matt and Perry launched into a furious rant about the signs posted after John's funeral. While the incident between Janey and Randy Keener had been downplayed for her father's benefit, Perry did tell Dad about it. Dad chewed her out for not calling him first, but after seeing how upset he got just hearing about it, she was grateful Gemma called her brother that day.

Janey's sleep devolved into a mélange of bad dreams about war-razed fields littered with wounded, dying soldiers. Their screams of agony drowned out her cries as she sought John, desperate to find him. In her worst nightmares, John appeared as a prisoner in an orange jumpsuit, captured by radical insurgents and tortured. The latter images came after she watched the horrid videos Randy Keener had mentioned.

The Iraqi warlord Farid Zaman's gruesome violence included the torture and murder of local Iraqis who'd dared to disagree with him. Janey also found the video where Zaman reiterated his *fatwa*. Seeing Zaman hold up grainy photographs of US soldiers, including John and Layton, sickened her.

Zaman's threat of continued vengeance on the survivors made Janey worry even more about the soldiers still overseas. Especially Layton. She'd heard nothing since the day of John's funeral and the longer he remained incommunicado, the worse her fears grew. Had there been complications after his last operation? More than ever, she longed to let him know how much she cared — no matter what — but how to reach him?

Her emails were returned as UNDELIVERABLE. All the soldiers' Myspace pages continued to be inaccessible, too. Sharlene Sweeney sent Janey regular emails asking if she had heard anything. Reading that Sharlene had no contact with Layton made Janey feel petty relief.

The McKays still had no detailed information regarding John's death. Dad remained in contact with Donald Livingston's father in Colorado, but the Livingstons were equally frustrated. The excuses both families received about ongoing investigations and national security grew tiresome. Even her father's pleas to their senator yielded nothing more than requests for patience.

That no one expected Janey to work was a small blessing. She went to the McKay store once but found the continual expressions of sympathy overwhelming. Her editor at the newspaper also urged her to take time off, which she resisted. Randy Keener's taunts about John being forgotten, becoming a casualty statistic, fueled a desire to commemorate her brother publicly, but privately she struggled with writer's block. The words which had always been her faithful companion deserted her, leaving her to question her self-identity. Who was she without a desire to create?

And who was she without a belief system? Everything she'd held as sacrosanct about life, God, good, and evil had collapsed. She begrudged her past naiveté, like the way she'd bought into John's

theory that they'd always have time before the final farewell. Life
didn't offer do-overs, and guilt provided continual reminders of every
argument they'd ever had, especially the ugly accusations she'd flung
at John before he deployed. She'd refused to speak of it unless he
apologized. Her self-righteousness had her thinking she'd won. But
what good to rule Hell?

At Perry's insistence that she leave the farm, Janey helped Lisa
paint her living room. When Janey burst into tears for no reason, Lisa
offered tissues and didn't pry. That Lisa didn't try to explain everything away with platitudes made Janey feel better.

It was late afternoon when she returned home, headed to the
bunkhouse. Just as she pulled into the farm, her cell phone rang.

"Would you come up to the house?" Dad asked. "Lloyd Nelson is
here."

"I'm covered with paint, Dad."

He paused. "It won't take long. Lloyd needs to tell you
something."

Janey held her breath. Despite her family's urgings, she hadn't
been back to the cemetery. Her dad went daily and probably thought
Lloyd could sway her with an update on John's headstone or
something.

Lloyd and her father sat at the kitchen table. Eileen wasn't
present, and the two men stopped talking when Janey came in. She
halted when she saw what sat on the table.

The last box from John.

Lloyd cleared his throat. "Janey, I came to apologize in person. I
don't know how, but this box was not placed in John's coffin. I just
found it today, in a supply closet. For the life of me, I don't know how
it got there."

"What about the other items?" Everyone had given Lloyd
mementos to be buried with John.

"I personally placed everything inside," Lloyd said. "Which is
why I'm baffled the box turned up. I know I put it in. I distinctly
remember moving items to make room for this. I've asked all the

others, but everyone swears they touched nothing, just as I'd ordered. John was completely my responsibility." His shoulders sagged. "In all my years, this has never happened. I feel terrible. Maybe I'm getting too old for this, Ward."

"Don't say that." Her father spoke up now. "It's a simple oversight. God knows, it happens to me frequently. We'll deal with it."

Lloyd picked up the box and held it out to Janey. "Regardless, I came here as soon as I found this. I can still bury it in the ground at John's plot. There are certain restrictions, but I'll make it right however I can."

She reached for the package. Goosebumps chased up her arm at the realization that this was the final thing John had ever sent to her — maybe to anyone. She rubbed her fingers across the surface where the address was printed. "This was the last time John wrote my name."

"Then maybe you should keep it," Dad said. "At least for a bit. We can bury it later if you want, right Lloyd?"

"Absolutely."

Janey gripped the box more tightly as the goosebumps spread, their intensity jolting her. "Thank you, Mr. Nelson. For now, I think I will hold on to it."

She took the box out to the bunkhouse and set it on her desk while she took a shower. When she came out, the box caught her eye. If John were here, he'd start making spooky sounds and telling ghost stories to explain why it hadn't gotten buried. She blinked away tears and moved to stare out the window. Outside, the sun dropped behind the tall rows of corn, backlighting the lush green fields that surrounded the bunkhouse. The otherworldly atmosphere teased out a memory.

As children, she and John spent hours sitting in those very cornfields, listening to the sounds of the growing stalks. John had taught her to close her eyes and concentrate on the subtle pops and crinkles as leaves lengthened and unfurled, seeking sunlight as they raced upward from the earth. He said the corn talked and swore it spoke loudest in August. He also bragged that he could decipher its secret language, and then spun glorious tales of corn dynasties, complete with ruling hybrids and armies. While no damsels in distress or princesses lurked in John's stories, Amazon-like, bad-ass girls were Janey's contribution to the tales. She built her own story world where cornstalks grew crystals with magical powers.

An unexpected urge to write had her turning on her laptop and when she started typing, words poured onto the screen in a stream of consciousness as she tried to capture her childhood memories. It was after midnight when she stopped. The flood of words dislodged her pent-up emotional energy, leaving her too tired to read what she'd typed.

Rubbing her neck, she checked email but was discouraged to find the last two emails to Layton had been returned along with the one she'd sent to Danny Carpenter. She let Fuller in and turned off the lights before falling back on her bed.

Sleep slammed over her like a wave and pulled her under. At some point she became aware that she was in a nightmare again, back in Iraq, bombs exploding, guns blasting. People screamed, calling out while she searched for John and Layton. Fear and helplessness smothered her with leaden bogs of desolation.

"Wake up, Janey!"

She bolted upright at the sound of John's voice, so real she expected to find him standing there. When they were kids, John would shout her name at the top of his lungs every morning – *Wake up, Janey!* — demanding she get ready for school. If she resisted, he would count to three. That never failed to get her moving because at the count of four, he would thump her arm, smack her with a pillow. Except—

No one was there. Tears streamed down her cheeks as the visions and sounds from her dreams replayed of their own volition. Is this what soldiers suffering from PTSD go through? An unrelenting horror show?

She reached for the tissues on her nightstand, but her hand hit an object. A book, she realized as it fell to the floor with a muffled crash. She snapped on the bedside lamp. Both the tissue box and book were on the floor, leaving only one item on her nightstand.

The box from John.

Seeing it there startled her. Hadn't she left it on her desk across the room? She heard Fuller's low *woof* and scrambled out of bed.

"Fuller?" She raced to her door and opened it. The collie was just outside, her tail wagging in greeting. "How did you get out?" She held the door open, but the dog whined and hesitated. Janey glanced around outside but saw no one. Her father must have come to check on her. "Come on, girl."

When Fuller obeyed, Janey shut and locked the door. The collie leaped on the bed and barked. Janey shivered when she saw why. The box was on the bed now. Was she losing her mind? Tentative, she touched the box. A tingling raced up her arm.

Open it. Once again, she heard John's voice in her head and felt a strong urge to hold the coins inside, to touch that which he'd last touched.

Tearing one taped edge loose, Janey tipped the box. A paper-wrapped packet slipped into her hand, heavier than expected. She unfolded the paper and found a strand of sparkling black beads. The contents surprised her. She'd been so certain the box contained more battle coins.

Shifting closer to the lamp, she spotted the crucifix and sucked in a breath. A rosary? Seriously? John's entire life had been lived in the shadow of the Catholic Church and now the last thing he'd sent home was a rosary. The circle of life. Well, the Catholic life at least.

Except this was no ordinary rosary. The beads were cut in a design that made them glow as if illuminated from within. Delicate, silver filigree encased the oversized beads, making the exquisite rosary look more like jewelry. Or sacred art. Where on earth had John gotten this?

She let the beads spill off the paper and into her palm. They felt almost hot. She hugged them to her heart. John had been the last person to touch this rosary, and she imagined him cradling it in his hand, warming the beads. Except he had likely mailed this over a month ago.

She picked up the box to check the postmark date and spotted a folded sheet of paper wedged inside. She yanked it free and stared at the lines of ink, recognizing John's slasher-like penmanship. Hand-written letters were rare as John mostly connected via email or Skype. Hands trembling, she dropped the beads in her lap and blinked, straining to read through her tears.

Dear Pest–

Greetings from the land of sand. Before you get all excited about what I'm sending, I'll warn you it's not a gift. I'm sending this rosary to you for safekeeping until I get home. There's something special about this piece. It's unusual and I hope you can dig something up on its origin. Mom said every rosary had a story, and I bet this one is epic. You'll never believe how I got it.

Heck, you'll never believe a lot of things. So much has changed since I've been here. I've changed. I once believed war was the only way, but the opposite is true. Peace is the only way. I mean it, so quit laughing.

I know you always keep me in your prayers, but today I have a special request: pray for peace, Janey. I swear God listens to you more than me. (Ha-ha.) Can't wait to get home.

Love you like there's no tomorrow.

The prophetic closing had her sobbing anew. There was no tomorrow for them.

Fuller scooted close and woofed.

"He was wrong, Fuller. I'm barely on speaking terms with God right now. God doesn't listen to me. If He did, John wouldn't be dead, Layton wouldn't be hurt, and Momma would still be alive." Her list of grievances weighed heavily.

Fuller laid her head on Janey's lap and remained still as she reread the letter. The line *I'll explain how I got it as soon as I'm home* was one more story she would never hear.

Setting the letter aside, she picked up the rosary again. Its warmth jolted her. An image of her mother kneeling in church flashed in Janey's mind. The scene expanded into a clear memory. Janey had been five years old, and she and her mother had just dropped John off at his second-grade classroom before walking across the street to the church, something they did regularly before her mother got sick. Janey usually played quietly on the kneeler while her mother recited the rosary, but that day it rained. Janey's shoes were wet, and the church was cold and damp. Uncomfortable, she'd grown cranky, wanting to leave.

Her mother switched from kneeling to sitting, pulling Janey into her lap as she sat back in the pew and snuggled Janey in her arms. Not missing a beat, her mother continued to pray her rosary. *"Hail Mary, full of grace."* The prayer fell from her mother's lips, repeated ten times with each decade of beads, as gentle as a lullaby.

As it had back then, a sense of peace and calm now overcame Janey. She fell back against her pillow, eyes closed as the memory lingered. Her mother's arms tightened around her, rocking her, warming her. She recalled her mother's soft cotton blouse rubbing her cheek. The faint scent of roses, her mother's signature scent, made Janey sneeze. *"Gesundheit, Sugarpuff,"* Mother whispered between verses as if that line had been part of the prayer.

The memory receded, leaving Janey with new tears and a cherished memory. Her mother had been the only one to call her Sugarpuff, and Janey hadn't ever recalled that specific memory before. It was as if the memory had sprung forth, shepherded through the depths of her mind by this strange new rosary.

Gathering the beads close, she shut her eyes and replayed the precious recollection from that long-ago day, desperately hoping for more.

———

SHE AWOKE to the sound of John's voice, this time as a soft whisper.

"Janey, pray for peace."

She jolted upright, disoriented. Her gaze fell on the alarm clock. That it was after nine o'clock surprised her. She hadn't slept this late since before—

John! Where was the rosary and his letter? Panicked, she felt beneath the bed sheets. Fuller moved begrudgingly, resettling at the foot of the bed, but Janey found nothing. She climbed to her feet, distraught to realize she'd dreamed the whole thing. Like the scenes of war, none of it had happened.

Then she spotted the box on the rug, caught in the morning light streaming through the window. She snatched it up and found the letter and rosary beneath the box. They were real and the beads still felt warm, as though someone held them all night. The rosary glittered, even more stunning than she remembered.

Over her lifetime, she'd seen many other rosaries that, while pretty, were always utilitarian. This one was oversized, as if meant for display versus personal use and the longer she studied the rosary, the more questions she had. Where had this rosary come from? How had her brother gotten it? And what type of information had he hoped she'd find?

She moved to her laptop and began doing research, but soon gave up. Most searches yielded rosaries for sale. She'd have to ask her uncle about it. Uncle Nick would be blown away by not only how the box escaped burial, but that it contained this unusual rosary.

Hoping for clues, she re-read John's letter. What stood out were the uncharacteristic lines. *I once believed war was the only way, but the opposite is true. Peace is the only way.* Her brother never waxed philosophical. Had something happened with this rosary to inspire him to write words of peace, or was he once again manipulating her? *I'm hoping you can dig something up on its origin.* John used to connive her into doing his chores and homework, making her feel guilty if she refused.

The last thing she needed was more guilt. She also didn't need another set of rosary beads. She'd received many rosaries over the years and John's letter stated it wasn't meant as a gift for her. *I'm sending this rosary to you for safekeeping, until I get home.*

Except... He wasn't coming home.

Grabbing the beads, she went into John's bedroom. She started to put the rosary on his trophy shelf but stopped, unable to shake the feeling that she was supposed to do something special with this rosary. Like it was John's last request.

The beads grew warm, as if in affirmation, which didn't help.

"What do you want me to do?" As she spoke to the empty room her gaze fell on the wall map studded with pins. Another of John's dreams that would never know fruition.

A line from his letter came to mind. *Pray for peace.*

"That's asking too much," she whispered. While she continued to attend Sunday Mass with her father because it was easier to go and avoid questions, she no longer prayed, uncertain what she believed.

There were, however, plenty of faithful people in the church who did pray. She stared at the rosary beads that seemed to pulse with approval of the idea formulating in her mind. With others' help, could she honor John's request and make sure he was never forgotten?

———

LATER THE NEXT DAY, Janey's website went live without fanfare. While the scope of the project exceeded her initial expectations, the mission statement remained simple: To pay homage to Army Specialist John McKay and the other soldiers who died courageously in battle on July 17, 2006, and to honor John's last request to 'pray for peace.'

After brainstorming with Gemma, Janey set a goal of having a rosary peace prayer service in every state. The tribute to her brother would be as big as the great country he chose to serve and that he'd planned to explore.

Uncle Nick suggested that the services be church-sponsored if she wanted the rosary physically present. It meant the rosary had to travel, which she didn't mind. Getting the rosary out of sight, where it didn't remind her of losing her brother and that she wasn't being a good Catholic right now, helped ease Janey's conscience, too.

Encouraged to be creating again, she tackled the project with fervor, welcoming the feeling of agency it gave when much felt beyond her control. She wrote the website's content. Gemma designed the layout and took photographs of the rosary. Their friend Ben Hufstedler handled the technical part of launching the site. Uncle Nick became the biggest supporter of the idea, offering to promote the project with other parish priests.

The website included a personal page honoring John and each of the other soldiers who died, and salutes to the squad's survivors. Janey sent messages to each soldier's family, inviting them to contribute photos and stories. The Livingstons responded within hours, promising to share pictures and anecdotes about their late son, Donald. While the Livingstons were Unitarians, they promised to pass information about the website to their local Catholic Church, hoping to have a rosary service in Colorado.

Janey also set up a blog to share stories about John. Her first post explained how she received the rosary and included an excerpt of John's letter. Ben devised an online form for churches to sign up to receive the rosary and have their scheduled service listed on the website.

She debated having the initial service in River Haven but decided to wait until October on what would have been John's twenty-first birthday. Uncle Nick signed up for the first rosary service, which seemed fitting. After carefully packing the beads, she sent them to her uncle's church in Chicago. While she had yet to find any information on the rosary's origins, Uncle Nick promised to check with some Vatican brainiacs.

The River Press newspaper agreed to publish an article Janey wrote about the rosary and her quest to have prayers for peace recited in every state. Her editor suggested she write occasional updates as part of her column.

Three days later, Janey met Gemma in town at The Pizza Barn.

The restaurant was packed, but Gemma had snagged their favorite booth. "Can you believe classes start in two weeks? My Dad and brother have promised to help us move."

Two weeks? Dejected, Janey dumped her bag on an empty seat. Would Layton return to River Haven before she left for college?

Before she could respond, Randy Keener moved into view, a rolled-up newspaper in his hand.

"Didn't know you wrote comedy," he said. "The piece on those rosary beads is flat out hilarious. Who makes a dying request to pray for peace? If you're dying, you ask to live."

Janey struggled to feign indifference. Perry warned that Randy would try to provoke her again. "Just stay clear of him," Perry advised.

She was grateful they were in a public place. "They let you out of jail? Pity."

Randy grinned. "Turns out my supporters have more clout than you McKays. All charges were dropped. And to prove no hard feelings, I thought I'd offer you an exclusive interview about the JFA's next protest." He slapped the newspaper down on the table, headline up.

IOWA MARINE KILLED IN IRAQ.

Janey felt like she'd been struck, her heart aching for the unknown Marine and his family.

"This poor, dead sap was from Davenport," Randy went on. "I'm posting notices about our rally, if you want to join us." He pointed to the bulletin board near the entrance where a bright red flyer hung.

"Leave that family alone," Janey said. "They've suffered enough."

"My point exactly. Enough is enough," Randy said. "These headlines won't stop until we quit sending soldiers to that God-forsaken country."

Mr. Markson, the owner of The Pizza Barn, hurried over to their table, a red flyer in hand. "Did you post this?" He thrust the paper at Randy. The restaurant grew quiet.

"Sure did. You want extras?"

"Take this garbage elsewhere and get out of my restaurant. And never come back," Mr. Markson said.

"I buy my pizza here," Randy argued.

"Not anymore. Buy it elsewhere." When Mr. Markson pointed to the door, the whole place applauded.

Randy glared at everyone, then shook his head. Before leaving, he looked back at Janey. "This isn't over," he mouthed.

CHAPTER SIXTEEN

August 2006
River Haven, Iowa

Randy Keener squealed his tires, leaving the acrid scent of burned rubber as he peeled out of The Pizza Barn parking lot. Screw Markson and everyone in that place, especially Janey McKay. One of these days it would be just the two of them. He'd teach her a thing or two and have fun doing it.

He grabbed a beer from the cooler on the seat beside him and popped the top. The McKay family needed to be taken down a notch or two after all the trouble they'd caused Randy's family over the years. His daddy said the reason the McKays went after them was that, back then, the Keener business was larger. *"McKays can't stand not being top dog. They lied and cheated to mow down any competition."*

Like most feuds, the origins weren't simple. Daddy said everyone cheated, but McKays were just better at covering their tracks. Daddy also swore Anna McKay had a thing for him before she married

Ward. *"Women act like they hate you to cover up the fact they want you really bad."*

Randy took a slug of beer. The thought of Janey wanting him eased his temper. He glanced at the clock, then quickly turned up the radio. They almost made him miss his show. Station KKKX, the syndicated voice of the Justice Freedom Association, was one of the fastest growing talk-radio shows west of the Mississippi, thanks largely to the popularity of shock jock, Hank – The DC Stank – Bogden. The Stank came on at five o'clock, the top-ranked show during happy hour, and preached to the underpaid, overtaxed, under-appreciated blue-collar workforce.

Randy drummed on his steering wheel as the show's introductory music played. At the stoplight, he rolled down the window and hollered, "Stank for president!" The old biddy in front of him looked in the opposite direction while someone else honked in solidarity.

Today, The Stank was on the warpath, ripping into a new bill on overseas spending. "Sources close to Senators Texton and Dent say the proposed bill is an elaborate scam designed to funnel close to twenty-billion — that's twenty billion of our hard-earned tax dollars, folks – over to the Saudi government. When we come back from a short commercial break, I want to hear what you think of this travesty."

"Those no-good politicians." Randy drained his beer after hitting two digits on his speed-dial. To his surprise, his call to the radio station went through. He typically got a busy signal.

He spoke with a call screener, who asked if it was okay to put Randy on hold. "After the commercial break, you'll be our first caller," the screener said.

"Heck yeah, I'll wait!"

Already downtown, Randy parked behind the JFA headquarters and hurried inside. The same commercial he listened to on his phone was playing on the radio in the front hall where a half-dozen guys were gathered around the pool table. He strode straight toward the refrigerator in the corner. Snapping his fingers to get attention,

Randy pointed to the speaker. "Listen up, all you patriots. You might hear something interesting."

Grabbing an icy beer, he retreated to his corner office and fired up his computer. The JFA's private online forums were always active, but comments quadrupled when The Stank started his broadcast. Right now, the chat boards were going nuts over the twenty-billion-dollars comment.

The commercial ended abruptly as Hank Bogden's deep voice boomed over the line. "We're back and you're live with Washington's most hated watchdog, The DC Stank. Our phone lines exploded over this one. Clearly my listeners, the true American patriots, are sick of these namby-pamby, far-left-over-the-edge-off-the-cliff, kowtowing-to-every-foreign-country-out-there, politicians. Our first caller is from southeast Iowa. Are you there?"

Randy grinned. "Oh, yeah. I'm Randy Keener, president of JFA local chapter 176 in River Haven, Iowa, and we don't care what it's for, we oppose this bill one hundred percent. Stinking government forgets where tax dollars come from — my wallet. Your wallet. That twenty billion needs to stay here in the USA. Heck, it needs to go back in our wallets."

From the front of the hall, the guys started cheering, whistling, and whooping loudly, stomping the floor and banging the walls. Randy moved to shut his office door but stopped when The Stank started talking.

"Wow, Randy. Sounds like you've got a lot of support there." The guys cheered even louder after hearing The Stank's public acknowledgment. "Stay in the USA, nails it. I read more of the bill during the commercial but had to stop when I got to this one line that states — and I quote — 'this funding shall be designated as support for the peace accords in the Middle East.'"

Randy scanned the recent comments being posted online. *Sounds like they have a big chapter down there in Iowa. This Keener guy must have clout.*

He focused back on the call. "Aid and support are their code words for political BS. Why do we care if they have peace in the Middle East? They've been fighting each other for centuries. We send all this money over there and nothing ever changes. I suspect many of those funds somehow find their way back into the politicians' pockets. It's probably given to some big corporation they own stock in, who pays them a huge fee for giving a dim-witted speech to their board at some swanky golf course on the ocean. Bunch of super liberals are probably in bed with the Saudis."

"Preach it," The Stank crowed. "Well, the US government says they're our allies."

"And I say they're the richest suckers in the world. If they want a peace accord in the Middle East, let 'em use their own money. It's their backyard that needs cleaning up, not ours. We shouldn't even be over there." Randy couldn't keep up with the new string of posts online, but the consensus leaned in his favor.

I'm with Keener, several people wrote.

Spoken like a true patriot.

This last comment got Randy's attention as Bill Heasly, president of the Detroit JFA chapter, the largest in the organization, posted it. If a person wanted to rise in the JFA ranks, Heasly had to be a supporter.

"Now you're talking," The Stank said. "Makes me wonder what the actual purpose of this bill is. We've paid off every country out there and called it aid, but who does it really benefit?"

"Exactly. We don't know where this money goes. We just know they keep pulling more of it out of our pockets. Washington is run by a bunch of brainless liberals. Just like here in River Haven. The McKays have tried to run everything since John McKay died over there—"

"Whoa. Hold on there, Randy. We can't use people's names on the air unless they're public officials. You've summed up the problems, but let's move on to another caller and see what they've got to share. Thanks for calling in."

Randy wasn't surprised when the call wrapped up. He'd listened to the show often enough to know endings were abrupt. Swiveling his chair, he scrolled back through the news feed on the private forum. Ninety-seven people had commented favorably, with several asking where the River Haven chapter was located.

The Stank kept him online longer than most.

Wonder if they're friends?

Randy typed a few words, then stopped. One thing he'd noticed when Bill Heasly commented on the boards: Heasly's posts always sounded humble. *For the people...* Was that why Heasly's name was always tossed around when JFA national elections were discussed? Randy crushed his empty beer can. No reason his name couldn't be tossed around, too.

> *This isn't about me, it's about us,* Randy typed. *It's about us taking back control of this grand country of ours. The doors here at JFA Chapter 176 are always open to fellow patriots. Come by. Be heard. Everyone matters here.*

Within seconds, others started liking his post. Randy's ego swelled as his likes surpassed the number given to Heasly's most recent post. The new comment notification icon flashed repeatedly as people responded to Randy's post. His smirk grew wider with each *high-five, right on, bro,* comment he read.

But one post had him sitting forward in his seat.

You're battling the McKays? We need to talk.

CHAPTER SEVENTEEN

August 2006
River Haven, Iowa

While the Army remained mute on specific battle details, they finally released the results of John's autopsy.

Janey kept a hand over her mouth as she read the cold terminology. *Catastrophic abdominal injuries from shrapnel. Un-survivable even with prompt medical attention.*

But a coroner's report wasn't what she'd sought. She wanted to know what her brother had been doing prior to the attack. She ached to know his final moments, thoughts.

Janey continued to send messages to Layton, heartened when they didn't immediately bounce back as UNDELIVERABLE, even though he still did not reply.

However, this morning when she checked email, she found a note from Teddy Fallon, who'd been deployed with John. Teddy's fiancée, Roxanne, had been the one who confirmed Layton was in Germany, but Janey's attempts to contact her again had hit a dead end. Was Teddy back in the States now? Oh, God, was Layton back too?

Janey did a double take when she noticed Teddy's email came in via the rosary website.

> A friend's aunt saw your website, Teddy wrote. I recognize that rosary and told my family all about it. I want to sign up for a prayer service at our church in Cincinnati. How soon can I get the rosary?

Her stomach fluttered as she reread the message. Had Teddy seen the rosary before? Did he know how John got it? She replied immediately with her phone number.

> Please call anytime, night or day. I want to talk with you about my brother and the others.

Minutes after she hit SEND, her phone rang. "Hello?"

"Janey? It's Teddy Fallon in Cincinnati. I served in Iraq with your brother." He sounded animated at first but there was also an undertone, a slight slurring of words followed by a sharp intake of air that sounded painful.

Janey recalled Roxanne saying that Teddy had lost a leg. "Yes, John mentioned you several times. He said you were going to be a new father, right?" She'd reread her brother's letters enough times to have them memorized.

"Two more months. A little boy. Teddy Junior."

"I spoke once with your fiancée, Roxanne, after she returned from Germany but haven't heard from her since and—"

He cut her off. "You talked to Roxanne? Man, people don't tell me anything." Teddy drew another uneven breath. "I'm so sorry your brother didn't make it. John was an honorable person and a good soldier. Always there for everyone. About eight months into our tour, I got word my dad died. It was the middle of the night, but your brother stayed with me until I could catch a flight home."

Janey and John had learned their mother died in the middle of the night. "I can imagine him doing that."

"Family was number one with John. He and Layton used to talk about you a lot."

Her pulse elevated at the mention of Layton. "Really?"

"Constantly. I remember John bragging about you taking college classes in high school. He claimed he tutored you, taught you everything, but Layton called him out on it. They were always doing that, you know?"

"Yes." She recalled the way John and Layton one-upped each other, like real brothers. That she'd never hear them do that again brought tears to her eyes.

"Those two were inseparable. You saw one, you saw both. Now?" Teddy paused. "Can't believe we lost so many that day. I'm so sorry."

Janey cleared her throat. Teddy was one of the last people to see John alive and she didn't want to waste time wallowing in grief. "I have some questions, but first tell me how you are doing. When did you get back to the States?"

"I'm not so good." His voice faded, then grew forceful. "I lost my right leg. And I hate when people make stupid remarks, like 'sorry 'bout your leg, but at least you're alive, man.' Now my leg won't heal, and the antibiotics quit working. Since I've been back from Germany, they've cut off more of it, twice, to stop the infection from spreading. Damn pain won't go away either." A woman's shrill voice in the background came through. "That's my mom. Sorry about my cussing. I spent fifteen months in a tent full of soldiers. Mom says it shows, too."

Janey gripped the phone tightly as the extent of Teddy's injuries sank in. "You've been through a lot. I hope your leg heals quickly."

"Thank you. I don't mean to sound ungrateful. I mean, some guys are still in the hospital. Corporal Lovett, Layton Burnet."

Janey sprang out of her chair. "Roxanne mentioned that you were in the same hospital as Layton. Do you know how he's doing? Have you heard from him lately?"

"I guess his shoulder and chest got messed up bad. The medics said they didn't think he'd make it. I've heard he had a bunch of surgeries. We were in different wards in Landstuhl, so it was hard to keep track. Nobody's heard from him since, but I know he'll call as soon as he can. Our squad promised to keep in touch no matter what."

She knew how easy promises were to make. John and Layton had both promised to come back safe and sound, as if either of them controlled life or death. "If you hear anything about Layton, please let me know."

"Sure." There was another deep inhalation like he took a drag off a cigarette. "Look, I saw your website and the tributes you posted on my squad. That's nice, but what I got super excited about was to see that rosary again. I wondered what happened to it. I should have known John would ship it to you."

"Do you know anything about the rosary? John sent it home but didn't say where it came from."

"I was there when your brother got it. Our squad had been in a tough skirmish in an alley that day. It was nothing compared to that last battle, but still, bullets were flying everywhere. Then John jumps up as if he was Superman and runs out into the middle of it to rescue this crazy, one-legged beggar. You should have seen John scoop the old man up with one arm while laying down suppressive fire with the other before dragging him off." Fallon's voice wavered, dropping from a manic high pitch to a choking wail. "It was awful. The bad guys were firing; everyone was screaming. Civilians ran into buildings, and you could hear kids crying inside. Afterwards, John acted like it was nothing."

Sergeant Boswell had mentioned the incident to Janey's family, but in general terms. The details Teddy added broke her heart. "I can see my brother doing that. John was fanatic about protecting innocent people, especially those who couldn't defend themselves." It was one reason she hadn't wanted him to join the military. There were parts of the world that were too big, too broken for one man to fix.

"I think the old man gave John the rosary as a thank-you for saving him," Teddy said.

"But why would an Iraqi beggar have a Catholic rosary?" Janey asked.

"I wondered the same thing. I remember the base chaplain, Father Donovan, saying maybe the old man was a Christian. But the story gets even more bizarre. I saw that old dude disappear in a flash of green light after he gave John the rosary. I mean disappear like beam-me-up, Star Trek stuff."

Star Trek? Had she heard right? Teddy's continued rambling sounded distant, like he'd set the phone aside. Then Janey heard a voice in the background again. It was Teddy's mother, telling him to stop, that he'd just taken medication twenty minutes earlier.

"Sorry." Teddy's voice came across more loudly. "What was I saying?"

Janey realized he was likely on some powerful painkillers for his leg. That explained his slurred words, but did it also affect his recollections? "The old beggar. Do you know his name? Or where he lives?"

"Nah. The alleys over there are full of beggars and none of them speak English, so you really couldn't communicate if you tried." It sounded like he took a sip of something. "There's more, Janey. That old beggar was at the last battle, too, even though it was miles from where we first saw him. I swear to you, I met him a second time, but no one believes me. I think he was looking for his rosary. I tried to get John's attention, to let him know the beggar was back, but with rockets and mortars going off and bad guys with RPGs everywhere, John couldn't hear me."

John. Teddy was talking about that last battle now. Could he share details of John's last moments? "Did you see my brother before he died?"

"No. Once that rocket exploded, I went down hard. I didn't see much else and the pain..." There was a pause, a sob. Then swearing. "Layton saved my life. If he hadn't stayed with me, I would be dead, too." Another reminder was hollered out on Teddy's end, telling him to watch his language. "Shut up, Mama. Geez, I'm sorry."

"It's okay." Janey's heart hammered as she tried to make sense of his rambling explanations. "You said Layton stayed with you? Then John must have been right there, too."

"No, I'm telling you, John was somewhere else."

Somewhere else? Was Teddy having another *beam me up* moment? "Are you sure? I mean, you just said they were always together."

"Not every minute. That day, Corporal Lovett split us up. John went off with Ollie Fitz, not sure where, but I saw the old beggar. He was there. I swear it! You got to believe me." Teddy sobbed, his breath anguished.

Janey felt bad for pressing him for answers when he was in a lot of pain. Tears trailed down her cheeks. "I can't imagine what you've been through, Teddy."

He cleared his throat. "That was the worst day of my life. I lost most of my friends and my leg. Now I'm afraid I've lost Roxanne, too. She's threatened to keep the baby away if I don't change. It feels like I'm losing everything, even my faith. But then I found your website and remembered that rosary. When John showed it to Father Donovan, I got to hold it and it was so weird."

"Weird like very warm?"

"Maybe. No. It was more like a shock. A zap. The good kind that makes you want to, I dunno, sing or something. I want to see that rosary, see if it will make me feel good again. Mom looked at your website and said we can get it sent here, yes?"

"Of course. There's a sign-up form." Forget the form. She would schedule Fallon's church herself. He was one of John's buddies. "My uncle is sponsoring the first service in Chicago, but I'll see that you get the rosary next. All I need is the name and address of your church."

There were muffled voices. "My mom's sending it to you now." Teddy's words were even more slurred. "Look, I have to get ready for a doctor's appointment. Please don't forget to send the rosary. And tell John I said hi and—" He caught himself. "Sorry. Oh, God, I'm so sorry."

The call ended abruptly. Janey stared at her phone. *Tell John I said hi?* Fallon was obviously highly medicated, but really?

She paced the room. The trauma in Teddy's voice left her struggling to comprehend his suffering. While he had not spouted the *under-investigation* line like others had, some of his explanations had been disjointed and out-there, making her question his lucidity and whether he recalled the incident correctly.

Once again, it seemed her sole chance at answers depended on talking to Layton.

———

WAITING to hear from Layton consumed Janey as another week passed. What was he going through? Had he needed more surgery? The thought of him alone, dealing with physical pain and emotional grief left her shaken.

Teddy called twice more to inquire when the rosary would arrive. "It should have been here by now. I've just got to see it again!" Both times his speech was slurred, his concentration erratic. He didn't remember that the rosary was headed to her uncle's church in Chicago first.

Nightmares of John's final battle continued to plague Janey's sleep, with her brother calling out her name. At times he spoke in a foreign tongue, throwing beads at her while beseeching her to find something that was missing. She knew that was a direct reference to the rosary, which had apparently gotten lost in the mail while en route to her uncle.

Guilt shadowed her at the thought of never again seeing the last thing her brother sent home. Hindsight left her regretting her idea to have a traveling rosary in the first place. She went to the post office only to be advised to give it a few more days to show up, followed by a polite lecture to insure future packages and require a signature to track the delivery.

Matt or Perry were still at the farm daily, helping Dad as they all struggled to cope with the void created in their hearts by John's death. The blessing-in-disguise of farm life was daily chores. Rain or shine, joy or grief, the animals needed care. Crops had to be tended, and the weather fussed over loudly, as if Mother Nature were listening.

Today Janey rode in the big air-conditioned tractor with Perry, keeping him company as he mowed hay fields. The scent of freshly cut grass brought back memories of doing that same task with John. As a child, Janey thought she worked harder than most of the population. John made her load twine and stack bales. He also made her open and close the gates, which she hated. How many times had he driven off laughing, making her run to catch up? Or demand a password to let her back inside the cab?

She and Perry listened to a baseball game on the radio, their companionable silence broken only by Perry's colorful swearing when the Cubs remained down at the bottom of the eighth. They finished mowing by three o'clock. Perry pulled the tractor into the machine barn. Fuller waited for them and barked twice.

Perry climbed down from the cab, upset that the Cubs had lost. "If they make it to the play-offs, I'll—" He cut off mid-sentence.

"What's wrong?" Janey turned, her gaze following Perry's.

Half of the machine barn housed the Boys' Toys. Motorcycles, four wheelers, and go-carts were parked everywhere, some working, some parts-donors.

But Perry stared at John's racing motorcycle. The last time John was home, he and Perry had replaced the engine. Then John washed it and covered it. He'd made a point of telling everyone to not let Janey ride it.

Somehow, the bike's tarp had come off. A shaft of sunlight speared through the bay door, spotlighting the frame. The navy-blue metal flake paint glittered with embedded flecks of gold. How many times had she watched John go airborne off a jump, that beautiful bike hanging suspended by sunshine before dropping back to the track in a burst of speed?

"He loved that thing," Perry said. "God, he was fearless on the racetrack, too. Same as you."

Janey's throat ached. "I had no choice. It was go fast or be left behind." By age ten, she could keep up with everyone on the motocross team, thanks to John, but no matter how hard she practiced, she couldn't match his skill.

Perry walked over, brushed the dust off the front fender before gathering up the cover. "Dad about had a stroke when he learned John taught you to ride motocross."

"Really? Why?"

"You were how old? Seven? And so tiny."

"John said I could make up for my size with meanness."

Perry laughed. "You'd believe anything he told you. Did you know that Dad refused to let you race? John badgered him into relenting."

She blinked back tears. She hadn't known that. After Mom died, she had begged John to let her ride with him. He'd been noncommittal at first, claiming he needed time to think about it. As if the entire decision was his alone. "Daddy said nothing to me about not racing."

"Of course, he didn't. Heck, none of us could tell you no. I'll tell you another little secret. If there was something we really didn't want you to do, we'd make John play the heavy."

"Gee, thanks. Do you know how much he relished telling me no?"

"He was the only one who wasn't afraid of your temper and the only one immune to your tears," Perry said.

But John wasn't immune. If she would cry at a race, he was merciless. *Never let 'em see your tears.* But if she'd cry at home, he'd do anything to make her stop. Usually. She learned to use tears judiciously. If she cried too much, he'd thump her arm.

Perry's cell phone rang. He handed her the tarp before stepping away to answer.

Janey stared at the silhouette of John's bike. Would it stay like that forever, a frozen tableau of time? Dad had promised John's belonging would remain untouched, but still she worried. Except for the garden Madonna and the big hand-painted sign out front, most of her mother's belongings had been packed away since Eileen moved in. How long before the same was true of John's stuff? Before they packed it up, too?

She covered the bike reverently.

"Okay, we're on our way." Perry disconnected. "That was Dad. There are two FBI agents at the house." The muscle in his cheek twitched.

"Why is the FBI here?"

"He didn't elaborate, but he sounds uptight."

"Let's go." More stress was the last thing their father needed. The doctor had switched his medications yet again after Dad's blood pressure spiked dangerously high last week. The unpleasant side effects of the new drugs had Dad threatening to quit all meds. Even Eileen seemed worried.

A few minutes later, Janey and Perry were back at the farmhouse. Two men in dark suits were seated at the kitchen table. Dad introduced Special Agents Holmes and Smith. "They're from the Des Moines FBI office."

"What brings you here?" Perry went straight to the point.

Agent Holmes took the lead. "We're following up on information regarding a Middle East radical group led by Farid Zaman. You've heard of him?"

"Yes." Perry scowled. "His group, Black Death, claimed responsibility for the attack on John's squad. What kind of information are you talking about?"

Agent Holmes motioned toward Janey. "The increased chatter we're hearing is about the website you've set up, Miss McKay."

Dad addressed Agent Holmes. "Back up a minute. Exactly what does increased chatter mean?"

"Chatter is communications intercepted between suspected groups and Zaman's known sympathizers," Holmes explained.

"Why would Zaman's followers care about my rosary website?" Janey asked. In the larger scheme of the Internet, her website seemed nonexistent, and outside of emailing a few churches, she'd done no promotion.

"They're most likely interested because John and members of his squad are featured on it, and Zaman had issued a *fatwa* against them. Zaman's followers take his edicts seriously," Holmes went on. "We think it would be wise if you temporarily take down your website."

"And let those lunatics have the satisfaction of pushing us around? No way," Janey said.

"Darn right!" Dad snapped at the agents. "My daughter's website is about a rosary. It's also a tribute to my son and the soldiers who died with him. Taking it down means giving in."

McKays never gave in. Janey shifted closer to her dad in a show of solidarity, Perry right behind her.

"Very well." Agent Holmes handed each of them a business card. "If you hear or see anything unusual or receive any bizarre requests through the website, we'd like to know right away. You can reach me at this number. We won't take up any more of your time."

"Hold up." Dad stood now, bracing his arms on the table, his face serious. "I need to know one thing before you leave. Is my family in danger?"

The two agents exchanged a look.

CHAPTER EIGHTEEN

OH. MY. GOD. Heaven is a cornfield?

John McKay took in the surreal green of the most perfect corn-field he'd ever seen. The tall stalks held fat, full ears; the promise of a bountiful harvest. The field spread out before him, the verdant rows racing without end toward the horizon. A slight breeze lifted the golden tassels in unison like fingers beckoning him forward.

He couldn't recall the sky ever being that vibrant, that blue. The color evoked a feeling of deep serenity. He relaxed against the wooden bench just like the one he'd sat on as a child with his mother. Her presence was powerful here.

Eyes closed, John listened to the wind singing through the leaves. The sounds were sacred. Blessed. Call it crazy, but he'd known his greatest moments of peace in a field like this.

Maybe Heaven was in Iowa.

"It's different for everyone," the man who sat beside him on the bench said.

"So not everyone visits the Field of Dreams movie set after they pass over? Figures." John was getting used to the way things like benches and cornfields and people simply materialized.

Up till now, he'd been visiting places in his past, reliving moments of happiness and even sorrow, but without the pain. Time had no relevance here, though he could follow its tracks across the physical plane in a life review. Except...which life to explore? There were many past experiences to choose from, but this one called most loudly. There were lessons yet to be mined here.

John turned back to the man, who he'd come to know as the one called The Nazarene. *Jesus. Emmanuel. Friend.* John's eyes widened. "It was you I saved in the alley, right?"

Now the old beggar sat on the bench. "Which time?"

A kaleidoscope of people flashed on and off the bench. John recognized each of them now, though at the time their paths crossed on the physical plane they'd all been disguised as strangers. *Entertaining angels unaware.* He had the impression that if he'd been Buddhist, he'd be engaging with Siddhartha Gautama. Or the prophet Muhammad, if a Muslim.

Since returning here – Heaven? — after leaving his physical body on the battlefield, John had a cadre of helpers, angels, guides, and spirits surrounding him with Divine love as they helped him reintegrate into non-physical.

He was in a transition state and would remain thus until he was ready to move on. From the eternal perspective, time was infinite, yet here in transition he felt its sway, its pull, and still felt connected to earth, especially his family, his sister. Though he didn't share their sadness, he felt compelled to linger, to resolve something. But what?

"This unfinished business," John began. "When will it be made clear?"

The Nazarene returned, his presence a peace-filled balm. "The choice is yours. When you're ready, you'll remember."

John nodded. "Then I think I'm ready now."

The Nazarene gave a wisp of a smile as he faded away.

John was alone on the bench when a lone stranger, a man, came out of the cornfield, leading a horse. The newcomer, a tall English knight, wore a patch emblazoned with a red cross on the front of his chain mail chest piece. His helmet obscured his facial features, but wisps of dark hair stuck out on one side.

The knight paused without speaking, as if waiting to be invited to step forward or to sit on the bench.

Hesitation clouded John's recall. "Do I know you? Are you here to protect my family?"

The knight shook his head. "You still don't remember."

As the knight turned to depart, the sun reflected a flash of green light off his helmet, just like it had eons before, and not so long ago. Images from a past war unfolded in John's mind.

Men on horseback.

Crimson stained tunics.

Bloody swords.

A promise made.

"Wait!" John stood and called out to the retreating Crusader. "I remember."

CHAPTER NINETEEN

August 2006
Chicago, Illinois

Father Nick Shelton surveyed the six-foot section of graffiti-covered brick wall in front of the Prince of Peace Youth Center. The spray-painted futuristic landscapes had been rendered in stunning detail, but the gang signs and curse words wouldn't be tolerated. Part of him longed to connect with the vigilante artists and funnel their amazing talent in other ways. Another part wondered who he was kidding.

Nick was barely holding his own with the students at the youth center, students who readily reminded him they were there under duress, fulfilling community-service requirements. They would leave as soon as their commitment was satisfied.

Nick's doubts about his transfer to Prince of Peace parish had grown exponentially over the past few weeks, leaving him more convinced that he was not the right priest for this job. Throw in his increasing bouts of high anxiety and those doubts morphed to whether he was the right man for the priesthood anymore. Oddly, those same doubts were his saving grace. That the thought of leaving was more painful than staying gave him hope. While the colloquial advice to 'pray through it' often produced more apprehension — how many times had he glibly offered that advice? — he didn't abandon his path. In fact, to combat stress, Nick had recently taken up jogging and discovered prayer and exercise were not mutually exclusive.

Out of habit, he checked his watch and spotted the Latin phrase he'd scribbled on the inside of his wrist with a permanent marker. *Acta non verba*. Deeds, not words. Actions, not thoughts.

Today Nick's actions were focused on one problem: get rid of the graffiti.

Fifteen-year-old Domingo Sanchez stopped working as soon as Nick walked up. "This cleaner isn't cleaning." Domingo tossed his scrub brush back in his bucket. Soapy water sloshed over the edge.

The two thirteen-year-olds helping Domingo threw down their brushes in solidarity. "Yeah. Isn't cleaning."

Nick plunged his hand into the bucket and grabbed a brush. He ran it lightly over the wall before handing it back to Domingo. "You're not trying to scrub the paint off. You're scrubbing away the dirt to prep the wall for primer. You're doing great, by the way."

With a teen-angst-perfected sigh, Domingo turned away and pointed the scrub brush at the younger boys. "You missed a spot. There. And there." Just like that, all three boys were working again.

Nick made a mental note to thank his best friend, Father Pete, for inspiration. Last time they spoke, Nick had openly groused to his friend. "I'm failing, Pete. Strike one: I don't speak Spanish, so seventy percent of my parishioners go elsewhere for Mass. Strike two: I'm fresh off the farm. What do I know about the lives of big city kids?"

Pete offered no sympathy. "The majority of your parish speaks English, though they prefer Spanish. Work your magic on them while you study Spanish. And as far as so-called big city kids, have you tried treating them the same way you treated Iowa kids?"

Boom! How had Nick treated his students in River Haven? He held them to a higher standard. And not just academically. He didn't make them janitors or exploit their labor, but he did require them to help with facility beautification. The difference was more than well-kept buildings. The exterior influenced the interior. As the students took more pride in their building, grades and attendance improved.

Though Nick had less than ten students in the after-school programs here in Illinois, he implemented the same philosophy. It was too soon to tell if it made a difference but judging by how Domingo insisted the younger boys do a better job, it maybe had some impact.

Domingo was a natural leader. Granted, this past year he had been more of a follower, which nearly landed him in juvenile detention, much to the dismay of his Aunt Constanza, who was the church's secretary. With Nick's help, they'd gotten Domingo assigned to Prince of Peace Youth Center for community service. More than an alternative to incarceration, the youth center offered neighborhood kids tutoring and counseling. Nick had also expanded the curriculum to include optional classes that students expressed interest in, like art and music.

"Don't know why you're bothering to paint this," Domingo said. "Just giving the taggers fresh canvas."

"We're sending a message by taking a stand against vandalism." Nick moved to a clean section of wall and pried open a paint can.

"You'll get a message right back," Domingo muttered. "In bright red spray paint."

Nick stirred the primer. By morning new graffiti might appear, but at least it would look nice for tonight's rosary service as he'd promised Constanza.

"If we get more tags, we'll paint over them," Nick told Domingo. "Change takes time. Keep the faith."

Hadn't that been the same thing Nick told Janey?

His niece's struggle with faith after John's death was a reaction so common that Nick considered *renouncing God* the missing step of grief processing. That he'd helped Janey work through those very doubts after her mother died made it tougher to be away from River Haven right now.

He'd talked with Janey yesterday, confirming that the rosary had not arrived here in Chicago, even though she'd mailed it over ten days ago. It made him sick to recall how hard Janey had taken its loss, and he felt bad for his part in encouraging her to set up a roving prayer campaign.

Nick had been ready to cancel the rosary service, but Constanza hadn't been swayed by the lost package and insisted they hold the prayer service as previously announced, which meant he needed to get busy rolling paint.

"Time's wasting," Nick said.

"All we got is time and we waste it." Domingo began rapping. "Wasting time. Chasing rhymes." His two helpers joined in.

A gifted musician and spoken word poet, Domingo could make a song out of any moment. When the teen seemed engrossed in creating music videos, Nick offered to institute a video production program at the youth center and challenged Domingo to help establish a curriculum. The teen's knowledge and passion for the project amazed Nick.

Domingo stopped singing and coached the younger boys on two-part harmony before the trio switched to the current hip-hop hit, Money Maker.

They were so good, Nick couldn't tell their voices from the original recording. When they hit the chorus, he even joined in. "Money maker. Life's a taker."

That fast the boys quit singing. Domingo grumbled under his breath. When the other two boys did the same, Nick laughed. *Follow the leader.*

The mail carrier pulled up to the curb just then. "Afternoon, Father Nick. Got a package for you. From Iowa."

"Iowa?" Domingo drifted closer and peered over Nick's shoulder. "That can't be cookies from those church ladies. Box too small."

Last week, the Ladies Society at St. Francis sent Nick a large package of homemade cookies. He'd left them on a table inside the youth center while looking for napkins, but by the time he'd returned, only one cookie had remained.

Funny how a single cookie evoked fierce homesickness. Back in River Haven, Nick had never cooked. He and Father Martin ate with parishioners who generously sent home leftovers. Here in Chicago, Nick lived on cereal and frozen microwave meals, which he didn't mind. What he missed was the company, the camaraderie of breaking bread together. Communion.

Nick accepted the box from the postman and blew out a sigh when he saw Janey's return address. His niece would be ecstatic to hear her package had arrived.

"Maybe it's diet cookies," one of the younger boys said.

"More like air cookies," Domingo joked.

"Let's see." Nick pulled the rosary out of the box. The afternoon sun made the beads sparkle.

Domingo's eyes widened. "Are those black diamonds?"

Nick shook his head, unable to draw his eyes from the rosary. The piece was even more exquisite than the photographs Janey had posted on the website. His curiosity surged. Janey shared the story about an old beggar giving John the beads, but where on earth had the beggar gotten a rosary like this?

The beads were warm from being in the mail truck all afternoon. Flicking his wrist, he allowed the rosary to untangle. The beads spun and swayed as he held it up, casting off light that seemed created from within.

Domingo reached forward, touched it, but quickly withdrew his hand. "Jesus Christ! They sent you a necklace?"

Nick frowned. "Domingo! You know that type of language is not tolerated here. Apologize."

"Sorry." If Domingo hadn't rolled his eyes, the apology might have come across as sincere.

"It's a rosary," Nick said. "You know, for prayer." The beads seemed to grow heavier, drawing his attention and amplifying his guilt. He released his irritation with Domingo. "I can see how a piece this beautiful could be mistaken as jewelry."

"You are mis-take-en." One of the younger boys snapped his fingers while singing an ad-lib tune.

Domingo's scowl deepened. "Whatever. It looks like a necklace to me. Something a girl would wear. Or a sissy."

Nick counted to ten. "Looks can be deceiving. Come to the rosary service tonight and I'll explain the story about this piece. Your aunt would be pleased. She's worked hard to put tonight's service together."

"Still sounds lame. And my time is officially up for today, so I'll leave you to gawk over that *necklace.*" Domingo stuffed earphones in before lumbering off.

The younger boys exchanged dubious glances. Nick cleared his throat. "If we can get this wall painted by four o'clock, we'd have time for a little soccer practice." The bribe worked. Nick paused long enough to send a text to Janey about the rosary and promised to call her after the service.

At five o'clock, he locked up the youth center and headed to the adjacent church, a short walk beneath a vine-covered pathway.

Built in 1910, Prince of Peace Church was in an older Hispanic suburb of southwest Chicago known as *La Frontera* – The Border. Founded by wealthy immigrants of an earthquake-stricken region of Mexico, the neighborhood flourished well into the fifties and sixties, with its own shopping district, two Catholic churches, and its own Catholic school system. However, by the eighties, only Prince of Peace Church remained open.

When jobs grew scarce in the seventies and crime rose, the well-to-do left *La Frontera,* followed by the middle class. The once vibrant business district was now a rundown ghost town.

How Prince of Peace parish kept going despite low attendance was no longer a mystery to Nick. An anonymous donor provided funding for the church with a generous stipend going to the diocese on the condition that Prince of Peace maintain a priest in residence.

Father Hernandez, whom Nick replaced, had been there over seventeen years. But when the diocese agreed to open a youth center — recommended and funded by that same anonymous source — Father Hernandez announced his retirement.

While Nick felt he was slowly establishing a rapport with some of the youth center's students, he'd struck out with the church's elderly population, who largely spoke only Spanish. It had been humbling to learn that many parishioners had boycotted Prince of Peace to protest his arrival. Though Nick resisted the transfer, he hadn't considered being unwanted himself.

Now, if many more parishioners quit coming, how could Prince of Peace remain open, donor or not? In these days of fewer priests, was it a waste of manpower and resources for Nick to remain here?

When he reached the church's front door, he groaned to read the flyer printed in English and Spanish, announcing tonight's *bilingual* prayer service for peace. He knew exactly who made the sign.

Inside, Nick headed straight for the front sanctuary where the church secretary, Constanza Sanchez, instructed two other women on setting up an easel.

In her early forties, Constanza had worked as a registered nurse before an inoperable tumor behind her eyes forced her out of her job at the hospital. She refused to let it stop her from fulfilling her duties as church secretary.

"I love what I do here, Father," she'd said. "And the wages help my family."

Though Constanza had no husband or children, she was the primary caregiver to Domingo and his younger brother, and her widowed father, an old curmudgeon who didn't seem supportive of his daughter or his grandsons.

How much longer Constanza could maintain the status quo was a question they'd have to deal with soon. Just last week the vision in her left eye vanished, leaving her with a thin sliver of vision in her right eye. "Enough to serve the Lord," she insisted cheerfully.

Her doctor, however, warned that sliver would also soon fail.

"Father Nick, you brought our rosary?" Constanza turned in his direction.

"Yes. And I noticed the sign out front says the service will be bilingual."

"Sí." Constanza smiled. "I will translate your words."

And remind everyone I can't speak Spanish.

Catching his own negative thoughts, Nick paused and repeated his mantra of late: *Father, forgive me.* "That's thoughtful of you, Constanza. Thank you." He handed her the box from Janey. "Here."

"Didn't I tell you this would show up in time?" Constanza made a clucking noise that sounded a bit like *oh ye of little faith.*

From the moment Nick shared Janey's rosary story, Constanza talked nonstop about the privilege of having the inaugural prayer service in Chicago. "How fitting to have prayers for peace at Prince of Peace Church," she'd said.

When the rosary did not show up in the mail on the day expected, her optimism hadn't wavered. She'd even predicted a told-you-so moment. Nick was grateful she didn't know about the backup rosary he had stashed in his briefcase.

Constanza's excited chatter ceased when she withdrew the rosary from the box. "Sweet Mary! It's exquisite." She held the beads an inch from her face to examine them. "These beads are so warm and bright. Miranda. Dolce. Come help me."

The other women came over and took the rosary. Constanza followed, instructing them on how to arrange it on the display board they had propped on an easel. "I want it pinned so everyone can see it as we pray."

Nick checked his watch and grimaced as he felt his chest tighten, the familiar opening salvo of an anxiety attack. He inhaled through his nose, slow breaths. He didn't need this right now. The service was scheduled to begin in five minutes. Perhaps it was a good thing no one had shown up.

No one? Forgive me again, Father. The four of them would do fine.

He heard Constanza laugh at something one of the others said. He moved forward. As he approached the completed display, the rosary's beauty struck him anew. A sense of calm settled over him as he gazed at the beads.

Even with the dim interior lights, the beads sparkled, making him wonder again about the rosary's origin. Nick's cursory research on the rosary had yielded nothing, but now that he had the actual piece, he could examine it for identifiable marks or clues about the maker.

His wristwatch alarm beeped, signaling that it was time to begin the rosary service.

"Constanza, if we can–"

The sound of the front doors opening interrupted Nick. He turned and smiled as two older couples entered the church. And then there were eight. *Thank you, Lord.*

"*Hola.* Welcome." Nick motioned them to the front pews before moving to help Constanza sit in a chair beside the rosary display. Then he addressed the small group.

"Before we begin, I'd like to tell you a story about this rosary." He paused to let Constanza interpret his words. "As you know, I came here from a small town in Southeast Iowa, where I was born. My last official duty at St. Francis' Church was a funeral Mass for my nephew, Army Specialist John McKay, who was killed in battle in Iraq. It is believed he received this rosary from a mysterious old man he saved in Baghdad. John sent the rosary home to his sister, Janey, asking that she pray for peace."

He stopped to allow Constanza to catch up. "Janey has launched a website to honor her brother's last request and wants to see the rosary prayed in every state. You see, John had a goal of hiking through every state in America, a journey this rosary will now make in his place. I am deeply honored that Prince of Peace is hosting the first service. Let us pray that the Lord will heal our world of the evils that rob His children of peace."

Just as Nick made the sign of the cross, a few more people

entered the church, slipping into pews in the back. He nodded but didn't interrupt the service to greet them.

He and Constanza found an even stop and start rhythm. He announced each mystery — a particular moment in the life of Jesus — and then listened to her reverent translation, her enunciation making each syllable musical. They prayed the Hail Mary in unison, in English and Spanish, their voices transcending the limitations of language. The smallness of the group gave the service the intimate feeling he recalled from childhood.

Nick had grown up in a devout family who prayed the rosary regularly, but it had been his Aunt Luanne who taught him to *feel* prayer. She'd explained the miracles of Jesus' life so rapturously that even as a child, he could envision each. That Luanne's stutter disappeared completely when she held her rosary was part of the magic.

By the time the service was finished, Nick felt filled with appreciation. He glanced at Constanza. "Please tell everyone I am grateful for their attendance tonight." He turned back to the audience as she translated. "And let us give thanks to our Heavenly Father for the blessing of peace."

Constanza spoke, but abruptly stopped. Nick looked over his shoulder just as she slumped forward, eyes closed. He dashed to catch her as she fell from her seat and eased her unconscious body gently to the floor. Gasps of alarm echoed in the church.

Nick felt for a pulse at her carotid artery just as Domingo rushed forward from the shadows. Dropping to his knees beside his aunt, the teen grabbed her hand.

"What is wrong with my aunt?" Domingo looked at Nick with panicked, tear-filled eyes. "She fainted last night at home but didn't want me to tell anyone."

"Her pulse is strong," Nick reassured. "But we need to get her to a hospital. Go into the sacristy and call 9-1-1. I'll stay with her."

Constanza's eyes fluttered open. "No ambulance. I'm fine, Father." When she spotted Domingo, her face broke into an enormous smile. She reached up to touch his cheek.

"You passed out seeing me in church, right?" Domingo tried to joke, but the tears in his eyes reflected love and fear.

"No." Constanza's gaze darted from Domingo to Nick before she started to sob. "You won't believe this, but I am seeing clearly. Quick, help me up."

"Take it easy, Constanza," Nick insisted. "You just passed out. I still think a call to the paramedics is wise."

Constanza shook her head and coughed.

Nick spoke to Domingo. "Get your aunt some water, please."

Constanza laughed. "Bring me holy water. You don't understand, Father Nick." She motioned to the small crowd now gathered around. Everyone had rushed forward when Constanza fell.

She pointed to where the rosary was mounted. "I looked at the beads during our prayer and they glowed. Did you see it? Then I felt a tingling in my head, so sharp I had to close my eyes. Now my eyesight has been restored. It is a miracle!"

————

LATER, when Nick was alone in the small rectory across the street from the church, he spread the rosary out on his desk. The incident left him shaken. Constanza, who had started using a white probing cane and took slow, cautious steps, charged forward unaided after the rosary service, wanting to see the stars in the night skies. "It's a miracle," she'd exclaimed over and over.

Was it? Had tonight been the first genuine miracle Nick had ever seen? Sure, he'd witnessed births and beautiful sunrises and doubters who'd embraced Jesus as their Savior, but those things had explanations. Constanza's now being able to see? No explanation. He touched the rosary. Warm again: always warm. It defied logic, but wasn't that very defiance a hallmark of the miraculous? Could this... this sacred piece...be the answer for him, too? The answer to his waning belief?

Doubt crept in as it always did when he contemplated his own faith. *This is about Constanza, not me. About a miraculous claim of healing.*

When he asked what Constanza remembered before fainting, she said the rosary had glowed with a green light before she blacked out. Prior to that, she offered a silent prayer of gratitude to Mother Mary. "I didn't ask for healing, Father. I asked for peace."

No one else reported that they'd seen the beads glow. However, even in low light, the black beads glittered. Had Constanza's compromised vision interpreted that as a flash of light? Everyone at tonight's service clamored for more details on the rosary. They'd also pleaded with Nick to schedule another rosary service so they could bring friends and relatives. Their excitement buoyed him and reminded him that he needed to ask Janey about keeping the rosary a few extra days.

He picked up his phone and called her. "How's my favorite niece?"

"Your only niece is fine." Janey let out a noisy breath. "I was so glad to hear the rosary wasn't lost. It's a miracle it arrived on time for your service."

"Speaking of miracles, something amazing happened this evening. Our church secretary regained her eyesight after tonight's rosary service. I can't quantify it as a miracle per se, but it's caused quite a stir here. My parishioners would like to keep the rosary for a second service, if that's okay."

"One of John's Army buddies has scheduled a prayer service in Cincinnati, one week from today and he's calling me daily to follow up," Janey said. "If you can arrange a second service within a day or two and ship it out immediately overnight, that should work. But the rosary must be in Cincinnati on the 6th. And ship it with signature required so we can track it. I never want to lose it again."

When they finished talking, Nick grabbed a magnifying glass to examine the rosary. Under closer inspection, the silver inlaid design appeared different on each bead, making him wonder if they were symbols versus decoration.

He pushed back to study the rosary from afar. Earlier, something about it struck him as odd. Now he realized the center medallion of the Virgin Mary looked out of place. Compared to the rosary's elaborate beads and crucifix, the medallion appeared rather plain, though it didn't detract from the rosary's beauty. There was something compelling about this piece, a magnetism that quickened the breath.

Tomorrow he would send detailed photos to one of his old professors from seminary who lived nearby but was currently out of the country. Professor Birdson claimed to know more about Catholic art and relics than the Vatican. If this rosary had a special significance, Birdson would know.

CHAPTER TWENTY

September 2006
Dallas, Texas

For Layton Burnet, going home meant taking a cab to the ten-by-twenty storage unit he leased near the Dallas-Fort Worth airport. It had been past midnight when his plane landed, and after twenty-four hours of flights and layovers in Europe and the United States, he was exhausted. He checked into a motel instead, hoping to catch a few hours of sleep, but insomnia had its own agenda. Then he'd made the mistake of responding to a text from his ex, Sharlene.

> I would have met you at the airport, she wrote. Given you a
> proper hero's welcome. Let's hook up. It's been too long.

He turned her down and ended up shutting off his phone. She didn't take "no" well and historically, Layton always caved in. He and Sharlene had been an on-and-off couple since ninth grade. He'd proposed in high school but realized his mistake at the same time she did. They shared a lengthy history that needed to remain just that: history.

By seven AM, Layton struggled one-handed to raise the garage door of his storage unit and current physical residence. It had been six weeks and five surgeries since that terrible battle and he still had a week of wearing an immobilizing sling. He wasn't sure the sling would survive that long. He'd already jarred his shoulder getting out of the cab and it throbbed like a jackhammer on a New York City street that had probably seen just as much reconstruction.

First thing, he eased his shiny black pickup out of the unit and let it idle. Even after sixteen months of non-use, his late model Ford F-150 cranked right up. It was the only useful advice his late father ever gave him. "Always buy a Ford pickup. It will outlast anything."

At the time, Layton Senior compared his own beat-up Ford to relationships. While it was true his father's F-150 had been with him for over thirty years, man and car had seen plenty of break-ups. When the truck wasn't in the body shop from the umpteenth fender bender, it was impounded for DUIs. The truck had been the only constant in Dad's life, right up to the day he died after totaling it.

Grabbing a broom, Layton attempted to sweep out the dead bugs accumulated near the unit's door, but with his arm braced, the motion was awkward.

Next, he rifled through the clothes packed away in plastic tubs. He'd lost weight in the hospital, so nothing would fit, but the sight of his favorite Tony Lama boots made him smile. Well-worn and comfortable, the boots slid on like sun-warmed butter.

Working slowly, he repacked his Army duffel, keeping out only the things needed for his trip. When his bag from Iraq first arrived at the hospital in Germany, he'd ignored it until it was time to find clothes for the flight back to the States. That's when he discovered a cache of John's stuff intermingled with his. They'd shared a foot-locker, so the mix up was understandable. However, seeing his best friend's belongings was a painful reminder of what had happened, those he lost, and what lay ahead.

After stowing his bags in the truck, Layton tried to straighten the storage unit. With the truck out, there wasn't much left. A ratty-looking sofa that doubled as his bed when he'd been forced to crash here in those last weeks prior to entering the Army. There were two bins of clothes, one for summer gear and one for winter. The cheap metal toolbox from his high school stint as a mechanic sat atop the tarp-covered wooden tool chest that belonged to his late grandfather. Only a few of Gramps' woodworking tools remained, but Layton treasured them.

He eyed the cardboard boxes along the back wall. One held personal memorabilia, mostly from the Army. The other boxes held some dishes and the few housewares he'd packed up from the last apartment his mom lived in before she OD'd. What little survived his childhood was in those boxes. An unfamiliar wave of nostalgia left Layton with the urge to open them and go through the old photos. Revisit the ghosts of the past.

He took a step forward and then stopped. When had he grown soft and sentimental? Something else to blame on John McKay. Layton shot a dirty look at the crude sign taped on the wall above the sofa. HOME SWEET STORAGE UNIT. John had put it there as a joke and at the time it seemed hilarious. Now it angered him. *Why did you have to die?*

That last battle took five of the finest and left three others critically wounded. Lives had been destroyed, families devastated. It was the only time Layton was glad he had no family. None that cared, anyway.

His cell phone buzzed. He glanced at the screen before answering. "Hey, Teddy."

"Dude! Where are you? I've been waiting for you."

Layton sank down on the sofa. He'd talked with Fallon twice yesterday. "I'm in Texas, man. I just got in last night, remember? I won't be in Cincinnati until next week."

Danny Carpenter hinted that Teddy Fallon was having issues.

Carpenter visited Fallon twice and both times Fallon's mother begged Carpenter to help her son, claiming he was mixing drugs and alcohol.

"Oh. That's cool. Hold on." Fallon lowered the phone and shouted at his mother to check the mail. "The rosary isn't coming here. It will be sent to the church," a woman's voice explained.

Fallon spoke into the phone again. "Hello? You still there?"

"Yeah, but I need to take off soon."

"Get here as soon as you can," Fallon said. "Janey McKay is sending me that rosary John had. Maybe you'll be here for the service."

Carpenter had also mentioned the rosary to Layton, but in a different context. Carpenter didn't like that Janey's website featured information on John's squad and hoped Layton could speak to her about it.

Layton tightened his grip on the phone. "Listen, Teddy, I'll call you when I'm headed to Cincinnati, but I won't be there for the rosary service."

He ended the call and climbed to his feet. At the door, he gave the unit one last look before locking it. Given his uncertain future with the Army — everything depended on his shoulder healing one hundred percent — he could live back here again. God, he hoped not. He was on medical leave while doing post-surgery care and was eager to begin physical therapy, to put all this behind him.

Climbing into his truck, he sped off. It felt good to be behind the wheel and in control. Twenty minutes later, he pulled into the Tall Grass Care Center, a small, private nursing home.

Betty Saunders, the woman who ran the facility, greeted Layton with a smile. "I almost didn't recognize you. Welcome back! But what happened to your arm?"

He hated the question. "Nothing really. A little break."

She ushered him into her office and motioned him to a seat in front of a desk. "Will you be in town for a while?"

"No. I'm headed back to my base in Illinois. How's my grandmother doing?"

Betty retrieved a file before sitting. "Her dementia has progressed, as the doctors warned. She has fewer lucid moments and is no longer responding to the standard prescriptions. Now that you're back in the States, I can arrange a phone consultation with her physician if you'd like."

Layton nodded. "Give them my cell phone number."

She handed him a stack of papers. "Here are the receipts for the last quarter. Let me know if you have questions."

"Thanks." He sent the facility monthly payments to cover what his grandmother's Social Security and Medicare did not.

When Betty opened the folder bearing his grandmother's name, he noticed his letters clipped inside. They'd gone unopened for nearly two years, ever since her dementia began. *"You still need to write her,"* John McKay had insisted. *"It's the right thing."*

Was it? It obviously didn't matter.

"Would you like to see her?" Betty asked.

No. "Sure." It was the right thing to say.

"I'll walk you—" Betty's phone rang, the sharp buzz catching her attention.

"You can take it." Layton pushed to his feet. "I'll find her."

Betty glanced at the wall clock. "This time of day, she should be in the rec room."

Layton strode down the hall. Even though he'd only been there once before, he remembered the layout. In the recreation room, he found his grandmother sitting in a wheelchair, staring out the window. She looked the same as last time, but frailer. And she'd hate knowing he thought that.

Or would she? A lot of time had passed, and people changed. He was proof of that.

He forced a smile. "Hi, Grandma! It's Layton."

At first, he thought she hadn't heard him. Then she turned her head and gave him a confused look.

"Laylon?"

"Layton," he corrected. She still did not recognize him, so he added, "Amelia's son."

At the mention of her daughter, Grandma nodded. "Amelia will be back soon. I don't know what's keeping her."

Layton let it pass. The last time he reminded Grandma that his mom was dead, she'd gone berserk.

"Are they treating you okay here?" This was the tough part, making general conversation. "Still playing bingo on Tuesday nights?"

"I don't like bingo. Amelia's told them that a dozen times." Grandma looked away now, uninterested in talking with a stranger. Heck, she hadn't been interested when she'd known him.

"All right. I'll head out, but if you need anything, tell Miss Betty."

Before he could escape, his grandmother transformed, a frown replacing the passive line of her mouth. Layton braced for it. He knew this Grandma.

"Go ahead and run off. Just like your father did," she hissed. "He treated poor Amelia horribly. Then you came along. Having a child so young ruined her life. She had such promise."

Grandma turned away in a huff and for a moment Layton remembered being ten years old, cruising back alleys in a stolen car, searching for his mother, desperate to find her before she scored another fix of meth. So much broken promise.

As he backed out of the room, his grandmother looked at him once again, but this time she was docile. And Layton was a stranger.

"Who are you?" Grandma asked.

Seeing her sudden confusion evoked sympathy. He snorted. He had the McKays to blame for that one, too. Their salt-of-the-earth goodness had rubbed off on Layton.

He released a breath, grateful to leave on a neutral note. "No one special. Just passing through, ma'am."

And thus begins the road trip through Hell, he thought as he fired up his truck a few minutes later.

His next stop was the Dallas-Fort Worth National Cemetery where the cremated remains of Chris Worth had been interred. The map Layton got from the cemetery's information kiosk led him to the exact location. Eventually there would be a flat bronze grave marker with Worth's name, like the others in this section. Tears filled Layton's eyes as he looked out over the gently rolling hills.

Worth died that day in a rocket blast that hit right in front of Layton. The same blast that injured Fallon. Layton gritted his teeth against the jarring last memory of that blast, recalling instead Worth's crazy Lone Star humor. *It's so hot in Texas, the trees are whistling for the dogs. It's so hot in Texas, the chickens are laying hard-boiled eggs.* Worth knew them all. And with his passing, Texas was not quite as big.

Layton saluted. "Rest easy, my friend."

He drove north for several hours to Wichita, Kansas, and the gravesite of Ricky Sturk. Sturk had been point man that day. The first to die. The tallest guy in their squad, Sturk joked about providing shade for the rest of them. Knowing that Sturk died instantly made his death no easier to bear. Just as knowing that Sturk's assassin died immediately thereafter brought no justice and left a hollow sense of vengeance.

Layton met Sturk's mother at a coffee shop. Despondent after losing her only child, Mrs. Sturk asked two questions: why were US soldiers there in the first place, and what purpose did her son's death serve? Layton's explanation about saving others from current and future atrocities in Iraq fell on deaf ears. Mrs. Sturk cut the visit short.

From Kansas, Layton drove west to Fort Collins, Colorado, where Donald Livingston had been interred in a private grave on the family's ranch. Livingston had been crushed along with Preach Sheridan when the school building collapsed. Livingston used to talk nonstop about doubling the size of his father's hardware store.

Livingston's family was warm and welcoming, his parents and two older sisters hungry for details. Layton tried to answer their questions with minimal deference to the ongoing CID investigation. The Livingstons insisted he stay and after a delicious meal, gave him a tour of the area. The Livingston family had established a homestead back in the eighteen-hundreds, and their sense of place within the community was tangible. The only sense of community Layton ever had was at the Second Precinct in Dallas where the cops fed him from vending machines as they waited on child services while his dad slept it off in jail again.

Layton left Colorado and drove through a fierce rainstorm before reaching the tiny town of Wall, South Dakota. Marc Sheridan, aka Preach, claimed Wall as his hometown. Preach took a lot of ribbing because of the way he tossed scripture around and mispronounced all the names in the Bible, but every head in their squad bowed when he offered prayer before and after each mission. Preach knew his way around a prayer and planned to use his GI Bill to attend divinity school. If the Hereafter was everything Preach believed, then Layton hoped The Man himself was schooling his friend. Preach deserved no less.

Unfortunately, there wasn't a grave to visit in South Dakota. *Yet.* Preach joined the Army straight out of foster care and had no family. Zero. At least Layton had Grandma and a crazy second cousin, someone to claim his remains and maybe publish an obituary before fighting over his truck.

Layton snapped a photo of the Wall Drug Store's oversized Jacka-lope statue. How many times had Preach and Layton debated which state had the biggest Jackalope? "You win, Preach."

Preach once said if he couldn't be buried beneath that statue, they could just scatter his ashes in a soybean field.

"I got your back." Somehow Layton would see that Preach got a proper grave.

Unable to sleep, Layton left South Dakota and drove eleven hours straight to Iowa, his next destination. The one he dreaded and craved the most.

It was midafternoon when he reached St. Francis' cemetery in

River Haven. He paused near the entrance, scanning the neatly manicured acres of eternal rest. Locating John McKay's grave had been as easy as finding the others. The telltale mound of fresh-tilled earth beneath a massive pile of rotted funeral flowers.

The enormity of what happened in battle that day, of all he'd lost, hit Layton like a wrecking ball in the solar plexus, leaving him sweating and nauseous, setting off his shoulder as if he'd just been hit. He came here alone to face down the demons eating his soul. His survival came at a cost: remembering it forever.

He sauntered to the gravesite, his boots feeling as if they were encased in cement. Once there, he dropped his backpack to the ground before shoving his good hand into his jeans pocket. The uneven spaded soil still had that ashes to ashes, damp smell that he associated with cemeteries.

Like the other graves he'd visited, a small US flag was staked into the ground where the headstone would eventually go. John's would be a massive marble thing, Layton guessed as he looked at the other headstones in the McKay family section. Seven generations meant they had a mini ranch right here.

He cleared his throat and focused on the flag as he talked. "Sorry, I missed your funeral, bro. I've been making the rounds, visiting everyone. Saved the best for last, though. Sergeant Boswell and Carpenter send their regards. They're already back at Fort DeWald. Fallon is at his mom's in Ohio and having a real rough time." Fallon had called a half dozen more times and after the sixth call, Layton let it go to voicemail. "I heard Corporal Lovett is still comatose. Not good, man. And Ollie Fitz, you'd never know he'd been injured. He's already back overseas. Never enough translators, remember?"

Layton looked around, confirming his truck was the only vehicle in sight. Then he kicked at a clod of dirt and stomped the ground, not caring if it was disrespectful. "You lied to me. Told me you were okay. It should have been me! Not you!"

Grief constricted his airway, cutting off his voice. *I should leave before someone sees me and thinks I'm desecrating your grave.*

Except his feet wouldn't budge. Sinking to his knees, he leaned forward as the memory of that last fight replayed. As man after man fell, Layton wanted to take out every single enemy fighter to avenge his friends. A sob rose in his throat. Unable to hold it off any longer, he gave in to misery, dropping his head as the tears flowed.

When a hand touched his shoulder, Layton sprang up, startled. The sudden move jarred his arm, leaving him wincing in pain. He turned, embarrassed, quickly wiping his face.

No one was there. And yet the touch had been so real. So familiar.

"Hello?" He looked around, but the cemetery was as deserted as when he'd arrived.

Must have been the wind. Or a muscle cramp. It didn't take much to make him jump these days.

Turning back to John's grave, he cleared his throat and straightened. *Sorry, bro. This sucks. I'm second-guessing myself on everything now. Should I have let Fallon die to save you? They all said I did the right thing, but what if I could have saved you? And what do I tell your family?*

The last time Layton saw John's family was just before they deployed. Everyone asked Layton to look out for John.

He'd let them all down.

But how had the McKay's responded? They reached out first, every one of them. Ward sent an email to "his southern son." Matt and Perry referred to him as a brother to John and by default to them. Janey flooded his email inbox with frantic queries after the incident, begging him to respond, to let her know he was okay.

He wasn't. Now, he was damaged goods with a sketchy future. What did he have to offer a woman like Janey – provided she could ever pardon him for not protecting her brother? Forgiveness was a rare trait in a McKay.

And reality check: the kiss he and Janey had shared, their agreement to talk later, meant little compared to Layton's promise to John to protect her.

Layton reached into his pocket and pulled out an envelope. He again focused on the flag stuck in the ground. John had been more than a best friend. He'd been a confidant, advisor. Moral compass.

"Dude, my re-up papers arrived while I was in the hospital, marked 'On hold pending medical review.' They're holding up my OCS application, too. I should have completed my associate degree this summer, but I missed all my class finals while I was in Landstuhl. My shoulder still isn't right. What do I do if the med board cycles me out?"

The wind caught the envelope. It flew from his hand and landed on a spray of dead carnations. As he bent low to grab it, his gaze leveled on a small, white cardboard cross sticking up on a wooden skewer, nearly hidden in the rotted flowers.

BURN IN HELL, GOVERNMENT PAWN, it read.

Layton snatched it. Even before spotting the Justice Freedom Association logo, he knew who had left it. The JFA were well known for leaving their blasphemous calling cards at soldiers' graves. Donald Livingston's father had a restraining order issued against a Colorado JFA group that continued to protest outside the Livingston's hardware store under the guise of free speech. *Right.*

Straightening, Layton methodically scanned the rows of headstones then quickly made his way around the graveyard, plucking up the white hate-filled crosses left at every headstone bearing a military emblem. He tossed them in the trash before returning to John's grave. Whoever did that better hope they did not run into Layton Burnet.

Opening his backpack, he tugged out a bottle of Gran Patron Platinum Tequila. As he had at his last four stops, he loosened the cap. "I dumped Preach's shot at the Jackalope's feet. Seemed fitting. I should have brought you a beer, buddy."

John had sworn off tequila after that last party, joked that just saying the word made him sick.

"Always said I'd buy your first drink when we were stateside. But you left the party too soon. You saved my life, bro, and I swear I'll never forget my promises to you. For you, my man." Layton held the bottle up in a toast and watched the sunlight refract through the clear liquor before tipping it and emptying it on John's grave. "To my hero."

CHAPTER TWENTY-ONE

September 2006
River Haven, Iowa

Janey ripped the plastic wrap from the case of motor oil before sliding it onto the metal shelf. Even sealed, the bottles emitted the pungent petroleum odor she associated with the parts department, a foul scent she couldn't wait to shower off each day.

This afternoon she worked in the oven, the rear section of the McKay Equipment warehouse that never cooled and never saw daylight. Perfect territory for trolls like her brothers.

Matt and Perry had gone into overprotective mode following the FBI's visit last week after Agent Holmes confirmed that Farid Zaman's previous retaliations had included family members of Zaman's sworn enemies. It didn't matter that the instance had occurred 6,500 miles away, in Iraq. Janey's father and brothers closed ranks, refusing to let her out of their sight. Especially Matt. *Mr. I-smell-a-conspiracy* wanted her close by, but not out in public. Matt also suggested she stay home for the fall college semester.

She refused. "That's giving in. I won't let Zaman scare me.

Besides, Gemma and I have been planning this for months. I won't let her down."

Her brothers weren't above playing dirty. "Would you endanger Gemma?" Matt asked.

Then her brothers played the *we-can't-worry-Dad* card. Familial guilt trumped all. Janey's weakness was the people she loved. At the last minute, she enrolled in online classes, emphasizing it was only for one semester. Though disappointed, Gemma understood and easily found another roommate. That Janey's brothers acted as if they'd won made her mad, though.

She grabbed another case of oil and scanned the bar code to update inventory. Her name was being called across the intercom again, but this time she ignored it and slammed the last of the bottles onto the shelf. If her brothers would quit paging her every five minutes, she could have been done an hour ago.

Her hand caught the edge of the metal rack, slicing her finger. She clenched her fist against the pain as she bent over to gather the trash from the floor. When she straightened, she overcorrected and cracked her head on a shelf brace. Pain blasted through her skull.

Screw this. Her brothers were full of it if they thought she was doing this again tomorrow. In fact, as soon as she finished here, she'd page them and tell them that.

From the corner of her eye, she spotted movement one aisle over. Better yet, she'd tell them in person.

Misty, one of the cashiers from up front, called out. "Hello? Janey? Are you in here?"

She wiped her hands on her jeans and dashed around the corner. "Yes, and you can tell my brother I said—"

Janey jerked to a full stop after nearly running into Layton Burnet.

The room tilted as the weight of a dream come true hit her square in the abdomen. *Layton.*

"Hello, darlin'." He grinned, his smile the same kiss-me-now curve that taunted her sleep.

Afraid to blink for fear he'd disappear, she took in every detail. He looked taller than she remembered, his close-cut hair even more golden. Then he peeled off his aviator sunglasses, giving her a glimpse of the sexy green eyes she'd missed. Those precious eyes looked haunted, like they'd seen too much suffering, witnessed too much death. The black circles beneath his eyes attested to a lack of sleep, and his gaunt cheeks screamed tension. The button-down shirt he wore hung on his shoulders, emphasizing his weight loss and hiding God knew what injuries. His left arm was immobilized with a block and sling. Most important — he was *here. Now. Finally.* She trembled.

"Are you okay?" Layton's gaze dropped. "You're bleeding." He grabbed her hand. "Where's a first aid kit?"

"It's nothing. I'm so glad to see you!" She closed the distance, then stopped short. "Can I hug you?"

"Thought you'd never ask." He stepped closer.

Careful to avoid his bad arm, she moved to his right side and hugged him fiercely. *Do not cry. Do not cry.* "I can't believe you're here. Welcome home!"

Layton's good arm encircled her and drew her in. "That's so good to hear."

She melted against him, her eyes squeezed tightly shut to anchor the memory. Of all the hugs she'd received since losing John, *this* was the one she'd needed. The one she had longed for. Layton's embrace tightened, holding her against his side. She felt the warmth of his skin, smelled the spicy scent of his aftershave. The edge of his dog tags hidden beneath his shirt pressed against the half-heart pendant buried beneath her shirt.

Out of nowhere came the torrents of tears as weeks of unspoken apprehension sought release. She buried her face against his chest, her breath uneven between huge sobs. "I thought you forgot about me."

"Never." He pulled her even closer. His lips brushed her ear as he whispered. "I wish I could've been here sooner. God, I'm so sorry about John."

The thought that John could no longer come between them was a bittersweet reminder of why Layton was here now. Conflict strafed her senses. Was it wrong to be so excited to see him? Should she be more restrained, more respectful of the reason he'd come here alone?

Behind them, Misty cleared her throat. "Well, then, I guess I'll be going. But I'll let Matt know you came by."

Janey stepped back in disbelief as the metal door clanged shut behind Misty. "You haven't seen Matt and Perry? Have you been to the farm?"

"Nope. I was on my way there when I spotted your car out front and, uh, had to stop. I figured you'd be back at school already. The cashier said your brothers were on a conference call, but when I asked about you, you'd think I'd asked for the safe's combination. Luckily, Misty recognized me and gave an all clear. Is something going on?"

"Other than my brothers being McKays?" Janey held her breath when the overhead speaker cackled again, but the page was for someone else. Still, Misty would make sure her brothers knew Layton arrived, and Janey wasn't ready to share. "Let's go grab a cold drink." *And some privacy.*

"Is the Dairy Freeze still open? I could go for a Coke float."

She smiled. Her brothers were avowed root beer fans. Coke floats had been a Janey and Layton thing. "This way." She grabbed her bag and felt around for sunglasses as they ducked out the rear exit.

"I'll drive." They both said at once.

"Come with me." Layton pressed his key fob, unlocking the doors to his truck. "This sling impedes everything, but at least it doesn't interfere with driving."

That he drove his truck meant he'd already been to Texas. Had he gone to see Sharlene first? Janey fought a wave of jealousy as she settled into the passenger side of Layton's Ford. Before she could speak, her cell phone rang. Certain it was one of her brothers, she glanced at the screen.

"It's Teddy Fallon," she said.

"Before he asks, I don't want to talk," Layton said.

Janey nodded before answering. "Hi, Teddy. I'm at work, so I can't stay on long." Since they were still in the parking lot, it wasn't a lie. And she already knew why he was calling.

"I hate to keep bugging you, but I haven't received the rosary yet," Teddy said.

She and Teddy had this conversation daily and each time he didn't seem to remember previous calls. "They should deliver it to your church today. I checked on it before I left the house this morning."

"Thank you. I'll ask my mother to stop by the church," Teddy said.

That he hung up without further conversation also wasn't surprising. She muted her phone before putting it away, wanting no further interruptions.

Layton had pulled out and headed toward the Dairy Freeze Drive-In, less than a mile away. He cleared his throat. "Before you think I was being rude, I have talked with Fallon several times since getting back. But frankly, he calls a lot. I think he's having memory issues or something."

"I suspected as much. He sounds confused occasionally." And she didn't want to be rude, either, but Teddy wasn't the person she wanted to discuss right now. "Tell me about you. How long have you been back in the States?" *Did you see Sharlene?* Janey bit her tongue to keep from asking.

"Three, four days. I flew into Dallas and stayed long enough to grab a few things from storage and check on my grandmother. Then I headed out to visit the other families." Layton's voice lowered. "I needed to pay respects to the others we lost – Sturk, Livingston, Worth, and Preach."

Heaviness constricted her heart. It had been excruciating to lose

her brother, but what had it been like to lose five friends? Five broth-
ers-in-arms? "That had to be a tough journey."

"Yes." Layton took his eyes off the road and gave her a quick
glance. "But coming back to Iowa without John is the hardest." He
slowed at the Dairy Freeze. "Do you mind if we just stay in the
truck?"

"I'd prefer that."

Layton pulled into one of the drive-in slots. After he ordered two
large floats, he turned back to Janey. "I don't know where to start.
There's so much to say."

She motioned toward his sling. "Start with you. How are you?
And by that, I mean how badly were you hurt, and why were you in
the hospital so long?"

"You want more than 'I'm fine,' eh?" He held up his hand,
signaling a pause while he lowered the window long enough to
grab their floats and pay the car hop. "Cheers." He passed one
drink to Janey and then took a long sip from his before continuing.
"The first couple weeks in the hospital, I was out of it. I took two
shots in the upper chest and shoulder that day and I've had five
reconstructive surgeries. Doc says my scars have scars. I had a
couple setbacks with snapped tendons and bone fragments, but I
hope to be cleared next week to start physical therapy and then
return to active duty."

"Back overseas?" Her voice rose in panic.

"No. I'll return to Fort DeWald until my OCS application goes
through."

She fiddled with her straw. "Teddy Fallon said you almost didn't
make it."

"Take what Fallon says with a grain of salt. He's having setbacks
of his own."

"I realize that, but those first few weeks, the Army wouldn't
disclose anything, and I was so worried. Teddy's fiancée was the first
person to confirm that you were in Germany at the hospital. It was
awful not knowing what happened to you."

Layton grew serious. "I can't control what the Army does or doesn't do, but I wouldn't have worried you intentionally."

His words soothed her. "Outside of an autopsy report, the Army has disclosed little about John's death. I swear if I hear the words 'it's under investigation' one more time, I'll punch the person. Not you, of course." Janey couldn't keep the edge from her voice. "Sorry. My frustration level has been off the charts."

"Don't apologize. I'll tell you and your family what I know. Just keep in mind that what I share is my opinion only and shouldn't be repeated." He looked out the windshield, as if searching for thoughts he'd prefer to forget. Then he sighed and turned back to meet her gaze. "John was the bravest person I've ever known. Maybe the craziest, too."

"Both."

"The day he died..." Layton closed his eyes briefly. "Honestly, it happened so fast it's hard to recall everything. When adrenaline takes over, your focus narrows. We had been on patrol and stopped to check a school construction project. Almost immediately we came under a rocket attack."

"Was it a random strike? Or did they know you were there? I've seen Farid Zaman's video. I know about the *fatwa*."

"I don't believe it was random. More likely opportunity meets preparedness. Zaman has networks over there, fighters and weaponry cached at various spots to allow his followers to mobilize quickly. I suspect we were spotted at a public market earlier that same morning. Someone followed us to the school site and tipped off Zaman. His militia closed in quickly."

Janey kept quiet, not wanting to miss a word. After weeks of tortured waiting, she would finally get answers.

"We'd split into three groups before the attack, so it was hard keeping track of everyone once it started. John had the radio, so he and two others were with Corporal Lovett, but even they got separated. I heard Ollie Fitz shout that he'd been hit. I saw John pick Ollie up in a firefighter's hold and start running. We were all under fire at that point, and many men were down. I was helping Fallon, who'd lost a leg from a rocket explosion and was bleeding out. There was another explosion that leveled most of the building. When the smoke cleared, John was on the ground. I didn't know where Ollie was, but I've since learned your brother threw Ollie clear of the blast."

Janey could barely breathe. The scene he described mirrored the worst of her nightmares where she'd searched similar battlefields looking for John and Layton. "Did John die...immediately?"

Layton shook his head. "He was conscious and shouted out that he was okay. He even saved my life, shot an insurgent sneaking in from behind. At that point I had no idea John was seriously injured."

"Until you got to him?"

"I had to stay with Fallon." Layton pinched the bridge of his nose. "Danny Carpenter tried to get to John but took a hit. Then I went down. I honestly don't know what happened beyond that point. I was told support arrived, but the only thing I remember was being loaded onto a helicopter sometime afterwards. I didn't learn for days that John and the others had died."

A sharp rap on the window made Janey jump. She swiveled and found Perry and Matt outside her door. Layton was already climbing out of the truck to greet her brothers.

Janey got out of the truck and watched Matt carefully embrace Layton.

"Welcome home," Matt said before shooting Janey an accusing look. "Though God knows how long this one would have kept you tied up. If Misty hadn't tipped us off, you might have gone missing for hours."

"And Dad's eager to see you," Perry interjected.

"We all have been," Matt said.

Perry motioned Janey close before reaching out and brushing her jaw. He held up a finger dark with oil.

She caught her reflection in his mirrored sunglasses and grimaced. She probably smelled as bad as she looked.

"Perry will take me to get my car." She motioned to Layton. "You and Matt can go to the farm."

"Sure thing," Matt said. "I need to run back by the store first. Tell Dad we won't be long."

As soon as Janey was alone with Perry, he launched into lecture mode. She ignored him, still trying to process her emotions at seeing Layton and hearing about that final battle.

At the farm she rushed through a shower, eager to get to the main house. Her dad and brothers would ask Layton questions and she didn't want to miss a thing, didn't want to be away from him any longer than necessary.

Word of Layton's arrival had spread fast. Robin, Lisa, and Eileen zoomed around the farm's kitchen in full hospitality mode. A few minutes later, Matt and Layton pulled in. Janey dashed back outside just as Layton climbed out of his truck. Fuller ran up to greet him with a bark, before leaning against his leg.

Janey slowed. The only person Fuller ever did that with was John.

"Hey girl." Layton let his backpack slide to the ground before reaching down to scratch the collie's ears. "Have you missed me?"

"We all have." Her father came up then, his hand extended. "Welcome home, Son."

Layton glanced away, as if overcome with emotions. "Thank you, sir."

Matt moved close and grabbed Layton's backpack. "I'll set this in the kitchen for you."

Robin and Lisa moved in to greet Layton with joyful smiles.

"Where's the wild bunch?" Layton asked as he hugged Robin.

"At my mom's. Lisa's brat pack are with her folks," Robin said.

"We deserve breaks, you know," Lisa joked as she moved to hug him. "The kids will be overjoyed to see you."

Layton held out his hand to Eileen and introduced himself. "I recognize you from photos John showed me of the wedding. He looked forward to meeting you in person."

"I'm grateful John and I got to talk via Skype," Eileen said. "Now come on in the house. I have fresh coffee brewing."

Inside the kitchen, they gathered around the large oval table. "It smells like Heaven in here," Layton said.

"Eileen's put a beef roast in the oven for dinner tonight," Dad said. "Lisa and Robin brought pies and bread."

"The last home-cooked meal I had was here." Layton pointed to the table.

Here. With John. Her brother's absence dug sharp talons into Janey's skin as she slipped into the chair beside her father. This was the first time Layton had ever been at the farm without John. More painful firsts to endure.

Her father asked about Layton's arm, and how long he'd be in town.

Layton repeated his explanation about his shoulder. "I'll be around a few days. I have an appointment later in the week to have my shoulder checked at the VA hospital in Iowa City."

"Will you be stationed in Illinois again?" Matt asked.

"For now, yes."

Eileen moved in with mugs filled with coffee. When everyone had settled, Layton glanced about the table, making eye contact with each person. "I'm sorry I couldn't make it back for John's funeral. I can't begin to express my sympathy for your loss."

"Our loss," Dad said. "We know how close you and John were. I won't lie, it's been awful. I've buried my parents, my wife, some close friends. But to bury a child?" His breath caught, leaving him unable to go on. Eileen touched his shoulder, and Dad visibly relaxed. "Forgive my bluntness, but can you tell us what happened at that last battle? The Army gives me the run around, which is feeling like salt in the wound."

"John wouldn't have wanted that," Layton said. "He loved all of y'all so much, but when he said the words, 'my Dad,' his voice, his demeanor changed. Softened. And, yeah, I know he'd kick my butt if he heard me use his name in a sentence with soft."

Her brothers laughed, but the room grew quiet as Layton began recounting the same story he'd told Janey at the drive-in.

"How many were in your squad that day?" Dad asked.

"Twelve. We'd been on high alert since the *fatwa* was issued, so they beefed up the squad considering the threats. There were also a couple of Iraqi civilians present. A local contractor and his helper were moving a crane into place. They both were killed. I heard that John and another soldier, Ollie Fitz, rescued an Iraqi man and his child who came under attack."

A child? Janey's chest tightened. "Did they survive?"

Layton shrugged. "I think so. I saw a man approach John later, on the battlefield. Your brother identified him as a friendly, but honestly once the rockets and explosions started it was impossible to keep up."

"So, John was with another group when the attack began?" Perry asked. "Not with you?"

"Correct." Layton drew a diagram with his fingers on the table. "My group was here in the compound. Danny Carpenter's group was there, too. John and the others were out by the street. By the time they reached us, over half our guys were down. The blast that hit John took out most of the rest."

"That had to be horrific," Dad said.

"Yes, sir. Fallon lost a leg, and I had to keep pressure on the artery, so I couldn't get to John or anyone. Then I was hit. I understand backup arrived within moments, but I was unconscious." Layton cleared his throat. "Believe me, I've wished a thousand times I'd done things differently, tried to save John."

"Don't go down that road," Dad said. "You couldn't let Fallon die. From what I'm gathering, you were the last man standing in the middle of combat."

"I still should have been there for him," Layton said. "John was my best friend."

"You were there. Protecting the others," Dad went on. "Let me be clear on one thing. I'm asking about John to know what happened, not to question or blame. I've seen the autopsy reports. John's injuries were too extensive. Even with immediate help, he wouldn't have made it. But Teddy Fallon's life depended on you."

The compassion in her father's voice plucked at Janey, reminding her she wasn't always as forgiving. She leaned forward. "That civilian John called a friendly. Do you know who he was?"

Layton shook his head. "Ollie Fitz said the description sounded like the man with a child that he and John helped earlier."

"How long was he with John?" Janey asked.

"Not long," Layton replied. "I wouldn't attach any meaning to it. I don't think he harmed John, if that's your concern."

"My concern is whether someone was with my brother when he died." Janey's voice grew loud with emotion.

Dad put a hand on her forearm. "You got to let that one go, sweetie."

Eileen stood, interrupting the awkwardness of the moment. "Let me refill coffee cups."

Janey offered to help, grateful for a moment to pull herself together. The narrative she'd spliced together over the last few weeks to fill the gap of not knowing about her brother's last moments had unraveled. She hadn't considered that she might never get answers.

Layton reached in his backpack and withdrew a dented laptop. "If I can plug this in, I've got some photos you might like to see."

He placed a small black flash-drive on the table. "I made a copy for you. John and I go way back, to basic training, so I have a lot of stuff. And I apologize up front that some photos show him or others flipping off the camera, but I didn't want to censor them."

Janey picked up the flash drive. Desperate to preserve her brother's memory, she had gone through the digital photographs on her computer and even copied everything she could find off John's Myspace site. If a photo of her brother existed, she wanted it. "Thank you."

Dad motioned to Perry. "Can you hook Layton's laptop up to the new television in the living room so we can all see these photos?"

"Let me check if we've got the right cables." Perry picked up the laptop and he and Layton disappeared into the other room. A few minutes later Perry yelled, "Oh, yeah. Come look."

They filed into the living room. The photo frozen on the over-sized television screen was a shot of John leaned against a tan Humvee, one booted foot on the running board. He looked straight at the camera, laughing.

Janey walked up to the screen, her hand extended. *John.*

"That was taken the day he died. He'd just told some corny joke. That was his thing — get everyone laughing before we left base," Layton said.

She stared at the last photo ever taken of her brother. John used to say that the McKay men were tall, dark, and handsome. *"Perry's tall, Matt's dark, and I'm handsome."* God, she missed him.

Turning away, she sat in a chair and curled her legs beneath her knees. Layton sat on the sofa with Dad and Eileen while Matt and Perry claimed the two love seats with Robin and Lisa.

For the next few hours, they viewed scores of photos, some blurry, but most achingly clear. Layton paused at each one, telling them where it was, who else was in the photo and adding details that gave context. The stories and anecdotes he shared painted a picture of John's life overseas.

The photos included other members of John's squad, names he'd mentioned in letters and conversations. Janey wept anew for all the soldiers who'd died with John. Preach, Ricky, Chris, and Donald. Were their loved ones haunted like Janey over her brother's unknow-able final moments?

"We've spoken with all their families except Sheridan's," Dad said. "Do you have any contact information for them?"

"Preach had no family, or none he'd been able to locate. He'd been abandoned as an infant and spent his entire life in foster care. He'd started the legal process to have his records unsealed but put it on hold when we deployed. Now?" Layton shrugged, his expression sad. "Preach was an honorable man. Whoever his family was, they'd have been proud. I will do what I can to find his kinfolk and lobby for having him interred in a national cemetery in South Dakota."

"I don't know if it's possible, but we'd be honored to have him buried next to John," Dad said.

Janey hugged her knees tighter, unable to imagine life without her family. She looked at Matt, Perry, and her father. Then her gaze shifted to Layton. He had no proper family himself, yet he was determined to find Preach's next of kin.

Layton caught her eye and mouthed, "You okay?"

She knew that if she shook her head, he'd stop showing the photographs and there was no way she could miss seeing a single picture of John. She nodded slightly, then struggled to tamp down her emotions as he continued the slide show of photos.

By the time they finished she felt raw, as if every new picture of John flayed open another layer of her skin.

"I can't tell you what this means," Dad said as they regrouped later in the kitchen.

Janey helped Eileen, Robin, and Lisa prepare the evening meal. Despite the short notice, Robin and Lisa had fixed several of Layton's favorite dishes, which he praised. Dinner turned into a question and answer session as Layton expanded further on the everyday aspects of life during deployment.

"What was the food like over there?" Lisa asked.

"Compared to this? Warmed over sawdust. Actually, the chow was decent. But John would torment us by reading descriptions of Sunday dinners at the farm." Layton pointed his fork at Janey. "She would recount the full menu in her letters. I found it especially tormenting to hear details like 'Lisa picked apples for her pies and green beans from Robin's garden.' Or John's favorite, 'slices of Dad's tomatoes the size of saucers.' I missed those meals as much as John did."

"Stick around and we'll make up for it," Robin said.

By the time the dishes were cleared, it was dark outside. Eileen brought out pies, but Layton begged off. "I'm stuffed. But I'd take a piece to go."

"Go? Stay here," Dad said. "Janey's taken over the guest room in the bunkhouse, but we've got plenty of space upstairs. Or you can stay in John's room."

"I'm already checked in a motel for tonight, but I'll take you up on that tomorrow. Before I go, though, I have a few things to leave with you. I know the Army would have returned John's personal effects, but we shared a footlocker and I ended up with some of his stuff. You might have found some of my stuff mixed with his, too."

"I've left his bags untouched," Dad said.

"No worries. There's nothing I need. Just letting you know." With his good arm, Layton reached to tug something out of his backpack.

Janey let out a cry at seeing the small stuffed bear she had sent to John. The bear wore a camouflage uniform. John must have added the American flag tie-tacked on the bear's cap. She hugged it close. "Oh my! I smell John's aftershave." Her dad, Matt, and Perry all leaned in.

"This is for you, sir. Careful." Layton handed her father a small black Bible. "There are loose clippings and notes tucked in the pages. Exactly like John left it. Open the front cover."

The Bible had belonged to Janey's mother. Dad had given it to John when he enlisted. Inside the front cover was a list of dates John had inscribed. *Gift from Dad. Graduation from Boot Camp. First tour of Iraq.*

"He read it regularly, sir," Layton said.

Dad held the Bible reverently. "That makes me happy."

"You saw all those photos of John wearing these in the barracks." Layton handed Matt and Perry each a Cubs baseball cap. "I'm not sure which one each of you sent, but folks sure enjoyed razzing him about his team."

Perry took the cap from Layton's left hand and looked at Matt. "I didn't know you'd sent one, too."

Layton grinned. "John joked about that. Said as hard as you two tried to be different, you always made the same choices."

Matt pointed to the inside of the cap where John had scrawled MCKAY with a permanent marker, and then he fingered the American flag pin stuck into the bill. "Just like your bear, Janey."

"I have one last thing." Layton reached into his bag and withdrew some envelopes. "John wrote these when we first arrived overseas. It's standard practice for all soldiers to write letters to loved ones — just in case. John gave me his. And he had my letters. In fact, you may find mine in his stuff."

Janey stared at them, recalling an essay she'd read about soldiers going off to war. How they acknowledged death by writing letters they hoped would never be delivered. She wondered whom Layton had written. Who had he cared enough about to share last thoughts? His grandmother? Sharlene?

"I'll get your letters back to you," Dad promised.

"Thank you, sir." Layton handed her father five white envelopes, one each for Dad, Matt, Perry, Janey, and Uncle Nick. "John and I promised each other that if anything happened, we'd deliver these in person and leave before they were read. They're meant for family only. So, good night, y'all."

They followed Layton out onto the porch, then one by one, they hugged him. Janey was last.

"We need to talk more," Layton whispered as he pulled her close. "Tomorrow?"

Tears welled in her eyes. The urge to demand answers, to demand kisses, left her trembling and confused. "Tomorrow."

She stood with her family in the dark, watching as Layton backed his truck out. As he'd done so many times with John, he honked three times as he pulled away.

"Well, I'm going with Lisa to get the kids," Robin said to Matt. "I'll see you at home later."

"And I'm headed to bed," Eileen said.

"Whoa!" Dad held up a hand. "You guys are leaving before we open John's letters?"

"Yes." Lisa stepped closer to hug Perry. "The three of us decided this needs to be a private moment for you. We know you'll tell us about it afterwards."

"That's extremely thoughtful," Dad said. "But don't feel you have to leave."

"We don't. That's the best part." Eileen kissed Dad and smiled at each of them before leaving.

The kitchen was quiet as Janey, Matt, Perry, and their father circled the table. Though each person in the room now stood behind one chair, no one made a move to sit. They simply stared at the envelopes. John's death letters. The last words any of them would hear from him, a makeshift farewell.

One thought kept swirling inside Janey's head. *I'm not ready to say goodbye.*

CHAPTER TWENTY-TWO

September 2006
River Haven, Iowa

The lump in Janey's throat doubled in size as she stared at the envelopes at the far end of the kitchen table. The unexpectedness of them — a gesture from beyond the grave — left her torn between eagerness and dread. According to Layton, these letters were written right after they had deployed. Right after that last terrible fight she and John had over a year and a half ago.

A lifetime ago. The burden of guilt made it difficult to breathe.

From outside came a low *woof.* "Let Fuller in," Dad said to Perry.

The collie trotted up to Janey and whined softly before ducking under John's chair and stretching out.

"Now that we're all here." Dad picked up one envelope and set it aside. "I'll mail this to Nick."

"I wish Uncle Nick were here tonight," Perry said.

"Me, too," Her father pointed to the remaining four envelopes. The top one bore a single word on the front. DAD. "While I respect that you may want to keep your letters private, I'd prefer to share mine."

"We're in this together." Matt pulled out a chair.

Perry did the same. "Good times and bad."

Janey hesitated. Had John mentioned their argument or her feelings for Layton? Maybe. And maybe this letter held the answers, the goodbye she longed for.

She exhaled. "I'm in, too."

They all took seats as Dad slid reading glasses on. He used his pocketknife to slit the edge of the envelope before withdrawing a single sheet of paper.

"What's this?" Dad tugged a second, smaller envelope free from the one he'd already opened. "It's for Layton. I'll give it to him tomorrow. I guess John would have felt awkward handing Layton a letter with his name on it."

"Yet he didn't forget him," Perry noted.

If Layton were here, would he read his aloud? Janey guessed he wouldn't. He was more private.

Dad unfolded his letter. "It's handwritten. Dear Dad." He cleared his throat before going on.

If you are reading this, it's because the worst has happened. I knew when I took my Army oath that this was a risk, especially since I enlisted during a time of war. Still, I went gladly, proud to serve my country. And if I had to make this decision again, I wouldn't change it.

I want you to know how often I've thought of you since enlisting. I don't know what I did to deserve it, but I'm lucky to have been raised by a man like you. The important stuff in life — honor, courage, and compassion – I learned at your knee. Thank you for your steadfast love and quiet patience, even when I disappointed you. You always encouraged me to pursue my dreams, and quite selfishly, I did. If I have any regrets, it's only that I didn't ask for your advice more.

What bothers me most is the thought of you grieving. I remember how much it hurt to lose Mom. But I also remember you telling me that all things happen for a reason, even if we don't know or like it at the time.

I cannot tell you not to mourn, but please find peace with my passing. Because of you, Mom, and Uncle Nick, my soul is right with God and if I face eternity, I do so in good conscience.

Until we meet again, your loving son,

Dad placed his letter back on the table before fumbling with the envelope as he tried to catch his breath between sobs. "I can't imagine what it must have felt like to write this."

Janey glanced at her brothers. They all cried now, wondering what last message John had for each of them.

The next two envelopes were addressed to Matt and Perry. John thanked his brothers for different things – Matt for listening without lecturing and never tiring of throwing football passes. Perry got credit for teaching John everything about racing motorcycles, fighting, and for their long talks when they'd go running.

Only the closing line was the same. "Mother once told me she was twice blessed to have had twins. I completely agree. I feel twice blessed to have you both for brothers." Matt wept as he read.

The last envelope on the table bore Janey's name. Her hand trembled as she reached for it. Would this be the goodbye John had pledged? Would he apologize for stealing that letter? *Did he know she loved him?*

She unfolded the letter slowly. "Dear Janey."

You are the one I didn't want to write. I wondered if it would be

better to spare you. Then I realized you'd be hurt if the others got
final letters and you didn't. So, I write this in hopes you will never
see it.

Most of my pre-Army memories center on you. Yes, we were
always there for each other, but I swear, you were there for me
more. You cheered me on, you helped me out. You were the light
that kept darkness at bay, especially after we lost Mom.

You know I'd do anything for you, but now, I must ask you to do
one more thing for me. Live the way we raced, Janey. Full out. No
fear. Go for the win. You always did the right thing, no matter how
I tried to dissuade you. Keep that up and you won't fail.

I asked Dad to see that my life insurance proceeds go toward
your college expenses — a full ride. Earn a degree for both of us.
We both know you're the closest I'll ever get to higher education.
Seriously, you're a McKay. Make us proud, Janey.

Your loving brother,

She stood, sobbing uncontrollably before pointing to the letter.
"John swore he'd come home. I wish he'd kept that promise."

The legs of Dad's chair scraped the tile floor as he rose and
tugged her in his arms. "You can't look at it as a promise. It was an
intention, a noble one. But it was made on circumstances John
couldn't control. We have to accept that."

Matt and Perry stood too, joining them in a family hug. Fuller
moved in, whimpering. Perry bent down to stroke the collie's head.
"We know, girl. We all miss him."

Janey swiped at her eyes. "It's so hard."

Dad nodded. "Who said it would be easy?"

"Not John." Matt's eyes were red as he stepped away.
"Remember all his crazy rules? 'McKays don't do easy.'"

"Who could forget?" Dad pointed a finger toward the ceiling. "He's probably looking down from Heaven and feeling embarrassed that we're crying."

"He'd tell us to act like McKays." Perry laughed.

"You okay, Janey-girl?" Dad asked.

"Yes." She motioned toward the table. "But I'm in shock about the insurance money. Did you know? I don't mean to sound ungrateful—"

Dad cut her off. "That's something else we discussed before he deployed, even though he hoped it would never come to pass." He made a sweeping gesture. "That none of this would come to pass. Honestly, I'm relieved he spelled it out in his letter, because I've been uncertain how to bring it up with you, especially with you staying home this semester."

"He talked about it with Matt and me, too," Perry said. "We supported his decision one hundred percent."

But he never talked to me about any of it. How many other conversations had she been excluded from? Too numb to argue, she sat back down.

Her father spoke again. "As much as he despised being called Johnny, did you notice he signed each one, Love, Johnny?"

"He must have been thinking of Mother when he wrote these letters," Matt said. "No one but Mom and Janey called him that."

Janey sniffed back tears. "After Mom died, John told me that 'Johnny' reminded him of her passing, so I started calling him Bob. You can imagine how that went over."

Matt chuckled as he stuffed his envelope in his shirt pocket. "Let's call it a night. Layton will be back in the morning and I want to be here early."

After telling everyone goodnight, Janey made her way to the bunkhouse with Fuller. Usually, she slipped into John's bedroom to check everything before going to bed, but tonight she was emotionally exhausted and couldn't face the reminder of John's absence.

Fuller followed her into her bedroom and jumped up on her bed before circling and collapsing.

Unable to sleep, Janey sat at her desk and reread John's letter. That he hadn't asked for any final forgiveness didn't bother her nearly as much as the fact that she never got to retract the horrible words she'd yelled that night before he deployed. *"I'll hate you forever."* She'd been confident they'd have a chance to hash it out once and for all when he was home. A battle royal between two worthy opponents.

Except he was never returning.

THE NEXT MORNING, Janey awoke before dawn. Her father was up, too, sipping coffee when she slipped into the kitchen.

"Morning, Janey-girl." Dad seemed extraordinarily cheerful. "I don't know about you, but John's letter gave me a sense of peace."

Eileen moved in and gave her father a peck on the cheek. "You seemed to sleep better, too, Ward. That's the first night in weeks you haven't been up pacing."

The look that passed between them reminded Janey that Eileen was an important part of her father's life now. Like it or not, much had changed in the McKay family hierarchy. With John gone and Dad remarried, where did Janey fit in?

From outside came the sound of a truck pulling in the drive. Eileen shifted to peek out between the lace curtains. "It's Layton."

Janey's pulse elevated as he entered the kitchen. He moved slightly slower, as if in pain. He also seemed distant, closed, and radiated a stay-away vibe.

Dad didn't appear to notice and greeted Layton enthusiastically. "You always were an early bird. We'll make a farmer out of you yet."

"Rancher," Layton corrected. Farmer versus rancher had been a running joke since the first time Layton visited. "Good morning, Eileen. Janey."

"Hope you're hungry," Eileen said. "Breakfast will be up shortly. I've got sweet rolls in the oven."

"I could smell them baking a mile down the road." Layton sat where Eileen placed his coffee mug — next to Dad.

"I can't thank you enough for John's letters," Dad began. "Heck, for everything you shared yesterday."

"I hope they gave you solace," Layton said. "And some closure." He looked at her. "You too, Janey."

She wasn't sure she wanted closure. "I don't ever want to forget."

"You won't," Dad said. "None of us will." He held out an envelope to Layton. "This was in my letter from John."

Layton stared at the envelope for long moments. His lips curved down in profound sadness. She longed to move closer, to offer comfort, but that back-off sense shrouded him again.

"I don't know what to say." Layton looked uncomfortable. "I didn't expect this."

"John only wrote the people he cared most about," Dad went on. "That would include you."

"Thank you, sir." Layton thrust the envelope in his pocket.

Dad changed the subject. "Has Janey told you about the rosary John sent home? It's causing quite a stir."

"Teddy Fallon mentioned the rosary a couple times." Layton looked from Janey to her dad. "But what kind of stir do you mean?"

"For starters, it was supposed to be buried with John, but wasn't." Dad explained about Lloyd Nelson finding the box. "John wrote about praying for peace, so Janey's started a website and now some people who attended rosary prayer services are reporting miraculous cures. Nick had two services in Chicago, and three people claimed healings."

"I wonder if that explains Fallon's obsession with it," Layton said. "Does he know about that?"

"Yes," Janey said. "When he first asked for the rosary, the miracle claims hadn't yet occurred. There have been some comments online since then, though." Janey turned to Layton. "Do you know how John got the rosary? Teddy's story about how John got it changes each time we talk. Sometimes he even talks about people disappearing in flashes of light."

Layton took a sip of coffee before replying. "I was there when your brother got the rosary, and there was nothing supernatural about it. John saved an old beggar who stumbled into a firefight. That the old coot wasn't blown to bits was amazing. Afterwards, the old man insisted John take the beads as some sort of thank you gesture. John didn't realize until later that it was a rosary. He seemed surprised by it."

"But why did the beggar have a rosary in the first place?" Janey pressed. "Do you think the old man was Catholic?"

"Who knows? John had questions about it too. He even looked for the old beggar, but we never saw him again," Layton said.

"Do you know why John wanted to find the old man?" Dad asked

"Or even how I could find this beggar?" she added.

Layton looked at her father. "No, sir, I don't." Then he turned to Janey. "You'll never find him. The old man took off as soon as we turned our backs. That's a mode of survival over there."

"Teddy said he has contacts still in Iraq who can find the old man."

"Teddy sometimes forgets that most of our squad, the ones who survived, are back in the States now. He rambled on and on the other day, telling me Chris Worth had come to Cincinnati to visit. But Worth is dead."

Janey recalled the time Teddy said, 'tell John.' The back door slammed as Perry and Matt came in and started talking. She still wanted to ask Layton about the old beggar, but she'd wait for another time.

Both Matt and Perry had questions about some photos Layton had shared the night before. Perry also asked for updates on the surviving soldiers in their squad.

As soon as Eileen started setting plates on the table, Dad proclaimed, "Enough talk. I'm starving."

Matt and Perry moved to carry steaming food dishes over, while Janey poured orange juice and milk. Then Dad offered a blessing before picking up the bowl closest to him. Dishes and silverware clattered as compliments were heaped onto Eileen.

Layton asked her brothers about the new store being built across the river in Quincy, Illinois. Coffee flowed in earnest as Dad started talking about farm equipment sales. Crop prices came up next, discussions of soybean futures passed alongside platters of bacon, ham, and sausage. When Layton asked about projected corn yields, Dad took over the conversation again as freshly scrambled eggs were served up with a crispy hash brown casserole.

Janey unwound a cinnamon roll as her gaze drifted around the table. Dad and Matt parried on ten-year averages, while Perry gestured with a butter-covered knife. Layton held his own, listening and nodding, leaning in when he had a different take. Fitting in like he'd never been gone. Like he belonged here.

Did he feel that, too? Or was Texas still home? With everything else going on, she hadn't thought about his future except with her. Layton said they still needed to talk, but now Janey worried about the topic. Layton had gone to Texas before coming to Iowa. Had he and Sharlene rekindled their romance? Did he plan to let Janey down easy?

"Earth to Janey." Matt pointed to the sausage plate in front of her. "I'll take that last patty if no one else wants it."

Eileen laughed. "There's more in the skillet, keeping warm."

Matt and Perry both said, "Dibs."

It was a typical McKay family meal. The first one not shaded by sadness.

Janey's throat dried, and she grabbed for her juice. Life was doing what it had done for eternity. Moving on. Whether or not she wanted it to.

Layton's cell phone rang. He held up a hand before tugging his phone from his pocket. "Excuse me. I'm expecting a call from my grandmother's doctor." He stood, stepping away from the table as he answered.

Janey felt a stab in her heart as she overheard his next words.

"I can't talk right now, Sharlene."

Sharlene, Sharlene, the rodeo queen. How many times had John made a big point of teasing Layton about his girlfriend whenever Janey was close by?

"I'll call you tonight. We'll talk then. Promise," Layton said.

Before he deployed, he promised Janey they'd talk. Now he'd just made that same promise to Sharlene. Jealousy morphed to anger.

Layton disconnected and turned back to the table. "Sorry about that. False alarm. What were you saying, Matt?"

Matt checked his watch. "Perry and I have a meeting with our contractor. But we'll be back as soon as we can."

"And I've got an early doctor appointment," Dad said to Layton. "I shouldn't be gone long."

Janey stood, eager for everyone to leave. "I'll clean up."

"I'll help — as best I can with this." Layton pointed to his sling.

It didn't take Janey long to load the dishwasher. Layton grabbed a sponge and wiped down the stove top. When he finished, he tossed it in the sink. "That's done. Do you have time for a ride now?"

Janey's hand paused over the soap dish. Part of her wanted to say no, to tell him to go call Sharlene. Another part, the part that cared deeply, wanted a chance to talk. "Sure."

"We have to go slow-poking," Layton said. "No racing for me for a while."

"We'll take Dad's cart." Dad's cart was a four-wheel ATV with bench seats. With its high suspension and souped-up engine, her father joked that even he could keep up with the grandkids.

"I'll drive," she said as they walked out to the machine barn a few minutes later.

A light breeze had her grabbing her long hair and twisting it back in a knot at her nape. Fuller followed them and jumped into the back seat. Layton awkwardly climbed in the passenger side and put a booted foot on the dash.

"You sure you're good?" She couldn't stop worrying about him.

At his nod, she backed out and drove off, away from the house.

The sun hung on the morning side of the sky, not too hot. She sped up carefully, steering around ruts in the roads to avoid jarring his shoulder.

Layton pointed east. "Let's see how well I remember things."

Her cheeks flushed. Did he remember their kiss?

"Is that the trail that leads to the pond?" he asked.

Disappointment had her slowing. "Yes."

He pointed again. "And straight ahead goes to the tree house, right? Let's go there. It took me forever to figure these trails out, you know. Your brother loved to lose me in the back forty."

"When we were kids, John would lead me in circles and try to give me the shake. He usually succeeded, but in the end, he'd always be here waiting for me." Janey pulled up beneath the largest oak on the property and shut off the engine before looking up at the wide branches supporting the tree house. How many times had she raced up to this exact point, excited to think she'd beat John? Only to find him up there, leaning over the rail and waving.

Never again. A lump formed in her throat.

Layton cleared his throat. "Matt told me why you're not in school this semester. Until Zaman is captured or otherwise stopped, I think it's wise to stay close."

"Do you think Zaman will come after you and the others?"

"He might want to, but right now he's in hiding, a wanted man. I hope our guys overseas find him soon. Closer to home, though, I'd keep an eye on the local Justice Freedom Association. Matt also told me what happened after the funeral. I wish I had been there."

She tried to mask her disappointment. This was not what she wanted to discuss. "I'm sure Matt exaggerated."

"Oh yeah? He said you went gangster on Randy Keener, but warned me to not mention it in front of your father. Look, there's something you need to know about Keener. The night before John and I deployed, John kicked Keener's butt."

"I know. Randy's been vocal about the fact he ended up in jail afterwards."

"Have you had more than one dust-up with Keener?" Layton's eyes narrowed.

Why couldn't he look at her with that intensity, but talk about *them?* "Randy is the least of my worries. He's a moron."

"A moron with an axe to grind. If Keener gives you any more crap, let me know. Matt and Perry, too. I know you can take care of yourself, Janey. I'm just saying you don't have to do it alone. I'm here for you."

She sat up straighter. "Really? You promised we'd talk about us when you returned. Instead, we're talking about everyone else."

Layton shifted positions. "There's something you need to know."

Janey grimaced. She knew what came next, knew it would hurt less if she said it instead of Layton. "You're still involved with Shar- lene, aren't you?"

"I'm not involved with anyone right now."

"She posts about you a lot. Like she's your girlfriend."

"Former."

"Yet still she calls."

He didn't deny it further. "Janey, I'm not the same man you kissed in these cornfields a year and a half ago. I've seen too much... bad. Lost too many people. Physically, I'm damaged goods and not sure what the future holds. Your future is filled with potential, mine is filled with questions."

"The two of us can figure the future out together."

"There is no us. Not like you mean, anyway. You're John's little sister and I promised John I'd look out for you. And I will because I care about you and your family."

There is no us. His letdown crushed her heart. How could she get Layton to give them a chance? She wanted a romantic, undying love. A fair shot at an eventual happily ever after.

But apparently, she wasn't the only person wanting those same things from Layton. His answers about Sharlene hinted at something undone. *Former* wasn't the same as *finished*.

Layton's phone rang. He glanced at the screen and frowned. "It's your Dad. I have to answer."

Janey pretended to gaze out at the fields as she struggled against the urge to cry.

Layton's sharp exhalation got her attention. "Yes, sir. Thank you for letting me know. We'll be right there."

She reached for the ignition. "What's wrong? Is my dad okay?"

"He's fine. Teddy Fallon was attacked outside the VA Hospital in Cincinnati this morning. Your father just heard it on the news. I've got to get back."

"Is Teddy okay?"

Layton ran a hand through his hair and closed his eyes. "Your dad said Teddy died from wounds received in the attack."

CHAPTER TWENTY-THREE

September 2006
River Haven, Iowa

The grim news about Teddy Fallon's death pummeled Layton. Another friend and brother gone. He and Janey returned to the farmhouse and watched the news report replay with Ward.

The details were horrific. Fallon had been brutally attacked by a machete-wielding madman. Fallon had just finished physical therapy and sat in his wheelchair outside the VA hospital clinic, smoking a cigarette while waiting for a ride. His assailant had been shot and killed by a security guard. Fallon had been rushed into the hospital but died in surgery.

That Fallon's assailant also died was no comfort. The attacker's death had been easy compared to the multiple stabs and blows Fallon endured. Dead, the attacker couldn't give answers, couldn't be punished for his crime.

The motive remained unclear. One news report conjectured that because it happened at the VA hospital, the attacker may have been a vet suffering extreme PTSD. Authorities didn't even know the man's name. The incident had been captured on security cameras, and police released a portion of it asking for the public's help in identifying the deceased assailant.

That Fallon survived that awful battle in Iraq only to die like this angered Layton, especially when he thought of Fallon's unborn child. Fallon had been so eager to be a dad. He'd told Layton several times that the sheer determination to be there for his son kept him focused on recovery. Now that child would enter the world fatherless.

"I'm sorry, Layton," Ward said as they regrouped in the kitchen a short time later. "You've lost a lot of people."

Too many. Layton learned early in life to never ask *how much more?* No matter how bad things seemed, it could always be worse.

"I need to make some phone calls." He wanted to make certain Sergeant Boswell and Danny Carpenter heard. "I'm going to Cincinnati for the funeral."

"The rosary service is scheduled for tonight," Janey said. Her demeanor switched to sympathy once she heard about Fallon. "If we left now, we could be there for it. I'll drive."

Layton wasn't ready to contemplate what he wanted from Janey, but it damn sure wasn't pity.

He also didn't like the reminder that Fallon had died before attending that stupid rosary service he'd been so eager for. Guilt multiplied as Layton remembered how he'd avoided Fallon's call yesterday. If they'd spoken, would a crazy Butterfly Effect have changed the outcome?

Layton scowled at Janey. "I don't think that's a good idea. Fallon's family will probably cancel the service now. I would. Besides, I'm sure I'll be going with others from my squad." Too late, he realized his voice sounded harsher than intended.

Miffed, Janey stepped back. "Fine. I'm going into town to ship a package to Gemma. I'll be back later, Dad."

The door slammed as she left. Layton rubbed his aching temples. It seemed like every time she offered kindness and understanding, he flung it away as if she'd offered a poisonous scorpion.

"I was rude. I need to go apologize," Layton said to Ward.

Ward made a snorting noise. "You weren't rude. Janey pushes too hard sometimes and then gets her feelings hurt. Trust me, if you went after her now, she'd give you a whole new definition of rude. Give her a chance to cool off. Frankly, I'm glad to have a moment of privacy. I wanted to thank you again for keeping John's letters safe. I've re-read mine a half-dozen times, and each time I feel a bit more at ease. I hope the letter John left you grants you some measure of the same."

Layton held a breath, hoping Ward wouldn't ask what John wrote. Layton hadn't read his letter, wasn't sure he ever would. The pact between him and John was forged of war and death, of action. Words on paper didn't change that.

"I feel bad I didn't write one to him," Layton blurted, remembering the day they'd written those letters. He and John joked about not getting overly sentimental. John rolled out the gallows humor, making kissy noises and "*I love you, man,*" quips while writing.

Layton's retort had been equally flippant. "*Sergeant Boswell said to write to the people we care most about. I skipped you and wrote to myself,*" is what he told John when he gave him his letters. Had John been surprised to see who Layton wrote to? Had he been offended not to see a letter to himself?

Ward's voice lowered. "Who you did or didn't write doesn't matter. It was John's turn to give, our turn to receive. John only wrote to family. You're family, Layton. That doesn't change because John's not here."

"That means a lot, sir." The McKay family's acceptance had always been meaningful, and Layton worried how John's death would affect that. Ward's reassurance soothed something so deep down inside it was scary. Caring meant being vulnerable to more loss. And there was always more to lose.

"Right now you've got your buddy, Teddy, on your mind, but I want you to know one more thing," Ward said. "You always have a place here, with us. If for any reason you decide not to stay in the

Army, we'd be honored to have you join McKay Family Enterprises. Matt and Perry feel strongly about that too."

Layton's bones threatened to turn to jelly. He still had hopes for his Army career and OCS and wasn't sure how to react to Ward's words. Except for his grandfather, Layton's family's worldview was one-part suspicion and one part dog-eat-dog. The world he knew, the world where wars waged as easily in Cincinnati as in Iraq, didn't include family bonds. So why was he sobbing all of a sudden?

"Don't hold it in, Son." Ward's forthrightness undid the last of Layton's stoic composure, leaving no boundaries between the morass of guilt, grief, and anger that threatened to consume him.

———

EARLY THE NEXT MORNING, Layton headed out to pick up Danny Carpenter. When Layton had been hospitalized in Germany, he'd hated missing the funerals of his lost comrades. The hospital chaplain suggested it might have granted closure. However, it wasn't closure Layton wanted. It was justice. "Then you'll miss out on peace," the chaplain said.

Peace? You can't miss what you've never had.

Janey hadn't returned to the farm last night, opting to stay at Perry's. Layton couldn't blame her for avoiding him. Right now, things were a mess and he didn't deal well with messes.

This journey was tough enough as is. Layton glanced at the empty passenger seat. The last time he drove from River Haven, Iowa, to Fort DeWald, Illinois, John had been riding shotgun.

John had been unusually quiet on the drive back to base that day, his mood somber and wistful, which he blamed on his hangover. Later John said it had been difficult to leave his family, but Layton knew something more troubled his friend. Had John sensed he was not coming back?

The thought burned Layton's gut. If he'd known back then what the future held, could he have persuaded John to go AWOL?

Nope.

No more than John could have convinced Layton if the circumstances were reversed. McKays and Burnets had too much honor. They also believed they were bulletproof. Sweet Jesus, what else had they been wrong about?

Don't go there. The news of Fallon's death ripped open Layton's emotional battle wounds. Had Layton saved Fallon for nothing? Could Layton have saved John instead? If Layton had done anything differently, could both men have survived? Could the whole battle have been averted?

He was mentally exhausted by the time he pulled through the Army base's gates and headed to the bachelors' quarters. He'd barely climbed out of his truck when Danny came up.

"Welcome home, brother." Danny hugged him, careful to not bump his splinted arm.

The last time Layton saw Danny was in Iraq. Danny had been running towards John only to be struck down by an explosion. Layton hadn't known if Danny was dead or alive. Fallon had been screaming, rockets exploded. The smoke and dust had gotten so thick Layton could hardly see. He'd wanted to obliterate the enemy and save his friends, but ultimately, he'd been powerless to do either.

Danny's fingers gripped Layton's good shoulder tightly. He felt Danny's shoulders shake as both men contained the same demons. Loss. Remorse. Sorrow. Survivor's guilt.

"You look good, man." Layton's voice cracked as Danny stepped back. Danny had been trapped beneath rubble, pinned in place until backup finally arrived. He'd suffered a concussion yet refused to leave until everyone else in their squad had been extricated.

"You look good, too," Danny said. "Except for that sling. How much longer till it comes off?"

"Two days. Then after a little PT, I'll be back here, ready to wrestle."

Danny flexed his arm and pointed to the muscle. "Dude, Boswell and I have been hitting the gym. You won't find me so easy to whup next time. Provided you even come back here before Officer Candidate School."

Layton let the comment pass. Being back on base brought up all his fears about the future. *What if I can't get into OCS? What if they kick me out of the Army?* He changed the subject.

"What's the word on Boswell's wife?" Layton knew the sergeant's wife started chemotherapy for breast cancer while they'd been deployed. That Boswell wasn't attending Fallon's funeral didn't bode well.

"Guess they found another tumor. She's going in for more surgery." Danny shook his head. "They just found out she's pregnant again. Boswell's taking his kids to stay with their grandparents while their mom's in the hospital."

Layton grimaced. It can always get worse. "Hope it turns out for them."

After throwing his bag in the back seat, Danny buckled up as Layton pulled out. The drive to Cincinnati would take about five hours, which would still give them enough time to check in a motel and change before going to Fallon's wake later that same day. The funeral was tomorrow.

Layton tried to call Fallon's mother last night but had instead talked with a cousin who promised to convey condolences. Layton had been surprised to learn Fallon's family decided to go on with the rosary service as planned.

"We're holding it in Teddy's honor," the cousin explained. "You're welcome to attend."

The irony that Fallon died a day before the rosary service seemed particularly cruel, especially after Fallon had gone on and on about that string of beads as if it could restore his leg, his health, his sanity. While Layton didn't know much about religion and rosaries, he knew one thing. The blasted rosary hadn't saved John or Fallon, despite their obsessions with it.

"When was the last time you talked to Fallon?" Danny asked as they headed off base.

"Two days before he died. I was driving from South Dakota to Iowa." Once again Layton felt guilty over the call he'd ignored.

"Did he sound, I don't know... Weird? Strung out? Crazy talking?"

Layton glanced sideways and saw Danny's anguished expression. "Yes. He was taking some strong meds, though."

"Last time I visited, I brought up potential opioid problems, but Fallon vehemently denied it. Worse, he questioned my loyalty as a friend and brother-in-arms. Then he started sobbing and said the pills were the only thing that made life tolerable on the days he didn't think he could go on, when he couldn't get ahead of the pain." Danny sighed. "I backed off, but maybe I should have called him on it, insisted he get help, go into rehab."

Layton had the same thoughts after his mother overdosed. "I talked to Fallon's cousin, Manny last night. Manny brought the subject up, too. He said Fallon consumed painkillers like he was in a contest, often arguing with his mother if she tried to control his usage. The family even tried an intervention, but Fallon denied having a problem and refused to seek treatment."

Danny shook his head. "I hate that."

When they reached Cincinnati, Layton and Carpenter checked into a motel before donning full dress uniforms. With Danny's help, Layton was able to fully suit up, but still had to wear the arm brace.

They made their way to Fallon's wake in Cincinnati's rush hour traffic. The parking lot at the funeral home was full when they arrived. Two television news vans were double parked out front.

As they drove past, looking for a parking spot, Danny swore. "Can you believe them?"

Layton looked at where Danny pointed. A small group of men stood on the sidewalk across from the funeral home, holding up protest signs for the Justice Freedom Association. ANOTHER DEAD SOLDIER EQUALS SAVED TAX DOLLARS.

Layton did a double take when he saw who held the sign. Randy Keener.

Tires screeching, Layton pulled over, but Danny beat him out of the truck.

"How dare those commie cowards show up here," Danny raged as they crossed the street.

Keener moved to the front line and pointed at Layton's arm as they approached. "Well, if it ain't the McKay wannabe. Looks like the jihadists only got half the job done on you."

"Take your signs and get out of here," Layton said.

"Says you? We got permits that guarantee our God-given right to protest." Keener puffed his chest out. "Though this one isn't nearly as exciting as the one we threw for your dead buddy John McKay."

The thought of Janey facing down Keener left Layton wanting to smash the man's face. "You ever touch Janey McKay again and I'll put you down permanently."

"Challenge accepted." Keener spat on the ground.

"Easy dude," Danny whispered. "I'm pissed too, but here comes that news reporter and we're in uniform."

Layton had fought too hard to not care deeply about what his uniform represented. He gave Keener a dismissive glance before turning away.

"How do you know that JFA skinhead?" Danny asked.

"He's from John's hometown. They protested at John's funeral, too."

The reporter rushed forward with a microphone extended.

"Just keep moving," Danny said.

"Arlo Daines, TV43," the reporter said. "Are you gentlemen here for the Fallon service? Were you stationed overseas with him?"

"Yes, and yes." Danny nodded toward the door of the funeral home. "Excuse us."

"Can you comment on the reports that Fallon's attacker was connected with Farid Zaman's jihadist group Black Death?"

Layton jerked to a stop. The thought of Zaman claiming credit for Fallon's death was too bizarre to contemplate. He met Danny's gaze, saw the slight shake of his friend's head. *Don't overreact. Don't engage.*

"We have no comment," Danny said as they moved away.

Once they were out of earshot, Danny shook his head. "Obviously we've missed some big news."

"We'll ask Fallon's cousin, Manny." At the funeral home's entrance, Layton removed his beret. "Covers off." Right now was about remembering Fallon, not stewing over Keener or the reporter.

Inside, an usher directed them down the hall. As they entered Fallon's viewing room, the crowd grew quiet. People cleared the aisle, as if silently honoring them for their roles in the military. It hurt to straighten his shoulder, but Layton gritted his teeth and strode with Danny to stand at attention beside the open coffin.

Layton thought back on happier times. Fallon had been one of the first people Layton met in Advanced Training. Fallon recruited him and John for a baseball team. Fallon's pitching arm was good enough for the majors.

Layton reached out to straighten the Purple Heart pinned to Fallon's uniform. *Rest in peace, buddy. And if Zaman had anything to do with this, he'll pay.*

Stepping back, Layton surveyed the room and was surprised to see Army CID Investigator Lt. Santiago in the crowd. They'd met in Germany. When their eyes met, Santiago shook his head, waving off Layton from approaching or acknowledging his presence. If Santiago was here, there was more to the Zaman story than the reporter had suggested. Layton would call his CID contact later.

"Excuse me." A man their age came up. "I'm Teddy's cousin, Manny." His eyes scanned their name tags. "You're Layton? We spoke last night."

Layton shook hands and then introduced Danny.

"I'm sorry for the loss of your cousin," Danny said. "Teddy fought bravely in Iraq. I was honored to serve with him."

"Your presence means a lot," Manny said. "Especially with those protestors out there. And the news reporters. Do you think what they're saying is true?"

"We've been on the road all afternoon," Layton said to Manny. "Can you explain what's happened?"

Manny kept his voice low. "The leader of the radical group called Black Death identified the man who murdered Teddy and claimed the man worked for him. Can it be true? Foreign terrorists on our own streets?"

"Don't jump to any conclusions," Layton advised. Farid Zaman wouldn't hesitate to take credit falsely as a psychological scare tactic.

"I'm certain the US military and other Federal agencies are investigating the claim," Danny added. "They'll get to the bottom of it."

"Come. Teddy's mother is eager to meet you." Manny led them to a row of seats off to one side where a group of people gathered around a sobbing older woman. Manny addressed the distraught woman. "Aunt Sophia, these are the two soldiers I told you about. They fought with Teddy in Iraq."

Sophia Fallon stood and hugged each of them. "Thank you for coming. My son spoke of you like family."

"I'm sorry for your loss. It was an honor to have served with Teddy," Layton said. "He was the top sharpshooter in our squad and always first to offer help for anything."

As Danny moved in to offer condolences, Layton noticed an older man shift close, eavesdropping on the conversation.

Manny noticed too and offered an introduction. "This is my and Teddy's uncle, Merle Hammett."

Merle shook hands as if he was operating a water pump. "You were with my nephew in Iraq? Oh my God. You must have been there when Teddy saw the sacred rosary pass over from the jihadist. Let me find my wife. I'll be right back."

"Did I hear right?" Danny whispered. "He called the old beggar a jihadist?"

Layton grimaced as others pressed close, looking expectantly at Layton and Danny. "You were with Teddy overseas?" a woman asked. "Please tell us more about the miraculous rosary and the jihadist."

While Layton wasn't a religious person, he knew Fallon's family were Catholics and that the rosary service had just been held last night. For a moment, Layton wished Janey was present to field these questions. He turned to Danny, who gave him the *ball's in your court* look.

Layton cleared his throat. "There's not much to tell, ma'am. The beads came from a crippled old beggar. I wouldn't call him a jihadist, though. You can go to the rosary website for more information."

Merle Hammett returned, a woman with him. "The story posted on the rosary website about the beggar is wrong. We were there when Teddy told the truth of the rosary. He swore that the rosary was found on the body of the dead terrorist. Teddy believed the dead man was a closet Christian."

"Hold on there." Layton held up a hand in disbelief. "With all due respect to Teddy, that is not what happened. My friend, John McKay, was given those beads by an old beggar who John rescued during a gun battle. I know. I was there."

Merle dismissed Layton's explanation with a wave of his arm. "So was my nephew. Teddy told us all about the green flash of light. He said it saved his life on the battlefield. My wife saw that flash of light at the rosary service yesterday. It healed her." Merle motioned to the woman at his side. "Show them your neck, Lucy."

Lucy Hammett stepped forward and turned her head to expose her neck. She ran fingers over the skin. "You see how smooth this is? Two days ago, there were wide scars from where they removed tumors twice. There was also a large tumor here." Once again, she pointed to her flawless skin. "At last night's rosary service, I felt a burning on my neck, so bad I thought I would pass out. Then I saw a flash of green light. Just like Teddy described. My husband went to get me water, but when he returned, he nearly passed out to see that my scars were gone. It's a miracle."

Layton tried to quell his default disbelief. "I'm happy for you, ma'am, but the story of the rosary coming from a dead terrorist is false."

Merle made a derisive noise. "On the contrary, I think it explains why these jihadists targeted poor Teddy. They thought to stifle the truth about where the rosary came from. But we won't be quiet. I intend for the entire world to know the truth about this sacred piece."

CHAPTER TWENTY-FOUR

September 2006
Chicago, Illinois

The news of the soldier's death in Cincinnati stunned Father Nick.

Nick had just shipped the rosary to Teddy's church last week. How sad that he'd died before the service occurred.

The stories of more miraculous cures ascribed to the Cincinnati rosary service amazed Nick. That was how many now? Six or seven? At the second rosary service held in Chicago, there had been two more miracles: one for chronic migraines, another for severe arthritis. More were being reported in Cincinnati.

So far, the collective of miracles attributed to Janey's rosary defied traditional Catholic convention where miracles came as a result of intercessory prayers to a single saint. These new miracles differed because the recipients reported praying to a variety of saints. Or not. No two stories were alike.

As word spread, Janey's initial mission to pray for peace became secondary — practically forgotten — as people clamored to attend a rosary service in hopes of a miracle. Nick didn't fault anyone for that.

The need for healing was unending and, sadly, not everyone got big, flashy miracles.

Constanza's restored eyesight had baffled her doctors, who wanted to run more tests to confirm. She refused. "I have confirmation from God. What more do I need?"

Nick had been disappointed when attendance at Prince of Peace dropped back to the previous lows after a large turnout for the second rosary service. Any uptick he noticed — another soul or two showing up for Mass, someone besides crickets in the confessional — was because of Constanza's efforts. After their success with the bilingual rosary services, she pushed him to make a Spanish/English recording of Mass. He grumbled at first, but soon realized she was right.

They had started on the recording this morning but got sidetracked by the ringing phones. As news of the miracles in Cincinnati circulated, Constanza fielded a steady stream of inquiries about future services with the rosary. She referred callers to Janey's website and urged Nick to sign up for another service in Chicago.

Nick wondered what John would think of the notoriety his rosary had gained. Like Janey, Nick was curious to learn more about the rosary.

Shortly before noon, he locked up the youth center and headed to the church office. Today he was meeting an old friend, Dr. Ralph Birdson, for lunch. Ralph had just returned from a European lecture tour, promoting his latest book on Vatican art. Nick previously sent several close-up photographs of the rosary to Ralph, who was intrigued by the beads and promised to research their origin. They had spoken yesterday, but the fact that Ralph refused to hint at his findings didn't bode well. Typically, he would tease if he knew something. Perhaps the rosary was simply a rosary, albeit a beautiful one, but without a notable history.

As Nick approached Constanza's office, he heard loud voices, shouts. Concerned, he rushed inside and interrupted an argument between Constanza and her father, Eduardo.

Eduardo, one boycotter who went elsewhere for Mass, turned

and pointed his finger at Nick while yelling in Spanish. That Eduardo could have shouted in English was a slight directed at Nick.

"What's going on, Constanza?" Nick asked.

"My father wants me to go back to the doctor." She shook her head. "I refused."

Nick felt like a meddler. While he had encouraged her to embrace both God and medicine, he'd promised to back whichever decision she made.

Eduardo continued speaking in Spanish.

"He doesn't believe in miracles," Constanza interpreted. "He thinks they offer false hope."

As Eduardo continued his rant, Nick caught mention of Domingo's name.

"He also thinks you are feeding Domingo false hope of being a real musician," Constanza said. "My sister, Domingo's mother, moved to California to pursue a singing career. Papa blames her death on that. Like I tell Domingo, don't take his words to heart, Father Nick."

Before Nick could respond, Eduardo jerked his hat low on his head and stomped out of the office.

"Don't," Constanza said when Nick turned to follow. "He'll go for a walk, cool down, then return and apologize. Hopefully before he goes home and upsets my nephews."

That was another issue Nick needed to discuss with her. "Is Domingo home today?"

"He has school until three. I told him he has to come see you this afternoon."

Domingo was a touchy subject. The teen had skipped two work sessions this week. It was a three-strike program and if he missed one more, Nick would have to remove him, which meant Domingo would have to go back before the judge and risk a harsher sentence. That would be a blow for all of them. How could Nick make the center a success if he failed to help the kids he was supposed to serve?

Domingo hadn't completely disappeared. On the contrary, Nick knew the teen came into the youth center after hours to use the recording equipment. Nick had rewarded him with a key to the new studio after Domingo volunteered extra time to set up the audio/video equipment. Nick explained that any after-hours time Domingo spent in the studio would not count toward community service. Now Nick would have to rescind that privilege.

"If he misses another session, I must report it," Nick said.

"I beg you to bend the rules for all the kids, not just for Domingo. They are starting to trust you, and you are making a difference. I can see it at home, the way Domingo's more patient with his little brother. One of the other boys called me ma'am the other day. Give it time, Father. Please. They will turn around just as this church is turning around."

Nick's frown deepened. The changes she spoke of were invisible to him, which amplified his doubts about his transfer to Prince of Peace. His watch alarm beeped, reminding him of his appointment with Dr. Birdsong.

"Tell Domingo it's critical we speak this week," he said before taking off.

Thanks to a traffic snarl, Nick showed up at Ralph Birdsong's house ten minutes late.

Catherine, Ralph's housekeeper, answered the door but before she could greet Nick, Ralph hollered out, unseen. "Tell him to get his priestly arse in here. And for God's sake, bring the food, Catherine. Men my age have hypoglycemia."

"They also have poor manners," Catherine shouted over one shoulder. Turning back to Nick, she smiled. "He's in his study, Father. Barely alive from the sounds of it. First door on the left."

Nick had visited several years ago and remembered feeling book envy as soon as he entered Ralph's large private office. The walls were floor to ceiling bookcases, crammed with tomes.

Ralph Birdsong had two doctorates, one in theology and another in anthropology. Considered one of the top experts in the world on Christian iconography, he had a fondness for publicly debating

Vatican sources even though he considered himself a devout Roman Catholic. "The wolf keeps the shepherd vigilant," was Ralph's excuse.

Nick greeted his friend with a firm handshake. "Good to see you, Ralph."

Nick had barely taken a seat on the sofa in front of Ralph's desk when Catherine returned with a cart laden with food.

"I thought we'd eat in here, where I can access my notes." Ralph sat at his desk, a huge barge of solid oak.

"Heaven forbid he set foot in the kitchen," Catherine teased as she set a tray before each of them and left.

"Make your prayers quick," Ralph said as he folded his hands. "The Lord knows we're both good-hearted men."

Nick chuckled a rapid blessing, then admired the tray of food on the coffee table before him. An ironstone crock filled with a thick stew of braised beef, potatoes, and carrots. A small, napkin-lined basket held thick slabs of crusty Irish soda bread slathered with yellow butter. Next to that was a small plate layered with wedges of cheddar cheese and apple slices.

"The older I get, the less inclined I am to waste time on manners." Ralph shoveled food in his mouth, chewing as he talked. "I'm fine. You're fine. And if we're not, who cares? Let's talk about this rosary from Iraq. It's an intriguing piece."

Ralph hit a few buttons on his keyboard and the projection screen behind him lit up with shots of the rosary Nick had provided. Some had been cropped and enlarged.

"I'm sorry I wasn't able to examine the actual rosary, though I hope you can convince your niece to ship it back so I can. There are a couple things on the photographs I wanted to call your attention to. First, let me say that this rosary is not from any public collection."

"That's a relief," Nick said.

"That's no guarantee it wasn't stolen from a private owner, but the fact no one has come forward and made a claim makes its origins even more mysterious. There is no artist's mark visible, however, the combination of faceting and inlay is reminiscent of one jeweler who made pieces for a thirteenth century sheikh who ruled a small Middle Eastern kingdom ransacked during the crusades. Here are some of the jeweler's pieces from a museum in Turkey."

The screen changed and split, with close-ups of Janey's rosary beads on the left and secular jewelry from the museum on the right.

Nick noted the similarity of design between the etched rosary beads and the jewelry. "The materials look identical, too."

"As I mentioned, I need to examine the actual beads, but some inlay reminds me of an ancient Arabic script. I've asked a linguistics professor to examine the photographs, too. Here's another feature I want to point out." Ralph shuffled the photographs and zoomed in on a portion of the rosary's chain. "Judging by the twists in the metal, this rosary appears to have been rearranged. Which makes sense. In the thirteenth century, *pater noster* beads didn't have the layout of the rosary we use today. I'm guessing someone rearranged these beads later. It may have been altered more than once "

"Does that explain why the center medallion looks out of place?" Nick asked.

"You noticed that. The center medallion appears to be from the late eighteenth century, making this piece an odd mixture possibly spanning multiple centuries." Ralph shuffled the photos to a different close-up. "Did you notice that one bead is missing? Or rather, has been replaced?"

Once it was called out, Nick noticed the bead in question was not inlaid with silver. It also had a slightly different facet. "Could the old beggar have refashioned the piece?"

"I doubt an old beggar would have the materials and tools needed."

Nick sat back and narrowed his eyes. The differences on the screen blurred. "So there's nothing definite to identify this piece?"

"That's where it gets fuzzy." Ralph took a sip of coffee. "What I'm about to share is pure conjecture as I need to do more research. Years ago, when I was younger and studying at the Vatican libraries, I read a reference to a thirteenth century sheikh's offering that was delivered to Rome. It was vague, just a brief note in a bishop's records about a Middle Eastern emissary bringing a gift of beads. The bishop's guards were instructed to execute the man and destroy the beads, but the man apparently escaped and there were no further notes. I've always wondered what induced a call to murder. I searched for a record of the beads, but found nothing, which begs the question: were they destroyed? Or did they disappear with the emissary? A few years later in France, I read an ancient chronicle of a Templar escorting a Middle Eastern emissary to Rome with beads from a sheikh. It wasn't much more than a recording of payment for safe passage, but it happened around the same time as the bishop's records. When I tried to research it further, I found a third record of two men with beads who sought safe passage back to the Middle East with a caravan in North Africa. The fact that beads are specifically mentioned is of interest, but another note that caught my attention cited a legend about a prophecy of a lost offer of peace. Beads of peace, in fact."

"Beads of peace. Peace rosary." Nick leaned forward, his food forgotten. "A gift from a sheikh? Do you know which part of the Middle East this sheikh was from?" Back in the thirteenth century, there were many independent kingdoms in the Middle East.

"No, which is why I mentioned the master jeweler earlier. If I can confirm the rosary was crafted by that same jeweler, it would tie it to the same time period and give us a more exact place."

As Nick drove back to Prince of Peace a short time later, he pondered Ralph's words. How ironic to learn that seven hundred years ago, someone in the Middle East might have fashioned beads intended as an offer of peace to the church. Could Janey's rosary be related to that story? And as far-fetched as it sounded, could that offer of peace somehow be reignited now?

Back at the youth center, Nick hurried to prepare for the after-school crowd. To his surprise, Domingo waited in the shadows near the front doors.

Nick reminded himself not to launch into lecture mode. "I missed you this week. Everything okay?"

"I've been working on a special project." Domingo reached behind his back and pulled out a shiny DVD in a plastic case. "Here."

Nick took the disc. "What is this?"

"A video with some music I wrote. It's not for you, it's for your niece, Janey. I owe her something for sending that rosary here." Domingo looked Nick straight in the eyes. "My grandfather says we're all fools to believe in God and miracles, but I saw what that rosary did. It healed my aunt, and she means the world to my brother and me. This is a thank you song for Janey. For my aunt. Maybe even for God. You're always saying music is a prayer the soul sings, right? Do you think He would like it?"

Nick's heart turned to mush. "Absolutely. I'm touched by this. And by the fact you remembered something I said."

Domingo laughed. "Sometimes you make sense, Father. Can you upload the video and send it to her? That's my only copy."

"Sure." Nick held the case up. "May I watch it first?"

Domingo looked away before nodding. "If you don't like it, just remember it isn't for you."

Touché, Lord. "I'm sure my niece will be delighted. In fact, I'll send it to her this afternoon."

"Thanks, Father Nick." Domingo moved off. "I have to go see my aunt."

"Don't miss tomorrow," Nick said. "Three times, you know."

Domingo grimaced and rolled his eyes. "I can count. And tomorrow I will make up the hours I missed."

Curious about what the DVD held, Nick headed straight to his office computer. It took a few moments for the disc to boot up and play. He turned up the volume as the video opened with a flash of near blinding light. As the light faded, the setting came into focus. Nick recognized the deserted alley behind the brick buildings not too far from the church.

Domingo appeared in the distance, a dark silhouette striding toward the camera. He wore a black hoodie that nearly covered his face, his hands fisted in the front pockets. His jeans hung low, the denim making a *slishing* sound as he closed in and scowled at the camera. Sunglasses covered his eyes, but his features sharpened. Only the spare-wispy mustache hairs hinted that the tall boy was a juvenile.

Music started, the beat instantly mesmerizing, compelling. The opening riff had a powerful hook that repeated. Four other boys, all students from the center and all wearing the same dark hoodie and jeans, sauntered up beside Domingo, moving in a perfect unison that bespoke hours of practice. Nick marveled that the younger boys had not even hinted that they were part of this.

Domingo began to rap, the others chiming in with harmonies that gave Nick a thrill of anticipation.

"You say you're my homey, that I'm some child of the universe.
No! A freaking child of the most high God.
Yeah, right! Father who? Father who? Yeah, right!
I heard this tale all my life, growing up, getting beat down by those sworn to protect.
Yeah, right! Father who? Father who? Where were you last night?
Our Father who art in Heaven...hallowed be thy name.
Yeah right, yeah right.
Thy kingdom come, thy will be done...

The music pulsed. Nick stood, mesmerized. These kids had put hours into creating a video that appeared to be as professionally made as many he'd seen on YouTube.

"Does on Earth as in Heaven apply to me?
Father who? Father who? Hear my cry. Forgive me.
Give me, give us, our daily bread, forgive as we forgive others.
What? No!
Help me forgive those others... even when I can't.
When I don't want to. When I know they don't deserve it.
Lead us not into temptation — deliver us from evil.

Yeah, right! They say you died on the cross for all of us.
Me. Them. You. But I got to ask, did we deserve it?
The kingdom? The power? And the glory?"

The last verse was a string of "Amens," sung in four-part harmony. At the end, Domingo reached beneath his shirt and tugged out an oversized crucifix. The screen faded to black.

Nick hit REPLAY as tears of awe rolled down his cheeks. Was this yet another miracle of the rosary, one more person brought back into faith before God? This hip-hop version of the Lord's Prayer was musical genius. From the way it was filmed, to the raw emotion of a young person struggling to find God in the gloomy spaces of a tattered world, the video reflected Domingo's talent and his desire to believe.

When it finished, Nick stepped to the window and looked toward where he'd last seen Domingo. What other talents might the boy have? What else might Nick — and everyone else — have missed?

Nick could imagine what detractors would say about the video. Some people would never get hip hop, and this song differed greatly from any past words of worship. But then again, the times were very different. Kids today were on their own, with more peer pressure than ever before and less faith in the guidance adults offered. Could Domingo's video serve as a bridge between generations? Help win the hearts of the young?

Nick thought of Janey. She'd been the one to tell him to connect to his students through their music. What would her reaction be?

CHAPTER TWENTY-FIVE

September 2006
River Haven, Iowa

Janey loved Domingo's hip-hop video. The teen's lyrics — *yeah, right! Father who?* — reflected Janey's angst. She understood the feeling of being shut out of Heaven. Domingo's voice was strong, the beat unforgettable. She featured the video prominently in a blog post on her website.

Ben Hufstedler shared a link to the music video with an online college forum. The video quickly became the most viewed website page, getting so many hits their site couldn't keep up. Janey got Domingo's permission to upload the song to YouTube, where it climbed in popularity.

At home, the news about Farid Zaman claiming responsibility for Teddy Fallon's death took a grim turn when Zaman not only identified the attacker as a follower but also released a video snippet filmed by an unidentified third party.

The brief clip showed Teddy sitting helpless in a wheelchair, his arms thrust up to shield himself from the machete's blows as Zaman's interpreter gloated that Teddy's death fulfilled some crazy version of divine will. There were unconfirmed reports that the attacker had been after the bounty promised by Zaman's *fatwa*. The Cincinnati police announced FBI involvement as the case was labeled an act of terrorism.

Janey couldn't stop thinking about her last phone conversation with Teddy. He'd been so eager for the rosary service. "I know it will help to heal me," he'd insisted. She regretted not attending the rosary service in Cincinnati that was held in Teddy's honor. Layton had quashed her attempt to go with him, but in retrospect, she wished she had just gone alone. Especially after Merle Hammett, a prominent Ohio business owner, made his crazy claim. That Merle's wife received a miraculous cure seemed secondary to his assertion that the rosary came from a dead terrorist. If Janey had been present, she would have challenged Merle on the spot.

"That wouldn't have been appropriate, not at a funeral wake," Dad told her as they finished their evening meal. "And you can't deny the woman's claim of a miraculous healing. That's like questioning God."

Janey wasn't sure what to make of the reports of miracles, but it seemed that God definitely played favorites. She was grateful when Perry changed the subject.

Matt and Perry were gathered around the table with Janey, Eileen, and Dad. The farm's kitchen was their sanctuary, their waiting room and tonight they were expecting a call from Layton.

Layton had returned to Fort DeWald after Teddy's funeral, communicating with her father and brothers while ignoring Janey. She told herself she was ignoring him, too, which made it easier to nurse her bruised heart and ego. Layton had made it clear she didn't matter to him, except in terms of whatever obligation he felt toward John. That was the last thing she wanted. Now she hoped he'd stay away until she returned to Iowa City next semester.

Still, when the phone rang, Janey leaned close to eavesdrop as soon as Dad answered and said, "Hello, Layton. Yes. Yes." Then he put the call on speaker. "He wants to talk to all of us."

"Evening, y'all." Layton's lush drawl filled the room, tormenting her. "I wanted to let you know that Fallon's cousin, Merle Hammett, held a news conference about the rosary today. Part of it is posted online. His wife's doctor made a convincing presentation regarding her claim of a miraculous cure, but Merle continues to push his version of the rosary's origin. Another relative now sides with him, swearing that Fallon told them John recovered the rosary off the body of one of the terrorists killed that day."

"But you were there when John got the rosary from the old beggar!" Dad said. "You were an eyewitness."

Layton agreed. "Fallon told them he was an eyewitness, too. Danny Carpenter and I denied the story and reiterated the truth, including the fact that Fallon wasn't even present when the old beggar first gave John the rosary. Fallon's family, however, remains unconvinced."

Matt propped his forearms on the table. "It's tough to dispute the word of a deceased loved one."

Janey recalled the times Teddy sounded confused when they spoke. "They know he was taking a lot of medication, right?"

"Yes, but no one wants to speak of it now that he's gone," Layton said. "They're also dealing with the shock that Fallon's murder may be connected to Zaman's Black Death group."

"What's the Army's official stance on all this? Or is it 'under investigation?'" Dad made air quotes with his fingers.

"That's a SOP response in any situation involving loss of life," Layton said. "I doubt the Army will ever comment on the rosary beads, but they should confirm that only authorized personnel went near the bodies of the terrorists. There's strict protocol about that. Unfortunately, the Army is slow to respond, and in the meantime, Merle's version is getting circulated."

"Merle has no right to distort the truth about John and the rosary," Janey said. "I respect that Teddy's family has suffered a tragedy, but so did the McKays. After I watch Merle's video, I will post a rebuttal on the rosary website."

"Can you wait until after we talk?" Layton asked. "Another hasty reaction will only make it worse. I have a doctor's appointment tomorrow, then I'll head back to River Haven."

Until after we talk. The words riled her. Layton's promise to talk had carried little weight in the past. Was he blowing her off again?

"We'll see you tomorrow then," Dad said. "Take care."

As soon as the call disconnected, Dad moved to a desktop computer in the small alcove behind the table. "I want to look up this Hammett guy. His name sounds familiar."

Janey and her brothers crowded in as Dad did an internet search. Several images popped up.

"I knew I recognized him." Dad enlarged one photograph. "Merle Hammett's made a fortune in pork rinds and potato chips of all things. In the early days, he made his own commercials and called himself The Pork Rind King. Even wore a crown. It was hokey as heck, but he sold a lot of pork rinds."

Perry pointed to a link on the screen. "There's the one mentioning the rosary."

The title of the video infuriated Janey. *The Truth About The Miracle Rosary.* "It's the Peace Rosary," she muttered as Dad turned up the volume.

Merle Hammett appeared much older in the video. His hair was grayer, the skin on his face looser than in his publicity photos. He stood in front of a podium in what looked like a conference room. A large company logo appeared on the wall to the left.

"Leave it to the Pork Rind King to get in a little marketing," Dad fumed.

Merle glanced up from his notes. "You've seen the news coverage of my cousin, Teddy Fallon's murder at the hands of a zealot. Poor Teddy had lost a leg fighting in Iraq and was defenseless when attacked. I believe my cousin was killed in an attempt to stifle the truth about the miracle rosary recovered after a battle in Baghdad. A rosary that has already been credited with several miracles, including one that occurred at a recent prayer service here in Cincinnati that saved the life of my wife, Lucy."

Merle looked at the camera with a serious expression. "Before he died, my cousin Teddy shared stories about this rosary. With all due respect to the girl who started the rosary website, Teddy gave a very different accounting of how the sacred rosary was passed on, which I believe explains the reason my cousin was murdered. According to my cousin, the rosary came directly from one of the deceased terrorists who attacked Teddy's squad in a skirmish that happened ten days before the last battle that claimed so many of his comrades. When I questioned why a radical terrorist would have a Catholic rosary, Teddy suggested that perhaps the man was a closet Christian."

Merle shook his head. "I think it was more. What if that now-dead jihadist who had this rosary was trying to surrender to our troops? Maybe he hoped to come to America where he could freely practice his Christian beliefs? It's important to understand that one of those jihadists was the son of Farid Zaman. Think about it: it could have been Zaman's own son who possessed the rosary. A son who knew his own father would execute him for his Christian beliefs and I believe that's the real reason Zaman ordered a *fatwa*. To silence the US soldiers who knew the truth about where that rosary came from."

Janey couldn't believe what she was hearing. Perry put a hand on her shoulder as Merle's video went on.

A photo of the rosary appeared on the screen behind Merle. "My family will forever owe a debt to that precious rosary for healing my wife," Merle said. "Therefore, I'm announcing plans to erect a marker in Iraq, a small shrine at the exact spot where the rosary was found. I hope it will serve as a beacon of hope to other Iraqi Christians in the Middle East. If a terrorist's son could dare attempt to convert to Christianity, so can others."

As the video ended, Janey's temper spilled over. "How dare he make such bogus claims?" Merle's premises had been worded to include speculative modifiers. *Perhaps... Maybe... What if...* She glanced at the comments, which indicated most viewers had taken the outrageous and false claims as gospel.

Dad shut down the computer before turning to Janey. "I'll contact Dave Williams and see if we can do something legally to have Hammett's video taken down. I'm not about to let anyone call my son a liar."

Dave Williams was her father's corporate attorney. While Dad meant well, Janey knew the likelihood of getting it removed was slight. "Freedom of expression doesn't mean it has to be true," she said.

"I'd still let Dad's attorney look at this," Matt said. "Sometimes truth is best emphasized with legal threats."

———

BY THE NEXT MORNING, Janey had over one hundred emails requesting the rosary. Many included heartbreaking recounts of loved ones desperate for a miracle for a family member.

That the surge of requests was in response to Merle Hammett's news conference disheartened her. Every email she read referenced 'The Miracle Rosary.'

Janey posted a general update on the website and blog. First, she reiterated the correct name: The Peace Rosary. Then she restated the website's mission, to honor John's request to pray for peace. She emphasized that John's story about the rosary was correct and promised an updated statement soon.

She also disabled the online sign-up calendar that now blinked with an error message from too many requests. She highlighted details of the previously scheduled rosary services — one in Texas, one in Louisiana, and the one in River Haven on John's birthday. The Texas and Louisiana churches had signed up because of Uncle Nick's services in Chicago, before the Cincinnati service was even held, and she wanted to honor those requests. Once the sensation-

alism of Merle Hammett's claims died down, she'd reconsider scheduling future services.

When she came into the kitchen of the farmhouse, Dad handed
her a sheet of paper covered with names and phone numbers.

"These are reporters and press outlets who'd like to speak with
you about the rosary," he said. "Your brothers suggest we hold our
own press conference and let Dave Williams field questions. I think
it's important we respond quickly. Those fools at the Justice Freedom
Association have jumped on the bandwagon now, too, and I won't
have the likes of Randy Keener belittling John."

Janey set the list aside. The thought of the JFA using the incident
to further their cause riled her as much as Merle Hammett's false
claims. "What has Randy said now?"

Dad ran a hand through his hair. "He's referring to John as a religious martyr. Keener also claims tax dollars were used to allow
soldiers to bring home religious icons from jihadists."

Janey picked up the list and scanned the names of reporters. "I
don't care what Layton said, I'm formulating a rebuttal. The truth is
on our side. I will give an exclusive interview to Frank Delloyd at
DNN news. He lost a nephew in Iraq a year ago and is supportive of
the troops."

———

LATER THAT AFTERNOON, Janey went to the Quincy, Illinois,
news affiliate and taped a remote interview with Frank Delloyd. By
that time, the Iraq ambassador had officially renounced Merle's
claims as false and insisted that no shrine would be permitted within
Iraq's borders.

When Janey finished the interview, she found three missed calls
and a text message. All were from her friend, Ben Hufstedler.

We've got a problem with the rosary website. I've taken it down
until we talk, Ben's message read.

Janey called Ben right away. "What happened?"

"The rosary website was hacked. A statement denouncing the rosary was posted along with a graphic video of a beheading and a reference to the *fatwa* declared against John's squad. Whoever did it covered their tracks well. I traced it to a server in India then hit a wall."

Janey groaned. "Any idea how many people saw it?"

"Over two thousand according to the stats. The mailbox is at its limit as well. I suggest we keep the website offline for a few days to give me a chance to beef up security and upgrade the email system. I also need to make sure no Trojan backdoor viruses were uploaded."

"To allow the hackers future access?" Janey asked.

"Exactly. Look, I know it's discouraging, but we'll be better prepared in the future."

After Janey disconnected, she concentrated on driving as she left the television station. Mentally, she seethed. First Merle's claim, then the Justice Freedom Association's asinine response, and now someone hacked her website. That she couldn't control any of the events added to her frustration.

As soon as she was out of the Quincy city limits, she sped north. Her father was meeting late this afternoon with his attorney, but it would be tomorrow before the McKays could schedule their own press conference.

When she crested a hill near Keokuk, Iowa, she slowed. The mighty Mississippi River came into view, a dark moving ribbon that edged the valley below.

When she and John were young, they'd beg their mother to drive this route for another round of *who could spot the river first*. The contest always ended in a fierce argument with John claiming Janey cheated if she yelled "There it is!" before he did. She made the same accusation when John yelled out first.

Mom would threaten to head back home if they kept arguing. That always shut John up. For a few seconds anyway. Then he'd switch to begging Mom to stop so he could hunt for crawdads. One of her brother's get-rich-quick schemes included raising crawdads in the farm pond, and they needed an endless supply of breeding stock. A willing partner in John's every idea, no matter how ludicrous, Janey would join in begging.

On impulse, she slowed and took the next exit. At the access road, she turned left and watched for the dirt road that would lead to the scenic pullover that Mother used to take them to. Driving by instinct, Janey turned down a deeply rutted road that cut through bottomland. The road cut left, then right. Then—

There it was.

Mom's secret place was a long-forgotten picnic area abandoned when the new highway was built back in the sixties. Since Janey hadn't been here since Mom died, she was amazed she found it.

At the small parking lot, Janey climbed out. Nothing had changed. A half-rotted picnic table, a rusted trash can chained to a pole. She wondered if that trash can still held the remnants of their last picnic.

Janey could barely see the river through the dense stand of papery-bark river birch that lined the banks. She found the short path between the trees and remembered how she and John would race toward the water.

While she and John waded and turned over rocks, snatching up the wily crawdads, Mom would tell stories. Her recounting of Tom Sawyer inspired John's next big idea after he figured out that the bass in the farm pond devoured those crawdads as fast as they dumped them in. "We'll build a raft and float down to Hannibal, Missouri," he promised Janey.

They spent most of that summer building that raft at the farm, skinning logs with old butcher knives, never once questioning how they'd transport it to the river. The finished raft turned out to be huge. When the adults forbade the trip, John launched the raft on the pond, which hadn't made the adventure any less grand. The pond became an ocean and when they later added a sail, the raft transformed to a pirate ship.

The memories had bittersweet tears brimming in Janey's eyes. She would have followed her brother anywhere and defended his grandiose schemes with the fervor of a TV lawyer. When had that undying loyalty faded?

It hadn't.

That realization had her sobbing more fiercely. No matter what her brother did, she loved him. That was the gift of family.

Maybe it was time Janey returned to the cemetery and made peace with John's – and Mom's – passing.

As she headed back toward the parking lot, her cell phone rang. When she glanced at caller ID, her pulse quaked. It was Layton Burnet.

"Hello."

"Janey, where are you?" His voice sounded distant. "I'm at the farm, but no one's here. Matt and Perry weren't at the store, either."

She climbed inside her car and cranked it up, suddenly eager to get back. Whatever resolve she'd mustered to not care fled at the sound of Layton's voice. "Go on in the house and make yourself at home. The door's unlocked. I'll be there in fifteen minutes."

"Let me meet you." His voice sounded odd.

"Is something going on?"

He exhaled sharply. "A bomb was left at Sergeant Boswell's home. It was discovered before it detonated, but the FBI believes it was sent by one of Zaman's followers. And they're warning everyone connected to our squad."

CHAPTER TWENTY-SIX

September 2006
River Haven, Iowa

A bomb. At Boswell's house. Janey clutched the steering wheel.

When Sergeant Boswell had called her family after John died, there had been children's voices in the background.

That Boswell's family had been targeted — *with a bomb* — horrified Janey. She had been raised by tough men, who joked about fear. But the McKays had one common vulnerability: Family.

"We've got to warn Matt, Perry, and Dad." Janey's voice quavered as she spoke.

"They're not answering their phones. Do you know where they are?"

She rubbed her forehead. "They had a meeting scheduled with Dad's attorney. Perry sent me a text about an hour ago. They probably have their phones muted, but I can call the office to verify."

"If you've heard from him that recently, it's fine. I've left detailed messages for all of them," Layton went on. "Right now, I need to know exactly where you are."

Janey glanced out the windshield at her deserted location. Moments ago, she'd felt secure. Now she felt isolated. "I'm at a riverfront park, off the grid. But leaving now." She put the car in reverse.

"Don't start your car!"

Layton's command had her slamming on the brakes. "I already did. Are you worried about car bombs?"

"Sorry. No. Yes. I'm worried about everything when I don't have eyes on you. Is anyone else nearby? Could you have been followed?"

Her eyes darted around. She didn't see anyone, but a herd of hippos could have followed her for all she knew. Who paid attention to that kind of stuff?

"There are no other cars around. I think I'm okay." She needed to hear herself say that.

"You said you're off the grid. I need more than that to find you. Describe your surroundings."

"This place isn't on a map and telling you I'm surrounded by cornfields isn't helpful. I just left and am going back to the main highway."

"What main highway? I'll head that way."

"You don't need to."

"Yes. I do. Humor me, Janey. What road did you take out of Quincy?"

"Highway 61. I was north of Keokuk when I turned off." She tried to recall landmarks. "I'd already passed Montrose but hadn't yet reached old Ortho Road."

"Good. That gives me a bearing. Just keep talking to me. Calm me down." His voice was lower, deeper. Soothing.

Calm him down? She was the one hyperventilating. She checked her rearview mirror again, but at this speed the dirt road behind her was a dust cloud. If someone followed, they had a perfect cover. *Keep talking to me.*

"Did everything look okay at the farm when you got there?" she asked.

"Yes. Fuller was on the front porch. She gave me her glad-to-see-you yap versus her Timmy's-in-the-well bark."

"She wouldn't let a stranger on the property." Janey paused at a crossroads, uncertain what direction to turn. She spotted a familiar stand of hickory trees to the East and headed toward them.

"I remember the first time I came home with John. Fuller didn't growl, but she blocked my path until your brother vouched for me," Layton said.

Janey remembered the first time Layton visited the farm, too. She had met him briefly when her family attended John's graduation from basic. While she didn't believe in love at first sight, meeting Layton Burnet had robbed her of breath. She'd been ecstatic when John invited Layton to the farm for a few days leave before they reported to advanced training at Fort DeWald. Had that really been almost three years ago?

Layton asked for an update. "Where are you now?"

"I just turned onto Highway 61." That she knew where she was helped her relax. "Where are you?"

"Just passed the Catfish Café."

"The Racetrack gas station will be about three miles on your right. I'll meet you there."

At the station, she drove to the far side of the store's building where Layton was parked. As soon as he climbed out, she noticed that the awkward block and sling were gone, a reminder he'd been scheduled to begin physical therapy.

She threw her car in PARK and opened the door. The anxiety she'd been fighting surfaced, leaving her trembling. Layton closed the distance and tugged her into his arms, hugging her to his uninjured side.

Janey tightened her grip around his waist, drawing strength from him. When he held her, she felt safe. Grounded.

"I didn't mean to frighten you," he whispered after a few moments. "But I feel better knowing where you are."

His phone started ringing, shattering the moment. She stepped back as he checked the caller ID.

"It's Matt," he said. "Hello."

She wrapped her arms around herself, holding in the warmth he'd offered, as she listened to Layton talk to her brother.

"Here's what I know. Sergeant Boswell came home this morning to get his son's bike and spotted a box left on the front porch. They live off base, but his wife is recovering from surgery, so their kids are staying with her parents in Peoria. As soon as Sarge pulled in, a neighbor came over to complain that a delivery van clipped one of his sprinklers driving off too fast. Sarge took one look at the box's label and called it in. His name was misspelled with two e's instead of two l's — the same way Farid Zaman misspelled it. The base dispatched a team, found an incendiary device inside. They had to detonate it but sent what remained to a crime lab. The Army's got all of us on high alert. I came straight here from the VA hospital in Iowa City."

An incendiary bomb? The thought of what that could have done to Boswell or his family chilled Janey.

"I'm with Janey now. We'll meet you back at the farm." After Layton disconnected, he turned back to her. "We need to go."

"I can't stop thinking about what could have happened to Sergeant Boswell." She closed her eyes, recalling visions from her worst nightmares.

Layton's hand cupped her chin gently, his thumb stroking the skin beneath her jaw. "Breathe."

She met his gaze, which only made it harder to breathe.

"Focus on facts," he went on. "Boswell is okay. Period."

"But Teddy—"

"We're not discussing Teddy right now. Look, ride with me. Perry and I will get your car later."

As tempting as it was to go with him, she stepped away. Being this close to Layton made her feel vulnerable. At any moment he could cut her off and retreat behind that impenetrable wall of his. "I'm okay. And I'd rather not leave my car."

"I'll follow you back to the farm. Matt said the FBI is on their way, too. They're coming to tell your father about the incident."

Janey took the bypass, avoiding town traffic, and made it to home in record time. Matt and Perry pulled in right behind them, followed by two black Suburbans. Eileen looked shaken and stood close to Dad.

Fuller moved in beside Janey and woofed. She bent down and hugged the collie. "Easy, girl."

"That's the FBI," Dad said. "Apparently they came by while we were gone, but Fuller wouldn't let them near the house."

"Good girl." Layton and Perry spoke at the same time.

Four men climbed out of the Suburbans. The two agents in suits had visited before. The other two were dressed all in black, like SWAT team members.

Fuller growled. "It's okay," Janey said.

Special Agent Holmes introduced everyone. The two men in black were part of the bomb squad. "As a precaution, these two would like to look around while we talk."

Perry stepped forward. "I'll go with them."

Dad frowned as the other agents walked toward the house. "Are they looking for another explosive device? Have we been targeted, too?"

Agent Holmes shook his head. "Not that we're aware of. They will look for anything suspicious and offer safety tips. This is a precautionary measure, but keep in mind there was no warning of the attack on Teddy Fallon or the bomb left at the Sergeant's. Army CID has asked us to help notify all the families in your son's squad and connect with local law enforcement. On a separate note, we also have reports that a grave of one soldier in Kansas was desecrated."

Layton leaned in. "That had to be Ricky Sturk. What happened?"

"Police believe someone may have tried to exhume the remains. The ground was disturbed, and a shovel was recovered as evidence. It happened late at night. Apparently, some thrill-seeking teens taking part in a Halloween-type dare scared the perps off."

Dad's expression grew intense. "Farid Zaman's behind all of this, isn't he?"

The Agent's demeanor remained unreadable. "There has not been another claim by Zaman since Teddy Fallon's death. However, the Army is trying to contain information about the bomb at Boswell's and asks that you not speak publicly about it. It's not unusual for a terrorist organization to claim credit for an incident they hear about in the news."

Perry returned with the other two agents. "Everything looks okay. They've given me some pointers that we can discuss later." He leaned down and scratched Fuller's head. "Janey's dog gets high marks for alert fierceness."

Agent Holmes passed out business cards again. "If you see or hear anything unusual, let us or your local sheriff know immediately. We're headed there next for a briefing."

Inside the kitchen, everyone gathered around the table. Janey listened as Layton reiterated the full story on Boswell for Dad and her brothers.

"A misspelled name?" Dad rapped his knuckles on the table. "A *faux pas* that may have saved his life." He nodded at Perry. "What did you learn from the bomb squad guys?"

"Nothing new. That being rural means more exposure. We live on farms, with no close neighbors. We're surrounded by fields that offer multiple access points to the property. They said Fuller's protectiveness is a plus. I guess she charged the agents, growling and baring teeth, when they climbed out of their cars. It persuaded them to retreat. They suggested having security cameras and alarms installed. I'll ask the sheriff's department to increase patrols, which will be another deterrent." Perry looked at Janey. "They also suggested you move back in the house, kiddo. The bunkhouse is too isolated."

"I'm not afraid," she said. Worried? Yes. But not for herself. The thought of her family or Layton being harmed terrified her.

"A little fear is not a terrible thing, even for a McKay," Layton said.

Dad scowled. "I hate that any of this is necessary, but I agree, Janey-girl. You need to move back in here until this Zaman character is locked up."

"Speaking of locks, that also means locking doors. Cars and houses," Layton went on. "When you go out, stick to main roads. Park in highly visible areas, as close to an entrance as you can get. Cell phones should always be charged and on your person. And no going off alone. Everyone needs to buddy up. I'll be around as much as possible to help, too."

Dad pointed to Layton's arm. "I forgot to ask about your shoulder. Did you see the doctors in Iowa City? The sling is gone, but you're still favoring your arm."

Janey noticed that Layton straightened before answering. "I'm supposed to wear the sling for shorter periods each day until I start physical therapy. Doc won't release me back to duty yet, so I'll be on medical leave at least another two weeks."

"Stay here," Dad said. "We have plenty of room. And we're closer to Iowa City than Fort DeWald for therapy."

"We'd feel better having you close by," Perry added.

"I could make you more of a target by staying here," Layton said.

"No more than we already are, though, right?" Matt asked. "Who knows you would even be in Iowa? We won't advertise it and I'm guessing your Army records list Texas as home."

"True." Layton looked at Janey for a moment before turning back to Matt.

She held her breath, wondering what he was thinking. This afternoon she'd sensed his concern for her. His relief at seeing her at the gas station had been tangible. Had she given up on him too soon? If he was around the farm more, could they recapture the ease they once had? Would he be willing to give them a chance?

"Thank you. I'd be glad to stay," Layton said.

Eileen stood. "Well, then. I better start dinner and get linens on the beds upstairs."

"I can take care of the beds." Janey's pulse elevated to realize Layton would stay upstairs, too.

"There's one more point we need to discuss, Janey," Layton said. "You need to take the soldier photographs off your rosary website. After Merle Hammett's crazy claims, your website will be under more scrutiny. The less that's known about the others in the squad, the better."

"The entire website is down right now." She explained about the site being hacked. "I'll have Ben temporarily disable the Soldier's Tribute page before putting it back online."

"I'll let the Army CID know about the hack," Layton said. "Tell Ben to preserve whatever cyber footprints he can."

Dad pushed to his feet. "I'm going to head out to the cemetery before it gets much later. I won't rest easy until I've checked on John."

Perry stood. "Matt and I are coming, too."

"I'll keep an eye on things here, sir," Layton said. "I need to make a few phone calls."

―――――――

THOUGH JANEY HAD MOVED to the bunkhouse after Dad and Eileen married six months ago, Dad had insisted she keep her room upstairs. He'd made the same request when John moved out to the bunkhouse, but John hadn't complied. Declaring a need for newness and independence, John transported everything he owned to the bunkhouse. In the end, he recreated the same bedroom, with the same furniture and layout. While Eileen converted his old bedroom in the main house to a guest room, Janey still thought of it as John's room. Memories were powerful binders.

Wanting to keep a connection to the farmhouse, Janey had left her furniture upstairs along with most childhood mementos. When she moved out to the bunkhouse, she'd taken over the already-furnished second bedroom because that was where Layton had stayed whenever he visited. She'd drawn comfort and heartache from the thought of sleeping on the same mattress Layton had.

Upstairs, Janey rifled through the linen closet for the softest sheets she could find before putting them on the guest bed, taking extra care to smooth the fabric and tuck it tight. She'd bet Layton slept on the side closest to the door, but she wasn't sure if he slept on his back or side. Regardless of preference, he was likely stuck on his back because of his shoulder injury. She fluffed the pillows and arranged the chenille spread before going in search of extra pillows he could use to prop his arm.

In the upstairs bathroom, she set out clean towels and a basket with travel spares like a razor and toothbrush. When she slid a fresh bar of soap into the shower, she paused, not knowing whether to laugh or cry over the realization that she was excited to think they would share soap. *I need a life.*

By the time her father returned, Janey had moved some of her belongings from the bunkhouse to her room upstairs. Dad confirmed that everything appeared fine at the cemetery. They watched the evening newscast, but Janey's interview with Frank Delloyd was cut because of breaking news that an airplane had crashed in Los Angeles.

Disappointed, Janey helped Eileen prepare supper. Eileen made spaghetti with meatballs. Janey diced vegetables for a tossed salad while Eileen sprinkled grated Parmesan cheese and chopped parsley on garlic bread.

A lump formed in Janey's throat as she watched Eileen move between the oven and stove. In the year before Mom died, when she'd been sick, the family ate mostly frozen TV dinners. John claimed to give Janey cooking lessons by telling her how to unbox an entrée, which areas of the cover to pierce, how many minutes to set on the timer. That she couldn't cook had never bothered her before. Now she wondered how she'd prepare meals for her own family one day.

Her own family? Flustered, she grabbed a stack of plates and moved to set dishes around the table.

"I'll help." Layton came up beside her with a handful of silverware. "You have to tell me which side the fork goes on. I'm better at using utensils than setting a table. My, um, parents didn't do family meals."

Janey recalled a similar remark he'd made once, about how he was used to eating meals while leaning against a counter after his family's kitchen table was destroyed during a fight.

"Don't laugh, but for years John was my sole etiquette tutor," Janey said. "It was as bad as it sounds. He said to put the silverware closest to a person's dominant hand, so they could eat faster. It wasn't until Perry married Lisa that I learned fork on the left, knife on the right."

"Fork on the left it is." Layton grinned. "Now I'm wondering what else he told you."

———

AFTER DINNER, Perry dropped off an apple pie from Lisa but didn't stay long. Janey cleaned the dishes, then headed upstairs to unpack her suitcase. Staying in her old bedroom evoked memories from when she and John were children. Her own motocross trophies and 4-H ribbons still filled the shelves above her desk. John had been there for every single win. While she'd raced motocross as fiercely as he had, those wins never meant as much.

She touched the largest of the 4-H trophies. John had declined to take part in the livestock shows, claiming no time between football and motocross, but he'd encouraged Janey and even helped when she was raising calves and sheep in junior high. She quit 4-H, though, after overhearing John tell a friend that farming was for losers.

She stared at the rows of livestock photos, longing for simpler times. Swiping at the tears streaming down her cheeks, she grabbed her robe and headed for the bathroom.

As soon as she stepped into the hall, she collided with Layton. "Oh! Did I hurt your arm?" She scrambled away so quickly she hit the wall behind her.

"Easy. I'm fine. You clipped my good side." He narrowed his eyes. "Are you okay?"

He wasn't wearing a shirt and had obviously just taken a shower. She couldn't stop staring at the way his chest was now divided by violence. One side was muscular, in that way that had always weakened her knees. The other side was an angry quilt of stitch marks, the scars still red, the contractures from damaged skin and grafts tight. Her hand moved forward.

He caught her fingers, preventing her from touching his scars, but not letting her go. "Tell me why you're crying."

She shifted her gaze to meet his. "It's been a wild day. I guess everything just hit me."

He moved closer and ran light fingertips through the tears beneath her eye. "It's been nonstop for a while, hasn't it? That you handle it with such poise amazes me."

She couldn't help herself. She leaned in and dropped her forehead to his shoulder. "I haven't handled any of it well. I'm—"

From below, her father's voice called up the stairwell. "That you, Janey-girl? You sleep well. See you in the morning."

Layton backed off immediately, breaking the delicate thread between them.

"Good night, Daddy." She replied even though she knew her father had already moved away.

"Good night, Janey," Layton whispered before turning and disappearing into the room down the hall.

She exhaled. For a moment she thought he might kiss her. Or was that just another dream? Either way, she would not get any sleep with him so close...yet so far.

CHAPTER TWENTY-SEVEN

September 2006
Baghdad, Iraq

The backdrop of gunfire, the sound of revolution, soothed Cleric Ibrahim Yassin as he contemplated the latest news.

Farid Zaman would be furious to hear the rumors touted by Westerners that his late son had been a Christian. Just a week earlier they had been celebrating the news of the machete attack. The soldier's death was even more gruesome for having been carried out on US soil. That the attacker hadn't lived to collect the bounty promised by the *fatwa* proved provident. Dead, the attacker evoked even more anxiety and questions. Fear was a powerful ally.

Zaman's claim of having masterminded the attack had increased his stature in the Middle East, securing them greater funding and weapons from supporters. Zaman swore that his promise to "rain down fire on the bases in Iraq" had barely begun.

As always, Yassin remained in the shadows, content to let Zaman take credit. *"Fear the hand of Zaman. It has far reach!"*

This latest news, however, threatened Yassin's hard-won

advancements. The story of the rosary was especially troubling. Its connection to Zaman's son was as false as the western ideology of praying for peace in the Middle East, but that was not what worried Yassin the most.

The beads needed to be discredited before they were tied to an old prophecy. *When two men rise and meet again, the circle for peace will be restored.*

That it was an obscure prophecy didn't make it any less repugnant. There would never be peace in the Middle East as long as there were infidels on Islam's soil. He needed to redirect attention away from those cursed beads.

Yassin steepled his fingers beneath his chin. A swift rebuttal by Zaman would shore up support of the local warlords until their latest retaliations went into effect. Shock and awe weren't exclusive to the West.

A harsh knocking sounded just before Yassin's assistant entered. "Zaman demands your presence immediately."

Yassin stood. "I will go. But first, I have a very important job for your spies."

CHAPTER TWENTY-EIGHT

September 2006
River Haven, Iowa

Janey laid awake most of the night, unable to stop thinking that Layton was just down the hall. So close, yet so unreachable. Would he be around long enough for her to convince him to give her — them — a chance? To hear him talk, he expected to be cleared for a return to duty soon. If he got accepted into OCS, he'd leave Fort DeWald, which would end his frequent visits.

She recalled his scars, a hellish map imprinted on his flesh that detailed every hurt he'd suffered. What he'd endured physically and emotionally was beyond her comprehension. He'd see those scars in the mirror daily and would carry them on his body for the rest of his life. When she'd tried to touch him, he'd stopped her. She longed to help him heal, but how?

The door to Layton's room was closed when she passed by the next morning. Was he sleeping in? Downstairs, the kitchen was deserted. She heard voices in the living room, muffled by the sound of the television.

Layton appeared in the doorway and motioned to her. "You will want to see this, Janey."

She hurried to the living room. Dad motioned for silence as he turned up the television's volume. The logo of a major twenty-four-hour cable news network flashed briefly. Behind the reporter was a split screen showing photographs of Merle Hammett on one side and Farid Zaman on the other. Dread poked sharp spines between Janey's shoulders as she listened.

"Yesterday, Mr. Hammett announced that over a quarter-million dollars had been raised to support his quest to establish a Christian shrine in an alley in Baghdad, where a rosary was purportedly obtained by a US soldier, John McKay," the reporter said. "That rosary is at the center of a controversy that includes a growing number of claims of miraculous healings, like the one in Chicago that inspired a hip-hop version of The Lord's Prayer which is smashing records on YouTube. There are differing accounts of how John McKay came to possess the rosary. The rosary's website purports that the beads were a gift from a beggar whom John McKay rescued in a gun battle in Iraq. Mr. Hammett asserts that the rosary came from a terrorist killed in that same battle."

Trepidation pooled in Janey's stomach as she waited for the reporter to continue. "This morning there is a new video from Farid Zaman, denying that the rosary was associated with the deceased terrorists. It includes footage of the old beggar who originally possessed the rosary."

The video, captioned in English, showed an elderly man walking slowly. He wore rags and his face was bruised, his arm tied in a makeshift sling. The man nodded vigorously when shown a photograph of John McKay.

"Yes, yes." The old man's words were captioned in English. "That is the soldier who beat me and stole the beads I found earlier in the trash. He said I should be grateful I wasn't dead like the others they had slaughtered that day."

Rage clawed at Janey. How dare anyone falsely accuse her

brother of such atrocities? She glanced at her father. Dad's nostrils flared, his face growing redder as he stared at the television. Eileen had one hand over her mouth, the other resting on Dad's knee.

Before moving on to another story, the reporter remarked that the Army had no comment on Zaman's "unsubstantiated accusations."

Layton pointed to the screen, his eyes dark with anger. "That was *not* the beggar who gave John the rosary. The old man John rescued was missing a foot. He had a cut on his forehead, which Danny Carpenter treated, but no broken arm. That man's black eye and facial contusions looked recent, as if incurred in the last day or two."

"How can they broadcast such blatant lies on national television?" Dad raged. "I ought to sue them for slandering my son's name." The phone rang, and Dad pushed to his feet. "I hope that's a reporter asking for a comment. Boy, have I got a lot to say."

"Dad, wait." Janey followed him. "We're angry and upset. Is that the position from which we want to field questions? What have you always told me?"

Her father made a huffing noise, then nodded. "Never react to provocation with emotion. Never react in defense. I never dreamed one of you kids would parrot that back to me, but you're right. I will let calls go to the answering machine, if you can figure out how to mute it so I don't have to hear it. There goes my cell phone, too, but that's Matt's ringtone."

While Dad answered his cell phone, Janey moved to the kitchen alcove and adjusted the controls so calls went straight to voicemail without ringing. She jumped when Layton came up behind her and touched her arm. She whirled to face him.

"Sorry. I wanted to make sure you were okay after watching that," he said.

"Did you already know about it?"

"One of my buddies on base called me this morning. And no, I know nothing more than what was reported on the news." Layton stopped talking as Dad's voice grew agitated.

Janey waited until her father ended the call. "What's wrong with Matt?"

"Apparently Randy Keener sent out a JFA press release that basically agrees with Zaman's accusations," Dad said. "Matt says that for all Keener's talk about being an American patriot, the statement reads like he supports a terrorist. Apparently, the national JFA organization thought so, too. They issued a retraction, stating that Keener does not have the authority to release official statements on the JFA's behalf."

Dad shook his head before continuing. "Matt is on his way over to see Layton. I'm going out to the barn to get a few chores done. Work off a little steam."

Janey tried to act casual as she moved to follow her father. His stress level worried her. "Wait up, Daddy. I need to get a few things from the bunkhouse and feed Fuller."

Outside, they walked together without speaking. Then Dad reached for her hand. "I'm glad you're here, Janey-girl. I miss our private time."

Up until the time Janey left for college, she'd always helped with evening chores. She hadn't hated farm work, like John, in part because Dad called it "their" time.

By the time they returned to the house, only Matt's truck was in the drive. "Layton took off to meet some of his Army buddies to see what they can do to refute Zaman's claim," Matt said. "Ace Sentry Services is on their way to install the security cameras we discussed. As soon as we finish with them, we can do a conference call with your attorney."

———

JANEY SPENT the rest of the day researching an article for the newspaper and catching up on classwork, but she worried about her father. Dad continued to fret over Zaman's claims, which kept his blood pressure elevated. Eileen hovered closer than usual, a sure sign that she was concerned, too.

Later that afternoon, Dad's attorney, Dave Williams, released a statement on behalf of the McKay family that restated the actual story of how John came to possess the rosary and dismissed all other claims.

Layton finally called Dad just before supper.

After hanging up, Dad exhaled. "Apparently, Danny Carpenter's family has some pull with a Chicago television station. He and Layton recorded an interview this afternoon that's supposed to air on the news tonight. Layton also said he'll be late getting in."

In a continuing ritual, Matt and Perry came by the farm in time for the evening news. Janey perched on the edge of her chair as the newscaster summarized local events before mentioning the upcoming segment with Layton.

"In an exclusive Channel 32 interview, three US Army soldiers weigh in on the recent controversy surrounding an extraordinary rosary," the reporter said.

The taped interview began with a recap of events. The reporter then introduced Sergeant Boswell, Danny Carpenter, and Layton. Janey's heart leaped when the camera closed in on Layton's handsome face.

"The three of you served in Iraq with John McKay," the reporter said. "You told me earlier that the claims made by Merle Hammett and Farid Zaman about the rosary are incorrect. What's your basis for that claim? Do you know how John McKay got this rosary?"

Sergeant Boswell spoke first. "The three of us were with McKay when he risked his life to rescue an old beggar caught in the crossfire during a skirmish in Baghdad. Layton and I were the first to reach McKay and the old man after the battle ended. During the entire ordeal, McKay was not out of my sight for more than a few seconds."

"Did you notice any injuries on the old man?" the reporter asked.

"He had a minor cut on the bridge of his nose, which could have happened when he fell in the alley to begin with. Overall, the old man seemed in good spirits. Danny Carpenter, our medic, treated the old man's cut. The claims that John or anyone in my squad mistreated the old man are lies. John was respectful of all the locals we encountered during our deployment."

The reporter nodded. "When did John receive the rosary?"

"When I came up, the old man was badgering McKay, insisting he take the beads," Boswell said. "I assumed they were Muslim prayer beads and urged McKay to accept them so we could treat the man and move on. I don't think anyone realized it was a rosary."

The reporter turned to Layton. "I understand you and Specialist McKay were close friends. You were the first person to get to John after the gunfire ceased. What did you see?"

"As Sergeant Boswell said, the old beggar was very animated and insistent that John take the beads," Layton said. "I couldn't understand a word the old man said, but he seemed pleased when John finally relented and accepted them. The old man seemed especially happy when Sergeant Boswell retrieved his crutch. Which is a point I'd like to emphasize. The old man John rescued was missing a foot. The person Farid Zaman presented walked in on two feet. That old man was not the same beggar John rescued."

Danny Carpenter was the next to speak. "After the battle, I examined the beggar. His only injury was a quarter inch cut near his left eyebrow, which I cleaned and disinfected. I specifically checked him for broken bones. He had none. The old man was lively and seemed grateful for my attention."

The reporter turned back to the Sergeant. "Even before Zaman's most recent claims, the rosary was making news. There have been many claims of so-called miraculous healings attributed to it. Are you aware of the claims put forth by the family of the late Teddy Fallon, who was violently murdered by a man claiming to be a Zaman supporter?"

Sergeant Boswell grimaced. "Teddy Fallon was a brave soldier who was injured in the same battle that took the lives of five members of my squad, including John McKay. The news of Specialist Fallon's death was horrifying. Any claim that the rosary came from someone other than the old beggar is untrue. No one in my squad went near the bodies of the attackers that day. There are standing orders regarding that. To be clear, the story posted online by Specialist John McKay's sister is the only true narrative. McKay received the rosary from the old beggar. Period."

The interview ended. As the programming switched to a commercial, Janey sat back. The tightness in her shoulders had started to ease as soon as Sergeant Boswell finished speaking.

Dad looked relieved, too. "In less than five minutes, they set the record straight on Farid Zaman and Merle Hammett."

Before getting ready for bed, Janey sent emails to Danny Carpenter and Sergeant Boswell thanking them for their part in the interview.

Then she texted Layton. That he didn't respond could mean a lot of things. It was late. He could be driving. His phone battery could be dead.

Or he didn't care.

At least not in the way she wanted him to.

———

THE NEXT MORNING, Janey learned that Layton had not returned to the farm. He sent her father a text explaining that he stayed overnight at Fort DeWald.

"He'll be back later today," Dad said.

That Janey had spent most of the night listening for his truck meant she was exhausted, cranky, and tired of playing the lovesick fool. She'd sent Layton three texts last night, and he hadn't responded to a single one, yet he'd sent her father a message, which was an indirect message to her.

Take a hint. Give up.

"I'm going to meet Gemma," Janey said.

"In Iowa City?" Dad frowned. "I don't think that's a good idea. Have you talked to Perry or Matt about this?"

"Gemma's home for the weekend. I'm just going to her house, Dad."

"I overreacted, didn't I? I know you're probably feeling penned in. We've asked you to give up a lot and you haven't complained once."

His contrite tone soothed her. "Thanks."

"You have your cell phone with you, right? Fully charged?"

Don't scream. "Yes, Daddy. I'll text you when I get there and when I'm headed home."

Janey's sense of irritation swelled when she noticed that she checked the rearview mirror continually while driving the short distance to River Haven. When had she grown paranoid?

When she pulled into Gemma's drive, her friend ran out and gave her a fierce hug. "I've missed you!"

"Me, too." Even as children, she and Gemma had never gone more than a week without seeing each other. Their plan to go off to college together had been nurtured since junior high.

"You look ready to cry. Come on. My folks are gone, so we've got plenty of privacy."

Gemma's room was the entire bottom level of the house, a daylight basement set up like an apartment. Gemma's house was Janey's second home, and she hadn't realized how much she'd missed it. She flopped onto the sectional couch with a groan.

"What's wrong?" Gemma asked. "Layton?"

"Everything. And yes." She and Gemma talked every day or two, so her friend was up to date. But a lot had happened in the last forty-eight hours.

Janey recapped the latest news about the bomb sent to Boswell, and Layton's return to the farm. "One minute I think I might have a chance, then the next he's distant and pushing me away. I'll get fed up, write him off, then boom! He's there asking what's wrong."

"Men!" Gemma said. "I know you're sick of hearing me tell you to give him time, but he's only been back a few weeks, right? He's endured a war, the loss of friends, plus he was critically injured. Your life hasn't exactly been easy either. Maybe you need to cut yourself some slack, too."

Janey slumped further down on the couch. "You always know what to say, especially when no one else knows or understands."

"We are doomed to be misunderstood. Such is the plight of forgotten children." Gemma delivered the line with such an overly dramatic British accent that Janey laughed.

Family hierarchy was another thing they had in common: both were the youngest and only daughters in families that had older parents and sizable age gaps between siblings. Matt and Perry were eighteen years older than Janey. Gemma's brother was twenty years older. Janey and Gemma jokingly referred to themselves as lost or forgotten children. Their parents, while loving, were too tired to go through all the hoopla again.

Gemma's phone dinged with a text message. "It's from Ben. He wants to meet for lunch. You up to it?"

"See if he'll come here and we'll get pizza delivered."

An hour later, Ben wheeled down the ramp with two pizza boxes balanced on his lap. Janey grabbed the boxes while Gemma held the door open. Gemma's parents considered Ben a part of the family, too. So much so, they'd had a wheelchair ramp installed after Ben's accident.

"As of this morning, the rosary website is back up, but without the soldiers' page and sign-up section," Ben said to Janey. "We're getting more traffic than ever. The comments in the guest book are overwhelmingly supportive. There's at least twelve more people claiming miraculous healings, but get this. Several of those miracles are from a church that was unable to sign up for the rosary and instead printed one of the photographs from the website. They held a rosary service using the paper facsimile. That's launched a whole new level of discussion in the comment sections, though people still ask when their churches can sign up for the rosary."

Janey crumpled a napkin. The claims of miracles ate at her. Why did some get miracles, but not others? And what about her original intention to honor John's memory with prayers for peace?

"The rosary will be back here in a couple weeks for the service at St. Francis. Between now and then, I'll decide how to continue. Not to take away from anyone who's claiming a miracle, but the reason I started this website has been buried beneath controversy." Janey's phone rang. She glanced at caller ID. "It's Perry. Hello?"

"Janey. You still at Gemma's?" Her brother's voice held an edge.

Mild panic had her sitting up straight. "Yes. What's wrong?"

"Layton just called. Another bomb was discovered. Authorities intercepted it before it detonated. Layton's on his way to the farm, but Dad wants you home, pronto."

Anxiety flooded her veins. Two bombs, neither had detonated. How much longer could that continue? "Was it the Boswells again?"

"No. It was Danny Carpenter's fiancée."

"I'll be home in a few minutes."

Janey explained the situation to Gemma and Ben and grabbed her bag.

"You want me to follow you home?" Ben asked.

"No. But thanks."

Gemma hugged her. "Text me as soon as you're at the farm."

The first thing Janey noticed when she returned home was Layton. He stood alone on the porch, his cell phone pressed to his ear. Had he stepped outside for privacy? Was he talking to Sharlene? As soon as Janey climbed out of her car, he tucked his phone away and strode toward her.

"I'm gone less than twenty-four hours and you take off." The muscles in his cheek clenched.

So did Janey's. "Oh, hi. I'm fine. Thanks for asking." She walked past. "PS, you don't get a say in anything I do."

"This is serious, Janey."

She whirled to face him, ready to battle. "I never said it wasn't. Give me some credit and quit treating me as if I'm a little kid.

Gemma lives two miles from here and I watched traffic like a paranoid drug dealer."

Layton put his hands on his hips and looked up at the sky for a
few seconds before exhaling. "I give you a lot of credit. Unfortunately, I must give the enemy more. I know I sound overbearing. It's
my knee-jerk reaction to threat, to circle the wagons. I can't bear the
thought of losing anyone dear to me. And PSS, I'm well aware you're
not a little kid, Janey. So aware it's driving me crazy."

For a moment she glimpsed a raw ache in his eyes, felt his strain.
He cares. She reached for his arm but stopped when her father called
out behind her. She dropped her hand.

Layton straightened, all business once again. "Give me your keys
and I'll pull your car into the garage while you talk to Ward."

Janey released her keys before heading to the house. What she'd
complained to Gemma about — *get fed up, write him off, then boom!*
— just happened again. But what did it mean?

————

DETAILS on the bomb sent to Danny Carpenter's fiancée were
limited, which frustrated Janey. All they knew was that the bomb had
been in a smaller package that contained an incendiary device like
the one left at Sergeant Boswell's. Because Danny had warned his
family to be watchful, his fiancée was immediately suspicious of a
box left at their front door.

At Matt's request, Deputy Blake Evans came by the farm a short
time later. Blake reviewed the security cameras installed around the
property and discussed additional measures. Some were no-brainers
like not accepting packages from strangers and staying clear of
anything left at the door. He also reiterated that the sheriff's department had increased patrols at the farm, the stores, and Perry's and
Matt's farms.

"We're still not around twenty-four hours, so the moral of the
story is, you can't be too cautious," Blake advised. "You need to

rethink your routines. Ward, everyone in the county knows you attend ten o'clock Mass every Sunday and that you get there early to get a front parking spot. Change it up until this is resolved. No one wants their freedom curtailed, but I suggest you adhere to the buddy system. No going off alone, even around the farm."

Layton's cell phone rang, and he stepped away to answer it while Blake answered a few more of Janey's father's questions.

Layton returned a few minutes later, his mouth set in a stern line. "That was my contact at Army CID. It hasn't been publicized, but Merle Hammett received a bomb, too."

"Did it detonate?" Dad asked.

"No. According to the bomb squad, all three bombs were set to explode when picked up. The worry is that future ones could be remotely detonated."

"Future ones?"

"Yes, and they're concerned we're the next target."

CHAPTER TWENTY-NINE

October 2006
Chicago, Illinois

Saturdays at Prince of Peace Church fell into a quiet pattern for Father Nick. An early riser, he dressed in old work clothes and headed to the church, toolbox in hand. There was no morning Mass, and both the youth center and church office were closed.

He still marveled at the notion of a day off. In Iowa, his weeks were overfilled, commitments slotted months in advance and reshuffled daily, as additional needs popped up. Back in Iowa, sleep qualified as time off.

Chicago was the polar opposite. During the week, Nick stayed busy at the youth center, but the absence of weddings, baptisms, and funerals on the church calendar seemed yet another statement of his shortcomings. Constanza urged him to be patient. "Your schedule will pick up, Father. One day you'll look back and long for these quiet times."

Initially, Nick thought he'd catch up on all the reading he longed to do, but after the first week, the stillness drove him crazy. Even the silence of prayer felt unnatural until he recalled that he'd become accustomed to praying around the edges of nonstop motion. His longing for constructive activity led him to take on the role of handyman at the church. Physical labor had always been his panacea for stress, and once Nick began looking critically at Prince of Peace's physical structure, he found myriad opportunities for working through frustration.

With her vision restored, Constanza's boundless energy had her tackling projects as well, like going through the old boxes piled everywhere. She inventoried and labeled the boxes before sealing them for storage. While most boxes held accounting and administrative records, one file contained a few old photos of the church.

Nick barely recognized the building. In its glory, Prince of Peace had been magnificent. Now, with so many things in a state of disrepair or neglect, the church looked more like the Pauper of Peace. Its white steeple hadn't been painted in years. Constanza guessed that the old-world statues shown in the photographs had been moved to one of the newer churches when the diocese reorganized. The graceful arched windows that previously held stained glass were now a barren hodgepodge of Plexiglas and plywood that was watertight and functional, but austere.

While a full church restoration was beyond Nick's skills and budget, in the four months he'd been there, he'd already tackled a couple major projects that proved deeply satisfying. The church's front doors, two huge oaken monoliths, had pigeon-poop coated sheets of Masonite nailed over them. When he pried the ugly, rain-warped sheets loose to replace them, he'd been stunned to find ornate carvings of scenes depicting the Garden of Eden. The artistry was fabulous. While the wooden doors were scratched in spots, the carvings had remained intact. Had they been covered to protect them from the bird droppings and weather?

Nick repaired the leaking overhang and bird-proofed the eaves before refinishing the doors. The renovated doors looked so striking that he repainted all the exterior entry trim to showcase their splendor.

Another extensive project came about as the result of an accident. While painting the entry, a can of turpentine tipped over inside the church foyer. By the time Nick discovered it, the turpentine had softened the paint on the tile floors. As he wiped up the solvent, he uncovered exquisite mosaic flooring.

The mosaics turned out to be exacting works of biblical history that swept through the church's interior. It began in the foyer where the floor art depicted Genesis – God created earth from the blackness of nothing before calling forth water and light. The mosaic of the seventh day, the holy day when God blessed His work and rested, spilled into the main aisle of the church.

Stripping the remaining paint from the floors was painstaking, but Nick worked nights, eagerly looking forward to the work as he uncovered scene after glorious scene up the center aisle. Working steadily, he exposed tiled illustrations of the Old Testament stories of Abraham, Moses, and Noah. In the very middle of the main aisle was a wider circle that featured the nativity. When Nick had stripped that spot, a cramp in his back muscles left him rolling in pain on the floor. When the pain subsided, he looked straight up and noticed a circular hole in the ceiling that was boarded over. Had glass been there once, allowing light to shine down on the nativity mosaic?

Constanza shared Nick's enthusiasm and promised to research more of the church's history. "Many of the old timers moved across town and now attend St. Ignatius, which is where my cousin goes. He'll help me get in touch with them."

This morning as Nick carried his toolbox into the church, he admired the gleaming tile floors before making his way toward the basement door in the back that supposedly led to a storage space. His goal today was to move the boxes that Constanza had piled in the hall. Not only were the boxes a trip hazard and unsightly, they hindered Nick's plan to paint the walls.

Constanza could not find a key for the basement door, but when

Nick went to remove the doorknob, he found the screws were stripped.

"Get thee behind me, doorknob," he muttered as he put a special bit in his power drill. A minute later, the knob fell to the floor.

Nick's cell phone rang. He was surprised to see a call from Father William at the diocese office. The two priests had spoken several times since news of the rosary and the phenomenon that was Domingo's song hit the Internet. William had been very supportive of the music video. While some people believed that a hip-hop version of the Lord's Prayer was sacrilegious, William had become a champion for the huge teen and young adult audience the video reached.

"I've got some news that I couldn't wait to share." William began speaking as soon as Nick answered. "The bishop has received a special request from the Vatican. The Pope has invited your students to sing The Lord's Prayer before his Mass in December. Turns out The Holy See has a fondness for certain hip hop songs."

Nick almost dropped the phone. "Tell the bishop I am honored as I'm certain my students will be when they hear this news."

"There's more. The Pope would also like to see a peace prayer service scheduled at the pre-Mass events. The Vatican extended an invitation for you and your family to attend a private meeting with the Pontiff. Can you make the arrangements with your niece?"

Tears welled in Nick's eyes at the thought of being included. "Yes, I will speak with her this evening." The McKays would be stunned to hear of this rare privilege.

"I must emphasize that this in no way indicates the church has taken an official position on the rosary. Personally, though, I think it indicates that interest has been piqued at the higher levels. The number of miraculous claims has grown to the point that I don't think the church can remain mute on the matter much longer," William said. "I'll follow up next week with details."

Nick grinned after disconnecting. What spectacular and unexpected news. He usually talked with Janey on Saturday nights, but tonight he would call at supper time and speak with the whole McKay family.

He wanted to call Domingo right away, though.

Domingo had changed since the rap video's popularity skyrocketed. The sullen, irritable teen who reported to the youth center because it was court-ordered now showed up early to work at the center. He also exhibited a previously uncharacteristic humility, insisting that the music video was a group effort. The youth center's video production class had a wait list and Domingo was lobbying to add music lessons.

Constanza reported that Domingo's near-flunking school grades had risen significantly. "And he asked about college," she said.

When the teen answered his phone, Nick told him about the Pope's invitation.

"Wow," Domingo said. "I know that's a big deal, but have you checked out the number of views on YouTube lately, Father Nick? We're almost at seven hundred thousand! Can you believe it?"

Chuckling, Nick hung up and looked down at his toolbox, then back at the door. Those boxes would not move themselves.

He finished removing the doorknob, but it took another ten minutes to pry the paint-encrusted door free. When it swung open, he peered into the dark basement. Musty air wafted forth, making him cough. No light came on when he flipped the switch. He stared into the void, unable to see beyond the first step. Navigating these stairs in the dark would be treacherous.

Grabbing a flashlight from his toolbox, Nick shined it down the staircase before testing the first tread. It was solid, but he advanced downward cautiously until he reached the bottom. He swept the flashlight's beam around the room and spotted a ladder near a small workbench. Spare bulbs were there, too.

He changed the bulb at the base of the stairs. While not bright, the light provided enough illumination for Nick to see more of the room. One wall had shelves lined with file boxes like the ones upstairs. He rearranged the boxes, shifting them closer together and stacking them to make space for more.

Behind one shelf, hidden by boxes, Nick found a bank of four light switches. He flicked them up. The basement lit up as bulb after bulb pinged on overhead, revealing an area much bigger than expected. Curious, he moved beyond the storage space into a cavernous hall-like expanse that branched in several directions. His flashlight beam revealed more rooms and alcoves off to the sides. He tried to estimate the width and length. Even with most of the space still unlit, the basement appeared considerably larger than the church above.

He spied another bank of light switches on a far wall. When those were turned on, he frowned. Wooden crates and boxes filled the space. Judging by the accumulation of dust and cobwebs, Nick guessed they'd been there for years, probably emptied and shoved down here for storage.

Unfortunately, it was a fire hazard he'd now have to address. Discouraged, he paused at an alcove crammed with items covered by filthy sheets of canvas. More trash? Lifting the edge of one tarp, he shined his flashlight beneath it and found two elaborate floor candelabras.

Surprised, he flipped the tarp free, coughing as dust filled the air. He ran his hand over one and found it steady. Heavy, the pieces appeared to be solid brass. He moved to another tarp and found two massive votive light stands. Recalling the old photos Constanza had found, he believed these had once been bolted to the walls on either side of the altar. Why were they down here?

Stepping away, Nick surveyed his surroundings with fresh interest. Returning to the row of wooden crates, he knocked on the side of one. The lack of echo indicated it wasn't empty. He tried to lift the top but found it nailed shut. Backtracking, he raced upstairs for his toolbox.

It took a while, but eventually he pried the top loose. Inside were gorgeous cherub statues, nestled in straw. Nick touched the plaster reverently. He worked to remove the top of the next crate and found statues of sheep and a camel, obviously part of a nativity crèche.

He eyed the other crates, feeling like he'd stumbled across Santa's bag. Did these crates hold more of the church's old furnishings? Some were so tall he'd need a ladder to open them. Could they hold the statues of saints that had once been upstairs?

Wiping his brow, Nick moved back into the center aisle. Before he opened any more crates, he wanted to explore the rest of the area. Exactly how far back did the basement go and how much stuff was down here?

He shined his flashlight toward the farthest end and jumped when he saw a man step out from the shadows and quickly duck back out of sight.

Startled, Nick called out. "Who's there? Come on out." When no one responded, he tried again. "This is Father Nick of Prince of Peace Church. You shouldn't be down here, whoever you are."

The man stepped forward now, crunching a hat between his hands. "Father Nick?" His voice was low and he sounded relieved.

"Yes." Nick moved closer. The man appeared older and looked harmless, but he was still a stranger. While Nick had yet to meet everyone in the neighborhood, this man wasn't familiar.

The man closed the distance slowly, leaning on a cane. "You're not wearing your collar, Father. I was afraid you were a thief."

"I could say the same. These are my work clothes." Nick held out a hand. "You already know my name, but I didn't get yours."

"Benito Alvarez. Benny to my friends. I'm one of the last of the church's old guards." Benny coughed and nearly doubled over.

Nick rushed to steady him. "Are you okay?"

"I just got out of the hospital. I developed pneumonia after hip surgery, then fell and went back to surgery, so I haven't been to Mass since before Father Hernandez left."

"All this dust can't be good for you. Let's go back upstairs." Nick pointed to the cane. "How did you get down those narrow steps?"

Benny looked sheepish. "There is an entrance with a ramp

hidden behind the old school. I come down and check things periodically."

Nick tried to guess the other man's age. Eighty? "I'm curious what you know about all this stuff. I don't know any of the church's history and frankly the records are in a bit of disarray right now."

Benny pointed upward with his cane and made a *pfft* sound. "I was baptized at Prince of Peace and I'll be buried here. No time soon, the Lord willing. My great-grandfather helped build the church, so you might say I was born into its history. Follow me for one moment." He motioned to the crates as he ambled toward a row of shelves. "Shine your light over there, Father."

Nick did as Benny requested. "What are you looking for?"

Benny pointed to a cardboard box with his cane. "That. If you'll grab it, we can go upstairs. Does Constanza still have a coffee pot in the office?"

————

NICK LEARNED a lot over a carafe of coffee. Benny was eighty-two years old. His wife died thirty years ago, preceded in death by their only child.

"I never remarried," Benny said. "Sonia is waiting for me in Heaven."

The box Nick carried upstairs turned out to be a mini time capsule with documents and photographs showing the church under construction.

Nick pointed to the back side of one photograph. "I appreciate that someone dated these pictures and listed names." How many times had he heard surviving families lament the lack of context for older photographs left by a deceased loved one?

"My father spent hours going through these photos with his grandfather before he passed," Benny explained. "He knew the knowledge, the oral history, would someday be irretrievable. I'm grateful he took the time, just as I'm grateful you're taking the time,

Father Nick. I'm the last of my family who is still a member of this parish. This branch of history ends with me and I want to leave a mark."

The words gave Nick a chill. With his parents and sister gone, Nick was the last direct line of his family tree, too. Did that realization underscore his longing to make a difference?

As it turned out, Benny's ancestors had done more than help build Prince of Peace Church. Over one hundred years ago, a small Mexican village inhabited by artists, relocated to the Chicago area after an earthquake destroyed their town. Benny's ancestors, two brothers, had literally owned a gold mine and financed the move after the Mexican government refused to help the village rebuild. One brother was Benny's great-grandfather.

"The church's beauty was crafted by those very artisans who moved here," Benny said. "After losing much of their past in the earthquake, their desire to reach into the future through their art was apparent with every piece created."

"Did your great-grandfather's brother settle here, too?"

Benny grimaced. "Unfortunately, there was a falling out between the brothers. My great-great-uncle died before the church was completed. My father said my great-grandfather carried a burden of guilt after his brother passed, which led him to make the church even more grandiose."

Nick motioned to one of the photographs taken after the church first opened. In comparison, the current building looked like a dried husk. "Your great-grandfather must have been proud when it was completed."

"Everyone was. Every person in that village took part in establishing this church and dreamed their gifts would endure beyond their and their children's lifetimes." Benny paused and sipped his coffee. "It grieves me to see how the church, the area, has succumbed to disrepair, but with so few left here, who cares? Besides you, Father. When I heard you refinished the floors, my heart rejoiced to hear the church finally has a champion."

"I'm hardly that," Nick said. "Before I entered seminary, I worked construction, but my skills are limited and more than a little rusty."

"Yes, but that background means you know what it will take to restore this church, right?"

Nick set his coffee mug down harder than intended. The magnitude of work needed at Prince of Peace was more than a single man could do, and he didn't want to give Benny false hope. "A full restoration is beyond my competency. I'm more of a handyman/painter/duct tape/save souls kind of guy. That said, I think we could look at bringing up some original pieces from the basement. Speaking of which, do you know what all is down there? Is any of it damaged?"

"There is a complete inventory in here." Benny tapped the box for emphasis. "Except for a few broken items that need repair, everything you've seen in these photographs is intact downstairs. Even the stained-glass windows."

The news stunned Nick. "I don't understand why everything was removed and hidden down there in the first place. When I first arrived, I thought the church had been desecrated."

"According to my father, back in the early nineteen hundreds, a mobster threatened to burn down the area churches unless a very high ransom was paid. The brave priest here refused to be extorted, but when he saw another church in town destroyed by the mob, he ordered his parishioners to dismantle everything and hide it." Benny shook his head. "My family feared the mob for a long time after that. Gradually, many other families moved away and the church's grandeur was forgotten. No one is left who remembers."

Nick picked through more of the photographs. How could anyone forget such exquisite beauty? He looked at the windows in an exterior shot, then shuffled excitedly back to another photograph taken inside the church. "I just noticed that the stained glass mimics the Bible scenes on the floors!" The details in the stained glass, the way the intricate scenes in the window complemented the floor mosaics astonished Nick.

"There was even a circular window set above the center aisle," Benny said. "It is the simplest of all the stained glass, its sole feature a large star. When backlit by the moon, it shines brightly over the Nativity scene below."

Nick quoted a Bible verse. "We saw his star when it rose and have come to worship him."

"Exactly."

Nick shuffled through the remaining photographs. His hands paused at a shot of an enormous statue of the Risen Christ in all his glory. Undefeated. "This might be my favorite. So many statues concentrate on the passion and crucifixion."

"That one graced the bay above the altar, behind the crucifix. A larger-than-life reminder of resurrection. Of victory and hope over death."

As Nick stared at the picture, he felt a desire to bring Prince of Peace back to life. Spreading the photographs out, he tried to arrange them in the proper visual sequence. His mind raced, trying to weigh what he could and couldn't do. "I can't restore everything, but for these pieces to be packed away, forgotten, is wrong."

"If you're serious about seeing it through, I can muster some helpers." Benny pushed his coffee mug away and stood. "I must go for now, but I will be back in touch soon."

"Can I give you a ride home?"

Benny shook his head. "The doctor says I'm supposed to walk as much as I can. When the weather is good, I'll walk to morning Mass, Father. You can, however, escort me out the front door and show me what all you've done so far."

As the two men sauntered down the church's center aisle, Benny's eyes filled with tears. "I haven't seen these floors except in photographs. And they are even more beautiful than my father had described. You are a blessing to Prince of Peace, Father Nick."

Outside of Constanza, it was the first time anyone expressed appreciation since Nick had arrived. The feeling was...uncomfortable for someone who wasn't sure they belonged there. "I'm not sure everyone agrees but thank you."

When they reached the front doors, Benny ran his hands over the carved panels, marveling over the workmanship. "You did a nice job refinishing these." Then he pointed to the eaves and gave a thumbs up to the bird-proofing. "Maybe the pigeons will take a liking to the Methodists."

After the older man made his way down the sidewalk, Nick turned back to the church, still determined to move the boxes as originally planned. The sun glinted on the varnished doors, making them sparkle. Benny's words echoed in Nick's mind. *"The church finally has a champion."*

Undoubtedly, this church and its parishioners needed a champion.

But was Nick the right person for this job?

CHAPTER THIRTY

***WHEN THE CRUSADER** first stepped out of the corn-field, John McKay sensed their connection.*

Had they fought together in the past? That was another recurring theme in John's previous incarnations. Battles. Challenges. Revenge. Yes, he could choose to not remember the past. He could choose the traditional one-life belief — with death, Purgatory, Heaven — had done so before.

But those two words, *I remember,* opened the door of possibilities.

And in that instant, John recognized the Crusader as a paternal ancestor. Their bond, a virtual multiverse woven from the strands of familial inheritance, had been passed down through the McKay DNA for centuries. They shared the same burden: guilt and an obligation to honor an oath. *Promises made* had been a persistent theme, a lesson John kept repeating. He wanted to get it right this time.

"You are the story's beginning," John said.

The Crusader nodded and extended his arm. "Do you want to know more?"

"Yes." John touched the Crusader's hand, the contact allowing them to venture backwards into the past and relive it as one.

Immediately their surroundings transformed to a thirteenth century battlefield in the ancient Kingdom of Jerusalem.

The vile stench of death mingled with an impenetrable mist. A vat of oil that had been heated to provide their enemy a smoke cover, had spilled and ignited. Flames enfolded the battlefield, the thick smoke making it impossible to tell friend from foe. Men screamed in agony and frustration, killing blindly before they were killed.

The Crusader knew the man he'd just dispatched had been an enemy, but as his opponent's final scream faded, an eerie silence settled in. A breeze from the west cleared the haze, giving the Crusader full view of the war field and the savaged corpses that lay strewn across the ground like macabre trash.

There was nothing holy about war. Men of God had bled out beside men of Allah and in death they all looked alike: Lost. Fallen. Abandoned. Where was the sweetness of victory?

He was the last man standing. The king of nothing ruled an empty win.

The Crusader touched his side, felt the slick seepage where he'd been jabbed in the abdomen. The wound was not enough to kill him right away, but he'd seen men swell up full of pus, lingering days before dying of fever. He wouldn't make it out of this country alive. If the wound didn't kill him first, he'd stand no chance alone against an enemy army. He was the reviled, the interloper — an enemy to be kept alive only for torture.

The chuffing, impatient whinnies of horses drew his attention. In both directions, horses gathered warily at the edge of the field, waiting for men who'd never return. He needed to find a hiding place before nightfall. A place to make his peace with God before dying.

He looked at the sky to get his bearings. Buzzards circled, prepared to battle the jackals for the feast below.

A sound, half cry, half groan, had him spinning around. "Who's there?"

An arm raised and quickly fell. Hoping for a companion, the Crusader rushed to render aid. His hand went to the hilt of his sword when he discovered the survivor was a Moor. A younger man knelt beside the Moor, frantically trying to free the Moor's leg from beneath the carcass of a dead horse.

The Moor's eyes mirrored the Crusader's revulsion. They were the sole survivors out of scores of men, yet both reached for ingrained hatred as surely as they reached for a sword.

The Moor spoke to the younger man, the words foreign. The younger man, a servant or slave, nodded and translated. "My Master asks that our deaths be swift."

That the servant spoke English surprised the Crusader as much as the request for mercy. He released his grip on his sword. He had no hate left. "I've seen enough killing for this lifetime." The Crusader assessed the other man's wounds. The dark stain on the Moor's tunic foretold death. They were both dying, both far from serenity. "If I free you, will you direct me out of this country? That we may both draw our last breath in peace, at home?" *Home.* The Crusader would never make it.

As the servant translated, the Moor searched the Crusader's gaze. He nodded before replying.

"He gives his word," the servant said. "No further death by his sword as well."

After freeing the Moor, the Crusader helped the man to his feet. "There are horses on both sides of the field," the Crusader told the servant. "We should leave before night falls."

The Moor spoke.

"My master would know what land you travel to," the servant said.

Ingrained caution had the Crusader weighing his reply, but a lie didn't come forth. For the rest of his days — hours — truth would prevail. "I left my sons with my wife's family in Bordeaux. I am English by birth, but desire to be buried in French soil, beside my beloved wife."

The Moor and his servant exchanged more words. Then the Moor ripped a metal insignia from his vest and held it out. "Master says to ride east. You will come to a riverbed before the sun sets. Follow it north to the border. There will be tribesmen there. Show them this and they will let you pass unharmed."

The Crusader looked from the insignia to the Moor, expecting animosity. Instead he found an emotion long absent from his life: compassion.

At the Crusader's hesitation, the servant spoke again. "Take it. My master speaks true."

The Crusader accepted the offering. He reached beneath his chain mail and withdrew a string of *pater noster* beads that had belonged to his late wife. Her faith, her generosity, had always been stronger than his. She'd have gladly helped a stranger in need without question or hesitation.

"If you run into a Christian army, show them this." The Crusader held out the string of beads. "Tell them you converted to Christianity. My God will forgive the minor lie."

The Moor took the beads into his fist as the servant repeated the instructions. "Allah would forgive as well," came the translated reply.

As the Crusader turned away, he pitched sideways, dizzy. He touched his side. Freeing the Moor had restarted the bleeding.

The servant moved close. "Your wound. My Master bids you to let me treat it."

The Crusader knew it would do no good. "I must go."

"You won't make the riverbed," the servant warned.

The Moor spoke, drawing their attention as he lifted a pouch that hung from his belt. The servant took the pouch and lifted his master's shirt, exposing his wound. The servant sprinkled a black powder directly onto the Moor's wound. The bleeding stopped.

"I have seen this bring men back from the edge of death," the servant said. "It will help you."

What do I have to lose? May the Lord give me strength. The Crusader loosened his jacket to expose the gash on his side before allowing the servant to treat it. The mysterious powder stung, but not for long.

The servant wiped his hands on the ground as he listened to his Master. "He wants to know if you were praying, just now, in Latin. *Pater Noster*? Should we know these words if we are questioned?"

The Crusader shrugged. "It is prayed on the beads I gave your Master, but I don't have time to teach him."

The servant smiled. "My ears never forget. *Pater noster qui in coelis est.*" He recited the Lord's prayer in perfect Latin. "If anyone questions you, tell them you spared the life of Sheikh Hamid and his faithful servant, Samir."

ONE YEAR LATER, the Crusader sat opposite a priest in a plaza in Rome. Now fit and hale, his businesses prosperous, the Crusader was eager to share his extraordinary tale.

The priest's expression could have curdled milk as his gaze went from the Crusader to the simply dressed Samir. "How many slaves did you bring back from your campaign?"

"None. Samir is a free man."

When no further explanation was offered, the dour priest sat straighter and lifted his shoulders as if to embody his role as gate-keeper. "Tell me exactly why you are requesting an audience with the Pope. You said this pertains to your last battle. Does this man," the priest sneered in Samir's direction, "have information that could be of value to the church?"

The Crusader nodded. What was more valuable than peace? "I spared a man, a Moor, on the battlefield. He gave me a token that not only assured my safe passage back to France but brought me aid to speed my journey. In turn, I gave him my wife's *pater noster* beads, not expecting either of us to live beyond the night."

"Did the infidel renounce his sins and convert?" the priest asked.

Samir shook his head, but the priest didn't notice.

The Crusader shrugged, noncommittal. "I survived and returned to France. To my surprise, Samir showed up at my door a fortnight ago, having tracked me down through the maker of the very beads I gave away. The Moor I spared is a sheikh, and he attributes my beads to saving his life not once, but three times. Besides returning my wife's beads, the sheikh had an elaborate set of *pater noster* beads made as a token of peace. It's an exquisite piece, and I thought to offer it to his holiness, the Pope, along with the sheikh's hope of accord."

Samir reached into his bag and withdrew an elaborate carved box. He opened it and reverently offered it to the priest. Inside the box, on a bed of white silk, lay a circle of sparkling black beads made from precious jewels and polished silver filigree. The workmanship bespoke an artistry reserved for royalty.

Samir held out a scroll, too.

"This tells the story of a vision for peace that came to the sheikh in a dream," the Crusader explained.

The priest ignored the scroll, his eyes widening to take in the beauty and obvious value of the beads.

"What is this?" The priest frowned as he pointed to the center medallion, a heavily engraved, puffed silver cabochon much larger than any of the beads.

The Crusader rushed to explain the secret of the beads and waylay the priest's concerns. "The centerpiece is two-sided. On this side are the names of Allah in five languages, but on the other side—"

The priest slammed the box shut and shoved it away before jumping to his feet. "This is blasphemy! How dare you bring such a profane abomination for the Pope? It must be destroyed, and this man arrested for heresy."

"Let me explain." The Crusader had worried the gift might be misunderstood, but the priest's violent reaction surprised him.

The priest departed the room, shouting to summon an assistant.

Samir looked frightened as they heard the priest's voice rising, demanding Samir's head on a pike.

"Get the beads and follow me." They needed to flee before a full hue and cry was raised. The Crusader led Samir into the hall and down a dark passageway that lead to the kitchens.

He tossed a handful of coins onto a table in front of the startled servants. "This is for your silence."

A woman snatched up two coins, then rushed to open a door.

The Crusader pushed Samir outside. They ran a scant distance down the alley and ducked into a crowded marketplace, weaving through streets until they were far away from the center of town.

When they stopped, Samir had tears in his eyes. "I failed. I was sent to deliver the beads and the scroll, yet both remain in my possession."

"The priest's ignorance is not your fault." If the priest had heard the entire story, would he have understood? Or would the priest have declared the Crusader a heretic as well?

The Crusader had been amazed to see Samir again and to learn that the sheikh's experience with the *pater noster* beads had closely mirrored his own. On two different occasions when returning home after that fateful battle, the Crusader had held the sheikh's metal insignia aloft and passed through a crowd of Moors undetected. Apparently, the sheikh and Samir did likewise with the beads. Both men had prayed for safety, but while the Crusader prayed to God, the sheikh prevailed on Allah. That the men not only survived, but subsequently grew stronger in their respective faith, had the Crusader wondering if there were not many roads to Heaven as the sheikh had so eloquently stated in the prophetic scroll. Did God's children come to know each other through their journey back to eternity?

Samir trembled. "If I am captured, can you get word to my family? Tell my sons not to come after me."

The Crusader straightened. "You will not be detained. I need to get a message to my own sons, then I will personally see you back to the sheikh, to thank him for this gift."

———

THE JOURNEY back to the Middle East took months. Disguised as desert nomads, the Crusader and Samir traveled by caravan from Morocco. But just before reaching Samir's homeland, the Crusader took sick from a pestilence sweeping the continent. As fever ravaged his mind and body, the Crusader talked only of miracles and holy beads before finally succumbing. Samir buried him in the desert.

When Samir finally arrived home, he found his village under siege as well. He made his way to the sheikh, who lay dying from the fever.

Samir rushed to his master's side and ripped open the box he had guarded on this journey. "They rejected the beads, but I will not fail you again. Now I will take you to safety."

"Death awaits me, but not you." The sheikh took the beads and broke the strand in two pieces. He handed Samir the smallest section. "I have seen the future. Two heroes will rise again from the sands. Once the circle is completed in the West, peace will begin in the East." The sheikh closed his eyes. "Promise you will keep this section safe. As guardians, your line will be protected."

"Safe for whom?" Samir pressed.

"There will be a time when this symbol will be understood. When mankind is ready to find true peace, the pieces will be reunited."

————

JOHN RELEASED the Crusader's hand.

Instantly, he was back in the cornfield, near the farm. The Crusader was gone, but John recalled his last words. "You are the end of this story."

John knew what needed to happen next.

CHAPTER THIRTY-ONE

October 2006
River Haven, Iowa

Though Janey had been unhappy with Merle Hammett's false narrative about the rosary, the news that he had been targeted by the bomber evoked compassion.

The FBI grew more secretive about their investigation, but Layton gleaned some information from his Army CID connections.

"Thanks to security cameras at Hammett's, the authorities have a description of the man and the vehicle he drove," Layton said. "That may be the clue that breaks this case."

Janey hoped he was right, but as the weeks dragged by without an arrest, the strain grew exponentially. If she felt restricted before, she now felt smothered.

Matt and Perry hired private security for the farm, their homes, and the stores. Instead of feeling safer, the heightened defense measures increased Janey's anxiety.

That she could go nowhere without an escort rankled her. She spent most of her days sulking in the back sunroom where she could let Fuller in while she did schoolwork. The rotation of unfamiliar cars driven by the security team kept Fuller agitated, and Janey confined the collie at night.

Layton continued to stay at the farm, but most mornings he was gone by the time she got up. Whether going to physical therapy or helping Dad around the farm or her brothers at the stores, Layton seemed to go out of his way to avoid her. Ignoring him made it no easier to not think about him. Some nights she'd hear muffled conversation through the walls and wondered if he was talking with Sharlene.

The Vatican's request for a peace prayer rosary service in conjunction with the papal visit in Chicago surprised Janey. Her father had been over the moon to hear that the McKay family was invited to a private meeting with the Pope. For a Catholic, there was no higher milestone.

Janey confirmed to Uncle Nick that the rosary would be available. It was being returned to her next week for the rosary service scheduled for John's birthday. Since there was nothing scheduled after that, she would keep the beads until the Pope's visit in December.

Suppertime at the farm turned into family feasts. Lisa and Robin called it stress-cooking and came over early each afternoon to plan and prepare the evening meal with Eileen. Janey's job was to keep her rambunctious nephews out of the kitchen, and Fuller was glad to help.

Today, they played in the backyard on the massive wooden jungle gym. The play set had safety swings for the babies on one side, with regular swings and roughhouse gear for the older boys on the opposite side. The youngest ones clambered for Janey's attention, while the older ones begged her to intercede for motorcycle time. She understood their frustration. Her nephews all loved to race. Their freedom had been curtailed, too, with the boys only allowed to ride if two adults were present.

It was past six when Perry and Layton came into the kitchen that evening. The rest of the family was already eating.

"Sorry we're late," Perry said. "Matt's on the phone and will be right in." He circled the table, patting each child's head in greeting before settling into the chair beside Lisa and pressing a kiss to her cheek. "Pass the roast beef, honey."

"There are plenty of potatoes," Eileen said. "Finish that bowl and I'll get more."

Perry looked at Dad. "Merle Hammett abandoned his plans to build that shrine in Baghdad. He released a statement saying the funds he raised will be donated to his local diocese's missionary fund instead."

"That's good to hear," Dad said. "Just wish he'd done it sooner. The man's caused us — especially Janey – a lot of grief. Pass the mac and cheese to Layton when you're done."

The news made Janey wonder if Merle also renounced the troublesome story about the rosary.

Though the table was laden with food, she had no appetite and covered her lack of consumption by feeding her ten-month-old nephew. Samuel was Matt's youngest. She handed him a green bean before leaning over to kiss the top of his head. The scent of baby shampoo had her fighting tears. Samuel had been born while John was deployed. She glanced across the table at Perry's youngest, thirteen-month-old Josh. An unseen fist crushed her heart. Neither of these babies would ever meet John.

Matt came in then and made a semi-circle around the kids' side of the table before sitting next to Robin. Bowls were shuffled in his direction.

"I just got off the phone with Uncle Nick," Matt said. "He sends his love to everyone. Janey, he said that kid's song has hit big overseas now. He thinks all the claims of miracles are getting Vatican attention, too, though they're keeping it down-low because of all the negative stuff."

With everything else going on, Janey hadn't given the rosary much thought. Last time she checked, the growing list of miraculous claims had completely buried the rosary's original purpose. Someone had even set up a different website dedicated to miracles attributed to the rosary — using photos from Janey's website. Her proprietary feelings seemed selfish one moment, sanctimonious the next. Maybe talking to Uncle Nick about it would help.

As soon as the meal was finished, Janey moved to clear dishes while Robin recapped dessert choices. "Banana pudding!" her nephews shouted in unison.

It was dark by the time her brothers and their families left. "I need to let Fuller out to run." Janey grabbed a flashlight. "Make sure she's got food and water."

"I'll go with you," Layton said.

She paused, not in the mood to put up a front. "You don't need to. It won't take long. And we've got security out the wazoo these days."

Ignoring the hint, he grabbed his own flashlight and followed her. Outside, they walked in silence to the kennel. Fuller woofed softly as they approached.

"Glad someone's speaking to me," Layton said.

Janey refused to be baited and opened the gate. "Come on, girl. Don't go far."

Fuller trotted into the backyard, toward the swing set Janey's nephews had been on earlier. Good hunting grounds for dropped cookies and potato chips.

Janey stuffed her hands in her pockets and followed. Even in the moonlight she was aware of Layton's every move.

He sat in one of the big kid's swings. "Man, I would have given anything to have a setup like this when I was little." He shoved the adjoining swing toward her.

Stifling a sigh, Janey caught it and sat. "John used to say the same thing. We inherited Matt and Perry's rust trap. When we complained about the swings being busted, Dad hung old tires in the tree. John eventually converted the rusted out set into a mini-obstacle course.

Once my nephews started coming, though, Dad couldn't get new play equipment in here fast enough."

Layton laughed, then grew quiet. "You looked upset at dinner. Anything in particular? Or everything in general?"

From out of nowhere, tears filled her eyes. She clenched her fists around the swing's chains, grateful for the cover of dark. "Sammy and Josh will never meet John. Adam and Eddie won't remember him because they were only two when he deployed. I don't want anyone to ever forget, yet I don't wish this grief of missing him on anyone."

Layton's hand closed over hers. "You'll keep John's memory alive for them to know. Right now, your heart's too tender, but eventually you'll tell your nephews about all the wacky stuff your brother did when he was younger. Heck, the tales you've told me over the years are epic. Have you considered writing them down?"

That he kept his hand over hers had her heart beating erratically. How long before he drew away? And how sad that she expected rejection.

"I thought of that," she admitted. "It's just too soon."

"It won't always be. Maybe writing about what hurts will accelerate its healing."

Which hurt would she even start with? She stood, needing distance before she did something stupid like ask about *them*.

"Dad will worry if we stay out too long." She turned and whistled softly. "Here, Fuller."

Layton stood, too, but instead of moving away, he shifted in closer, right behind her. His hands speared through her hair, smoothing its length all the way to the curve of her back. Chill bumps chased down her spine. The urge to lean back, to surrender, weakened her knees.

"We will get through this," he whispered.

Did he mean we-as-a-couple, or we-in-general, as in he was still out to save the world? The reminder that there was always something more important than talking with her stung.

She jerked forward, away from his reach. "Let's go, Fuller."

———

LIVING on high alert kept Janey on edge as another nerve-wracking week lurched by. Layton learned that all three bombs appeared to have been made by the same unknown individual. While Farid Zaman remained quiet, the FBI warned the McKays not to let their guard down. Knowing that Zaman might strike at any moment kept Janey jumpy with adrenaline overload. At night she crashed, sleeping deep and blessedly dreamless.

Three times a week, Layton went into town for physical therapy, and then kept to his routine of helping Dad, Matt and Perry, while avoiding Janey. When she checked on Fuller at night, he followed, but hung back, guarded.

She longed for the BK days – Before the Kiss – when her feelings for Layton were secret. Back when their relationship had been effortless. BK Layton had been funny, tender, sincere. Now he was cautious, distant, formal. The war had changed him. It had changed her, too, but if she could take back that kiss, would she?

No.

After Sunday Mass, Janey changed into jeans. Outside the fall air was clear and sweet. Harvest was wrapping up, most of the fields shorn as the earth prepared for a long winter's rest.

Perry and Matt had promised to let the boys ride motorcycles and ATVs later today and before her nephews arrived, she wanted to make sure all the vehicles had full tanks of gas.

Layton stood when she passed through the kitchen.

"I'm headed to the machine barn." She grabbed the keys from the rack by the door.

"Mind if I help?" Layton asked.

Before she could reply, a beeping noise indicated a car had pulled into the driveway. Janey glanced out the window, expecting to see Matt's or Perry's car.

Instead she saw a familiar black SUV stopped in the drive, talking with security. "That looks like the FBI."

Dad came into the kitchen and confirmed it. "Agent Holmes just called. Apparently, there's been a break."

Janey set the keys aside and glanced at Layton. Did he know what this was about? He shrugged and followed Dad into the living room.

Agent Holmes came in a few minutes later. He was training a new partner and made introductions before addressing Janey's father. "A security camera at Merle Hammett's house caught video of the man who planted the bomb. Our investigators identified the suspect and confirmed he'd been in Illinois, Connecticut, and Ohio around the time when each bomb was delivered. He's been on the run but, last night, federal agents tracked him to a cabin in southern Utah. The suspect refused to surrender and ultimately committed suicide."

Dad shook his head. "I don't feel a bit of sympathy. If one of his bombs had gone off, he could have killed or injured many people."

"Was he acting alone?" Layton asked.

"It appears so," Agent Holmes continued. "I understand that bomb making equipment matching the explosives at Boswell's and the others has been recovered. They also found copies of Zaman's makeshift wanted posters and a list of names that included the McKays and you."

Janey felt giddy with relief. "So we can resume our normal lives?"

"Not so fast," Dad said. "If this guy was one of Zaman's followers, are there others we need to worry about?"

Agent Holmes shrugged. "It's still an open investigation, but I feel confident we've apprehended the perpetrator. The suspect was a lone wolf type. Survivalist. Anti-government. Guess he tried to enlist in the Army a few years ago but failed the psych exams. He had an axe to grind with the military, and he needed money. His mortgage is in default."

"That's no excuse," Dad said.

Agent Holmes nodded. "I'll be back in touch to give you another update. A press conference is planned for later this evening, so you should see more on the news tonight."

Dad walked the agents to the door before turning back to Janey. "I need to call your brothers. They'll be glad to hear this."

Janey watched out the front window as the black SUV drove off. She wrapped her arms around herself. All the tension she'd been holding in suddenly released, leaving her jittery.

"You okay?" Layton moved closer. "You're trembling."

"It feels like everything unwound all at once. I'm relieved, but part of me still feels tense."

He shifted in front of her and rubbed her upper arms. "Muscle memory. Give it time."

At his touch, she started to shake violently.

Layton enfolded her in his arms. "Shhh." His whisper was low, his lips brushing against her forehead as he held her close.

Lulled by his strength, she leaned against his chest. Her arms encircled his waist. Her defenses crumbled as she sank into the moment, reveling in his touch, his caring.

The driveway alarm sounded but he didn't let go.

"It's just your brothers," Dad called out from the kitchen.

Janey dropped her arms and took a step backwards. "Thank you."

"Look, I know we still need to—"

She pressed a finger to his lips. She didn't want words to spoil the moment, didn't want to hear another empty promise of talk. "The correct response is, 'you're welcome.' Coming, Daddy."

———

OVER THE NEXT FEW DAYS, life resumed its former pace. The FBI identified the deceased bomber who had a troubled history.

Private security at the farm and store was discontinued. Janey moved back out to the bunkhouse, which meant Fuller could stay with her at night once more. After weeks of living on alert, she still felt a residual tension.

Layton took off for Fort DeWald, promising to return at the end of the week. She overheard him telling Dad that he hoped to get a medical clearance at this next doctor visit so he could report back to duty. She understood his eagerness even as she dreaded the thought of him leaving for Officer Candidate School. Though he didn't talk about it much, Janey sensed Layton's determination. She admired his ambition and wanted him to achieve his goals and dreams, even as part of her wished he'd...what? Love her back? Give them a chance?

It seemed like every time she thought they were drawing nearer, he'd retreat and go stoic. Yet if she ignored him, he drew close again. It wasn't the relationship she'd dreamed of, but at least he hadn't withdrawn completely and left her out in the cold. For all her eagerness to talk, she did not want to hear *I care for you, but not that way.*

With the summer internship at the newspaper long ago finished, Janey looked forward to returning to part-time work at the store. With the cooler weather and the liberty to do as she pleased, she chose to work on the loading docks again, welcoming the physical activity, especially on days like today when she felt antsy.

It was Thursday. Layton was finally returning today and the more she told herself to not think about it, the more she obsessed over it.

After work, she raced home. Layton's truck was in the driveway. She fought the urge to run straight into the main house. Instead, she headed for the bunkhouse and showered. When she entered the kitchen a short time later, Layton turned and smiled. Her vision tunneled. He looked more handsome than ever. In the course of a week he'd regained some weight and seemed to move his arm more naturally.

"There's my girl," Dad said. "You can keep Layton company while I help Eileen."

She moved to grab a soda from the refrigerator. "How long are you here for?"

"I've got a doctor's appointment at the VA hospital tomorrow. I'll be here for the weekend, but if the doctor clears me, I'll return to duty Monday." Layton pulled out the chair next to him. "Feel like riding to

Iowa City with me in the morning? Thought the drive would give us a chance to talk."

A chance to talk, plus an entire day alone with Layton. Janey choked on her soda. Her cheeks grew warm as she nodded. "What time?"

"Six-thirty. My appointment is at ten. We can have breakfast along the way."

Breakfast? Did people eat in dreams? She reminded herself to breathe and nodded as the slow-motion sensation dissipated. "Sounds good."

Dad and Eileen returned just then. "What sounds good?" Dad asked.

Before she could answer, the driveway alarm buzzed, signaling a car entering the highway. From outside, Fuller barked.

Eileen looked out between the kitchen curtains. "I'm not sure who it is, Ward. Looks like a woman in a red pickup."

Layton frowned and moved closer to the window. "That's Sharlene, a friend of mine from Texas. Excuse me."

Unable to stop herself, Janey crowded in behind her father and watched through the window as a petite blond climbed out of the truck and literally launched herself at Layton. *Sharlene, Sharlene, the Rodeo Queen,* was every bit as gorgeous as John used to tease Layton about.

"So that's Sharlene," Dad said. "She's a spunky little thing. I'm guessing by the look on Layton's face, he didn't know she was in town."

Layton had caught Sharlene with his good arm and swung her around. When he set her down, she pushed up on tippy-toes and pulled him close for a kiss. Janey stiffened, her fingers curling into fists.

She turned away, struggling to batten down her emotions. It was one thing to envy a virtual stranger via their online posts, but the jealousy surging through Janey bordered on wildness. *He's mine. Even if he hasn't admitted it yet.*

"Uh, oh. Something's wrong." Dad continued to report from the window. "Sharlene's got her hands on her hips. Sounds like they're arguing. Wow. Did you know she's pregnant?"

Janey rushed back to the windows. Sharlene had moved away from the truck now, her protruding belly unmistakable beneath her tight shirt. Janey's pulse sped up and her throat constricted as Sharlene moved to hug Layton again. Did he look unhappy or shocked?

Janey tried to calculate how long Layton had been back, but all she could think was that he'd gone to Texas first. Was Sharlene carrying Layton's child?

"They're coming in now," Dad said. "Act normal."

He scooted away and brushed a hand over his hair. Janey retreated to the corner near the computer alcove while Eileen moved to fiddle with the coffee pot.

When Layton and Sharlene entered the kitchen, his expression was tense. "Ward, Eileen, Janey, this is an old friend of mine from Dallas, Sharlene Sweeney." Layton made introductions. "She's brought the news that my grandmother passed away."

Janey's stomach clutched in sympathy. From the bits and pieces Layton had shared, she knew he and his grandmother had a strained relationship. Regardless of their lack of a bond, she had still been family, the only blood tie to his late mother.

As Layton spoke, Sharlene shifted to grab his arm. Resentment swelled anew as Janey realized the breadth of their shared history. Had Sharlene and Layton's grandmother been close?

Sharlene smiled at Dad. "I apologize for barging in unannounced, but after everything he's been through, I didn't want to break that kind of news over the phone."

"That's understandable," Dad said. "I'm so sorry, Layton. What can we do?"

"Thanks, Ward. I'm Grandma's only kin, so I need to go to Texas and make her final arrangements." Layton rubbed the back of his neck. "I've got an appointment tomorrow in Iowa City that's critical for my medical clearance, but then I will take off."

"I'll go with you to the doctor," Sharlene said. "We can leave from Iowa City as soon as your appointment is done. One of us can sleep while the other drives. It'll be like old times."

Layton gave Janey an *oops, sorry* look. Just like that, she was uninvited.

Janey nodded, looking one last time at Sharlene's belly. Had that been why Layton wanted time alone with Janey? To break the news that Sharlene was pregnant? Sharlene knew when Layton was at the McKay farm, more proof that the two of them spoke regularly.

Any lingering uncertainty about Layton's feelings shriveled. Janey had been kidding herself, thinking she had a chance with Layton.

Layton looked at her father. "Do you mind if I leave my truck here, Ward? When I get things wrapped, I'll fly back and pick her up."

"Sure."

Janey turned to her father. "Ben needs some information for the website. I'll be back later." She forced a smile. "Nice to meet you, Sharlene."

Then she made a break for the door.

CHAPTER THIRTY-TWO

October 2006
Dallas, Texas

The scenery beyond the windshield barely registered as Layton drove toward Dallas. His hometown shimmered Oz-like on the horizon. Cruise control was on to avert speeding tickets, the radio low enough he could still think. That he was alone, in his own truck, suited him just fine after the last few days' fiascos.

Sharlene showing up in Iowa had been the first domino to fall. Seeing her pregnant had been a surprise, but not a shock. She had gotten pregnant once before — not by him — but when her then-boyfriend skipped town, guess who she had sought out for help? Layton had been in basic training then and sent her money for an apartment. Next thing he heard, she'd miscarried and taken off for Vegas with her newest true love, a professional poker player. Layton had wished her well, not expecting to see her again, but three weeks later, she called him sobbing because her winner had turned out to be a loser.

Layton couldn't *not* help her. Back in high school, Sharlene had been his lifeline, feeding him, sneaking him into her house when Layton had nowhere to go but the streets. He wouldn't have graduated without her help and persistence. He owed her.

From what he'd gathered via Sharlene's scattered conversation, the father of her child, her latest *true love*, had moved to Sioux City, Iowa, for a construction job. She'd balked, not wanting to spend winter in a snowy climate.

Then the nursing home called Sharlene with news that Layton's grandmother had passed away. Sharlene had been listed as an emergency contact while Layton deployed, something else he'd forgotten to amend upon his return. When Layton pointed out that she could have phoned him with the news, Sharlene feigned concern. "I wanted to offer comfort."

Layton called her on it. "You know how Grandma felt about me."

"She must have reconsidered. There's also a lawyer who needs to speak with you about her estate."

A blind man could read between those lines. "My grandmother had no estate, Sharlene. They're probably looking to collect on bills or to cover her funeral expenses."

The two of them had been out to eat in River Haven. After leaving the McKay farm, Layton had put Sharlene up in a motel. However, after learning his grandma's estate was a bust, she decided to head for Sioux City after all. "I'm already in Iowa, right?"

Layton felt better after she left. Once upon a time, he cared enough to overlook her gold digger nature. Now he just felt sorry for her.

He stuck with his plan to drive to Texas after his doctor appointment but hoped to talk privately with Janey first. He felt awful that he'd invited her to go to Iowa City, then had to rescind. And he knew how it looked with Sharlene showing up pregnant. Ward acted as if nothing was amiss, but he'd seemed relieved when Layton explained that he wasn't the father.

Layton wanted to make amends to Janey, but she steadfastly ignored his texts and phone calls. He'd returned to the farm after

Sharlene left, only to learn that Janey had gone to visit Gemma for a few days.

Before leaving the next morning, Layton and Ward went through John's duffel bags. Layton was searching for files that contained admission papers from his grandmother's nursing home. He was embarrassed to admit he'd read none of it, but now wondered if she'd expressed any preference about burial.

He and Ward found several of Layton's belongings mixed in with John's, including a framed photograph of their squad on their first day in Iraq. The fact half of the men were gone now made the photo priceless. Ward found the files Layton needed on his grandmother, plus the death letters he'd entrusted to John. Layton was grateful to get those back.

He ended up headed to Iowa City alone, but the news from his doctor yesterday morning had been disheartening. Layton's latest x-rays indicated more surgery might be required.

"That shoulder will never pass the physical endurance test," the doctor said. "I'm recommending medical discharge."

The conversation hung like a guillotine over Layton as he drove into heavier traffic. He'd half-expected to hear the unwelcome news from his doctor, especially after his physical therapist expressed concern over Layton's diminished range of motion. "It will improve gradually, with continued therapy, but I don't see you doing push-ups for a long time — maybe never."

What now? Layton's determination to get into OCS, to retire as a career officer, meant he'd never considered a Plan B. He still didn't want to consider it.

"Don't forget, you always have a place in Iowa," Ward reiterated. Would he have made that same offer if he'd known Layton struggled with feelings for Janey?

His cell phone rang as he took the next exit. It was Betty from the Tall Grass nursing home.

"I've been on vacation and just got your message," Betty said. "Condolences on your grandmother and I apologize that you were not contacted directly. She passed in the early morning hours and the staff followed the correct protocol, but apparently the files still showed your girlfriend as an emergency contact."

"Ex-girlfriend," Layton corrected. "I understand the confusion. I'm on my way there now. Can we meet in an hour? I don't even know which funeral home my grandmother is at."

Betty was quiet for a moment. "I'm sorry, but per your grandmother's advance directives, her remains were to be cremated immediately and her ashes interred beside your grandfather's grave. Her funeral expenses were prepaid with Dowden's, and they've handled everything. She even furnished an obituary which should be in today's newspaper, but she wanted no service, no memorial and she stipulated that any belongings be destroyed or donated, which we've done. As you know, she owned little when she came here, and she wasn't the type to keep mementos. However, per our policy, we inventoried everything as her room was emptied. Outside of her final billing statement, which won't drop until the end of the month, there is nothing left here."

When the call ended, the empty feeling caught him off guard. *Nothing left here.*

Layton pulled into a gas station and parked. He hadn't needed to come to Texas after all. As long as he was here, he'd go by his storage unit. But first, coffee.

———

LAYTON CARRIED a large coffee and a sausage biscuit into his storage unit and collapsed on the sofa. For all its austerity, everything looked the same, which was comforting. He'd rented this unit three years ago, which was the longest his belongings had ever been in one place. With his parents constantly on the move, he'd never known continuity as a child. The Army and *Home Sweet Storage Unit* had represented stability.

He took a bite out of the lukewarm biscuit and opened the newspaper he'd picked up at the gas station. He flipped to the obituary section. LOIS ANN BITTNER MORGAN had a short listing near the top of the third page.

BITTNER. He'd never known his grandmother's maiden name. According to his mother, Grandma had been an only child whose parents died in a train wreck. Who raised Grandma after that varied depending on Mom's temperance. Mom told him once that an elderly aunt raised Grandma. Another time, she'd been in an orphanage. As a child, Layton told himself the latter explained Grandma's lack of caring. Except Grandma adored Layton's mother.

The obituary listed Grandma's date of birth, in Olathe, Kansas, another fact he'd never known. It mentioned she'd been preceded in death by her husband, Jonathan Morgan, and a daughter, Amelia Morgan. *Amelia Morgan Burnet*, Layton corrected. That had been a familiar argument between his parents: Grandma's refusal to acknowledge their marriage.

The obituary's ending line left Layton cold. *She leaves behind no living relatives.* Even in death, his grandmother shunned him.

He folded the newspaper and set it aside with the rest of the uneaten biscuit. Growing up in the shadow of his grandmother's loathing, he'd never expected the least bit of common decency from her. So why did the obituary's words sting? And why did he continue to wonder what made her hate him? Had the transference of aversion from father to son really been that strong?

Restless, Layton pushed to his feet and unloaded his truck. He dropped the cardboard box he'd packed at the McKay's and winced at the sound of shattered glass. Opening the box flaps, he carefully removed the framed photograph he'd retrieved from John's duffel bags, shaking out the glass shards that hung haphazardly from the frame.

He set the photo aside, then retrieved a trashcan and picked out the larger fragments of glass. The smaller bits scattered everywhere. He grabbed the file containing his grandmother's papers and dumped it into the can. Then he fished through the remaining items, shaking them within the box to contain the shattered glass.

At the very bottom was the packet of letters Ward had given back. Layton's death letters. The one to his grandmother would have ended up with the other unread ones. However, the one to Ward contained thoughts that Layton preferred to keep private. Shaking off the glass slivers, he tossed them in the trash can. A flash of color caught his eye. Another envelope, a red one, was stuck between them. He pulled it free.

The red envelope had LAYTON written in big curlicues across the front along with a line of hand drawn hearts. Layton knew exactly what it was.

Once as a joke, John listed Layton in a singles ad, under the heading 'Desperate Texan Seeks Love,' with a list of crazy require-ments. John collected the responses and would read them aloud to the whole barracks. Finding one last letter was like being pranked by the afterlife. God knows he needed a laugh.

He ripped open the envelope and yanked out the folded page. His eyes skimmed the first line, **My dearest Layton**. He frowned. The singles ad hadn't mentioned his name. And this handwriting looked familiar. Simultaneously, he caught a faint whiff of perfume that reminded him of the rose scent Janey wore.

He searched for the signature at the end. **Love forever, Janey**.

Janey? It couldn't be.

Layton turned the envelope over in his hands. He'd received several letters from Janey while overseas. They'd all been stamped, postmarked, and bore his full address. This envelope had his first name only, written in big, flowing letters which made the red enve-lope look festive. Special.

There was only one reason John would have a letter for him, from Janey. It must have arrived that last week overseas when things had been so crazy, Layton reasoned. He'd been stuck in quarantine while John and the others pulled double shifts. Maybe Janey heard Layton was sick and sent a *get well soon* letter.

He moved back to the sofa and sat down before unfolding the letter completely. He did a double take when he saw the date. May 7, 2005. That was before they deployed. They'd still been in Iowa then.

Confused, he began to read.

My dearest Layton,

I have re-written this letter a dozen times since learning you and John were going overseas.

It's hard to describe what I am feeling. Part of me is worried sick, part of me is confident that all will be fine. I know you — and John — are well trained and highly capable. And as you've both told me more than once, this is what you signed up for.

However, it's not what I signed up for. My heart is breaking right now because I think I love you, but I could never find the courage to tell you that in person. I wanted to tell you at the county fair and chickened out. Now, the thought of you leaving without knowing how I feel breaks my heart.

I never intended to fall for you. Maybe at first it was a crush, but as I got to know you, my feelings grew and intensified.

We've had so many fun times together, racing, picnics at the river, counting stars and meteors. Fishing and dancing down at the pond.

Layton had to take a deep breath. How many times had he replayed those same memories while overseas? Nights when sleep evaded him? He focused back on her letter.

You always listened to my opinions and shared your own. That we value the same things — family, honor, and loyalty — added a specialness to every conversation.

I could go on and on, but I won't. The purpose of this letter is simply to tell you that I care for you with my whole being. And that devotion will only grow while you're overseas, even though my heart aches at the thought of you being so far away for so long. Whatever will I do?

This is what: I'll save all my kisses, all my hugs, all my affection for you, Layton Burnet. Please be careful and hurry home to me.

Like the little heart trinket you won at the state fair, my heart will never be whole without you. You're my everything.

Love forever, Janey

Tears blurred Layton's vision as he thought back to that last day before he and John deployed. Janey had kissed him and gently held out a promise. She had stars in her eyes and Layton didn't want to promise anything in case he didn't make it back.

Instead, her brother hadn't made it back. Layton had contemplated his own demise overseas many times, but he'd never once considered that John would not have returned.

"If anything happens to me..." How many times had John said that? And how many times had Layton promised to protect Janey? To look out for her. Would John have asked that if he had known Janey's feelings? Or knew Layton wanted to be more to her than just a protector?

Or had John known all along?

Had Janey entrusted this letter to her brother to deliver and had John withheld it on purpose? Had he known it was a love letter, but deemed Layton not good enough for Janey? How many times had Layton heard John say that no one in his squad of ground pounders was good enough for his sister? John regularly referred to Layton as a player, the exact type of male deemed most unsuitable for Janey. So why had John insisted Layton swear to take care of her? And why had John kept this letter from Layton? It made no sense.

He pushed to his feet, suddenly angry that John wasn't there to answer questions. Layton re-read the letter. It was the most beautiful note he'd ever received, but it had been written over a year and a half ago. Janey had written him dozens of times since he'd deployed and never hinted at this in any of her letters or emails. Maybe it had been a passing crush.

Then he remembered how he'd promised her they'd talk—

He groaned. Another promise broken. Could she ever forgive him?

Could he ever forgive John?

Layton glanced at John's sign on the wall. HOME SWEET STORAGE UNIT now seemed a mockery. Layton reached to tear the sign down but paused when he spotted a tiny word at the bottom right corner. *Over.* That it was so small explained why he'd never noticed it. But now that he saw it…

He ripped the paper from the wall and flipped it over. A second message was scrawled hastily in John's handwriting: Face it. Your real Home Sweet Home will always be in Iowa, bro.

Layton staggered backwards and tripped on his bag. An invisible hand seemed to catch him. He kicked the bag away, then buried his head in his hands. The Lone Star State was part of his DNA — part of his spirit, but his future and everything he cared about was in Iowa. Janey made him want to redeem himself. She made him long to do good, settle down, build a home, start a family. All the stuff Layton did not understand how to do. But if she'd give him a chance, he'd learn.

He tugged out his phone but didn't use it. The next time he talked to Janey, it needed to be in person.

It took Layton less than five minutes to pack up a few things, but before he loaded his bag in his truck, his cell phone rang.

The number on the screen had a Dallas area code. He answered, "hello?"

"This is attorney Gerald Neilson calling for Layton Burnet."

He frowned. Sharlene mentioned a lawyer, but she hadn't given him the contact information before she left. "This is Layton. How can I help you?"

"My firm Brandt, Cobb and Neilson, handled your grandfather's trust. We were notified that his wife, your grandmother, recently passed away. My condolences on your loss, but I'd like to set up an appointment with you to execute the settlement of your grandfather's estate."

Layton pressed the phone closer to his ear. "I'm not sure what you're trying to pull, but my grandmother had no estate. If you have questions about her personal effects, I suggest you contact the care center."

"I spoke with Miss Betty at the Tall Grass center, which is how I got your contact information. And I am talking about your grandfather, not your grandmother." Neilson sighed. "I understand there was family animosity, so you may not be aware of the estate's terms. Your grandfather left his property to you, with the stipulation that your grandmother have lifetime rights. Those assets have been held in trust, to be transferred to you upon your grandmother's death. While your grandmother couldn't dispose of the property without your consent, she could prevent us from contacting you on matters concerning the property."

Layton sat back down, thoroughly confused. "What property? My grandfather's farm was lost to foreclosure." Grandma had complained bitterly to Layton's mother about having nothing but legal problems from the farm. "The last time I drove by Grandpa's place, the roof was caved in and there were No Trespassing signs all over. The locals said it was tied up in a court battle."

"We posted those signs to keep out vandals, but the property has remained a trust asset. Your grandfather left enough to cover taxes, insurance, and legal costs but not major repairs. A storm damaged the place a few years ago, but your grandmother took the insurance proceeds and abandoned the house, which was within her right. I can review those details and the property offers we've received when you come in."

"I'm still lost. What offers are you talking about?"

The sound of shuffling papers came across the line. "We've received various offers to purchase your grandfather's property over the years. Initially, they were for the agricultural value of the acreage. However, since then, some tracts of oil have been discovered in the surrounding properties. Your grandfather's acreage is rare in that he retained all mineral rights. The last offer we received, two years ago, was over two hundred thousand, but nearby tracts have sold for twice that much. I suggest you get a current property appraisal."

Layton closed his eyes. That was a lot of money. And if it were true, it might explain why his grandmother hated him. Still, Layton's inner skeptic wasn't totally convinced. There had to be a catch. Words were cheap.

"Can we set up an appointment for tomorrow?" Neilson asked. "I can review all the papers with you then."

"If we can make it early, yes. I need to head out of town." More than anything, Layton needed to return to Iowa.

All the money in the world didn't mean a thing compared to making things right with Janey.

CHAPTER THIRTY-THREE

October 2006
St. Louis, Missouri

The more Randy Keener tasted the power of his supporters in the JFA, the more he craved it. His new mentor coached Randy on how to inspire others, and he'd followed that advice to the T: *Speak like a leader of strong, worthy men — men who would look to you for wisdom and advice.*

His mentor instructed Randy how to post online, giving him words that reflected a *we* attitude and to speak only of solutions that embraced the code of the JFA.

"No more going off script," his mentor advised. "Follow my lead. Show the JFA you're a company man."

And boy, had it worked. Randy's online stature on the Justice Freedom Association forums had grown exponentially.

With his mentor's help, Randy parlayed his fifteen minutes of fame on the radio station into what his mentor called an *elevated conversation* that promised results. *People will rally around a winner.* And right now, online, Randy was a winner. One person had even referred to him as a visionary. Someone else mentioned that he was exactly the type of farsighted leader the JFA needed in the twenty-first century. Heck, it wouldn't be long before even Bill Heasly called Randy for advice on how to lead.

His mentor warned not to let it go to his head, which was hard but not impossible. Except for the ill-timed press release, which his mentor had subverted favorably online, Randy had stayed the course. He'd sucked up and gone along with the current JFA powers that be, telling them what they wanted to hear, just like his mentor had advised.

And every bit of advice his mentor offered had paid off. Randy now sought the man's counsel on everything before proceeding. The questions his mentor asked were exciting. *Do you want to be top dog? Are you ready to be president of an organization that will grow to be one of the most influential in the USA? Are you ready to take on the hard tasks and do whatever is necessary to get the job done?*

Yes. Randy wanted it all. When he was on top, he'd crush the nay-sayers and direct the powerful legal forces of the JFA toward more worthy causes instead of slapping the wrist of someone within the organization who had the balls to speak out. People outside the organization, like the McKays, would bow down, too.

Randy had been secretly pleased to hear that his mentor wasn't happy with all the brouhaha over the Vatican's interest in Janey McKay's stupid rosary. It seemed like as soon as the guy in Ohio dropped his plans to build a shrine, the Pope stuck his nose in, keeping the rosary in the headlines.

His mentor counseled Randy to keep focused on the object — the rosary — not the person – Janey. *Emotions have no place in politics. That's why it's important to separate God from State, to make way for the one true way. The rosary is nothing more than static, making it tougher for a clear signal to be heard.*

As promised, his mentor also found alternative sources of revenue for Randy's campaign in the form of anonymous donors who wanted change within the organization. His mentor also advised

Randy on how to handle the personal offers that came in. *People will seek your favor with gifts. Accept, but don't commit. Keep it private. Don't post about anything you acquire, how it came from others. Let folks think it's part of your everyday lifestyle.* Randy's favorite form of favor had been trips to the casinos, courtesy of gift cards that let him drink and the chips left in his room for gambling. *Be smart. Gift cards and cash can't be traced. Checks, money orders can be.*

That Randy sought his mentor's advice on the topic to begin with had proved brilliant, too. *Some of those favors have been tests from the higher-ups. Certain people want to see how you handle the behind-the-scenes stuff that no one knows about. These are some of the most powerful men in the organization and beyond, who want the same reform as you and I.*

Trying to guess which powers that be supported Randy was a full-time job. He was sure one of his supporters was Bill Heasly, the powerful leader of the Detroit chapter who regularly liked Randy's posts on the JFA online forums. Maybe his mentor would reveal some names today.

Randy was on his way to the Cuivre River State Park, north of St. Louis, for their first face-to-face meeting. This was an enormous step. It meant he'd earned his mentor's full trust. More excited than nervous, Randy practiced some of the lines he'd written himself. *Glad to meet a fellow visionary. Your faith in me is humbling. I'm ready to prove myself one hundred percent committed to the cause.*

Inside the park, Randy headed to the designated trailhead parking lot. This time of year, fewer people hiked, so just as his mentor had predicted, the place was deserted. Randy arrived early, which gave him time to circle through the park to assure no one had followed him. Watching his tail was another topic his mentor had counseled on. *Powerful men cover their tracks.*

At precisely 11:30 a small Winnebago pulled in and parked opposite of him. The driver flashed his headlights twice. Randy flashed back before climbing out of his truck. As he approached the RV, the side door opened.

A tall, dark-haired man with sharp features stood inside, the top of his head almost brushing the roof.

"Thanks for driving all this way," the man said. "I've got meetings at a political rally not too far from here, so it saves me time. I'm Tom. And welcome to my traveling office. Come in."

Randy shook the man's hand and sat where directed at the camper's dining table. The RV had been customized with computer monitors and high-tech equipment that screamed *important*.

"I'm glad to finally meet in person," Tom said.

"And I'm glad to meet a fellow visionary." Randy motioned to the interior. "Nice set up."

"When you've got back to back, high-level meetings, it's required. Here's an insider tip: this rig gives me the home field advantage. I control this environment. That's an aspect I don't think the current JFA leadership fully grasps. When they go call on politicians in DC, guess who's turf they're on?"

Randy grinned. "Satan's. Just kidding. I know exactly what you mean and plan to use this model fully if I get elected."

Tom shook his head. "Not if. *When*. That's why today's meeting is critical. I've been authorized to go full out on getting you into the top slot. There are a few annoying loose ends your benefactors want to see wrapped up first, then they're eager to schedule a meeting, probably in Vegas." He put his hands palm down on the table. "What I need right now is to know you're serious about going all the way, Randy. It's time to put up or shut up, my friend."

"I just happen to be an expert at eradicating loose ends." Randy leaned forward, mimicking Tom's posture. "And I'm ready to prove I'm one-hundred percent committed to the cause."

"That's exactly what I needed to hear, brother." Tom stood and reached into an overhead cabinet. He set two glasses and a bottle of bourbon on the table. "First a toast, then we'll get down to business."

Randy's eyes widened as he read the label. The bourbon was the expensive stuff he and his pals made fun of at the liquor store. *What kind of idiot spends a hundred dollars on a bottle of booze?*

Tom poured a generous finger of bourbon into both glasses and handed one to Randy. "We are on the cusp of sweeping change in the JFA and I'm looking at the future. Here's to the American Dream."

Randy raised his glass, unable to stop smiling. He watched Tom swirl the liquor in his glass before taking a sip. Randy imitated his every move. The bourbon was a smoky, rich vanilla and soft as velvet. If he were with anyone but Tom, he might have howled over how good it was. *Guess I need a better class of friends, too.*

Tom settled across from Randy and looked him directly in the eye. "I apologize up front if it seems I'm throwing a lot at you, but if we play this right, we can kill multiple birds with one stone. I say, enough beating around the bush. Let's get on with it."

CHAPTER THIRTY-FOUR

October 2006
River Haven, Iowa

That Friday, Janey returned to the farm on what would have been John's twenty-first birthday. Remembering why her brother was not there cast a melancholy shadow over the day, making her question the wisdom of scheduling a rosary service that evening.

She had spent the last week in Iowa City with Gemma, nursing a broken heart. Returning home also held the bitter memory of the last time she saw Layton. He'd been standing next to a very pregnant Sharlene. Dad explained that Sharlene had taken off for north Iowa, to join the baby's father. Recalling the way Sharlene had kissed Layton with such easy familiarity still hurt and added nails to the coffin holding Janey's heart. If Layton and Sharlene were apart, it was temporary. Lesson learned: never again. Janey would not waste any more emotion on someone who would never love her.

She had also decided to return to Iowa City and rent something short term until next semester when she could room with Gemma. Getting over despair — *don't even think his name* — meant getting

away from the places that held memories and the farm held her best –
and now worst – remembrances. It was time to move on. In fact, once
Janey got through tonight's rosary service, she'd be free to take off
tomorrow.

She had decided to leave the rosary website active until the
Pope's Mass in Chicago but beyond that she wasn't certain. It was
difficult to deal with her own lack of belief in light of the cascading
reports of miracles. Many healings were attributed to services where
a photocopy of the rosary had been substituted for the actual thing, a
practice dubbed the *Praycebo Effect*.

Today, the River Press printed Janey's last piece for her column.
She had originally planned to write a once-and-for-all recap of the
rosary's purpose, emphasizing John's request to pray for peace, with
no mention of the miracles.

The scope of her newspaper article changed, however, after her
family received two posthumous awards for John. One was a Purple
Heart for wounds received in battle. The other was a Bronze Star
Medal for acts of valor in combat. In the face of the two medals that
marked her brother's heroism and ultimate sacrifice, the arguments
over the rosary's origins and the debates of its powers were meaning-
less. Her final column commemorated her brother's life, not his
death.

That evening, Janey dressed up in a lacy skirt and top and pinned
her hair up to cascade down her back. She rode to the church with
her father and Eileen. When they arrived, a steady stream of headlights marked traffic pulling into the church parking lot. Janey had
dropped off the rosary earlier and learned that Father Martin
expected a full capacity crowd that night, with another rosary service
scheduled the following day.

Before they entered the church, Dad turned to her. "I wasn't sure
how to observe your brother's birthday, but this feels right. Thank
you for doing this, Janey-girl. You've made all of us proud."

Tears welled in her eyes as soon as Janey entered the crowded
church. A knot of people gathered near the altar where the rosary

was displayed along with photos of her brother. *This is for you, John. Happy birthday.*

Matt and Perry were already seated up front with their families. As soon as little Josh spotted Janey's dad, he shouted, "Grandpa!" before racing down the aisle, followed by as many of her nephews who could escape. Dad chuckled as he took Josh's hand and herded the others back in place.

Father Martin greeted Janey with a big smile. "We've set up overflow seating in the social hall and will beam the service over closed circuit television, to accommodate everyone. When we're ready to begin, I'll introduce you. You can tell John's story, then Mrs. Kendall will read some scripture."

Janey moved to set her bag in the front pew. As she turned back, she caught an image of a soldier in full dress uniform striding up the aisle. For a moment she saw John, his image shimmering like a ghost and swamping her with reminders of all she'd lost. She started forward, then stopped.

The image — a mirage — shifted yet again. It was Layton, in dress uniform.

She straightened, unable to move. It felt like she watched a movie and half expected Sharlene to sashay in, too.

Her father came up from behind and touched her elbow. "I wasn't sure he'd make it in time, so I said nothing."

"You invited him?"

"Sure did. Thought it would cheer you up. I'm not the only one who suspects you have feelings for Layton."

She stifled a groan. Too embarrassed to face her father, she watched Layton. Red hot awareness overloaded her senses. Would it always be like this? Impossible to breathe or think when he was around? While she'd seen him in Army fatigues many times, she couldn't recall seeing him in full dress uniform. He looked more handsome than one man deserved, smiling that smile she always thought was only for her.

It wasn't.

He looked happy, which also had nothing to do with Janey.

She wished she could hate him. Failing that, she wished she could bolt. Except McKays never ran. She straightened her shoulders and forced a calm demeanor as Layton drew close and invaded her personal space.

Even with heels on, he was a head taller than her. His hand went to her waist, his touch scalding even through her clothes.

"Hello, Janey," he whispered as he leaned close and pressed a kiss to her cheek.

Part of her longed to capture his lips, to claim one more of those kisses she'd waited her entire life for. Another part still smarted over his rejection. *Don't give an inch.*

"Hello, Layton." She made a show of peering around him. "Where's Sharlene?"

"Don't know. Don't care." He edged infinitesimally closer, his hand still at her waist.

She didn't move. "You didn't have to come all this way."

"Yes, I did." He tightened his grasp slightly.

Unable to take it, she shifted sideways just enough to break physical contact while remaining close. Regrouping wasn't the same as retreating. Avoiding his eyes, she stared at the medals hanging on his chest. A Purple Heart – like John's. A Bronze Star, too. Where was his heartbreaker badge?

He reached for her hand and squeezed her fingers softly, smashing her resolution to not look directly at him. It didn't help that he smiled when she made eye contact.

"That dress, your hair." His eyes dropped, then locked back on hers. "You look amazing, Janey. You always do."

"Thanks." She jerked her hand back. *Don't read anything into his gaze, his words. His touch.* "The service will start in a few minutes."

"I've really missed you."

She shrugged. *I didn't miss you.* "You weren't gone that long."

Her father's voice broke the spell. "Our family circle is complete now. Glad you could make it, Son."

She stepped away but found herself trapped against the end of a pew as Layton shook hands with Dad, Matt, and Perry.

Father Martin rang a set of hand chimes to signal the start of the service. The church was at full capacity, but immediately voices quieted. Layton motioned to the seat directly behind her father. "After you."

Janey shook her head. "Go ahead. I've got to do an introduction."

"I'll save you a seat."

Frantic for distance, she moved to the far side of the church and tried to focus on Father Martin's words as he greeted the crowd.

"I'd like to welcome everyone to St. Francis' prayer for peace service. Before we begin, I ask you to take a moment and reflect on what peace means to you, individually, as well as for our nation. For our world. While this rosary has become celebrated for other reasons, tonight we celebrate its original mission." Father Martin smiled and motioned to her. "I've invited Janey McKay to tell us more about this special rosary that is making quite a stir in the secular world as well our spiritual one."

Janey moved to the podium and stared at the framed photographs of John. It reminded her what the evening was about. Her lost brother. His last request to pray for peace. In a faltering voice, she repeated the story of how John had received the rosary after rescuing a beggar in Iraq.

"That the beggar disappeared after giving my brother the rosary makes this story even more compelling. The letter John enclosed with the rosary asked me to pray for peace." Her eyes teared up to recall that was the last letter she'd ever received. "Today would have been my brother's twenty-first birthday. My family chose to commemorate John publicly by honoring his last request. Thank you."

Mrs. Kendall stepped to the podium as Janey walked toward her seat. She debated slipping in the pew beside Perry's family, but Layton had already stepped out into the aisle to let her in.

She slid down the bench, leaving space between them. But Layton scooted so close his thigh brushed hers.

"John would be proud of you," he whispered.

She nodded once, then grabbed her bag and dug around for the rose-colored rosary beads that had belonged to her mother.

Dad leaned back across the seat and handed Layton a rosary. "I brought a spare for you."

"Thank you, sir." As Dad shifted forward again, Layton wound the rosary around his fist before slanting toward her. "You got to help me out. I'm not sure what to do with these."

Layton had attended Sunday Mass with John enough times that he wasn't totally unfamiliar with Catholic rituals. But a rosary service differed from Mass.

"Just follow the crowd. It's straight forward, mostly a call and answer. If you don't know the prayers, close your eyes and everyone will think you're praying. My mom said it's what's in your heart that matters." Janey regretted adding that last part. Too personal.

Layton knelt when everyone else did and made the sign of the cross but remained silent as Mrs. Kendall recited the Apostle's Creed.

With Layton so close Janey could not concentrate, her heart beating with an odd, broken rhythm. Why had Layton returned today? If he had waited another twenty-four hours, she would have been gone. Her thoughts leap-frogged, wondering how long he was in town and if he planned to stay at the farm tonight. Either way, she'd make a point of leaving before dawn.

When the service ended, several people approached Janey with questions. She welcomed the opportunity to move away. As soon as she did, her nephews swarmed in to surround Layton, which resulted in a shoving match in the middle of the church.

"Proving once again that McKay spawn are unholy," Matt said as he stepped between his youngest two who were now kicking each other.

Janey was discouraged that most of the comments and questions were about the miraculous healings that had taken place at other services.

"Do you think we'll have any miracles here tonight?"

"Did your brother witness any healings overseas?"

"Did John know about the rosary's power?"

Her answer was a repetitive, "I don't know." The crowd finally thinned, leaving only Father Martin, Janey's family, and Layton.

"Many people plan to return for tomorrow's rosary service, too," Father Martin said. "I may have to arrange more overflow seating in the school gym as well as the social hall."

Janey handed the priest her notes. "I won't be at tomorrow's service, so maybe Mrs. Kendall can read this before the service. If you would hold onto the rosary after the services are done, I'll arrange to have it picked up in a few days."

As soon as the priest left, Layton moved close. "Would you like to grab a bite to eat?"

"No. Thanks." She looked around, alarmed to find that her father and brothers were almost out the front door.

Layton touched her arm. "We need to talk."

His words were a flame to a short fuse. She whirled around. "Which talk do you want to have? The one you promised before deploying? The one you promised while in the hospital? The one you've promised since getting back? And if it's the one about you and Sharlene, I'll take a hard pass." Memories of heartache crowded her mind. She wouldn't fall for his promises again. "I have to catch my family."

"Actually, we need to talk about this." Layton reached into his jacket and withdrew a red envelope.

Janey's soul lurched. *Red envelope. Flowers. Hearts. Layton's name in big curlicues.* The curlicues she had practiced for hours. *Her love letter.* The one John had claimed to have destroyed.

Recalling what she wrote made her feel dizzy. She had poured her heart out, certain that Layton was her *one*. Certain he'd feel the same way. How many times since then had she felt relieved that he'd never seen it after all?

"Where did you get that?"

"I'll tell you over dinner." He slid the note back inside his jacket.

"Did you read it?"

"Do you really want to discuss this here, in front of them?" Layton hooked his thumb toward the altar where Father Martin and Mrs. Kendall were moving the rosary display. "Go to dinner with me."

"This feels like blackmail."

"Is it working?" Layton exhaled sharply. "Give me one more chance, Janey."

She bit her lip. Part of her still wanted to flee. But a bigger part wanted to hear him out. She tugged out her cell phone. "Let me tell Daddy."

"Um, I told him I'd bring you home later."

She narrowed her eyes. "Don't ever do that again."

Outside, the parking lot was practically deserted except for the McKay family vehicles. As she and Layton exited the church, Perry drove by, honking his horn once, Matt and Dad following close behind.

Layton pointed to where his truck was parked. "The service tonight was nice, Janey. I won't pretend that I understood any of it, but the reverence, the atmosphere was moving."

"Thanks. But small talk isn't helping."

At his truck, Layton's arm brushed past her as he reached to open the door. Ever the gentleman, he held out his hand to help her step onto the running board. In the past she'd always grabbed his hand eagerly, thrilled for even the briefest of touches. Now she held back.

"Please," he whispered.

That he was aware of her hesitation rattled her. And her tight skirt meant she could use a hand to avoid literally showing her butt. Eager for the moment to pass, she took his hand and climbed into the truck.

"Perry recommended Butch's Steakhouse," Layton said once he was behind the wheel. "How does that sound?"

Butch's was River Haven's finest restaurant. That she'd long ago dreamed of going there with him on a proper date stung. "Too public."

Layton cast her a sideways glance. "Drive-through it is, then. We can sit in the car and talk about it while we eat."

It was the last thing she wanted to discuss. *It* was a monstrous hurt.

Layton took her silence as affirmation and went on. "I read your letter, Janey, and I'm touched and flattered. But there are parts I don't understand."

Here it comes. Guys didn't use the words touched and flattered except for excuses. Blow offs. She rallied her pride — *never let 'em see you cry.* "Look, that letter was written long ago. I wish you'd never found it, and I'm embarrassed you read it."

"Wow. I'm still confused. Why did John have the letter then? Did you give the letter to him to give to me?"

She gritted her teeth. "Not exactly."

"I'm sorry if I'm prying into something private between you and John, but—" He looked away for a moment, his handsome profile half in shadow. "What you wrote in that letter— I didn't deserve any of it. Back when you wrote it, I was a mess. I wasn't even sure I'd make it back alive. Or if John and your family would ever see me as a worthy suitor. And now?" He held up his injured arm. "I'm still a mess. The Army will likely roll me out because I'm damaged goods, which means my dream of OCS is over."

A worthy suitor? The phrase made Janey want to scream. It was something her brothers had teased her about all her life. "My family can't dictate my feelings, which never stopped them from trying. And if the OCS dream is over, build a new one."

"I already have." He pulled into Char Grill Burgers and parked. He started to reach inside his jacket but paused. "Look, if you can tell me that what you wrote isn't true, I'll give this letter back and never speak of it again. But first I want you to know—"

Janey's cell phone rang.

So did Layton's.

He tugged his phone out and glanced at the screen. "It's your brother, Perry."

Janey scrambled for her phone. "Matt is calling me." She answered immediately. "Hello?"

"This is urgent, Sis," Matt said. "There's a fire at the farm."

"Oh, no! How bad?"

"No details. I'm just pulling in."

"We'll meet you there," she said.

"We're on our way!" Layton had already dropped the truck back in gear. "Buckle up and hold on."

"Matt said there's a fire at the farm."

"Perry said he followed your dad and Eileen home and noticed smoke."

It seemed to take forever to reach the farm. Flames lit up the sky behind the house as they pulled in.

"The bunkhouse!" She leaped from Layton's truck, her heels skittering on the gravel.

He caught up, matching his pace to hers as they darted between Matt and Perry's pickups. Both trucks were running, their headlights illuminating the scene. The back half of the bunkhouse was a barn. It held hay — easy fuel — and was engulfed in flames. Perry shoveled at the fire's base. Dad and Eileen were on the east side, frantically digging a fire break between the bunkhouse and the main house.

Matt had cobbled together enough garden hoses to reach the bunkhouse, but she knew it wasn't enough. Out in the country, fire posed a catastrophic threat. No fire hydrants meant their only water supply was the farm's wells.

"Go help Dad!" Perry shouted at Layton.

Janey grabbed a shovel from the pile of tools by the truck and fell in a few feet from Perry. She shoveled dirt as fast as she could, hoping they could control the fire before it destroyed the bunkhouse — hers and John's bedrooms — or reached the main house.

In the distance, she heard sirens.

"Fire department's here!" Perry shouted as headlights flashed behind them.

The area was served by volunteer firemen. While the county would respond with trucks, cadres of local volunteers were pulling in. Two men rushed up beside her. Janey recognized her neighbor's sons.

"Check on Dad and Eileen," Perry said as more help swarmed in, men and women bringing shovels and axes. Someone shoved a flashlight into her hand as a fire engine pulled in and cut its siren.

As Janey moved away, a sound caught her attention.

"Woof."

"Fuller!" Janey turned in a circle, listening. "Fuller! Where are you, girl?"

No sound came. *Oh, God.* Where was her dog?

She heard another soft bark and dashed toward the far side of the barn, nearly tripping as her heels sank into the ground.

Flashing her light, she spotted the collie lying on her side, near the open fence.

"Fuller!" She raced to the dog and dropped to her knees. The collie whined and panted, her coat stained dark with blood.

"Hold on, girl." As gently as she could, Janey lifted the dog and struggled toward the bunkhouse.

She heard Layton frantically shouting her name. "I'm over here!" she called. "Fuller's hurt!"

Layton ran up, his arms extended. "Let me take her."

"I've got her. She needs a vet."

Layton waved her toward his truck and yanked open the passenger door. Janey laid Fuller on the seat. The collie whined again, confirming she was alive.

Janey looked back at the fire. Flames shot up, the hay barn fully engulfed. If the fire jumped to the house and other barns, everything could be destroyed. And if Fuller didn't get help—

"Keys are in the ignition," Layton said. "We'll get the fire under control, Janey. Go save Fuller."

CHAPTER THIRTY-FIVE

October 2006
River Haven, Iowa

"Hold on, Fuller." Janey's headlights barely penetrated the cottony bands of smoke that had drifted across the dark highway and clung to the night mist.

Their veterinarian, Dr. Wiseheart, had a clinic at his farm just down the road. While Dr. Wiseheart specialized in large animals, he'd always made an exception for Fuller, keeping the collie up to date with vaccines, treating her every mishap like when she'd tangled with a porcupine or gotten kicked by a cow.

In the rearview mirror Janey caught glimpses of the orange glow on the horizon. Her heart ached for her family. Her home. Her beloved dog. She glanced at the seat beside her, barely able to make out Fuller's silhouette in the dim reflection of the dash lights. The dog hadn't made a sound since they left the farm, but Janey kept talking to her. "Dr. Wiseheart will fix you up, girl. He'll know what to do."

When Fuller was born, she'd been half the size of her littermates, a sickly runt not expected to survive. John and Janey had begged their parents for a chance to save her. Then they'd besieged Dr. Wiseheart for guidance on coaxing the tiny collie back to health. "All creatures thrive on love," the kindly vet advised. "And goat milk."

John rode his bicycle to a neighbor's farm twice a day to get goat's milk, which they fed to the puppy a half-dropper at a time. Against all odds, Fuller grew fat and happy. Dr. Wiseheart dubbed himself the collie's godfather. That had been nearly fourteen years ago, and the collie had been at Janey's side in good times and bad.

"We're almost there, Fuller." As soon as she reached the Wiseheart farm, Janey started honking the horn. Despite the late hour, the porch lights were on. The front door opened as she threw the truck into PARK.

"It's me, Janey McKay," she shouted as she jumped out. "Fuller's been hurt, Dr. Wiseheart."

The vet dashed down the porch steps followed closely by his oldest son, Frank, who served as his assistant. Janey opened the passenger door. Fuller still hadn't moved, and in the pale interior lights she could see the dog's side barely rise and fall.

"There's a fire at the farm." Janey wept as she spoke. "I found Fuller out behind the barn."

"Let's get her inside. Get a table ready, Frank." Dr. Wiseheart's unruffled voice eased her trepidation. As the vet lifted the collie, Fuller whined. "Easy, girl."

Janey followed the men to the clinic. Inside, Dr. Wiseheart tipped his head to the reception area before heading down a corridor. "Wait out here, Janey. You can't help her any more than you already have."

Unable to sit, Janey stepped back outside and scanned the horizon. From here the awful orange glow was not visible. She longed to know what was going on back at the farm. Was the fire out? Had the bunkhouse survived? The thought of John's room being damaged or losing her mother's precious memorabilia weighed heavy, but much worse was the thought of the fire spreading to the house and the other barns, destroying the farm. Destroying her home, her heart.

She wondered how Fuller had gotten hurt. Had she been sleeping in the hay barn and gotten trapped? Had a burning timber fallen and struck her? Janey searched Layton's truck for her cell phone but couldn't find it. In the hectic scramble to battle the fire, she must have dropped it. Back inside the clinic, she paced and fretted. That it was taking so long meant the dog had a fighting chance, right?

When Dr. Wiseheart finally came back out, he wore an expression of grim sympathy. "I'm sorry, Janey. There's nothing I can do. Her injuries, the cuts and stabs, are too extensive. There's been too much internal bleeding and organ damage."

"Cuts and stabs?" Janey rushed forward, her hand pressed to her heart. "What happened to her?"

"I thought you could tell me. You mentioned fire, so I expected burns." Dr. Wiseheart rubbed his forehead. "Fuller's alive, but not for much longer. We need to talk."

No, they needed to act. "You have to make her better. Please. I'll do anything."

"I know what Fuller means to you, and I'd do anything to save her, but I can't. And she's suffering." Dr. Wiseheart paused, not speaking the rest.

"Let me see her." *Let me take her home and care for her and she'll be fine.* Janey would never put Fuller down.

Dr. Wiseheart led her back to the exam room but didn't enter. Frank was inside the room with Fuller. The collie lay quietly on a stainless-steel table, covered with a bloodied blanket. A phone rang in another room. Frank gave Janey a sympathetic look before moving to answer it, leaving Janey alone with her dog. Once again she felt cut off from Heaven, an outcast whose prayers had been rejected. Like when Mom died. Like when John died. Like just now.

Janey stepped close to Fuller's head. The dog's eyes fluttered open but remained unfocused. Janey gently stroked her muzzle before lowering her cheek to rest lightly against the dog's face. "I love you, Fuller." Her voice splintered beneath the weight of anguish. "Please hang on. Don't leave me."

The dog let out a pain-edged whimper that stabbed a dull knife in Janey's chest. She didn't want Fuller to suffer, but how on earth could she say goodbye? Was this why Mom never said goodbye? And John? Had they known the pain of parting would be unbearable?

Yet, how agonizing was the fight to stay when they couldn't go on? Janey's greatest gift to them could have been the simple act of letting go with grace and love. And forgiveness. She stroked the soft spot behind Fuller's ear, wishing for a strength she didn't have.

"I'm sorry, girl. You're the best dog in the world. Nothing will ever change that." Tears streamed down Janey's face, into the dog's fur as she repeated those words over and over, soothing the collie and wishing she could soothe herself. "Thank you for always being there. I love you."

Fuller's tongue licked her cheek one final time. With a weak sigh, the dog stopped breathing.

Janey wrapped her arms around Fuller as pain ripped through her heart.

Dr. Wiseheart moved in and placed a hand on her shoulder, his touch conveying compassion. "She was a mighty fine dog."

Janey straightened, wiping her cheeks. Disbelief had her shaking her head. First the fire, now this? "I don't understand how she got hurt."

"The only thing I can figure is that she got impaled on something, maybe trying to get away. Had she been inside?"

"No. When we left, she was on the front porch."

Frank came back in and held out a cordless phone. "Janey, it's your sister-in-law."

Janey pressed the phone to her ear. "Hello?"

"It's Robin. Thank God I reached you! We've been worried because you weren't answering your phone."

"I lost my phone." Static interrupted. "Robin? Are you there?"

"Yes. Listen, sweetie, your father is at the emergency room. Matt and Eileen are with him.'"

Janey's knees buckled. Dr. Wiseheart tugged her toward a chair. "What's wrong with Daddy?"

"He was being treated at the farm for smoke inhalation when he started having chest pains. The paramedics took him to the emergency room."

"I'll go straight there. What about the fire? Is it out? Did they save the bunkhouse?"

"I'm afraid the bunkhouse is lost. The fire's under control, but there's lots of smoldering embers and the wind has picked up. Perry and Layton are still at the farm helping the fire department." Robin paused. "How's Fuller?"

For a moment, Janey couldn't speak. "She's...gone."

"I'm so sorry. Do you want me to come get you?"

"No. I've got Layton's truck. Would you let him know I'm headed to the hospital?"

Janey disconnected and handed the phone back. "I have to go. Dad's at the hospital. Can I come back for Fuller in the morning?"

"Of course," Dr. Wiseheart said. "And Frank can drive you into town."

Janey shook her head. "Thanks. I'll be fine." *I just need to be with my family. With Layton.* And nobody could out-drive a McKay.

Grateful for the powerful engine in Layton's Ford, she sped toward town. Earlier she'd thought the night couldn't get any worse. But she'd just been reminded that she still had much to lose.

Dashing away tears, she took shortcuts. The new hospital had been built on the city's outskirts to better serve the three-county area, but tonight it felt as if it was in Alaska.

When she finally reached the emergency room entrance, she wheeled in and immediately hit the brakes. The drive was backed up with traffic. As she inched forward, she noticed a police cruiser and two sheriff cars parked at the front entry, too. The emergency room was packed tonight.

She circled the parking lot twice before giving up and heading to the overflow lot behind the building, the car behind her doing the same. Though the overflow lot was desolate and unpaved, it was packed with cars.

She considered double parking, desperate to get to her father. She couldn't handle another goodbye. *If anything happened to him...*

She found a spot on the back edge next to the tree line and parked. As soon as she stepped away from Layton's truck, someone came up from behind and grabbed her elbow, forcing her to straighten.

She turned and came face to face with Randy Keener.

"Almost didn't recognize you in the wannabe's truck." His words were slurred. "Until I saw you leave the vet's place."

"You followed me?" She yanked her arm free. "Get your hands off me, creep."

"Think you're something special, don't you?"

"You're drunk. Get out of my way."

"Nope. You're coming with me." Randy grabbed her from behind, this time locking both of his arms across her chest, pinning her arms at her side. Even inebriated, he was stronger than her. "We're going back to the farm, so you can find my cell phone."

His demand made no sense. Why would Randy's phone be at the McKay farm?

He'd been there.

Rage seared Janey's veins. Had he set the fire? Hurt Fuller? "What did you do to my dog?"

"Screw your stupid dog! She tore a hunk out of my calf muscle. I've got bone showing. I'm going to sue your family when this is done." He tightened his arms as she struggled. "Hold still!"

Janey stopped writhing immediately. Feigning compliance, she cowered, lowering her center of balance.

"That's better," Randy sneered.

The moment he dropped his guard, she jammed her elbow backwards as hard as she could into his gut. Breaking free, she shot forward.

He closed in and grabbed her hair.

Her scalp burned as he yanked her back and used the long strands to careen her sideways onto the trunk of a car. Pain exploded in Janey's rib cage. She tasted blood as her jaw slammed the car's frame.

Before she could react, Randy pounced, shoving her down against the car. Intense pain shot through her ribs as he leaned over and pinned her in place. She wanted to throw up when he ground himself against her.

"It will be fun putting you in your place," he hissed.

John's voice echoed in her mind. *Don't go for vengeance. They expect that.*

She forced her muscles to go limp all at once, exhaling through her mouth as she pretended to pass out. Randy made a scoffing noise of victory, then shifted his weight off before shoving one hand beneath her skirt.

With a scream, Janey bounded straight up, throwing her head back and catching him under the jaw with a satisfying *crack*. He groaned in pain, flailing off balance. She swung her leg, tripping him.

As Randy fell backwards, she kicked him in the groin as hard as she could before turning and running. She tried to scream, to call out for help, but the knife-like pain in her side took her breath.

"Janey! Over here."

Just ahead, Layton and Perry barreled toward her across the dimly lit lot. Perry stopped when he reached her.

But Layton kept going. "You can't outrun me, Keener."

"We're outside, in overflow parking!" Perry shouted in his cell phone. Then he focused on Janey. "Are you hurt?"

"He killed Fuller." Janey glanced back just as Layton tackled Randy.

"How dare you touch her," Layton shouted. He and Randy rolled down a slight incline, but Layton ended up on top, fists flying as he punched Randy's face.

Janey tugged at Perry's arm. "Don't let Layton hurt his shoulder."

"I'm sure it feels pretty good right now," Perry said.

A deputy came running up behind them. "Sheriff's department! Stop!"

"Yes, sir," Layton acknowledged as he shifted to his knees, both hands held aloft.

Perry shouted to the deputy as he pointed to Layton. "He's one of us. Keener attacked my sister."

"She had it coming," Randy shouted as the deputies yanked him up. He attempted to break free but was quickly forestalled.

Layton hurried to where Perry and Janey stood. He reached out toward, but didn't touch, Janey's cheek. "You okay?"

She wasn't. Her side and back hurt and her lip felt swollen, but she nodded. "How's Daddy?"

"Not sure yet," Perry said. "Let's get inside and find out."

Janey took a step, but the pain in her side had her doubling over.

Perry and Layton practically collided trying to get to her. "Let me," Perry said. "Your shoulder has had enough." He picked her up, then shouted back to the deputies. "We're going inside. Janey needs a doctor."

At the emergency entrance the glass doors slid open automatically. A nurse waved them through a second set of double doors and led them down a hall. "This way. Deputy Williams said you were on your way. Set her on the exam table."

Layton turned to Perry. "I'll stay with Janey. Go check on your dad."

"I don't have my phone," Janey wailed.

"I'll call Layton," Perry said before disappearing.

The nurse pulled a privacy curtain around them before sticking a thermometer in Janey's mouth. "What happened?"

"She was attacked out in the parking lot," Layton said. "By a guy twice her size."

The nurse finished gathering her vitals, then stepped away. "The doctor will be right in."

As soon as they were alone, Layton came up beside her, his brow furrowed as he gently traced the tips of her fingers. "I should have been there to protect you from Keener."

The look on his face, the tender-harsh note in his voice undid Janey. "Fuller's gone. I think Randy hurt her." Her voice broke as she relayed what happened at Dr. Wiseheart's.

"I'm sorry. I know how much Fuller meant to you. Perry and I raced to get here as soon as Robin told us she'd died." He leaned against the table. "After you make a statement to the cops, they'll charge Randy. Which doesn't bring Fuller back."

"How bad is the farm?"

"The hay barn is gone. Most of the bunkhouse, too. It got one of the calf sheds, but we were able to keep it from spreading to the main house and the other barns. The fire department was still there when we left, wetting everything down, but it will be tomorrow before we can fully assess."

The curtain parted as the nurse returned with a man who introduced himself as Doctor Geddins.

Janey struggled to rise, but the pain made her stop. "My father, Ward McKay, was brought in earlier by ambulance. Can you tell me how he is?"

The doctor moved close. "Easy. We'll see about getting an update on him after we check on you. It's your right side that hurts?"

"Yes." She yelped as he found a tender area.

"Maybe a cracked rib. Or three," Dr. Geddins said before pressing gentle fingertips to her cheekbones. He flashed a penlight in her eyes and listened to her heart. "I need x-rays and blood work before I can give you anything for pain."

As soon as the nurse and doctor left, Layton moved back beside the exam table. "I want to find Keener again and kill him, but I don't want to leave you."

Janey noticed that he rubbed his shoulder as he spoke. "Did you hurt your arm?"

"It's fine." He reached forward and brushed the hair from her eyes. "I want to hug you, but I'm afraid I'll hurt you."

After all she'd been through tonight, she wanted to curl up in his arms and never move. "Hug raincheck?"

"A thousand rainchecks." He picked up her hand and carefully threaded his fingers with hers before brushing a kiss across her bruised knuckles. "We still need to talk."

The touch of his lips on her hand made it difficult to think. Just a few hours ago — a lifetime ago — they'd been discussing her letter. Then the fire. Fuller. Keener. *Daddy*.

She pulled away from him. "I can't do this right now."

"Payback, right?" Layton stuffed his hands in his pockets. "God knows I said that to you enough times."

"Too many. Help me sit up." Janey gritted her teeth against the effort it took to swing her feet over the edge of the table.

"What are you doing? Do you need to use the bathroom?"

"No, you big dork. I'm going to find my father." Tears pooled in her eyes. Dad had been her parental North Star since Mom died. Her chest ached to recall how she'd been kept from seeing her mother until it was too late. "I'm scared that they're not telling me anything because something bad has happened."

"Aww, Janey. Please stay put. I'm calling Perry now." He tugged out his cell phone.

The ache in her head escalated when she nodded. "Thank you. And I'm sorry I called you a dork."

Layton moved in front of her and gently cupped her chin. "Big dork. And if you really meant stupid SOB, I agree. Look, I can't get a phone signal in here, so I'll go find out about your Dad right after this."

He leaned in to kiss her.

Without warning, the curtain snapped wide open as a technician crashed in with a metal cart. Layton pulled back and straightened.

The tech gave them each a *what's-going-on* look. "Um, I need to draw blood samples before they take you to x-ray."

"Raincheck," Layton whispered before he slipped away.

CHAPTER THIRTY-SIX

October 2006
River Haven, Iowa

Randy Keener didn't question his luck when he made bail two hours later. He limped out of the county jail as fast as he could.

His leg had been bleeding so profusely in the hospital parking lot that the deputies had to take him into the emergency room in handcuffs. The dog bites took forty-seven stitches to close. The six shots of Novocain had long since worn off, but Randy wouldn't take something for pain until later.

Now he needed to get away before the cops changed their minds. Randy had only been charged with assault initially. Just enough to hold him while the deputies cleared the backlog of calls from double-header bar fights. God bless all the rowdy drunks who'd practically overwhelmed law enforcement tonight.

Still, Randy knew it was just a matter of time before more serious charges rolled in. *Breaking and entering. Arson.* If the cops found his cell phone, they'd have proof that he'd been at the McKay farm. He'd been ready to film the blaze when Janey's dog attacked.

Gary Pickett, the treasurer of the River Haven JFA chapter, waited outside the jail. Gary hadn't argued when Randy told him to use special funds for bail. "Get an extra fifty for yourself for coming to get me."

Next, Randy instructed Gary to drive through the overflow parking lot at the hospital. If the cops were still tied up with calls, maybe his truck had not yet been impounded.

Lady Luck kept smiling as Randy drove off a few minutes later, headed for his makeshift apartment above the JFA headquarters. He'd fixed the place up on the sly, not wanting to raise eyebrows over the fact that the chapter paid his living expenses.

This time of night, downtown was deserted. He parked behind the building and slipped in the back door. His head felt ready to explode and his jaw ached where Layton had landed a punch. As soon as Randy was on the road, he'd take something for pain.

Upstairs, he quickly stuffed clothes in a backpack. Then he hurried downstairs and unlocked the safe in his office. He crammed handfuls of loose cash into his pack. He'd only been paid half, but five thousand was more than enough to get him to Arizona. He had a prepper pal there who owed him a favor and knew a lot about life south of the border.

Since Randy was never coming back, he helped himself to the JFA dues, too. As a wise man once said, cash didn't leave a trail. Randy zipped his pack and stood.

Tom stepped into the open doorway. "Going somewhere?"

Randy jumped backwards and grimaced when he jarred his leg. "Tom. You scared me."

"I could say the same about you. I've been calling your phone all night. Were there problems?"

Randy tightened his grip on the bag. If Tom was asking about problems, then he had no idea Randy had been arrested. He ran excuses through his head. Tom had gone over the procedure count-less times. *Set the timer for ninety minutes. Place it under the bed. Get*

in, get out on foot. Film of the aftermath would mean a bonus, but
don't risk being caught.

"Their dog attacked me while I set the timer. I may have hit the
wrong numbers." The lie came easy. Randy set a twenty-minute
timer. He wanted the film bonus, but not at the cost of murder. He
hated Janey McKay, but he wasn't up to killing her. "The bunkhouse
got destroyed like you wanted, but then I had to drive across the river
to find an ER to get my leg stitched up."

Tom's expression remained unreadable. "You need to get away
from here and lie low for a while."

Thank you, Jesus. Randy lifted his bag. "Great minds think alike.
If you've got the rest of my cash, I'll be on my way."

"It's out in my truck. But first I need to check something on your
phone and laptop."

Stalling, Randy patted his pockets. "Phone must be out in my
truck. I silenced it before the job which is why I didn't hear your
call." Tom frowned now, so Randy wasn't about to mention that the
laptop he'd used had been borrowed. "Let me go check outside."

Randy headed down the hall. Tom followed closely. In the alley,
Randy made a big show of searching his truck for his phone, checking
between and under the seats.

"Dang. Maybe it fell out of my pocket at the hospital. I can go
check." He backed out of the truck and straightened.

Tom had a pistol pointed at him. "We'll go together. In my car.
But first, give me your laptop."

CHAPTER THIRTY-SEVEN

October 2006
River Haven, Iowa

Stones of grief and pain crushed Janey as she lay in bed the next morning. She awoke before dawn, not wanting to move. Not wanting the day to begin *without*.

One morning she'd awoken without her mother. Another morning, without John. Now...Fuller. Her heart broke remembering the events of the night before.

Her recollection seemed surreal, thanks to the pain medication they'd given her at the ER. She'd been so out of it last night that Perry had to carry her upstairs to her old bedroom in the main house. Lisa had been there and helped Janey change into an oversized sleep shirt and get into bed.

Layton had been there, too. He'd covered her with an extra blanket when her chills wouldn't subside. Then he sat beside her and told her over and over that everything would be okay. She'd drifted off to the sound of his voice.

Now Layton was gone too, and Janey felt alone. The scent of

smoke clung to her skin, her hair, reminding her of the fire. She'd already lost so much and yet...there was always more to lose.

Like Dad.

She'd been told he suffered a major heart attack, but now she regretted letting her brothers talk her out of visiting intensive care last night. It had been late when they finished giving statements to the deputies.

Perry had cajoled, "It's past midnight, Janey. Dad will be asleep."

Matt had been blunt. "Dad will take one look at your face and want to go hunt down Randy Keener. Give us a chance to explain first."

Screw the explanations. She was going to the hospital. She moved to sit up. The sharp pain from her fractured ribs made her cry out.

"Easy. I'm right here." Layton's sudden appearance at her bedside startled her. He snapped on the lamp. "Sorry. I didn't mean to scare you."

She blinked against the brightness. Layton hovered over her. The top button of his jeans was unfastened, and he wasn't wearing a shirt, exposing the network of scars across his upper chest.

"Were you sleeping on the floor?" she asked.

"Just outside, in the hall."

"But the guest room—"

"I needed to be close. Perry's downstairs on the couch. How are you feeling? Do you need something for pain?"

"No. Pain killers make me feel like a desiccated zombie."

"The doctor said you could take ibuprofen and use ice packs for pain. I can get either if you like."

"I'm fine."

"Liar." He straightened the blankets.

"I—" Janey coughed, her throat parched.

"Hold on." He handed her the glass of water that sat beside a prescription bottle on the nightstand.

She drained half the glass, then closed her eyes as a wave of nausea hit.

"Breathe." Layton pried the glass from her grip and set it aside before helping her ease back on propped pillows. "Better?"

"Yes. Thanks."

"I like your pajamas."

Janey looked down. She wore a burnt orange Texas Longhorns T-shirt. *His* Longhorns T-shirt. Her cheeks flushed. "Sorry. You left it behind in the bunkhouse. I, um, liked it because it's oversized." She didn't want to admit it had smelled like him, his cologne.

"I'm not complaining. It looks good on you."

Self-consciousness flushed over her. What did she look like? And how bad was her morning breath?

"I need to use the bathroom." She struggled to sit up again.

"Hold on." Layton flipped the covers back, exposing her bare legs. He offered his arm, helping her to her feet with a minimum of discomfort then hovering close as she took a step. "Go slow. You suffered a concussion, so you might feel unsteady."

In the bathroom, she grimaced at her reflection. Her cheek was bruised, the skin beneath her eye darkening with the promise of a shiner. Mascara, mud — maybe both — streaked her skin. Brushing her teeth and washing her face made her feel more human, however her hair looked like she'd weathered a tornado in a pigsty. A smoky pigsty. She opened the drawer, searching for a hairbrush.

A wave of light-headedness had her grabbing the edge of the counter. The brush fell and skittered across the tile floor.

There was an immediate rap on the door. "You okay in there?" Layton asked.

Janey opened the door. "I dropped a hairbrush. I'll get it later."

Layton caught her as she dipped sideways, off balance. "Let's get you back to bed."

In her room, she pointed to the chair by the window. "I'd prefer to sit. I really do feel better." She tugged at the shirt, trying to keep it from riding up.

Layton grabbed a blanket and draped it across her lap. His thoughtfulness had her blinking back tears of self-pity again.

"I smell coffee brewing," he said. "If you promise not to move, I'll go grab some."

When he was gone, she wrapped the blanket around her legs, trying to remember if she had left any clothes in the drawers. She'd already been warned that the bunkhouse had been heavily damaged. Had any of her and John's possessions survive?

Layton wore a shirt when he returned. He held out a coffee mug but didn't release it until he was certain her grip was solid. "Two sugars. Lots of cream."

Janey took a cautious sip. "Perfect. Thank you."

"Perry just called the hospital. They said your father had a restless night but is sleeping now. Matt is headed there and will call as soon as the doctor makes rounds."

"I want to go to the hospital."

"Perry said the fire marshal and sheriff will be here shortly to wrap up their investigations. Then he'll take you." Layton reached around and pulled her hairbrush from his back pocket. "How about I tackle the rat's nest while you work on the coffee?"

Having seen her hair, she couldn't fault his description. She nodded and then braced for discomfort as he separated a thick hank of hair.

"You've got beautiful hair, Janey," he said.

The compliment warmed her. "Says the man who just called it a rat's nest."

To her surprise, he started brushing at the ends, expertly working his way through the tangles and snarls with no painful tugging. Then he divided off another section and repeated the slow process. He wasn't a stranger to a woman's hair.

"Did Sharlene teach you that?" Immediately Janey regretted the words. "Sorry."

"My mother had long hair. When times were good, she kept it perfectly groomed. When she drank too much, she'd have me brush it out before Dad got home. She cut it all off when she started doing meth." His next words surprised her. "I owe you an explanation about Sharlene."

"No. You don't. It's none of my business."

"It affects us, so I'd like to clear the air. Sharlene and I dated off and on since junior high, however we haven't been together since before I deployed. She was listed as an emergency contact for my grandmother and came here thinking I might come into an inheritance. Apparently, my grandfather left me some sort of trust, which I'll sort out later, but right now I need you to know that you're the only person my heart is interested in." He had finished with her hair and dropped on one knee before grasping her hand.

"Knock, knock." Perry rapped on the door frame as he came into her room. Layton didn't move. Perry's gaze went from their joined hands to Janey. He gave her his patented canary-eating-cat smirk. "How you feeling, kiddo?" He looked around for a place to sit.

Your timing sucks, bro. "Don't get comfortable. I'll be fine after a shower and then I want to go to the hospital."

"Judging by your bossiness, you must feel a little better. Lisa will be up in a minute. She brought you some clothes, Janey. Not sure what we can salvage from the bunkhouse yet." Perry started out the door, then turned back. "Layton, come on down and get a ham biscuit."

"He'll be down shortly," Janey said. When they were alone, she looked at Layton. "You're lucky to be an only child."

"That's debatable." He pressed a kiss to the top of her hand.

Footsteps ascended the staircase. "My family is determined to interrupt us."

On cue, Lisa knocked on the door frame. She had a large bag in one hand. "Sorry to interrupt, but Perry said you might need help to get changed."

Layton squeezed her fingers before climbing to his feet. "I'll wait downstairs."

When they were alone, Janey spoke to Lisa. "I guess I should explain about Layton."

"Nope. I know you've had a crush on him for a while and I'm tickled for you," Lisa said. "I'm probably not supposed to tell you this, but your Texan asked your father and brothers for permission to ask you out. Probably not so much asked as told, but you get the gist. He's such a gentleman."

This surprised Janey. "When?"

"Before coming for the rosary service."

Twenty minutes later, Janey made her way slowly down the stairs. Thanks to Lisa's help, she'd been able to shower and dress.

Layton stood when she came into the kitchen and pulled a chair out. "One warm biscuit coming up."

"It feels better to stand, but I'll take a couple ibuprofen now." She moved to lean against the counter. "Where's Perry?"

"Fire marshal just showed up." Layton held out her cell phone. "Perry found this in the bed of his truck."

Janey remembered setting it down when she'd grabbed a shovel. She took a few bites of food and swallowed the pills before heading for the back door. Outside, the sun was up but had not yet burned off the morning fog. The stench of charred wood lingered in the damp air. Layton came up behind her and wrapped a jacket over her shoulders.

She couldn't turn away from the darkened skeleton of the bunkhouse. Half of the roof had collapsed. The walls were heavily carbonized, but intact. A van marked *Crime Scene* was parked next to the fire marshal's truck. Perry walked toward her.

"Is there anything left of John's or my rooms?" she asked.

"I'm not sure. The wall on the other side has questionable integrity and there's a lot of smoke and water damage. After they complete their investigation, we'll assess how stable the structure is. You ready to see the rest?"

"There's more?" She followed her brother and Layton around to the front of the house where a technician snapped photographs. A vehicle had spun large ruts in the lawn before plowing through the flower beds. The edge of the front porch had been clipped, taking down part of the railing. The sight of the flattened rose trellis and smashed concrete Madonna sickened Janey. Why had Randy Keener been determined to destroy their home? She turned away and spotted more damage.

"Mom's sign!" Ignoring the pain in her side, she started down the driveway.

The big McKay Family Farm sign was knocked down, the poles snapped. Her mother had designed the sign after she and Dad married. Mom called the sign a work in progress. It mainly featured the farm, but in front of the house she'd painted her and Dad. Years later, she added Matt and Perry and eventually John and Janey. As Dad built bigger barns and added acreage and silos, the background behind the house filled in to form the portrait of their life.

It hurt to see Mom's beautiful artwork splintered, muddy tire tracks across it.

"It's ruined." Janey reached for it, but Layton caught her hand.

"Don't touch it until the crime techs are finished," he said. "Then we'll check it."

She didn't release his hand as they turned back to face the farmhouse. Their beautiful farm looked like a disaster zone.

Six of the seven generations of McKays whom had farmed this land had lived in this house. Her father spoke often of how each family proudly preserved that heritage while updating and expanding for future generations.

"Dad would be sick if he saw this," Janey said as they returned to where Perry stood.

"Agreed," Perry said. "Then he'd roll up his sleeves and start cleaning up."

"Which is what we'll do as soon as the investigation is complete," Layton added.

A tan pickup pulled in. Janey recognized Dr. Wiseheart's son, Frank. He climbed out and shook hands before surveying the damage.

"You folks didn't deserve this." Frank turned to Janey. "I brought

Fuller back. Dad and I made a pine box for her. She was a good dog and, well, she didn't deserve what happened to her either."

"That means a lot." Janey wiped her eyes. "Thank you."

"Where do you want to bury her, Janey?" Perry asked.

She didn't need to think about it. "Beneath the maple tree by the pond. That was her favorite spot."

"We can take her out there now, while they finish their investigation," Perry said. "Matt called and said Dad's resting. Doctor hasn't been by yet, though."

Frank transferred Fuller's box to the back of Perry's truck before leaving. Then Janey, Perry, and Layton drove out to the pond. Even driving slowly, the slightest bump sent pain shooting up her side.

At the pond, she watched Layton and Perry dig a hole. Memories of Fuller tugged at her heart. The dog had been a constant companion for John and Janey, especially after Mom died. Fuller saw them off each morning when they left for school and waited at the drive each afternoon. She accompanied them to do chores, and then morphed into a cowboy dog, a pirate dog, a spy dog as needed for the day's games. Thanks to the hours John spent training Fuller to respond to hand signals, the dog developed stealth capabilities an invisible man would envy.

Perry and Layton placed the pine box in the ground and stepped aside. The lump in Janey's throat swelled.

"I can't believe she's gone." *I love you, Fuller.* Janey grabbed a shovel, wincing as she scooped up a bit of dirt and let it fall into the hole. She didn't resist when Layton took the shovel and finished the job with Perry.

"I can make a marker if you want," Perry said as they prepared to head back.

Janey looked around, remembering how Fuller always circled the tree before lying down. "That big maple is the marker."

When they returned to the farm, the fire marshal and crime scene vans were gone. Matt's truck was there along with a sheriff's vehicle.

Deputy Blake Evans greeted them as they came up. "They

finished processing the crime scene and sent samples to the lab. The fire marshal believes an accelerant was used, which will prove arson. They also recovered a cell phone they believe belonged to Keener."

Perry swore. "So help me—"

Blake nodded. "Good thing Ward left the security cameras up. Matt and I just checked and found footage showing Randy Keener carrying a package into the bunkhouse, then leaving without it. You don't want to see it, Janey, but Fuller attacked at that point, took him down to the ground. Even injured, she gave chase. Then Keener came back in his truck and tried to run her down."

Layton moved in closer behind Janey. "Jail is the only place he'll be safe."

"Yeah, about that." Blake exhaled loudly. "Keener made bail last night before more serious charges were drawn up. Believe me, I hate it as much as you do, but five new warrants have been issued. He'll be back in jail within the hour and the DA will ask the judge to deny bail."

"Keener better hope I don't find him first," Perry said. "I made him a promise."

"There will be a deputy here at the farm until further notice," Blake said. "I hope that will ease some of Ward's concern."

"Speaking of Dad." Matt checked his watch. "He will be transferred to Iowa City for heart surgery later this afternoon."

"Surgery?" Janey panicked. Dad had been adamant that going under the knife was his last course of action. "Is he worse?"

"He's got a lot of blockages and will probably need a pacemaker. Doc says the cardiac unit in Iowa City is one of the best in the country." Matt looked at her. "He refused to go anywhere until he sees you, Janey. I promised we'd meet him in Iowa City before surgery."

Lisa had joined them. "How's Eileen?"

"She's a champ, but she won't leave Dad's side and plans to ride in the ambulance with him," Matt said. "We should get going, so grab what you need. It will be a late night."

"I'll pack a few things for Eileen," Janey said. "She's already spent one night at the hospital."

"And will likely spend a few more in Iowa City," Lisa said. "I'll grab her knitting bag and phone charger."

Layton took Janey's hand. "Go with your brothers. I'll look out for things here and get the evening chores." He nodded to Matt and Perry. "I'll go check on Robin and the kids, too. Tell Ward I'm confident everything will be fine."

———

TWO HOURS LATER, Janey and her brothers were at the hospital in Iowa City. Dad had arrived thirty minutes earlier and was being prepped for surgery. When they could finally see him, Janey pushed into the room, ignoring the pain in her side.

Dad had wires and tubes and IV lines snaking out beneath the covers. His skin had a gray cast to it.

As soon as he spotted her, he held out his hand and rasped, "Geez. Look at your eye. You okay, Janey-girl?"

"The other guy looks worse." She took his hand. His firm grip reassured her. "You're where I get my strength."

"And you're where I get mine." He pointed to Janey's bruised cheek and his nasal cannula. "Some of us are a little worse for the wear and tear — and nothing brings Fuller back — but all that matters is that you're okay. I couldn't bear to lose another one of you kids."

She squeezed his hand, unable to speak. *And I couldn't bear to lose you.*

Dad looked at Perry. "How bad is the farm?"

"The hay barn is gone, lots of damage to the bunkhouse, but we'll salvage what we can," Perry said.

"We're stronger than our losses. We'll rebuild." Dad coughed and shut his eyes for a few seconds. "Doc says I'll be better than new after this."

The cough worried Janey. "You need to rest, Daddy."

"In a minute. Is Layton out in the hall?"

She shook her head. "He stayed at the farm."

"There's something you kids need to know," Dad said. "Layton was next to me when I started having trouble. I think he knew what was coming next. He pulled me away from the fire and made Eileen go for help." He paused. "I wasn't happy he made me stop, but I might not be laying here if he hadn't. By the time the paramedics got to me, I was in serious distress and couldn't breathe. As soon as the paramedics took over, Layton jumped back in to battle the fire."

Perry came up behind Janey. "I can see him doing that."

A nurse leaned in. "We'll be taking him up shortly."

"We'll give you and Eileen a few minutes alone," Perry said. "We'll be in the waiting room."

Janey kissed her dad's cheek, then followed her brothers down the hall. The spacious surgical waiting room had multiple television sets and a refreshment center. A few minutes later, Eileen joined them.

As soon as Eileen sat down, tears filled her eyes. "Sorry. It's been a long night."

Compassion had Janey offering a box of tissues. "He'll be fine. He's a McKay."

Eileen wiped her cheeks. "That's the same thing he told me about you."

Perry shifted close. "Lisa's dad had open heart surgery five years ago. Now he jogs five miles a day and is in better shape than me."

Uncle Nick called and Janey passed the phone around so he could speak with everyone. Then she flipped through magazines and fidgeted, while Matt and Perry settled in to watch television. Eileen had been glad to see her knitting bag and moved closer to the window before pulling out her needles and yarn.

The time passed slowly. Despite everything that had happened in the last twenty-four hours, the only thing Janey could think about was her Dad and how much he meant to her. If anything happened to him—

She checked the clock constantly, which didn't help. They had been told the surgery would take at least four hours but worry chewed on the fragments of her nerves.

At five and a half hours, the McKay family was paged. Janey stood as a grim-faced hospital clerk approached them.

"There have been complications," the clerk told them in hushed tones. "And more damage than expected. Mr. McKay will be in surgery for a while yet."

CHAPTER THIRTY-EIGHT

October 2006
River Haven, Iowa

The news about her father's surgery left Janey with a familiar ominous feeling. The one that preceded loss.

No. Don't take Dad!

While the others were on their phones, giving updates, she slipped out of the waiting room to pace. A short distance down the hall she paused at a door marked CHAPEL. She yanked the door open and found the small room deserted. The chapel looked very different compared to St. Francis' vast interior, yet it felt every bit as holy...and lonely.

Janey went up to the front of the room where a large, simple cross was mounted on the wall. She stared at it as tears ran down her cheeks.

Then she turned away. What was she doing here? Chasing faith?

Her cell phone vibrated, signaling a text message. She tugged her phone out, half afraid to read the text. Would it be from her brothers, asking her to return? This soon, it would not bode well.

But there was no message, only a photograph. Of John's rosary.

She drew a sharp breath and heard John's voice in her head. *"Ask for a miracle, Janey."*

She buried her face in her hands. Asking for a miracle required faith. She had none.

Once again, she heard John's voice in the silent room. *"Ask anyway."*

She turned back to the front of the chapel with an anguished cry. "God, please help my father."

A warmth spread up her hand, nearly causing her to drop her phone. She glanced at the screen again, but the picture of the rosary was gone. Had she conjured it up in desperation? Did its disappearance mean disaster?

Frightened, Janey hurried back to the waiting room, but there was no news. She settled into a chair and closed her eyes. Layton texted a short time later, wanting an update.

Nothing yet, she texted.
Keep the faith, Layton sent back.

An hour later, Dad's surgeon came in and introduced himself. "Ward is in recovery and doing well considering what he went through. As we neared the end of surgery, your father's heart stopped. I shocked him three times, to no avail, and was ready to call it. Then his heart restarted. Call it a miracle because I can't take credit. It will be a while before you can see him, so you might get a bite to eat."

Ask for a miracle. "I'll meet you in the cafeteria," Janey told Perry.

She returned to the chapel, grateful to find it still empty. She walked up to the cross and stared at it. Then she bowed her head and offered a heartfelt prayer of gratitude.

"And I apologize for my lack of faith, my lack of belief."

She wanted to apologize to John, too, but knew an apology to her brother needed to take place somewhere else. With a lighter heart, she went to find her family.

———

IT WAS LATE before Janey and her brothers could see their father. That Dad remained in intensive care meant their visit was short. They got hotel rooms in Iowa City and went back to the hospital early the next morning.

Dad had better color but would remain in intensive care for at least another twenty-four hours. Eileen declined to leave but gave Janey a list of items to bring when they returned.

As they drove back to River Haven, Janey told her brothers about the incident in the chapel the day before. That she had found the rosary photo in a website file on her cell phone didn't make its appearance in the chapel any less inexplicable.

"Well, the doctor said he couldn't take credit for it," Perry said.

"Maybe this is why so many people are seeking the rosary," Matt added. "Hoping for their own miracle."

Matt's words haunted Janey. What if her original intent to pray for peace wasn't the rosary's true purpose? Maybe its purpose was beyond her comprehension. The website continued to get scores of requests for the actual rosary despite the reports of miracles coming from people using facsimile copies like the one that had appeared on Janey's cell phone.

How could she stand in the way of anyone hoping for a miracle?

"You're right, Matt. After the service in Chicago, I will let the rosary travel again."

It was noon when they got home. It hurt to see the farm's sign gone. With the Madonna statue destroyed, too, it felt like Mom had been erased from the farm. That Fuller didn't run to greet her was another knife in the heart.

Layton came up to help her climb out of Matt's truck. "How's Ward?"

"He's ready to come home," Janey said.

Matt stepped up to Layton. "Dad told us what you did, making him stop and getting help. It likely saved his life."

Layton's brow furrowed. "He may not remember, but he called out my name, otherwise I might not have noticed he was having trouble breathing. I was just glad paramedics were already here."

"What's with all the people?" Perry swept an arm toward the house. The driveway was filled with cars and trucks, some parked along the shoulder of the highway. "I swear half the county is here."

"They came to help," Layton said. "You've got fantastic neighbors, and each one has told me a story about Ward helping them out. They're all glad to return the favor. The guy wearing the red hardhat is with the insurance company. When he's done, we'll assess what can be salvaged."

Layton stepped aside to give Janey a full view. The bunkhouse remained roped off with yellow crime scene tape, but while they'd been gone, the charred remnants of the hay barn had been hauled away. Already a new structure had been framed out, the plywood being readied for metal roofing. A group of men from Dad's Tuesday morning coffee club loaded a trailer with burnt timbers while others unloaded new lumber.

The front porch of the main house had been leveled and new railings were being painted. Someone had smoothed the ruts in the lawn and laid squares of dormant sod atop the damaged lawn.

Layton hovered close. "You wince with every step you take. Maybe you should go inside."

"I'll grab a couple ibuprofen, but I'd rather be out here."

Someone shouted for Layton. "I have to haul these poles out to the hay barn." He pressed a kiss to her forehead. "Please take it easy."

As Janey made her way to the house, she spotted Ben Hufstedler. Ben's wheelchair was on the sidewalk next to the front flower gardens, beside a pile of leaves and grass he'd raked up.

Ben's two younger brothers gathered the broken bricks that once edged the gardens.

"Our dad's bringing over new bricks. He's got a bunch of them," the taller of the boys, Nathan, said.

"Mom's digging up some of her flowers, too," the youngest, Markus, pushed Nathan out of his way. "She said we're not supposed to ask nosy questions about the fire, but she didn't say anything about your black eye. Does it hurt?"

Ben hissed at his brother.

Janey ruffled Markus' hair. "It's not my first shiner, so I know it gets better. And thank you for all you're doing." She turned to Ben. "This is all amazing."

"Amazing is what we do in Iowa. How's your dad?"

"Okay for someone who just had heart surgery. The doctor says in time he'll be better than ever with those blockages removed."

Ben's father came up just then with a wheelbarrow of bricks and a shovel. "Good job, guys. Let me get in there to dig out that busted bush."

"No. Leave it, please," Janey said. "It was my mom's rosebush. Maybe it will come back."

Broken stems were all that was left of the climbing rose that once covered the trellis over the Madonna statue. Mom had planted the rose the year she and Dad married, and its profusion of blooms meant Dad had to reinforce the trellis several times. After Mom died, the bush grew and provided greenery, but the flowers never again bloomed, as if unable to overcome its grief. Until Layton visited the farm, that is. Overnight, yellow roses opened, and Janey knew its rebirth was her sign. That Layton was her *one*.

Perry called out for Janey.

"Go on," Ben said. "We'll leave the rosebush. I bet Dad can salvage some trellis, too."

Perry met her as she walked toward the driveway. "We will empty the bunkhouse and haul whatever is salvageable into the machine barn. I thought you'd want to supervise on that end. I'll warn you, there's not much."

Perry's assessment was accurate. Janey's room was a total loss.

What hadn't been destroyed by flames was water or smoke damaged. Though she reminded herself that things could be replaced, it hurt to see what couldn't be saved. The losses from John's room were harshest — irreplaceable.

Tables were set up so wet items could be spread out to dry. Janey spent the rest of the afternoon sorting through scorched heartache. Her mother's ceramic canisters were shattered, however she'd cried out in joy to find one of Mom's crockery mixing bowls had survived.

It was late afternoon when Layton and Perry came into the machinery barn.

"You look exhausted, kiddo," Perry said. "Why don't you call it quits for today? I have to head to the store. Lisa is hoping you and Layton will stay with us tonight. She's not above using the kids as pressure, you know."

"That sounds good to me." Layton turned to Janey. "We could get a good night's sleep and be back early in the morning."

She shoved her hair away and stared at the dark line of soot beneath her nails. Her clothes were coated in grime and ash and she had nothing to change into.

She nodded. "Tell Lisa we'll be over later. I need to go into town and pick up a few things." She had a few items in her room at the main house, but all her clothes had been destroyed.

"I'll see you at the house," Perry said as he left.

Layton moved in and brushed his fingertips softly across Janey's brow. "Got a few minutes for us?"

Us? The word was a balm. "Yes."

He reached for her hand and pressed a kiss to her knuckles. "Fair warning. If one more person interrupts us, I'm going ballistic. We still need to discuss your letter." He released her hand and reached into his shirt pocket before withdrawing a one-inch charred section of red envelope. "Your letter fell out of my pocket last night. This is all that's left."

"It's probably just as well."

Layton shook his head. "When I first read your letter, I was angry to think John might have hidden it from me. Then I realized he was simply being himself. Your brother didn't think anyone was good enough for you. Frankly, I'm not sure I'm good enough."

She started to speak, but Layton cut her off.

"I won't let my doubts keep me from trying to win your heart. And speaking of hearts." He reached in his pocket and withdrew the half-heart necklace stamped FOREVER still dangling from its chain. Heat had discolored the finish, but the pendant was intact. "I found it when clearing the bunkhouse. I'm surprised you kept it."

Her hand shook as she reached out. She'd taken the necklace off the day Sharlene had arrived at the farm. "I kept it because you gave it to me. When you were deployed, I wore it every day." Her fist closed over the pendant. "It might have meant nothing to you, but it was epic to me even if I misread the intent."

"It had meaning for me, too." Layton reached beneath his shirt and tugged out the Army dog tags he still wore around his neck. He peeled away the edge of the black plastic sheath that covered one metal tag. A small, metal half-heart fell into his palm, the word TOGETHER barely visible.

Tears filled her eyes. "You kept it."

"Close to my heart. It reminded me I should have kissed you longer that day. That I should have told John I was drawn to you." He shook his head. "If you'll give me a second chance, I'll prove that I love you, Janey McKay. I think I have for a while and—"

"Wait." She waved a hand to interrupt. "You love me?"

"I do. And you don't have to say anything—"

"Shut up and say it again."

"I love you, Janey McKay. And..."

She closed the distance between them and kissed him. His fingers speared softly into her hair, cradling her head. Her eyes shut as his lips brushed lightly against hers, the first touch tentative. At her soft sighing sound, he deepened the kiss with a gentle urgency that made her feel cherished.

He finally pulled away with a series of tiny, brief kisses that left her breathless. "I've waited a long time for that kiss, Janey. I've dreamed of you nonstop since I deployed."

Before she could respond, Perry came back in, his expression grim. "Sorry to interrupt, but FBI agents are on their way here."

"What? Why?" Janey asked.

"The evidence the fire marshal collected indicates the fire was started by an incendiary device similar to the one sent to Sergeant Boswell."

"How can that be? The bomber died," Janey said.

"Maybe the FBI closed the case prematurely," Perry said. "Let's go up to the house. The agents will be here shortly."

When Agent Holmes arrived, he had four other agents with him. "The FBI is joining the search for Randy Keener. We think he's with an associate of Farid Zaman."

"Keener was stupid," Perry said. "But I wouldn't have taken him to be a terrorist."

"He may have been targeted," Holmes went on. "Terrorists have been known to monitor and recruit from hate groups. A riff on the common-enemy approach. As far as we know, nothing in Keener's past shows bomb making skills, so someone else may have supplied the explosives and used Keener to get close enough to plant it."

Janey moved closer to Layton. "Never underestimate your enemies."

Agent Holmes nodded at her. "Which is why we're here. Zaman has claimed responsibility for this fire and said he's not done yet. He's also called you out as the source of the rosary problem. The fire marshal says the bomb was planted under your bed. You were the target. I don't want to take any chances this time, so we need to take you into protective custody, Janey."

CHAPTER THIRTY-NINE

October 2006
Baghdad, Iraq

The shopkeeper below Cleric Ibrahim Yassin's window rushed to complete a sale before closing his shop. The call to prayer would temporarily halt the bustle of business.

It would also end Farid Zaman's tantrum. After prayer, Yassin would steer the conversation back on course.

When news of the fire at the McKay farm arrived, Zaman had celebrated before promptly taking credit and reiterating his promise to rain down fire on his enemies and bragging on the reach of his hand.

However, the Westerners proved fickle yet again as the death of a dog — a worthless animal — fanned an outcry in international news. The local tribal leaders were losing faith in Zaman's power to lead. The warlord Rehab had declared that the hand of Zaman could only kill dogs in the West.

Worse, the story of the rosary was once again spotlighted as the Vatican confirmed that the cursed beads would be present at an official event. The progress Yassin had made in disassociating Zaman's son from those beads was further threatened as word that a small enclave of Christians in Baghdad sought to have the abominable rosary sent to Iraq for a peace service.

"My son is dead while my opponents ridicule me," Zaman fumed. "I want them all destroyed."

"Our faithful supporters are still at work. The infidels will be dealt with." Yassin couldn't allow a full revolt. In fact, if he didn't hear from his private contacts, soon he would take matters into his own hands. "Your focus should be on reassuring the tribes. They are superstitious and seek a sign."

Zaman stopped his frantic pacing. "They want a sign? I'll give them a sign."

CHAPTER FORTY

October 2006
River Haven, Iowa

Layton Burnet went into full defense mode after the FBI whisked Janey away to an undisclosed location. Not knowing exactly where she was, kept him on edge. That he personally couldn't keep her secure added to his frustration.

Matt and Perry sent their own families out of town with a private security team, but at least they knew where their loved ones were.

For the first time since returning from Landstuhl, Layton was grateful to be on leave so he could remain in River Haven. He stayed at Ward's farm and kept up the chores, but the highlight of his day was talking to Janey for a brief time each evening on a secure phone connection. The irony that they'd been forced apart moments after agreeing to be together was especially cruel.

The sheriff's department increased patrols at the McKays' homes and business, but they couldn't be present around the clock, so private security was once again employed and the number of closed-circuit camera feeds doubled.

Randy Keener remained missing and none of Keener's family or friends had heard from him since he'd bonded out of jail. His truck turned up abandoned at a Burlington strip mall. The cell phone found at the farm belonged to Keener, however it yielded few clues, except to confirm that he'd been at the McKay farm the night of the fire. Most significant was the fact that many of his recent calls had been placed to an untraceable burner cell phone.

After five days in the hospital, Ward was released. He and Eileen were laying low with Robin and Lisa, but Perry predicted that wouldn't last long. "As soon as Dad feels better, he'll want to come back to the farm."

The stillness of the week was shattered when Deputy Blake Evans came by the farm to tell Matt and Perry that St. Francis' Church had been broken into.

"It appears the only thing stolen was Janey's rosary," Blake said. "Father Martin had kept it on display in the church, while waiting for Janey to pick it up. He feels terrible."

"Any clues?" Layton asked. "Could it have been Keener?"

"I doubt it," Blake said. "This was a pro job. No fingerprints. The alarm was overridden and only the rosary was taken."

"There has to be a special place in Hell for anyone who would break into a church," Matt said. "I hate to break this to Janey right now."

"She has to know, though, and I'd like to be the one to tell her," Layton said.

It angered him that Janey suffered yet another loss, and he wasn't there to offer comfort. Since texting was forbidden, he emailed asking her to call as soon as possible.

She called within an hour, her voice panicked. "Is something wrong with Daddy?"

"No, he's fine. Everyone's fine. It's the rosary. Someone broke into St. Francis' Church last night and stole it." Layton sighed. "I'm sorry, Janey. I know those beads meant a lot to you."

She didn't speak for a few seconds. "I'm stunned. Do you know what happened? Did they report it to the police?"

"Blake Evans said it looked like a professional job, so few clues. They came in through a rear door of the church and it appears the rosary was the only item taken."

Her voice betrayed her tears. "John entrusted that rosary to me and I lost it."

"It's not your fault. Given all the publicity about the miracles attributed to the rosary, the police think the thief may try to sell it to a private collector. Stolen religious artifacts are a popular commodity on the black market. Blake suggested that giving it a lot of publicity might scare off a potential buyer."

"I'll ask Ben Hufstedler to share it on the website and social media." She grew quiet for a moment. "How long will they keep me locked up? It's already been a week."

As long as it takes. "I don't have answers for that. I know it's tough."

"I want to come home."

"I get that." He wanted her back, too, but only if her safety could be assured. "Believe me, it's hard to be away from you."

"That's good to hear." A beeper sounded in the background. "My time is up for now. I'll call again tonight."

"I love you, Janey McKay," he whispered.

———

THE NEXT MORNING brought a double dose of grim news.

Hunters found Randy Keener's body in the woods. He'd been tortured before being shot. Rain obliterated any evidence, but the coroner believed he'd been dead nearly a week.

Word of Keener's murder was quickly overshadowed by a horrendous story out of Iraq. Farid Zaman claimed credit for executing ten people in a grizzly house fire in Baghdad. Zaman alleged that the victims were Iraqi Christians who had gathered for a private worship service.

"This purge has only begun," Zaman said. "I will not rest until only true believers remain on Islam's soil."

The news bothered Layton. Feeling restless, he climbed in his truck and drove around before ending up at Saint Francis Cemetery.

He hadn't been back to John's grave since he first arrived in town. There had been no more reports of desecrated graves since the incident at Ricky Sturk's grave, but the urge to make certain that nothing was disturbed weighed on Layton.

The parking lot was empty. Walking through the cemetery was oddly calming. When Layton reached John's grave, the first thing he noticed was the engraved gray marble headstone.

JOHN MICHAEL McKAY
BELOVED SON, BROTHER, UNCLE, NEPHEW, FRIEND

The funeral flowers that had been present before were gone, the ground more level. By spring the grass would fill in.

He placed a quarter on the headstone. "I guess you know I'm on thin ice with the Army. You probably know pretty much everything from your vantage point." Layton figured if there was a Heaven, John was there. "The fire, Fuller, your dad. You know I got Janey's letter, too."

Layton looked away, realizing why he'd come there today. "When we were in Iraq, I wanted to ask you about dating Janey, but the time was never right. Famous last words, eh? I've already talked to your dad and brothers, but I need to talk to you, too. I'm in love with your sister, John, and if she'll have me, I'll spend the rest of my days making her happy and keeping her safe."

He glanced up at the sky, then back down. "I found what you wrote on the note in my storage unit and you were right. My home is in Iowa. For sure my heart is. I love your entire family, John, and I want to be part of it."

A calmness came over Layton as he headed back to the parking lot.

The calm fled when he noticed a brown pickup parked next to his truck. Alert, Layton paused as the truck's door opened. A man about his age climbed out and looked around nervously before waving.

Layton recognized the man as one of Randy Keener's friends. The guy had been with Keener at Mohler's party the night before they deployed.

The man called out. "You're John McKay's buddy, right?"

"Yeah. Why?"

"I heard they found Randy. Heard his guts were carved up bad. I don't care what he did, he didn't deserve that."

Layton kept quiet. Karma had its own scales of justice.

"Randy called me the night of the fire at the McKays," the guy went on. "He kept leaving me messages, wanting me to meet him. I figured he was setting me up because he was pissed at me for something else, so I ignored his calls. When I heard he'd gone missing I left town for a few days, but now that he's dead, I'm thinking I should leave again."

Layton's instincts buzzed. "Do you know who killed Randy?"

The guy shook his head. "He had enemies, but not ones who'd break his bones and shoot off his kneecaps."

"You should talk to the sheriff."

"No cops. I don't trust them. I figured you're safe since you're not a McKay." The guy looked away for a moment, then looked straight at Layton. "I've got something Randy desperately wanted back. My laptop. I'd let him borrow it a few weeks ago and the next thing I know, my bank card's getting dinged for his porn movies. He kept promising to give it back and finally I just went in and took the laptop. It wasn't like I stole it because it was mine. But Randy really wanted it back the night of the fire. He said someone would kill him if he didn't get it. I figured they'd be willing to kill me for it, too. Now I'm wondering if it's got something on it that might be evidence."

"You're probably right. The police need to see that laptop," Layton said. "I'll vouch for you if you'll reconsider talking with them."

"And end up like Randy? No way. Look, I've been here long enough as it is. If I give you the laptop, will you take it to the cops?"

"Yes."

The guy opened the truck's door and reached beneath the seat. "Don't ask me what the password is. Randy changed it."

The FBI would get into it easily, Layton knew. "They'll figure it out."

"One more thing. I know the cops will want to know everything I said, so just give me a head start."

"Fair enough." Layton reached for the computer. "Thanks for coming forward with it."

Layton memorized the truck's make, model and wrote down the tag number but waited until he was back at the McKay farm to call Blake Evans. Blake had been keeping them in the loop and deserved to be the first person to know about this. And thirty-minutes was all the head start Randy's friend deserved.

———

BLAKE EVANS CONTACTED THE FBI, who immediately came and took possession of the laptop. It must have yielded clues because within forty-eight hours two arrests were made in Arizona. The men arrested were traveling with fake passports. They turned out to be Syrian terrorists with known ties to Farid Zaman. Both men were charged with Randy Keener's murder.

Layton was at the store with Perry and Matt when news of the arrests hit. Perry called Ward, who announced he would return that afternoon along with Robin and Lisa.

"The FBI will release Janey now, too," Matt said. "But I think we should maintain security for a while. Phase it out gradually."

Layton's phone rang. He glanced at caller ID. It was Sergeant Boswell.

Concerned, he stepped out in the hall before answering. "Hey Sarge. What's up?"

"I just learned that Farid Zaman was taken out in a Baghdad raid earlier this morning. Ollie Fitz wanted to be sure we knew first." Boswell exhaled. "It's the best news I've heard in a while. The story should be on the news tonight, so no public statements until then."

Layton's shoulder ached as he thought of his friends and squad mates who had died in Iraq. Zaman was responsible for a lot of death and destruction. "Understood. Thanks for letting me know."

A heaviness lifted from his chest as he returned to Perry's office. "Finally, some good news."

CHAPTER FORTY-ONE

November 2006
Chicago, Illinois

The time Father Nick spent on his knees, praying for the people he loved, became a soothing morning ritual. Praying for the people he didn't want to love was a challenge that kept him returning to his knees.

The news from Iowa had disheartened Nick. Watching the national news replay video of the destruction at the farm had tightened the vise around his chest. The fire, the assault on Janey, Fuller's death, Ward's heart surgery, the lost rosary — it was a lot for an already grieving family to handle. Yet the indomitable strength of the McKays rose to new heights as they regrouped.

He spoke regularly with Janey as she struggled to cope with all that had been lost.

Next time Nick was in Iowa, he'd go through the boxes at his parents' home. His late mother had not only kept all of his and Anna's childhood mementos, she'd also kept the drawings and photographs John and Janey gave her when they were small. Maybe sharing those would give Janey a tangible bit of the past.

The theft of the rosary was a huge blow, too. Having held the rosary and prayed with it, Nick knew its mystique firsthand; he had felt a connection to those beads. As the public outcry over the missing rosary grew, rewards for its return were offered.

Nick's friend, Professor Birdson had been disappointed to lose the chance to examine the beads to prove or disprove their origin. "If your niece's rosary was indeed related to the fabled one, then its disappearance oddly parallels the legend I mentioned," Ralph said.

The clues Ralph had unearthed dated back to the Crusades when the sole survivors of a battle in the Middle East, an English lord and a Persian sheikh, formed an unlikely truce on a battlefield. When the Englishman's rosary provided safe travel for the sheikh, he ordered a commemorative set of beads to be sent to the Vatican.

"There are notations in the jeweler's records for a commissioned work that required a call for peace, spelled out in Arabic. That could explain the unusual silver filigree markings," Ralph hypothesized. "But in those times of Holy Wars and failed campaigns, it's unlikely the Vatican would have viewed such a gift through tolerant eyes. With the rosary gone, we shall never know if my conjectures are correct."

Nick let the restoration of Prince of Peace Church become a sacred obsession. Besides being some of the most rewarding physical work he'd ever done, it provided lessons in faith and creativity.

His friendship with Benny Alvarez grew as they co-planned the renovations. Benny's promise to secure help for the project exceeded Nick's expectation. Carpenters, plumbers, and electricians showed up exactly as needed. Thanks to Benny's meticulous records and photographs, they kept to the church's original design, varying only as needed to comply with modern building codes.

Each crate unearthed from the basement contained a treasury of sacred artistry. Nick had been delighted to find all the exquisite stained-glass windows intact except for one, but even those broken pieces had been carefully saved. The section of wall that once housed that broken window turned out to be a perfect spot for a side entrance with a wheelchair ramp. A portion of the original stained glass was being reworked to grace the spot above that new entry.

The crevices on the outside of the building that once held massive oil lanterns were being wired to hold those same lanterns that had been retrofitted with solar-powered lights.

This week, the church's interior was being painted. When Nick entered the church after finishing at the youth center, he was amazed at the difference. The lighter-colored paint made the inside appear more spacious and was a perfect foil for the reflections cast from the stained glass.

Benny sat in a front pew, wearing a T-shirt that read BOSS. Nick knew the older man longed to be up on the scaffolding wielding a paint brush.

"I can't believe how much these workers accomplished today," Nick said. "Will your resourcefulness ever cease to surprise me?"

Benny winked at the double entendre. The older man had admitted that he was the anonymous benefactor who supplied funding for the church and youth center. Turns out his ancestors had also owned two gold mines in Colorado, which he was now selling to consolidate his holdings.

Benny's vision for revitalization didn't end with the church and youth center. The man also owned several buildings that encircled a nearby greenway. One morning while jogging past those vacant buildings, Nick envisioned the greenway as a local park that hosted shows for a community of artists and musicians. When he shared the idea with Benny, the older man embraced it as a tribute to his grandfather.

Benny also worked with Constanza on another project he wanted to fund — adult education. The classrooms that served the youth during the afternoon could serve double duty for adult evening classes. In between all that, Benny and Constanza worked on a narrative of the church's history and early founders.

"By the way, Constanza was looking for you a few minutes ago," Benny said. "There she is."

Nick moved to where Constanza stood near the side entrance. He knew by the way she wrung her hands that something was amiss. He prayed she hadn't received a bad medical report.

"Have you seen Domingo today?" Constanza asked.

"No. His regular workday is not until tomorrow. Is something wrong?"

She nodded. "He had a terrible fight with his grandfather last night, and I haven't seen him since. I just learned he didn't go to school today either."

"Do you know what they fought about?"

"When Domingo first told my father about the song video, my father ignored him. Papa is old-school, he doesn't even know what YouTube is, but Domingo took it as a slight and vowed not to mention it again. Apparently, Papa just heard that the Pope invited Domingo and the boys to sing. Papa accused Domingo of hiding it and forbade him from singing at the Mass. I wasn't there, but Juan said Domingo left and said he was never coming back. I'm afraid he's run away."

Juan was Domingo's younger brother. The siblings were exceptionally close, and Juan frequently stopped by the youth center to walk home with Domingo.

Constanza shook her head. "I should have seen this coming. My father is harsh when it comes to Domingo."

Nick checked the time. If Domingo had been gone the night before and skipped school, he had a sizable head start. "Have you checked with any of his friends to see if they've heard from him? Does he maintain contact with any old friends in California?"

"Not that I know of. And none of his classmates here are talking. I tried to talk with Juan, but he just blames my father. I think he blames me, too. Could you talk with Juan, Father? See if he knows anything?"

"Of course." Nick checked the time. Juan would get out of school shortly. "If I go to your apartment, can you stay here in case Benny needs something?"

A short time later, Nick knocked on Constanza's door. At first, he thought he was too early.

Then Juan answered the door. "Domingo's not here, Father."

"Actually, I came to talk with you. Do you have a minute?"

Juan shrugged and opened the door. The living room opened into the kitchen and Nick noticed several pieces of bread laid out on the counter along with peanut butter and jelly. Nick doubted Juan planned to eat all four sandwiches.

Juan's eyes followed Nick's gaze. "I need to clean the kitchen before my grandfather returns."

"I'll talk while you clean." Nick followed him. "I wanted to ask if you had any idea what's going on between Domingo and your grandfather?"

Juan seemed relieved that Nick hadn't asked where Domingo was. Wrapping the sandwiches in a plastic bag, he crammed them into his backpack before responding. "Gramps doesn't want Domingo to perform for the Pope. Gramps says that rap music is of the devil and that the devil will take our souls for singing it. Domingo told him the video had nearly a million views, which upset Gramps. He said Domingo is too much like our father and would probably end up in prison. Domingo called him a crazy old man and said he's never coming back. Gramps said he didn't care." Juan looked away for a moment. "I think Gramps hates both of us."

Nick grimaced. He'd seen Constanza's father angry before, knew the old man had a quick temper. "I'm sorry that happened. You must feel caught in the middle. Look, your aunt is worried about Domingo. I'm concerned that he'll violate his community service agreement if he doesn't come into the center. I don't want that to happen. If I could talk to Domingo, I think I could help him."

The front door banged open just then as Constanza's father Eduardo strode in. When he saw Nick, he paused. "What are you doing here?"

"I'm looking for Domingo," Nick said.

Eduardo looked at Juan. "You. Go outside while we talk."

"Your aunt is at the church," Nick said to Juan. "Go there."

Nick waited until they were alone to speak. "I understand you had an argument with Domingo."

"So? He doesn't listen to me. If he did, he wouldn't need to go to your center."

"Domingo has excelled at the center. He's extremely bright and tutors the other kids. He's been offered several college scholarships because of his musical abilities."

"You shouldn't encourage his frivolous dreams," Eduardo said. "He needs to learn a trade, work in something dependable."

Nick leaned forward. "Have you talked to him about that or do you just deride his music? Deride him?"

The older man started to reply, but suddenly winced as if in pain. Then he shifted to the closest chair.

Nick grew concerned that Eduardo had lost color. "Are you okay?"

Eduardo shook his head. "No. I'm not. And don't mention this to Constanza. She has her own health issues to deal with. I'll be gone soon enough."

Compassion filled Nick. "Are you ill?"

At first Eduardo remained quiet. "Bone cancer. End stage. I have no intention of telling my daughter, so save the lecture."

"How can I help? Have you looked into hospice care?"

"No." The other man grew agitated. "I just want to die in peace, close to my family. I don't want to go back to Mexico. I have no one left there."

Understanding dawned on Nick. Eduardo was an undocumented immigrant. "Are you worried they'll deport you if you seek medical help?"

Eduardo said nothing. Which said everything.

"You're worried that if Domingo performs publicly, you might be exposed?" Nick asked.

"My wife and I paid a lot of money for documents, but they were lost in a fire years ago. Our children were born here, so I don't worry about them. But my wife is buried here, and I want to rest beside her."

"We can make an immigration request for humanitarian reasons," Nick said. "I can ask around quietly if you like."

"I don't like any of it." Eduardo closed his eyes for a moment. "I am tired, Father. Please go so I can lie down."

"I will leave, but I urge you to consider telling Constanza the truth. She is stronger than you know."

Just outside the apartment, Nick found Juan waiting. The look on Juan's face confirmed that he'd heard Nick and Eduardo talking.

"Will they send Domingo and me back to Mexico, too?" Juan asked.

"No. Your Aunt, you, and Domingo were all born here. And I will find a way to help your grandfather. But right now, I need to find Domingo."

Juan's shoulders fell in defeat. "Come with me."

———

DOMINGO WAS HIDING NEARBY, in one of the abandoned buildings. He wasn't happy to see that Juan had brought Nick. "Traitor."

"Grandfather is sick and might have to go back to Mexico," Juan cried. "If you run away, who will watch me?"

Domingo moved forward and embraced his brother. "Don't cry." He met Nick's gaze. "What does he mean about my grandfather?"

"Your grandfather has cancer, and he's worried about being deported. In his mind, you appearing publicly could draw attention to him. Your aunt doesn't know any of this yet, and he's concerned about upsetting her, too. In his own way he's trying to protect all of you."

Domingo glanced up at the ceiling. "Why do I feel guilty when I have done nothing?"

"Sometimes concern feels like guilt," Nick said.

"Concern? Why should I care about him?"

"For starters, he's family."

"That doesn't give him the right to be a jerk."

"You're correct," Nick said. "In many ways you're the better man here."

"And what would a better man do?" Domingo sarcastically parroted back words they'd discussed a week ago in a session at the youth center. Then he pushed his brother upright. "Just to be clear — if I come back, I'm doing it for Juan and my aunt, not my grandfather."

CHAPTER FORTY-TWO

November 2006
River Haven, Iowa

Janey returned to the farm the day after Farid Zaman's death was publicly announced.

Unfortunately, Layton had to return to Fort DeWald the same day. They barely had an hour together before he left, and they spent the time walking around the farm. After being cooped up, she craved the outdoors. She also welcomed the chance to be alone with him.

As they walked, hands linked, Layton told her about the offers he'd received for his grandfather's property in Texas. "I never dreamed I'd inherit anything, let alone something worth almost a half-million dollars."

"Are you sure you want to sell?" Janey asked. "You once talked about buying it back and retiring in Texas, making it a working ranch again. Now you already own it."

Layton paused and took both of her hands in his. "That was before I fell in love with you. Before *us*. Grandpa's ranch represented roots to me, I guess it always will. But it's also the past. My future lies with you, Janey."

She knew that he still hoped to salvage his Army career, so that part of the future remained a question mark. That she would follow him anywhere was the only certainty.

Layton's words helped Janey get through the next weeks.

Her father had returned to the farm before she did. The fact that he looked a hundred times better than he had in ICU after surgery still didn't ease all her worry. He'd lost weight, which his doctors encouraged him to keep off. He started physical therapy, but still tired easily and had a lot of restrictions.

Dad groused over feeling helpless, which Perry said was positive. "It's a good sign that he wants to reclaim his usual routine."

A caution-laced stress continued to hang over Janey, though. An expectation of *what-next?* remained, even as reassuring news reports surfaced. Zaman's Black Death group was considered neutralized once it was confirmed that Zaman's top supporters had perished with him. US and NATO forces were optimistic about truces with the smaller warlords who'd previously supported Zaman.

Closer to home, the investigation into Randy Keener's past launched a probe into the Justice Freedom Association national organization. After two directors disappeared, the JFA filed bankruptcy amidst reports of secret overseas bank accounts. So much for their pro-USA sentiments. Overnight the local JFA chapters closed, including the one in River Haven.

Though the repairs at the farm had been completed, the underlying scars were visible if someone knew where to look. The rebuilt bedrooms in the new bunkhouse remained empty except for two carefully packed boxes of mementos in the closet. So little had been salvageable that packing it away seemed less painful than seeing it displayed.

Janey moved back into her bedroom upstairs at the main house. Dad encouraged her to pick out furniture for the bunkhouse but having to replace everything overwhelmed her. Most of her clothes, shoes, jewelry were new, which reminded her of all she'd lost. Anything familiar she found — the jacket she'd left hanging in the house, her muddy boots in the garage, Layton's shirt that she slept in — were treasured.

She grieved over the stolen rosary. With no clues, despite the offers of reward, the police deduced the rosary had most likely disappeared into the vault of a private collector. The rosary website received more visitors than ever, with reports of miracles associated with facsimile copies continuing to pour in.

Her friend Ben sent the hard drive from her ruined laptop off to a specialty firm hoping to recover her photos and documents, especially the new writing she'd done since John's death. That she'd backed-up her computer to an external hard drive was moot since that hard drive melted in the fire. All those lurid warnings about storing backups off site — in case of fire — turned out to be a valid concern.

Returning to work at the store with her brothers proved to be good medicine for Janey. Everything there was untouched, including her locker with a forgotten backpack that yielded a few more treasures like a pair of sneakers and a notebook with story ideas.

Friday morning, Janey was at work when Layton called to tell her he'd be back in Iowa that day. "It's official. The Army is medically discharging me, effective today. The base commander listened to my appeal, but after reviewing my records, he wouldn't sign off on letting me attempt the physical fitness test."

The disappointment in his voice tore at Janey. "I know how much you wanted to stay in and how hard you worked toward OCS. I may not know what lies ahead, but I know you'll be wildly successful at anything you choose."

"That means a lot," Layton said. "I've got a few errands to run, so it might be late afternoon before I'm back, but I should be there by dinnertime."

When Janey told her brothers the news about Layton getting rolled out of the Army, they seemed pleased.

"I'm sorry for what he's been through," Perry said. "But we would all be happy to see Layton settle here in Iowa. In fact, I'll call Lisa, so she can start coaching the kids on how to bombard him."

Janey worked until three o'clock, then raced home to get ready. The entire family was gathering at the farm for supper that night and Lisa, Robin, and Eileen planned a feast to celebrate Layton's return. Janey planned her own private, welcome-back ritual for later, too.

When she reached the farm and turned into the driveway however, she slammed on her brakes.

It was back.

The beautiful MCKAY FAMILY FARM sign was once again displayed in front of the farm. Whoever replicated the sign had done a near perfect job.

Disbelieving, Janey climbed out of her car. Standing close, she noticed shiny spots of newer paint and a slight unevenness to the surface and realized someone had painstakingly restored her mother's original sign. She ran light fingers over the images and felt her heart heal at each repaired spot she touched. Then she saw the addition. In the bottom right corner, beside the painted figures of her and John, was a collie. Whoever painted the dog had mimicked her mother's style perfectly.

"Fuller." Janey was still crying when she went inside the house. Her father was at the kitchen table, fidgeting with a cardboard box.

"I can't believe it, Daddy! The sign's out front again." Janey moved to hug him. "And it looks good as new."

"Don't thank me. Thank Eileen," Dad said. "She insisted we salvage it and found an artist who could fix it."

Janey turned to where Eileen stood quietly by the sink. Fresh tears tracked down Janey's cheeks. Eileen had steadfastly cared for Janey's father, before and since his surgery. She'd cared for all them and Janey made a silent vow to acknowledge that more frequently.

"Thank you, Eileen. That sign has been there every day of my life. To the cars that pass by, it's just a billboard. But for me it was a tangible reminder of my mom." Janey's voice cracked as she moved to hug Eileen. "I can't tell you what it means to have it back."

Eileen returned the hug. "I'm glad you're pleased. The woman who restored it went to high school with your mother. She termed it a labor of love. It's actually your Christmas present — albeit a little early."

Janey took a shower and changed clothes, then returned to the kitchen to help while waiting for Layton to return.

"Uncle Nick!" Janey squealed when she saw her uncle seated at the kitchen table with her father. "I didn't know you were coming!"

Nick hugged her. "It was a last-minute decision. The youth center was closed today, and it's only a four-hour drive."

Her dad held up an oversized envelope. "He brought our invitation to meet with the Pope. This is all because of what you did with the website, you know."

Because of John's rosary, she thought.

The afternoon exploded into chaos as her nephews trudged in after school. The cousins merged into a big knot in the kitchen, devouring a small mountain of snacks before moving to the backyard like a swarm of wildebeests.

When Matt and Perry came in, the conversation turned to football and the family's favorite team, the Chicago Bears. The kitchen was filled with delicious aromas by the time Janey finished peeling potatoes. She eyed the row of glass Ball jars and recalled all the hours Eileen had spent canning and freezing during the late summer and early fall. Every vegetable being cooked had been grown on the farm.

She checked the bread rising on a corner counter. Earlier she'd helped Eileen make the honey yeast rolls that Layton liked so much.

Janey knew the moment Layton pulled up. The jungle gym in the backyard emptied as soon as one kid shouted, "He's here!"

Perry stuck his leg out, blocking Janey's departure. "Give the little heathens a minute to calm down. Then you can have Layton's full attention."

Janey peeled off her apron and dashed to the bathroom to check her hair. When she returned, she followed her father out the back door. The sounds of her nephews squealing with delight made her smile.

Layton set Samuel down before moving to greet Janey with open arms. "I've missed you," he whispered before pressing a quick kiss to her lips.

"That goes double here." To freely show her affection made her feel giddy. *This is love.*

"Would you quit kissing her already!" Timothy looked beseechingly at Layton. "We got 'portant stuff to do!"

Janey knew her nephews wanted Layton to go riding ATVs with them. She backed away to allow her dad and uncle to greet Layton. But no one moved. In fact, everyone seemed to wait expectantly, especially her nephews who suddenly looked ready to wet their pants.

Layton cleared his throat. "Janey, I don't know what I did to deserve your affection, but I wanted to give you something as a token of my devotion."

Janey's heart pounded, her hands trembling with uncertainty over such a public declaration.

Layton nodded at her nephews who stood clustered behind him.

Screaming, "Wait for me!" at each other, the boys ran to the opposite side of Layton's truck.

"What in the world?" Janey asked.

A truck door opened and slammed. Then her nephews reappeared in a gaggle, shoving at each other as they moved forward in a group. One of the younger ones tripped and fell, but Janey ignored his cries, her eyes locked on the tiny collie puppy that Michael, Perry's oldest, held in his arms.

Janey's vision blurred with tears. The puppy looked just like Fuller did when she was a pup.

Layton took the dog and held it out. "This is from a litter born from one of Fuller's sister's offspring. She's got a better pedigree than me, but I hope you'll keep both of us."

When Janey took the puppy and scratched behind its ears, the dog sank fully into her arms. "I love her. Thank you." She pushed on tiptoes to kiss Layton, then she buried her head against him and wept.

"What are we going to name her?" Timothy demanded. "Can we call her Fuller?"

"There is no *we*, half-pint," Matt said. "It's Janey's dog. She'll name it."

Layton chuckled. "Speaking of Fuller, do you know what her registered name was?"

Janey swiped at her cheeks, then pressed a kiss to the top of the pup's head. "Fuller wasn't a show dog, so she didn't get a fancy name like the rest of Mom's champions."

"On the contrary, sweets. Perry dug out your mother's breeder files, so I could locate a pup from the same bloodlines." Layton withdrew a folded paper from his pocket. "Get this. Fuller's name on her registration papers was 'Full of Grace.'"

Dad peered at the paper. "I'd forgotten all about that. When you were little, you called her Full-of, which John turned into Fuller."

Janey looked at Layton again. "You gave me a double gift. A puppy and a story from my childhood."

"Can we play with her while you think of a name?" Timothy begged.

"Her name is Grace," Janey announced. "Let's take her out in the backyard so she can get to know the family."

––––––––

AFTER EVERYONE LEFT, Janey and Layton rode an ATV out to the pond. Layton started a bonfire while Janey spread a blanket on the ground. With the sun gone, the temperatures quickly dropped into the forties, so a fire would feel good. Grace fell asleep on the blanket.

"Your nephews wore her out," Layton said.

"I still can't believe they kept a secret." Janey had learned that her brothers had been in on it, coordinating with Layton, picking up the puppy and keeping it hidden at Perry's.

"The kids were properly bribed. I dropped a small fortune on video games."

Janey unzipped her backpack and held up graham crackers and marshmallows. "Can't have a fire without S'mores."

"Do you know I've never had one?"

"Seriously? We need to rectify that. First, I'll make one McKay style." She waggled her eyebrows as she stuck marshmallows on the prongs of a metal fork.

"Telescoping marshmallow sticks. You're hardcore." Layton moved closer beside her on the blanket. "I'm afraid to ask what McKay style is. Does it include gunpowder?"

Janey rotated the marshmallows over the fire. "Close. They vary depending on which McKay is making them. The key is getting the marshmallow golden on the outside, but melty on the inside. Like this." She slid the toasted marshmallow onto a graham cracker, then topped it with a peanut butter cup and another cracker. She handed it to Layton. "This one is Perry-style."

Layton ate half in one bite. "It tastes delicious. Is there a Matt-style S'more?"

"Of course. Matt's always changing his. Sometimes he uses M & M's. Other times he uses Mike & Ike's candies."

"Did John have a signature S'more?"

"He used dark chocolate, crispy bacon and a jalapeño slice jammed in the marshmallow."

"That sounds like one I would have invented. So, tell me. What is Janey-style?"

"You're fixing to find out." She reloaded the marshmallow fork and rotated it. At the last second, she let it dip close enough to the flame that the surface bubbled. She slid the hot, crispy marshmallow onto a cracker and topped it with milk chocolate and a second cracker.

"I'm a purist. Just the basics." Picking it up, Janey stuck a corner in her mouth, holding it in place as she turned toward Layton.

His eyes lit up with understanding. Leaning close, he bit into the graham cracker. Janey did likewise, cupping her hand to catch the bits between them.

When they finished, Layton pulled her close and kissed her. He tasted of marshmallow and chocolate and Texas and moonlight.

"That one is my favorite," he whispered. "But I can't believe your brothers let you invent that one."

"I never felt the need to invent one. Until now." She licked the chocolate from the corner of his mouth and was rewarded with another kiss.

"At the risk of sounding jealous, I'm glad to hear that." Layton hugged her. "I enjoy knowing that I'm the first to sample Janey-style S'mores."

And I hope you're my first for a lot of things, she thought as he kissed her again.

————

THE HOUSE WAS quiet as they crept upstairs. Layton kissed her goodnight then disappeared in the room down the hall.

Unable to sleep, Janey opened her new laptop. Out of habit, she clicked the new mail icon and scanned the list. Most were from the rosary website, letters of support and more reports of miracles. But one email caught her attention. **Rosary Reward**, the subject line read.

Janey opened the email, hoping for positive news. It was the opposite.

Your pleas have fallen on deaf ears.
The beads are destroyed. We will rise anew.

The blood drained from her face as the embedded video began playing.

The image was dark and grainy, then a flashlight beam spotlighted a close-up of John's beautiful rosary. A voice spoke in a foreign language, but even without captions, the loathing came through the speaker's tone.

The camera zoomed out as a bearded man picked up the rosary and began whipping the strand against a small brick wall. The man shouted the entire time, staccato words that she guessed were curses. The chain broke as beads shattered, the rosary disintegrating with each swing.

Janey flinched as the man dropped what was left on the ground before grabbing a rifle and using the butt of it to smash the remaining beads. Then he spat on them.

The video ended abruptly as voices off camera cheered.

Janey buried her head in her hands. Seeing the rosary defaced and destroyed left her feeling as if she'd been kicked in the stomach.

She headed for the door to find Layton.

CHAPTER FORTY-THREE

November 2006
Baghdad, Iraq

It was nearly midnight, but Jamal knew there would be no sleep tonight, the burden of honor too heavy.

He paced the small apartment he shared with his wife and son, grateful that his family slept. Grateful for silence to weigh what could be the last action of his life.

The soldier's prayer beads. The missing piece. Go.

The pressure had been with him all day, an annoying inner voice droning on nonstop. Jamal resisted, chanting prayers repeatedly in an attempt to drown the voice out. He found relief in short bursts, a mere pause between breaths before it started in again.

The missing piece. Go.

He glanced to his computer where the screen still flickered on the Al Jazeera news story about the soldier's sister. She looked distraught as she held up a photograph of the black beads and pleaded for their return.

The same beads that had been destroyed.

He shut off the computer before moving to retrieve a small, ornately carved wooden box hidden beneath the flooring. The box had been given from father to son for centuries. Before dying ten years ago, his own father passed the box and its horrible secret to Jamal.

"Our family was chosen as the prophecy's keeper through time. Good fortune is promised to the one who fulfills the prophecy's destiny," his father had whispered with fading breath. "I prayed it would be me. I wanted to end the onus of worry and fear, for discovery means certain death."

Jamal resented inheriting the burden. He was tired of living in fear of reprisal for everything. The ongoing war had left him bitter and hopeless.

Or it had until he met the soldier.

He opened the box. His father's secret, a silver cabochon and a single black bead, lay next to Jamal's secret, the photograph of the soldier, John McKay, and his sister. The blood-stained photo depicted happier times, before the soldier died, before the sister had been left to mourn.

Jamal stared at the photograph. He didn't like feeling indebted, but his son was alive, healed, because of this soldier — the soldier who'd come searching for the missing beads of the prophecy.

Shoving the box back into its place, Jamal moved to his son's bed. As he did every night, Jamal lifted the covers and stared at the smooth flesh of his son's arms. The unmarred skin of his son's stomach peeked out where his shirt bunched up. John McKay had saved Jamal's son twice in one day: first the soldier pulled his son from the burning cart. Then he'd sent the old man to heal his son.

The events of that awful day defied logic. Jamal's son had been badly burned, his flesh charred to the bone in places. Jamal had been desperate to get his son to a hospital when the unthinkable happened. His son died in his arms. Jamal tried to resuscitate him, but to no avail.

The old man had hobbled up and placed a hand on Jamal's shoulder. "The soldier sent me to help. Do not weep." As the old man spoke, he touched Jamal's son's forehead.

His son drew in a breath. Jamal blinked in disbelief. In the instant that his eyes were closed, his son's injuries *disappeared* along with the memory of the horror. Later, Jamal would learn that his son's misshapen foot had also been healed.

The old man had then insisted that Jamal go and help the soldier. "I will keep your son safe. Hurry."

In retrospect, Jamal realized he'd been mindless with shock. But he'd also been protected by Allah. How else could Jamal have walked unarmed into a raging gun battle without being harmed? He'd found John McKay wounded, dying. Jamal had expected the old man to show up, to heal the soldier as he had healed Jamal's son. But the old man did not show and there had been nothing Jamal could do except offer comfort.

Afterwards, he'd run from the battlefield, afraid he imagined his son's healing. He hadn't, and he felt bad that he had no means to compensate the old beggar for his aid.

"Your time to repay will be shown." The old man had then urged Jamal to take his son home.

With the miraculous healing of his son, Jamal realized he had received the good fortune promised by the prophecy. Was this his time to complete his part, fulfill his duty?

The pressure tightened around his rib cage in confirmation. *The missing piece. The soldier's prayer beads.*

The voice in his head grew louder. *Go. Now.*

The streets were dark as Jamal left his home, moving cautiously from shadow to shadow.

The spot where the beads had been destroyed was a familiar shortcut he used to get to the marketplace. Anyone in their right mind would avoid the spot for a while, the price of curiosity too high. Zaman Farid might be dead, but some of his followers, like the cleric who'd destroyed the beads, were still trying to make a name for themselves. To get caught crossing them could mean death for him and horror for his family.

Go!

When Jamal reached the alley, he remained hidden, watching and listening. The lack of noise offered no comfort. For the hundredth time he thought of ending this folly and returning home, but the longer he hesitated, the louder the voice in his head roared.

He'd come too far, to turn back. *Allah give me strength.*

Inching forward, Jamal squinted, trying to make out shapes in the shifting moonlight. Just ahead was the brick wall against which they had struck the beads. He glided closer, expecting at any moment to feel hands grab him from behind, to feel the sharp bite of icy steel slice his flesh.

Withdrawing a wooden match, Jamal lit it. He dropped to one knee to examine the ground. He swept his arm in a wider arc but saw nothing, not even the glimmer of ground up glass. Had they gathered the remnants to leave no trace?

He extinguished the flame, feeling foolish for coming. What had he been thinking? What sane person listened to voices in his head? Still crouching, he pivoted, poised to flee.

Something tapped his shoe. He glanced down, spotted a black shimmer and knew it wasn't a pebble. He snatched it up, rolling it between his fingers. The surface was polished, symmetrical.

Lighting a second match, he spotted another bead, undamaged. Then another. He followed the trail and found an entire section of beads still connected. Glancing over his shoulder continuously, he frantically scooped up pieces.

With his final matchstick, he caught a glint of metal embedded in the wall. A bit of chain with another section of beads was lodged in a crevice between bricks. He gingerly tugged to work them free. The section that came loose had a broken cross and a small bit of medallion.

A noise caught his attention, footsteps headed this way. Ducking behind the wall, Jamal hugged the ground and held his breath. If anyone caught him with his pockets full of beads—

Go! Now! The voice was back, this time encouraging instead of demanding.

Leaping to his feet, Jamal ran off.

CHAPTER FORTY-FOUR

JOHN MCKAY WATCHED *Jamal grasp another bead that John tossed his way.*

The setting shifted, reverting back in time to a field of war where a Crusader and a Moor once exchanged tokens for peace and where Samir later vowed to keep the legend safe. John saw glimmers of other past events. The rosary beads had been lost and found and refashioned several times as they waited for this moment of destiny to be fulfilled.

Time whirled and returned to twenty-first century Baghdad, to the same spot where the ancestors of these men met again to fulfill the prophecy, the first time their bloodlines had been reunited.

Two heroes will rise again from the sand...

"Does he remember?" John asked as he watched Jamal escape safely.

"The eternal part of him never forgets." The old beggar was back. "And the eternal part is all that really matters."

"This is why you saved me that night on the road. Driving home from the party." John recalled the bright flash of green light. He hadn't known it then, but he'd been saved from a fatal car accident.

"You hadn't yet fulfilled the destiny you chose," the beggar said.

The Middle East setting exploded into bright fractals that rearranged into a cornfield, that bit of Heaven in Iowa. In every place, really.

John felt a familiar sense of homesickness, but not for the farm or Iowa.

"The soul longs for the stars, for its true home." The Nazarene was present once again, sitting beside John on the bench.

"I'm forgetting details of this life," John said. "I don't want to."

"What you lose is only illusion. There is much to gain in letting go and what you'll remember — your true destiny as a child of God — is spectacular beyond words."

John hesitated, feeling torn as he took in the magnificence of this earthly plane. "Not yet. I have one more task."

CHAPTER FORTY-FIVE

November 2006
River Haven, Iowa

Heaviness shrouded Janey's spirit. With the rosary's destruction, she lost her final physical connection to John.

Layton kept her from falling back into depression. He sensed when she needed space versus hugs and reiterated his devotion in words and actions. This morning he'd surprised her with a card commemorating the three-year anniversary of when they'd first met. He didn't gloss over or glamorize their tenuous past. *Thanks to that day, I've come to find a love I never dreamed possible,* he wrote.

To celebrate, they were going out to eat that night.

Today, Layton and Dad helped Matt and Perry at the new store in Quincy. Janey stayed behind to spend time with Grace. Though it seemed only Layton and Grace could make her laugh these days, the dog's mischievousness had gotten out of hand. This week the puppy had terrorized the baby calves, run off with three pairs of Dad's work gloves and both of Eileen's rubber boots. Grace had also discovered an endless stash of old feed bags that she delighted in shredding across the front lawn, leaving Janey with a mess to rake up every day. Dad hadn't used that brand of feed in years, so clearly the puppy was wandering off the farm, stealing bags from neighboring barns, which meant Janey had to restrict Grace to the kennel more frequently.

After breakfast, Janey took Grace to the pond. She remembered all the hours Mom and John spent working with Fuller there. Mom said Fuller was one of those rare dogs who trained easily, eager to please, and wanting only praise for a reward. John took it one step further, teaching Fuller complex hand signals for herding cows back to the barns so he wouldn't have to.

Janey worked with Grace on basic obedience—sit, stay, come, drop it. Praise meant nothing to the stubborn puppy, but she'd do anything for a bit of hotdog. When they finally returned to the house, Janey headed for the bench in the backyard.

"Sit. Good girl." She surrendered the last bit of wiener before pointing to the backyard. "Go on. You deserve a break."

Grace took off after a squirrel. The squirrel seized the advantage and kept the dog circling the big oak for long minutes. On the last turn, Grace came around the tree carrying one of Fuller's old rope toys. The puppy dashed forward, nearly tripping on the rope before laying it at Janey's feet with a proud bark.

The toy was a piece of heavy rope that John had knotted the last time he was home so he and Fuller could play tug of war, a game the collie only played with John. Janey hadn't seen the toy since. Had Fuller secreted the rope away, keeping it as her own memento of John?

Grace barked again.

"You're good at finding things. Except for the stuff you drag off, like Dad's gloves."

The puppy cocked her head, then spun around and took off running with a high-pitch *yap-yap-yap*, before disappearing behind the garage.

"Grace! Come here!" Janey ran after the dog. She lost sight of her, but the yapping continued.

Janey followed the gravel drive past the calf pens, toward the silos. She glimpsed Grace beside them, racing along the backside of the machine barn. Then the dog dropped from sight again.

When Janey reached the machine barn, she discovered a sizable hole dug at the bottom, near a loose wall plank. Grace was inside the barn, still yapping.

Janey circled to the front of the barn and slipped inside. "Grace! Come here."

The puppy didn't appear, though her barking persisted from the back where all the junk was stored. Alarmed, Janey rushed to find the dog before she got hurt.

"Grace?" Janey wove cautiously between old farm implements, car parts, and motorcycle carcasses. She could hear the dog but couldn't see her.

At the rear of the building, Janey peered between the wooden slats of a wall that separated what used to be an old tool crib. Grace was in there, barking.

"Stay! I'll get you." A stack of crates blocked the door. Janey shoved, but they wouldn't budge, forcing her to move them one at a time.

The barking stopped just as she wrenched open the rickety door.

"Grace! Where are you, girl?" Janey stepped into the crowded, dusty room, praying the dog hadn't gotten hurt or escaped again.

A muffled growl sounded. She spotted the puppy in the far corner, tugging on an old tarp. A metal handle protruded from beneath the tarp. She scooped up the puppy and hugged her. Then she sat her down with a firm, "stay!" and stared at the metal handle.

It couldn't be...

Janey flipped back the tarp. Hidden beneath was a treasure from her childhood, an ancient Radio Flyer wagon. Empty feed bags like the ones Grace had shredded covered most of the wagon.

Grasping the handle, Janey yanked the wagon free. The tarp and old bags fell away as she dropped to her knees. Her trembling hands skimmed over the wagon's metal side, across the clouds and birds and angels painted by her mother.

As heavy as a Sherman tank, the wagon had initially survived Matt and Perry's childhood before being used by John as a BB gun target. John started racing motocross the year he'd turned eight, but Janey had been deemed too young to race. As a distraction, Mother suggested she and Janey makeover the old wagon.

"We'll make it magical, so it can take you on adventures everywhere," Mom promised. The word RADIO had long since faded, but Mom painted JANEY'S MAGICAL in front of the word FLYER along each side.

Mom hadn't tried to patch the BB holes. Instead, she outlined each hole with silver paint, "to let the starlight in."

Protruding awkwardly on either side were wooden wings. Wings John had added at Janey's request after Mom died. *I want to go and get Mom in my magical wagon.*

John tackled the problem like a NASA engineer, graphing trajectories and vertical axes instead of doing homework. *If we go fast enough down this hill, and hit the ramp right here, we'll launch into the sky.*

And we'll fly up to Heaven and bring Momma back, Janey would add.

How many times had John pulled this wagon up the hill, and pushed off from the top, hopping in at the last minute as they sailed downhill? *Again, again!*

How many times had he greased the axles in hopes the tires would spin swifter? *We need more speed!*

And how many times had Dad threatened to ground them for being out too late? *What are you doing out here in the dark? John, you know better.*

Or for being too reckless? *Dang nabbit, John, you're lucky she didn't break her neck.*

She spied the pile of broken wings sitting opposite an untouched stack of fresh lumber. How many pairs of wings had they wrecked flipping over? John had been undeterred. *Don't worry, I'll build stronger ones.*

Janey traced her fingers lightly over the clouds on the metal part of the wheels and the angels on the front and back panels. The wagon had been the last thing Mom painted. *It must be perfect for all the places you'll go.*

After her mother died, Janey was relentless. She wanted to go one place, to do one thing. Bring Mom back. It was the only idea of Janey's that John never questioned. From sunup to sundown, they hauled the wagon all over the farm, searching for the highest hill, the steepest drop, the best launch site. John tried countless times without complaint.

But after three weeks straight, following a tremendous crash, Janey just *knew.* "We'll never see her again, will we?"

John's silence had been the answer she feared most. Inconsolable, Janey had sobbed for a long time, until John hugged her and said, "New rule. McKays don't cry."

Remembering that now had her weeping even harder. Anything John didn't like, he'd make a new rule, but that had been the first one.

She looked at the unmarred wooden wings. The last time she saw the wagon, both wings were snapped in half after that final attempt at flight. She had pulled the wagon home and taken it straight to the trash heap. *If I can't reach Momma in it, I never want to see it again!*

John must have secreted the wagon away and repaired the wings before hiding it here. He would have gladly taken her to try again if she wanted, as if he knew her heart would break if *he* made her stop.

A wire bound notebook poked out beneath a coffee can filled with nails. She pulled it loose and blew years of thick dust from the open pages. John's sketches included stick figures of the two of them in the wagon, usually mid-way down a hill. Broken lines and arrows marked the flight path down, then straight up toward a stick figure with a halo, waiting on a cloud.

After all Janey lost, to find such a gift from John left her without words.

She glanced at where Grace sat curled on a piece of cloth, chewing on what looked like yet another of Fuller's old toys. Moving closer Janey found that the piece of cloth was an old racing jacket of John's. Judging by the thick coating of dog hair covering it, Fuller must have frequented this spot regularly.

Grace stood and shook her body. Janey motioned her forward. "Come on, girl."

Before obeying, the puppy tugged a leather work glove from beneath a feed bag. Janey lifted the bag and found the rest of Dad's missing gloves and Eileen's boots.

Grace squirmed up next to her and for a moment she looked just like Fuller had as a puppy.

Janey picked her up. "I have someone I want you to meet, Grace."

It took some maneuvering, but she got the wagon out of the tool shed and pulled it up to the house. Then she loaded Grace into her car and drove to St. Francis cemetery.

Despite her intentions, Janey hadn't been there since John's funeral and for several minutes she sat in the car, remembering that final, terrible day.

When Grace gave a five-seconds-before peeing whine, Janey leaped from the car and set the puppy in the grass. Instead of squatting, Grace darted toward the cemetery, barking non-stop in a frenzied run.

"Oh, not again! Come back!" Janey took off after her, praying the dog wouldn't startle any visitors.

Grace disappeared around a hedge row and when Janey caught up, she spotted the pup sitting on the next rise, at a familiar spot. When she reached the McKay family section, Grace was laying in the sun, almost asleep at the foot of a gray headstone Janey had never seen.

JOHN MICHAEL MCKAY
BELOVED SON, BROTHER, UNCLE, NEPHEW, FRIEND

She stared at the engraved lettering until it blurred from tears. She'd lost more than a brother. She'd lost a corner of her soul.

Sobs rose, unleashing geysers of grief, sadness, and anger.

Worst was the guilt. "I didn't mean the awful things I said that night, John. It was more than just the letter. I was mad at you for joining the Army and for leaving me behind. I wasn't ready to face my own shortcomings, and I was too proud to apologize while you were deployed. But I never dreamed you wouldn't—"

Unable to go on, she wept hard, bitter tears.

As if in a dream, she heard her mother's voice. *"Don't hold the poison in, Sugarpuff. Let the anger run out and clear the way for healing."*

Her mother had always encouraged her to deal promptly with pent-up emotions. To turn it around. But turn it around to what?

"It feels like I've lost my way," Janey whispered.

McKays always find a way. This time John's voice came through and she sensed his presence as strongly as when he'd been alive. Maybe even stronger.

"I'm sorry." She hugged her chest, desperate to hold on to the moment, the feeling that he'd been waiting for her to return. "Forgive me."

Nothing to forgive, Pest.

Then she heard him chuckle. Grace awoke with a start and began barking and yapping wildly at a shimmer of light that moved across John's grave and disappeared in the bright sunlight behind the headstone.

A peaceful ease washed over Janey as she pushed to her feet.

"Come here, girl." When the puppy bounced close, she swept her up. "I want you to meet my brother, John. He was — is — the best brother in the world."

Janey glanced from John's headstone, to her mother's and grandparents'. The markers engraved with names and dates served as reminders of cherished lives, people she'd been privileged to love.

"Let's go, Grace." Janey took two steps away, then looked back with a smile.

The next time she came, she'd bring flowers for all of them.

———

JANEY TOOK extra time getting ready for her date with Layton. The look in his eyes when she came down the stairs wearing an off-the-shoulders dress told her she'd made the right choice. Her Texan looked handsome in a button-down shirt and a sport jacket.

"You look beautiful." He nodded approvingly from her cowboy boots to his own. "How was your day?"

"Amazing." She told him about discovering the wagon. "I can't believe John kept it."

"I can. For all his tough talk, your brother was quite sentimental. I think some of John's talk about home and family rubbed off on me."

She recalled the funny and heartwarming stories Layton shared of his childhood at his grandfather's ranch. "Maybe you rubbed off on him, too. I also went to his grave today."

Layton paused. "And?"

"It was time." She shrugged, not wanting to dissect it just yet. "I felt at peace after leaving."

"I'm glad." Outside, he helped her into his truck, but before taking off, he leaned close for a kiss. "I love you."

The kiss warmed her to her toes as his words wreathed softly around her heart. "I love you, too. So, where are we going?"

"We have reservations at Butch's Steakhouse."

"Good. I'm starving."

The restaurant was crowded when they arrived. The hostess led them to a corner table. "Will this do?"

Janey could barely hear over the noise made by the people seated at a long table beside theirs. The presence of wrapped gifts and helium balloons indicated a birthday party in progress.

"Do you have something quieter?" Layton asked the hostess.

The woman nodded and glanced around. "Yes, but it's not as private as you requested."

"That's fine." Layton pressed a hand to the small of Janey's back. "Sorry, darlin'."

They ended up seated by a window, close to the Davidsons, an elderly couple who also attended St. Francis Church.

Mrs. Davidson perked up when she recognized Janey. "Is this your beau? Arlette was talking about him at the beauty shop last week. He's even more handsome than she said."

Janey made quick introductions, then stepped away when their waiter showed up.

"Not everyone gets discussed at Arlette's," Janey whispered when they were seated. "In a small town, that's high praise."

"I'm sure we'll be the talk of the shop next week." At Layton's nod, the waiter moved back in with a champagne bucket. "Alcohol free, but bubbly enough to mark the occasion." The waiter popped the cork and filled two crystal flutes before disappearing again.

That Layton had prearranged this touched Janey. She recalled the card he'd given her that morning. "It's a lovely way to celebrate three years. Thank you."

Layton raised his glass. "Thank you, for believing in me and for believing in us. I don't know what I did to deserve your love, but I'll spend the rest of my life working to keep it."

They clinked glasses.

Mrs. Davidson's voice interrupted. "Isn't that romantic? Why don't you order champagne for me, old man?"

"You don't like the stuff." Mr. Davidson gave them an apologetic look. "And it's probably more romantic without an old woman's commentary."

Layton couldn't keep a straight face. He looked at Janey and shook his head. "Where was I?"

She grinned. "You just pledged your love."

"Right." He cleared his throat and grew serious once more. "As a token of that love, I wanted to give you this." He reached into his jacket and withdrew a white envelope. WARD MCKAY was written across the front.

Janey couldn't disguise her disappointment. "A letter for my dad?"

"Open it."

She ripped the flap free and tugged out a folded sheet of paper. A smaller envelope dropped to the table. Her name was printed on the front.

Layton held out his hand. "Give me back the folded sheet. Only the small envelope is for you."

As she picked up the envelope, she realized its significance. "These were your final letters?"

He nodded. "We wrote them the first day we arrived in Iraq. I wrote three. One to my grandmother. One to your father. And this one to you. I didn't want your brother to see it, so I stuck it in with your dad's."

"Like John did with yours."

"At the time I wrote this, I had no idea John had the letter you wrote to me. Now I want you to know what I was feeling back then."

Janey stared at the envelope for long moments before opening it. My darlin', the letter began.

Once upon a time, an extremely stupid man blew the chance of a lifetime with the most incredible woman on earth. He ended up turning into an ogre and spent the rest of his life wallowing in sorrow, wishing he'd done things differently.

The ogre sorely regretted not kissing the woman back. He regretted not holding her longer and telling her how much their time together meant. But most of all, he regretted not telling her he had just realized he loved her, too.

I don't know if a man worthy of your love exists, Janey, but if he does, I hope you find him and live happily ever after.

Love forever, Layton

Tears filled her eyes as she met Layton's gaze. "I did find him, you know."

"And you saved him." Layton pushed to his feet and stepped closer. Then he dropped to one knee in front of her.

Janey trembled, afraid to think about what this meant.

He cupped her hands in his as he looked up at her. "I never wanted to move the earth and stars for someone. Until I met you. You're my happily ever after and I love you more than words can express." He reached in his pocket and withdrew a small box. Inside was a diamond ring and the half-heart they shared from the county fair. "You fill the missing pieces of my soul. Will you marry me, Janey McKay?"

"Yes." The word burst forth without hesitation.

He slid the ring on her hand but didn't get up. "I haven't been easy to be with these last few months, but if you'll forgive me, I'll spend the rest of my life making it up."

"Are you watching this, old man?" Mrs. Davidson's voice rang out in the nearly silent restaurant. "I can't wait to call Arlette."

The people at the surrounding tables first laughed, then cheered.

Janey leaned down to press a kiss to Layton's mouth. "You're the one who makes me whole. I love you, Layton Burnet."

CHAPTER FORTY-SIX

November 2006
Baghdad, Iraq

Long before his stint as a US Army Chaplain, Father Donovan taught at Boston College where he'd met a visiting professor from Baghdad, who shared marvelous stories of Islam. The two men became friends and remained in touch for over twenty years.

Donovan lost contact once the war broke out and had been eager to learn if Azim was still alive. The tales of torture were especially gruesome. Iraqi teachers who traveled to the US were considered potential spies and especially vulnerable.

His friend was alive and working at great personal risk as an interpreter for NATO forces. Azim also spoke French and had been the former head of language and translations at the University of Baghdad. Father Donovan helped Azim move his family to France, where he continued to work for NATO before getting on with Paris Dauphine University.

This morning Donovan received a meeting request from a former colleague of Azim's. It wasn't the first time Donovan had been asked to help again. With his Army stint wrapping up soon, Donovan vowed to help coalition supporters and their families however he could.

Donovan's assistant notified the priest that the visitor, Jamal, had arrived.

The priest invited the nervous-looking Iraqi man into his office. "Please have a seat. I understand you taught at the University with Professor Azim? Are you looking for work?"

"No. I need your help in returning a favor to this man." Jamal placed a laminated photograph on the desk and slid it toward the priest.

Donovan stared at the photograph of Army Specialist John McKay and his sister. Donovan had met John McKay several times and prayed over his body after the deadly ambush. Like many Catholics around the world, the priest also followed the articles on Janey McKay's prayer initiative and the miracles attributed to it. The terrible news of the rosary's destruction had been an ugly end to a beautiful story.

"Where did you get this photo?" Donovan asked.

"I was there after the soldier was injured. Earlier, he helped save my son when a rocket hit close by. He insisted I take this photograph, so it wouldn't fall into enemy hands."

Donovan tapped the photograph. "I'm sure his family will be grateful to get this back."

"There is more. You are familiar with the soldier's prayer beads?"

"The rosary? Yes, John showed it to me once and of course, I've followed the news about it."

"That is where I need your help." Jamal reached beneath his shirt and tugged out a strand of beads. He carefully laid them on the desk. "I went to where it was destroyed and gathered what pieces I could. Then I tried to restore it."

Donovan's eyes flickered over the refashioned rosary. At least a third of the original beads were missing. Some were damaged, chipped. Other, plainer beads had been substituted to complete the five decades. A round silver disc inscribed in what looked like Arabic now replaced the center medallion, and the broken crucifix was pieced back together with carefully whittled bits of wood.

A Frankenstein rosary, Donovan thought, yet still one of the loveliest sights he had ever seen. "You did this?"

"As best I could." Jamal said. "I am no artisan, and I know it looks — different. Misshapen. But I thought it might comfort his sister to have some beads returned."

"I'm sure she'll be overjoyed and will want to thank you."

"No." Jamal cut him off as he stood. "I took a substantial risk to my family going after those beads and I do not want to endanger my family further. I only want to repay my debt to the soldier."

Donovan wanted to ask what debt Jamal felt was owed, but his phone rang. He ignored it. "Thank you. I will make certain this is returned to his sister." He offered Jamal a business card. "I know you braved danger doing this. I have some connections should you want to leave Iraq."

Jamal shook his head, but Donovan felt the urge to press the card into his hand. "Keep it. Just in case."

"Very well. Thank you."

When Donovan escorted Jamal to the door, he found his assistant ready to enter.

"I'm sorry to interrupt," his assistant said. "But you are needed at the hospital, Father. A convoy was attacked."

"Tell them I'm on my way." Donovan crammed the rosary in his pocket as he bid Jamal farewell and rushed off toward the base medical compound.

A familiar triage scene greeted Donovan as he entered the hospital. The closest medic told the priest that two personnel transport trucks had been hit. Gurneys with injured soldiers were lined up as nurses and medics assessed injuries and assigned priority.

"We've got a DOA over there." The medic tipped his head toward a gurney with a sheet-covered corpse. "Dog tags say he's Catholic."

As Donovan made his way to the gurney, an injured soldier in the lineup reached out. "Please Father! Pray for me!" The soldier's voice was raspy, his breathing labored. His abdomen was heavily bandaged, the bloody blanket indicating more injuries to the lower extremities.

"Of course." Donovan took the soldier's hand in his own, using his free hand to reach for the rosary he kept tucked in a pocket. That he pulled out John McKay's rosary instead didn't stop him from quickly making the sign of the cross.

The soldier tried to mumble the Lord's Prayer, but before Donovan finished, the soldier's grasp loosened as he let out a final breath.

A medic came up behind Donovan and examined the soldier before shaking his head. "Time of death: sixteen zero seven hours."

Donovan glanced at the soldier's name tag before praying. "Lord, receive the soul of Private Paulson, that he may enter into the kingdom of Heaven."

When Donovan finished, he respectfully pulled the covering over Paulson's face and started once again toward the other deceased soldier.

At that sheet-covered gurney, Donovan began to pray over the body. Then he heard a moan and saw movement. Tugging back the sheet, Donovan checked for a pulse. This man was alive.

"Medic! Need help over here!" Grabbing the gurney, Donovan tried to maneuver it, but it wouldn't budge.

A soldier rushed up to assist him. "The wheel is locked, Father. There. Let's get him up to the front of the line."

"Thanks." Donovan glanced at the soldier who helped him push the gurney.

PAULSON, the soldier's name tag read. Donovan did a double take. *Time of death: sixteen zero seven.*

The soldier's uniform was caked with dried blood, but his injuries appeared healed.

The medic came up, relieving the priest. "I got it, Father." Private Paulson stayed with the gurney as it disappeared around a corner.

Donovan felt his knuckles grow warm and lifted his hand. John McKay's battered rosary was still wrapped around his hand. The very rosary that had been credited with miracles like the one he just witnessed.

As he stared at the beads, a verse from Corinthians came to mind. *The last enemy that will be abolished is death.* Donovan moved quickly from gurney to gurney and started to pray.

The church had not taken an official stand on the rosary before, but after Donovan reported this, the scholars at the Vatican would have to investigate.

CHAPTER FORTY-SEVEN

December 2006
Chicago, Illinois

Father Nick had been at the Donald E. Stephens Convention Center since two o'clock that morning. Anticipation crackled in the air with an underlying sense of joyous urgency. *The Pope would be there today.*

Thousands of chairs had been set up amidst the acres of flowers and greenery. Smiling people rushed about, executing tasks with a prayer-like fervor. Everyone wanted their personal contribution to this historic day to be perfect.

Similar scenes were unfolding across other venues in the city. The Pontiff would offer an early morning Mass at the Holy Name Cathedral, a second Mass for clergy, nuns, and seminarians at Queen of All Saints Basilica, followed by the televised service here at the convention center, and a final late afternoon Mass back at Holy Name. Crowds queued up outside the convention center even though the Mass didn't begin until three o'clock that afternoon.

At eight o'clock, Nick ate a breakfast sandwich before calling

Constanza. Most of his meals the last week had been eaten on the run as he rotated between his duties at the church, the youth center, and the papal Mass preparations.

Constanza had been a godsend this week, serving as the official youth group chaperone and helping coordinate schedules and permissions.

She reported that she and the boys were already on their way. "They are eager to get there early for their rehearsal."

While Eduardo hadn't relented in his stance against Domingo attending the papal Mass, he had told his daughter about his illness. Constanza accepted the news with her usual grace. "I will pray for the blessing of another miracle," she said. "And keep the faith."

Even though Domingo wasn't performing, the teen stepped up at the Youth Center to help the other boys rehearse, forcing them to practice over and over. "The Pope will be watching. The entire world will be watching!"

After disconnecting, Nick made his way to the temporary confessionals and reviewed the schedule of priests who would administer the sacrament. Kneelers and chairs had been set up in an adjacent room for contemplation and prayers of penance.

When he reentered the main hall two hours later, a sense of reverence stole his breath. The center had been converted into a holy place, the stage awash in white and gold. Through the magic of projection, statues and crucifixes appeared on the walls. The jumbo-sized screens showed an image of the Pope, his hand raised in blessing.

The significance of the day hit, leaving Nick feeling dizzy. To attend a Mass recited by the Pope was amazing in itself, but to also be included with Janey's family in a private meeting with the Holy Father was an honor.

Nick thought about the people and intentions that he would mentally carry into that private meeting. His parishioners from Prince of Peace. Domingo and the other students from the youth center. Benny, who was feeling under the weather. Nick's deceased loved ones, especially his nephew John, who'd started so much with the rosary and a simple request to pray for peace.

One screen blinked and in a play of light, the shape of a dove appeared over the Pope's image. It disappeared quickly, seeming to lift the tiredness Nick felt earlier. With a smile, he hurried off to find the music director.

———

NICK MET Constanza and the students in the lobby. He recognized several other parishioners who'd accompanied them as chaperones. There had been no problems enlisting volunteers for this event.

As Nick drew close, one of the younger boys charged forward, hands raised for a high five. "We've got a surprise, Father Nick!"

"Don't spoil it." Constanza raised her voice.

Confused, Nick watched as the circle of people behind Constanza parted. Hidden behind them stood Domingo and his grandfather.

Domingo's grin lit up the room. "He changed his mind! I get to sing!"

Nick looked from Domingo to his grandfather.

Eduardo frowned. "Don't read too much into it, priest."

"*Gracias*," Nick said.

"You'd be proud of them, Father," Constanza said. "They practiced the entire way over."

"Let's get over to the stage area," Nick said. "You'll get fifteen minutes of practice to find your marks. The stage director will tell you where to look, and how to enter and exit."

The boys cheered until Domingo hushed them. "Listen up. We will only have one chance to get it perfect. Let's get in as much practice as we can."

The boys clamored to follow Domingo.

And a child shall lead them, Nick thought.

CHAPTER FORTY-EIGHT

December 2006
Chicago, Illinois

The throngs of people lining the Chicago streets around the convention center amazed Janey. Despite the chilly temperatures, people crowded ten-deep, waiting to catch sight of the Pope's motorcade.

Outside the center she spotted several people in the crowd holding placards with an image of John's rosary. PRAY FOR PEACE, the signs read.

"What you started is powerful," Layton said. "Your brother would be proud."

Janey squeezed his hand. The rosary's destruction hadn't slowed the project's momentum — if anything, it made each believer's convictions stronger. It wasn't a tribute to John anymore. It was a tribute to the power of faith.

The VIP invitation from the Vatican meant that Janey's family waited in a shorter security line to gain entrance to the convention center. They also had reserved seats for the Mass for her, Layton, Dad, Eileen, Matt, Robin, Perry, and Lisa. While everyone was excited, Janey's father seemed to beam. As a lifelong, devout Catholic, attending a papal Mass was a bucket list item for her father.

Uncle Nick met them inside the center and hugged everyone. "Are you ready for this?"

Robin held up a small Bible. "This is my dad's. Would it be inappropriate to ask the Pope to bless something?"

"Sorry," Nick said. "At events like this, the Holy Father will come in, read a brief statement and then offer a blessing to the room at large. There isn't time for personal requests."

Janey had been disappointed to learn that a *private* meeting with the Pope could include several hundred people, a much smaller crowd than she'd seen outside, but not at all what she'd call personal.

Inside the meeting room, they received a small program with prayers printed in multiple languages. Many in the crowd held rosary beads and prayed silently as they waited. The room sizzled with a sense of reverent anticipation. More than one person had tears streaming down their cheeks, their faces lined with wonder. Their tangible belief humbled Janey.

As soon as the entrance doors closed, a priest moved to a podium at the front of the room and began to pray. When he said "amen," a door behind him opened and the Pope was escorted in.

The room gasped in unison and like everyone in the room, Janey let out a sound of awe. The Pope was smaller in stature than she had expected and yet larger than life. Dressed in elegant white robes that seemed to sparkle beneath the bright lights, the Pope greeted the crowd. Janey had never seriously considered auras, but if goodwill had a color, the Pope glowed with it.

The Holy Father read a statement in English on the meaning of peace. He spoke eloquently of hope overcoming fear. "Hope is real, our fears are not. Finding God is finding hope."

The crowd seemed to breathe as one, hanging by each word the Holy Father offered.

"We are not in this alone. God works in community. I would ask that you pray for peace and for each other. We see in others our sameness. And it is that sameness in which we find God," the Pope said in closing. "I offer this blessing in the name of our Heavenly Father, from whom all life and all blessings come."

Heads bowed as the Pope made the sign of the cross over the crowd. Then the crowd chorused, "amen," and shifted, blocking Janey's line of vision as the Pope disappeared behind closed doors.

She shook her head, stunned that it was over so soon, yet moved in a way she couldn't describe. The room buzzed with excited whispers as people turned en masse toward the exit.

Uncle Nick tapped her shoulder. "Janey, the Holy Father has asked to see you."

Two men in black suits quickly whisked Janey through the crowd with a practiced precision and escorted her down a short hall to a smaller room.

She sensed the Pope's presence as soon as she crossed the threshold. The man radiated a joyous hope. He motioned her forward as the others left the room.

Janey trembled with reverence, bowing her head as she stepped closer and dropped a slight curtsy.

"So, you are the girl who began the peace prayer project." The Pope spoke English with a slight accent. "My child, what you have done is a blessing to the world."

"I did it for my brother, never dreaming it would become what it did," Janey said. "I guess there was a bigger force at work."

"There is always a bigger force at work." The Pope reached for a small box on a table beside him. "This was received from Baghdad."

The Pope lifted a rosary from the box and held it out to her. At first glance it had looked like John's rosary, but some beads were different. Mismatched. The center medallion had been replaced by a larger piece.

Confused, she touched a familiar black bead. It pulsed with warmth. Despite its altered appearance, it felt *right* and was as beautiful as ever. "But my brother's rosary was destroyed."

"There is a letter here that explains the story. A man recovered the surviving beads and restrung them, making substitutions for the missing beads. It's an apt analogy for a story my father once told me. We find each other in the missing pieces of ourselves. God is in those pieces." The Pope closed her fingers over the beads.

A tear ran down Janey's cheek as she accepted the misshapen rosary. "I didn't think I'd ever see it again."

"This rosary was a gift from your brother. It must go back to you. Someone thought it needed to go to Rome because it's been associated with miracles. But those miracles continued even when the rosary was believed destroyed. The genuine miracle is the power of prayer. I'd like to see this movement go on, but without risking your beads again. To that end, I offer a rosary from my personal collection for the continued prayers for peace." The Pope smiled and held out another strand of beads. "I think it's fitting that one of these beads was carried by St. Francis. Go forth in peace, child."

The door opened without warning, and her escorts returned, a cue that Janey's audience was over. "Thank you," was all she could say.

When she was reunited with her family, she told them about her meeting. "I will show you the rosaries later."

"Another miracle," Dad said. "This story can't get any better."

Uncle Nick moved in and introduced another priest. "Janey, I want you to meet Father Dickerson. He is an editor with St. Ambrose Press."

Father Dickerson shook her hand. "I'd like to speak with you in the next few weeks about writing a book about your brother and this experience. I've read your blog posts and newspaper articles and I feel strongly about the project." He handed her a business card. "We don't have time to talk now, but I'd like to email you a few ideas if you're interested."

"I am." Janey accepted the card before the priest moved away.

Layton hugged her. "A book? Congratulations!"

She stared at the business card in disbelief. "I know all of this happened because of John's rosary, but part of me wishes it hadn't been so dramatic."

"Dramatic events force us to pause and reflect," Layton said. "If John had been given the rosary under different circumstances, there wouldn't have been a story to catch everyone's attention."

Before Janey could respond, an announcement was made that the Mass would begin soon. When they were seated, Janey leaned forward slightly and glanced down the row at her family, the people she loved. As she sat back, a feeling of peace settled over her.

Perfect peace.

And in that moment, she knew everything would be okay.

CHAPTER FORTY-NINE

December 2006
Chicago, Illinois

It was 11:00 PM, almost the end of one of the most meaningful days of Father Nick's life. His students had performed flawlessly to a receptive crowd. Constanza and her father seemed closer than ever. And the Mass had surpassed Nick's every expectation.

To hear the Pope's message of peace, hope, and the call to recommit to the church's tenets moved Nick to examine his own faith, his own failings. He'd left the Mass feeling reborn and immediately sought the sacrament of confession for himself.

Recalling the events of the day made him want to weep as he knelt alone in Prince of Peace Church – *his church* — and finished his evening prayers. He stood after making the sign of the cross and let his gaze sweep around the interior.

The decrepit building he'd walked into six months ago had transformed. The restoration of the church was magnificent, the restoration of the priest no less glorious. So why did part of him still feel blue? Feel like *now what*? Was it the natural letdown after the near mystical experience of today's papal Mass?

He stared up at the statue of the risen Christ, the representation of triumph over death.

Rise and start anew.

Rise.

Start anew.

Nick felt like laughing. With the church renovations nearly completed, he needed a new direction, a new passion. The question wasn't, "Now what?" It was, "What more?"

The community needed rebuilding. Rebirth. Families with young children needed better options for day care and primary education. Several people suggested reopening the parish school on a smaller scale. While Nick hadn't mentioned it to anyone, he'd toyed with the idea of a one-room school, a throwback to the eighteen hundreds' schoolhouses. He'd read many reports of families who homeschooled in that manner, with remarkable results. Could those principles apply to conventional education?

His phone vibrated. Concerned, he tugged it out. Calls this late at night were never good. "This is Father Nick."

"This is Father Romano. We met earlier today."

"Yes, I remember." Father Romano was part of the Pope's staff. He'd sought Nick out to ask specific questions about the church restoration. It turned out that the artist who had designed Prince of Peace's floor mosaics and stained glass had been a friend of the Pope's great-grandfather. Nick had promised to email photographs of the church's interior.

"I apologize for the late hour, but the Holy Father would like to see the church before leaving."

Nick glanced around the church. "When would his Holiness like to come?"

There was a pause, a muffled consultation. "We'll be there in ten minutes. I ask that no one else be present or even told. It will be a brief stop as we are headed to the airport."

After disconnecting, Nick rushed to turn on every single light, refusing to allow the smallest detail to remain in shadow. He lit candles in the gleaming candelabras before pausing to take in the unique loveliness of the church at night. The insides of the stained-glass windows were embedded with tiny mirrors and bits of glitter that made the windows come alive when lit up from inside.

Nick hovered at the front door until the Pope's motorcade pulled up. There was a flurry of activity as a security team swept into the church. Upon their approval, the Pontiff climbed out of the vehicle, surrounded by more security and assistants.

As the Pope drew close, he extended his hand.

Nick bent forward and kissed the Pope's signet, the official Ring of the Fisherman. When Nick straightened, he realized he trembled, but the full-blown anxiety he'd experienced in the past was gone.

The Pope embraced Nick briefly. "*Grazie* for accommodating us."

Nick could barely form words. "Our humble parish is honored."

Everyone stepped aside as the Pope moved into the foyer. Sweeping his hand toward the first tile scene he quoted the opening verse of Genesis. "In the beginning God created the heavens and the earth."

With surprising agility, the Pontiff continued into the church, naming each scene as he walked, his head swiveling to take in the stained glass that complemented the mosaics.

At the center of the church, the Pope paused. "My great-grandfather was lifelong friends with the mosaic artist. Pablo sent my great-grandfather sketches of his designs. Unfortunately, my great-grandfather died before the church was finished. Being here today, seeing this beauty, I honor my great-grandfather's memory. I inherited those sketches and would like to donate them to Prince of Peace. This is where they belong."

Nick could only imagine how excited Benny would be to hear about this. "Such a generous gift. We are compiling a history of the church, and your sketches will be a treasured addition. Thank you."

The Pope's gaze tilted up as he took in the circular stained glass in the roof above the nativity mosaic. In a moment of Divine timing, the moon was directly overhead, illuminating the star. "I am grateful for all you have done to preserve and rebuild this church, Father Nicholas. You've shepherded this splendor back to serve our Lord."

"I take little credit," Nick said. "Most of the work was done by the faithful in my parish."

"We need more selfless souls in leadership," the Pope said. "Father Romano feels you would do well in Rome."

It took a moment for the significance of the statement to sink in.

Leadership.

Rome.

The Vatican.

Nick looked back at the statue of the Risen Christ. *Rise and start anew.*

"I feel strongly that the Lord still has work for me to complete here, your Holiness," Nick said.

Father Romano's eyes widened, and Nick realized he'd blurted out a response without first offering thanks.

The Pope laughed. "Complete that work, for now. Just remember that the Vatican has special pull with Him, too." The Pope pointed upward and winked. "A blessing for this church before I go, then."

Nick bowed his head and felt a surge of certainty that he'd made the right choice. For now.

CHAPTER FIFTY

December 2006
River Haven, Iowa

After returning from Chicago, Janey's family learned that the cleric, Ibrahim Yassin, was killed by one of his own followers. The *fatwa* was voided, which closed that chapter of hate.

As Christmas approached, the days grew shorter and colder. Janey's life took on a sense of deep contentment. Her family thrived. Dad looked and felt better than he had in years. Matt and Perry announced that they were both going to be fathers again, both with twins. Four new babies at once had everyone giddy. Layton accepted an offer on his grandfather's ranch in Texas. He and Janey were buying the Clements' homestead next door, from her father.

Layton had moved into the big Clements' farmhouse. After the Christmas holidays, he would split his time between helping her dad and completing his degree. Janey would return to Iowa City in January to complete her degree, coming home on weekends. They set a late summer wedding date.

She and Layton planned to remodel the old farmhouse. That it would be their future home hit her hard after Layton showed her sketches and said, "We could expand the sunroom and make it your writing studio. That would keep the bedrooms upstairs for our kids."

Our kids. They both wanted a large family. "I can already imagine our kids at your dad's, playing with Matt's and Perry's crews," Layton went on.

Janey decided to keep the news about John's rosary private for a while. Uncle Nick had been excited to see John's restrung rosary, especially the center medallion. According to a translation her uncle obtained, the engraving on one side of the cabochon appeared to be The Lord's Prayer printed in Arabic. The other side bore names of God. That the rosary might be linked to an ancient prophecy for peace seemed fitting.

She and Uncle Nick were discussing a plan to have the Pope's rosary publicly displayed indefinitely at Prince of Peace Church in Chicago, with weekly prayer services scheduled there. The idea of the beads having a permanent home instead of traveling seemed safer.

The letter Janey had been given when the Pope returned the rosary was written by an Army Chaplain. Father Donovan had known John and shared how her brother frequently asked the priest to pray for his family back in Iowa. Father Donovan explained that the man who repaired the rosary requested anonymity. *The man felt he owed a debt to John. This was his way of repaying it.* The letter also contained a laminated photograph of John, Janey, and Fuller. To learn that her brother kept that photo in his helmet, touched Janey deeply.

Today was Christmas Eve and traditionally Janey's family gathered at the McKay farm for dinner and a gift exchange. Janey was at the Clements' farm with Layton, feeding Grace and Tex, a long-haired German Shepherd rescued from a local shelter. Daisy the cat, another rescue, walked circle-eights between Janey's ankles meowing loudly.

"You shouldn't have eaten your food so fast," Janey lectured.

"Sweetheart! Come here!" Layton yelled from the kitchen.

Concerned, Janey hurried inside. "Are you okay?"

Layton stood in front of his open lap-top and motioned her close. "This is one of your Christmas presents."

Puzzled, she looked at the screen. Skype was open and a black-haired man with intense eyes stared at her. He had a beard, the darkness of it interrupted by a scar across one cheek.

Layton put his hand to her back and stepped up behind her. "Can you hear us, Jamal?"

"Yes. We have a good connection." The man spoke formal English with a Middle Eastern accent.

"This is John McKay's sister, Janey," Layton made introductions. "Jamal found the rosary and repaired it. He also returned the photograph."

Janey drew a deep breath as the significance hit her. This was the man who'd been with John after he'd been injured. "Thank you for returning both items. They are priceless to me. The fact you had the photograph means..." Her voice faltered. "Did you see my brother before he died?"

"Yes. I stayed with him until he drew his last breath."

To know John hadn't died alone had Janey blinking back tears. "Can you tell me anything about his final moments? Was he in much pain? Did...did he suffer?"

There was silence, the image frozen, and she worried the call had disconnected.

Jamal nodded. "Your brother seemed to realize he would not recover. I think he was beyond pain. He asked me to take the photograph he kept in his helmet — he worried it would fall into enemy hands. His last breaths were shallow. He did not struggle until the very end, when he seemed frantic to give me a message for you." He leaned very close to the camera. "Your brother said, 'Tell Janey I'm sorry. I was wrong. I love you more.' That sounds strange, but given the circumstances, I could only pray that I heard him correctly."

Janey swiped her eyes, remembering the last time she'd seen John in Iowa. She'd run after him for one last hug. "*I love you more*," her brother had whispered.

"Those words make perfect sense," she said. "Thank you. You can't imagine what this means."

"Your brother saved my son's life. I am indebted to him," Jamal said. "And I must keep this time short. My family and I are staying with friends in Jordan and I don't want to abuse their hospitality."

When the conversation ended, Janey collapsed in Layton's arms, sobbing. "I don't know how you arranged that but thank you."

"I had help," Layton admitted. "A friend, Ollie Fitz, is still stationed in Baghdad. Though I didn't know his name at the time, I realized Jamal was the only person who could have gotten the photograph from John's helmet. Ollie reached out to Father Donovan, the chaplain. It turns out Father Donovan helped Jamal immigrate to Jordan and felt it was safe to contact him now that he was out of Iraq."

Janey put a hand over her heart. "I need to tell my dad and brothers."

"Then let's go, darlin'."

Outside, Janey paused. Large snowflakes were falling, drifting down from billowing clouds that promised more. John had once proclaimed that if it snowed on Christmas Eve, all sins were wiped away. He called it an extra measure of grace and it was one more story to write about her brother.

"Our first white Christmas," Layton said.

She looked up at the sky. "It's a good omen."

CHAPTER FIFTY-ONE

JOHN MCKAY HELD out his hand and caught a single flawless snowflake.

Did Heaven hold all his favorite things? He let the flake complete its journey.

His mother used to say the first snow was magical. When John sought a sign about whether to enlist in the Army, he'd been given snowflakes. In July.

He turned to face the farmhouse where he had grown up. Four inches of sparkling snow covered the roof. Inside the house his family gathered, celebrating their love; their lives.

The image wavered like a mirage. John's connection to this life was fading.

The old beggar appeared beside him. "They will be fine."

"I know." John turned to the man, who wasn't the old beggar now. "The only thing I don't understand is the prophecy. I mean, where is the peace that the prophecy promised?"

"It's coming. And it will be glorious. Watch." The Nazarene waved his arm and showed John a glimpse of the future.

"Oh! Wow!" What John saw was magnificent. An awareness, a

certainty, rushed through him. Love, peace, and prosperity would ultimately prevail, the future as spectacular as it was inevitable. *On Earth as in Heaven.* Indeed.

Perfectly content, John looked back one last time, at the farm, the fields, and the memory of the bluest sky he'd ever seen. Joy filled him. Peace, too.

He was ready to go now. To his real home beyond the stars.

"Come on, girl." John whistled. "Want to race?"

Fuller ran up, barking with timeless vigor. And they ran into the light together.

ACKNOWLEDGMENTS

Writing is a solitary endeavor, yet no author completes the journey alone.

Heartfelt thanks first to my husband, Nolen Holzapfel. Your contributions to this manuscript are immeasurable. More thanks to those who read early versions or brainstormed issues: Michael Desmond, Karen Ashley, Kaye Trevarthen, Beth Skarupa, Mark Boss, and Tony Simmons. Milinda Stephenson, your fingerprints are all over this project.

Much gratitude to the writing friends and colleagues who keep me grounded: Jenn Stark, Lori Harris, Michael Morris, Lois Lavrisa, Natalie Jessen Freese, and a shout-out to The Cheshires Writing Group, Panama City, FL.

Kudos to the professionals: Sheila Athens, book coach extraordinaire; Cat Parisi, Cat's Eye Proofing; Susan Keillor, beta reader; and Deb Rhodes, beta reader.

As always, any mistakes are mine.

ABOUT THE AUTHOR

N. K. Holt has traditionally published multiple books, under different names. This is her first independently published novel in the family saga/inspirational suspense genres. A former accountant, she traded numbers for words and never looked back. She's also a Life Strategies Coach and enjoys hiking and being outdoors. She reads a wide variety of books and doesn't have a favorite. Born in Fort Madison, Iowa, she's been making up stories all her life and is busy working on her next novel. For more information, visit her website, www.nkholt.com, and sign up for her email list.

DEAR READER,

Thank you for reading **Missing Peace**. As readers, we have more books than time, and I appreciate that you choose my novel. I'd love to hear from you. Please connect with me via my website, or on Instagram at nkholtbooks. And if you enjoyed **Missing Peace**, I'd sincerely appreciate your review at Goodreads, Amazon.com, or your favorite sharing place.

Made in the USA
Coppell, TX
18 January 2021